Acclaim for Radclyffe's Fiction

In **2012 RWA/FTHRW Lories and RWA HODRW Aspen Gold award winner** *Firestorm* "Radclyffe brings another hot lesbian romance for her readers."—*The Lesbrary*

Foreword Review Book of the Year finalist and IPPY silver medalist *Trauma Alert* "is hard to put down and it will sizzle in the reader's hands. The characters are hot, the sex scenes explicit and explosive, and the book is moved along by an interesting plot with well drawn secondary characters. The real star of this show is the attraction between the two characters, both of whom resist and then fall head over heels." —*Lambda Literary Reviews*

Lambda Literary Finalist *Best Lesbian Romance 2010* features "stories [that] are diverse in tone, style, and subject, making for more variety than in many, similar anthologies... well written, each containing a satisfying, surprising twist. Best Lesbian Romance series editor Radclyffe has assembled a respectable crop of 17 authors for this year's offering." —*Curve Magazine*

2010 Prism award winner and ForeWord Review Book of the Year Award finalist *Secrets in the Stone* is "so powerfully [written] that the worlds of these three women shimmer between reality and dreams...A strong, must read novel that will linger in the minds of readers long after the last page is turned."—*Just About Write*

In **Benjamin Franklin Award finalist** *Desire by Starlight* "Radclyffe writes romance with such heart and her down-to-earth characters not only come to life but leap off the page until you feel like you know them. What Jenna and Gard feel for each other is not only a spark but an inferno and, as a reader, you will be washed away in this tumultuous romance until you can do nothing but succumb to it."—*Queer Magazine Online*

Lambda Literary Award winner *Stolen Moments* "is a collection of steamy stories about women who just couldn't wait. It's sex when desire overrides reason, and it's incredibly hot!"—*On Our Backs*

Lambda Literary Award winner *Distant Shores, Silent Thunder* "weaves an intricate tapestry about passion and commitment between lovers. The story explores the fragile nature of trust and the sanctuary provided by loving relationships."—*Sapphic Reader*

Lambda Literary Award Finalist *Justice Served* delivers a "crisply written, fast-paced story with twists and turns and keeps us guessing until the final explosive ending." —*Independent Gay Writer*

Lambda Literary Award finalist *Turn Back Time* "is filled with wonderful love scenes, which are both tender and hot." —*MegaScene*

By Radclyffe

Romances

Innocent Hearts	Fated Love
Promising Hearts	Turn Back Time
Love's Melody Lost	When Dreams Tremble
Love's Tender Warriors	The Lonely Hearts Club
Tomorrow's Promise	Night Call
Love's Masquerade	Secrets in the Stone
shadowland	Desire by Starlight
Passion's Bright Fury	Crossroads

Honor Series   ## Justice Series

Honor Series	Justice Series
Above All, Honor	A Matter of Trust (prequel)
Honor Bound	Shield of Justice
Love & Honor	In Pursuit of Justice
Honor Guards	Justice in the Shadows
Honor Reclaimed	Justice Served
Honor Under Siege	Justice for All
Word of Honor	
Code of Honor	

The Provincetown Tales

Safe Harbor	Winds of Fortune
Beyond the Breakwater	Returning Tides
Distant Shores, Silent Thunder	Sheltering Dunes
Storms of Change	

Visit us at www.boldstrokesbooks.com

CODE OF HONOR

by

RADCLY*f*FE

2013

CODE OF HONOR

ISBN 13: 978-1-60282-885-8

This Trade Paperback Original Is Published By
Bold Strokes Books, Inc.
P.O. Box 249
Valley Falls, NY 12185

First Edition: July 2013

Credits

Editors: Ruth Sternglantz and Stacia Seaman
Production Design: Stacia Seaman
Cover Design by Sheri (graphicartist2020@hotmail.com)

Acknowledgments

I waited to write more in this series until my characters had new challenges to face, personally and professionally. Fiction affords us many opportunities to dream, explore, imagine, and triumph in worlds that perhaps represent more "perfect" versions of our own. In writing the Honor series, I don't think I've strayed too far from the possible in terms of the challenges or the outcome, and while the events are fictional, the struggles and sacrifices of the real men and women of the military and justice systems are not. To them I offer my upmost respect.

Thanks go to Sandy Lowe for the support that keeps me going; to Ruth Sternglantz for a stellar job; to Stacia Seaman, for keeping me on track; and to my first readers Connie and Paula for invaluable feedback.

Special thanks to Sheri for a great cover once again.

And to Lee, for always believing—*Amo te.*

Radclyffe, 2012

For Lee, for a new day every day

Chapter One

L oren rolled on the throttle on the straightaway and the speedometer slid to sixty. The crisp night air sliced at her throat and froze the breath streaming through her nostrils. Her skin tingled. Adrenaline surged through her bloodstream. The macadam unraveled beneath her headlights like a silver ribbon swirling through dark chocolate, a seductive tease urging her to indulge in private pleasures. One mistake, one miscalculation, and the big bike would career off the twisting road into the dense, dark forest. Loren laughed into the wind—she never felt more alive than when in danger.

A faint vibration against her left thigh signaled a call on the cell phone tucked into an inside pocket of her leathers. Whoever was calling wasn't one of the Renegades. No one from the club would be calling her in the middle of a run. She'd spent two and a half years working her way up the club hierarchy, from prospect to voting member, but she was still a lieutenant. If the club president wanted to call off the run or change the orders, he'd be calling Quincy, his VP, not her. And Ramsey sure as hell would *not* be calling her on the burn phone he didn't even know about.

She put the call out of her mind and held the throttle steady. She was finally getting close to her objective, and everything else could wait—especially a sit rep to keep the bureaucrats happy. The big Harley purred contentedly between her thighs. The highway curved north into the Bitterroots, and at 2330 on a frigid December night, the roads were deserted. She liked riding at night, even in winter, but night maneuvers were always trickier. The three of them were out there alone, miles from any backup, about to meet with a bunch of fanatics who would outnumber and outgun them. Loose cannons with short fuses.

The uninformed often lumped paramilitary organizations and

motorcycle clubs into the same anarchistic pot, pegging them all as rebels and outlaws who lived on the fringes of society, ignoring law and order, threatening the status quo. In some ways the comparison was true—both groups eschewed laws imposed by a government they didn't recognize and guarded their territory with guns and blood. Internally, though, the groups were fundamentally different. Within the club, absolute loyalty was a given. No one betrayed the club, no one turned on a brother or sister, no one indicted a fellow club member. Self-sacrifice for the good of the whole was ingrained.

The militia was different. The first thing she'd noticed when dealing with right-wing paramilitary groups like the Forces for a Liberated America was the power-hungry competitiveness seething beneath the rigid hierarchy. The general might command obedience through force, but the internal cohesion that made a family out of the club was missing in the compound. Somewhere she'd find someone willing to deal for money or power, and those internal chinks in the militia's armor were exactly what she needed to get inside.

Ahead of her, Quincy's taillight blinked and he slowed. Loren throttled back, falling into single file between him and Armeo, who rode rearguard. They turned off the main road onto a packed gravel single-lane, slick with ice from a recent flurry. Her rear tire skidded on the glassy surface, and she put down a leg to help stabilize the Harley as it fishtailed back into line. The surge of adrenaline left her momentarily high. She loved the freedom of knifing through the dark unencumbered by metal and glass barriers, despite the risk. She didn't fear death, only a life of no consequence.

She pulled up behind Quincy in a semicircular turnoff and cut the engine, kicking the stand down as she dismounted. Two Humvees idled at the far end of the turnoff, their exhaust streaming into the frigid air like breath from some prehistoric monsters. During the tourist season, the area would be crowded with sightseers, but now, in the middle of the night on a road that led nowhere except higher into the nearly deserted mountains, they might have been on a faraway planet. Towering pines crowded up to the road on all sides, dwarfing them in the tiny clearing. The overlook gave way to yawning darkness. She balanced her helmet on the tank and settled her thin black watch cap over her ears. Her short, shaggy hair curled out from under the edges along her neck. Armeo, almost the same height and nearly indistinguishable in black cap, leather pants, jacket, and boots, stepped up beside her.

"I don't like this," he muttered.

"Just be cool, but be ready," she murmured. When Quincy started toward the Humvees, she slid her hand into her right front jacket pocket, gripped her Glock, and fell into step with Quincy.

A clean-shaven man in a flight jacket, fatigues, and paratrooper boots stepped out of the first oversized SUV. Six-three, looking trim even in winter clothes, he was hatless, his dark hair clipped short, making his lantern-jawed face and head appear bullet-like. She hadn't met him, but she knew his dossier, what there was of it. Augustus Graves—sixty-one, ex–Army Special Forces, ex–land speculator. He'd made a killing in a land deal with developers of a resort community on Bear Lake in the mid-nineties and then dropped out of sight. A decade later, he'd resurfaced as the self-appointed general of FALA, one of the largest and best-organized right-wing paramilitary organizations. He was rumored to have powerful backers on both sides of the law, and Loren's job was to find out who they were. And just what kind of security risk FALA represented.

Two younger men in similar military garb, each with an assault rifle slung across his chest, climbed out after him and took up positions slightly behind and off to his sides. The two triads approached steadily but cautiously, reaching at exactly the same time the center of the cone of light thrown off by the Humvees.

"I see the weather didn't slow you down," Graves said, his voice a gravelly baritone. His arms rested loosely at his sides. He didn't offer to shake Quincy's hand.

Quincy shrugged, his leathers creaking in the frigid air. "Not much slows us down."

Graves smiled thinly, his pale blue eyes scanning Loren and Armeo. Nothing registered in his expression, but his gaze lingered a moment longer on Loren than Armeo. She stared back, unblinking. After a second, he switched his attention back to Quincy. "Have you got the samples?"

"Right this way."

Loren took a step back, Armeo followed, and Quincy waited until Graves stepped up beside him. The two men strode toward the bikes in tandem, and she and Armeo kept them and the FALA guards in sight as they followed. When the group reached the bikes, Loren moved to hers and unstrapped the bedroll from the back. She rested it on the broad seat of the Harley and, under the light of the moon, unrolled the blanket to expose a Kalashnikov assault rifle. Quincy and Armeo did the same, exposing semi-automatic handguns and submachine guns.

One of the younger men with Graves whistled under his breath. The other one said, "Pretty."

Graves extended a hand toward the rifle resting on Loren's seat. "May I?"

"Be my guest," Loren said, easing her hand back into her jacket. She didn't expect any trouble at this juncture—a double-cross was more likely to occur when they transferred the full shipment—but she wanted to even the odds, just in case.

Graves hefted the rifle, worked the slide, and looked through the attached night scope. His expression didn't change. "How many can you get?"

Loren didn't answer, even though she had the arms connection. Club rules. Quincy was in charge. He said, "As many as you can handle."

"How much?"

"Fifteen hundred for the big guns, eight hundred for the handguns."

Graves looked through the scope again. "A thousand and five hundred."

Quincy was silent for a moment, then one quick nod. "Agreed."

"Let's start with a hundred of each."

"No problem," Quincy said, like they moved a few hundred thousand dollars' worth of illegal guns every day. That was a big order, bigger than any Loren had witnessed. Wherever these guys were getting their money, it was someone with clout. And what were they going to do with a hundred assault rifles? Start World War III? But she kept her expression neutral and took the opportunity to get a good look at each of the three men, committing their features to memory. Her memory was eidetic—she never forgot a detail of a conversation, could sketch the exact specifics of a face, and was able to accurately pinpoint her location without GPS to within a few hundred feet, even after an hour's ride. Those traits, her genetic inheritance from her mathematician mother and artist father, made her the best at what she did.

"Then we're done here." The general glanced at Loren. "Merry Christmas."

Loren stared back. *Ho-fucking-ho.* She hadn't even remembered they'd scheduled the meet for Christmas night. It wasn't as if she'd been planning to spend the night cozied up in front of a fire with anyone. Like there could even be someone—at least anyone she could risk seeing for more than a quick tumble in the back room of the club. She did have to prove she was one of the guys, after all. She looked at Graves until his smile grew predatory and he finally turned away.

Quincy and Graves traded a few more comments about when and where the exchange would occur, while she and Armeo wrapped up the merchandise and secured the bedrolls back on their bikes. Five minutes later, they saddled up and turned around for the two-hour ride back down the mountain to Silver Lake, the home base of the Bitterroot Renegades. Her home, for the last two and half years. The burn phone vibrated against her leg again. A call from Skylar Dunbar, the only person with the number, could only mean trouble.

Loren ignored it.

❖

"Merry Christmas," Cam said to Brock Nunez, the newest member of Blair's security detail, as she closed the door to the condo and left him outside in the hall. She shrugged out of her black wool topcoat, hung it on a coat tree, and leaned back against the door to watch Blair kick off her heels and drape her coat on the back of the sofa that faced the floor-to-ceiling windows. Beyond the glass, the White House glowed like a jewel backdropped against black velvet. They'd just left there and hadn't been alone since the Christmas festivities began more than twelve hours before.

For the president and his family, private traditions often gave way to public ceremonies. Even though today's event, with only a few dozen of the family's friends and supporters, had been a smaller, quieter affair than the official White House party that had hosted hundreds a few weeks before, politics was a silent, ever-present undercurrent. She didn't care for politics. She'd grown up in a political world. Living abroad with her ambassador father, she'd learned young that every message had subtext and often another meaning entirely than what was said aloud. Nothing was as it appeared on the surface, anywhere but at home. In the laughter- and art-filled villa with her painter mother and a father who adored them both, she'd been safe and protected and loved. All that had ended the morning he'd gotten into a car that exploded before her eyes, destroying the myth of security her parents had so painstakingly created for her. From that moment on, securing the lives of those entrusted to her had become her life.

Blair threaded her arms around Cam's neck and kissed her. Leaning into her, molding herself to the angles and planes she knew so well but never grew tired of exploring, she rested her cheek against Cam's shoulder. "What is it? Something's making you sad."

Cam wrapped her arms around Blair's waist and stroked the soft skin above the scooped back of her silk dress. She kissed the golden hair at Blair's temple and nuzzled the fragrant waves. "I'm sorry. I'm fine. You know how I feel about festivities."

"Oh, Christmas Grinch is back?" Blair laughed softly and smoothed her hands over Cam's chest. "I know you don't really mean it, there's something else."

"I was just thinking about being alone with you. Really alone."

Blair tilted her head back, studied Cam's face. "I'm really selfish. Sometimes I forget that I'm not the only one who lives in a fishbowl because of my father. I've dragged you right into it, haven't I? The wedding is just going to make it worse."

"Hey, no. I'm not complaining. I wouldn't change one single thing about being with you." Cam shook her head, trying to shake off the melancholy. "You were wonderful today, as usual. The press practically genuflects at your feet, although I can see why." She buried her fingers in Blair's hair and kissed her, slowly and thoroughly. Her heart beat hard when she pulled away. "You're smart, beautiful, charming—"

"Cameron," Blair murmured, nibbling on Cam's lower lip, "if you just want to get laid, you don't have to flatter me."

Cam laughed and the clouds lifted. "When you put it like that, who could resist?"

"Well, not you, I hope." Blair brushed back the black wave of hair that insisted on falling across Cam's forehead. "Are you sure you're all right? Is it the new mission?"

"I won't deny it's on my mind." Cam clasped Blair's hand and led her toward the bedroom. "Terrorism doesn't stop for holidays—in fact, holidays are a prime time to make a statement. I need to get my team together and start moving on this. Especially with Andrew scheduled to leave right after New Year's."

"You think they'll try again?" Blair didn't quite mask the tremor in her voice.

"No reason to think that." Angry at herself for worrying Blair, Cam yanked off her jacket and tossed it over a stuffed chair near the bed. "But we can't assume there isn't a backup plan, and we can't allow terrorists to believe they can launch an attack on the president of the United States without reprisal."

Blair nodded, her jaw set and her eyes clear of fear. "What do you plan to do first?"

Cam unbuttoned her shirt and stripped it off along with the silk undershirt. "First thing is to decide who I can read in on this. Then I plan to talk to someone who might be able to give me a closer look at what's going on with the militia groups."

"Unzip me." Blair turned her back to Cam. "Who?"

"I've got a few contacts who can put me in touch with other agents monitoring paramilitary organizations. I might have to call in some favors, but I'll start there."

"I guess you won't be able to stay away from fieldwork."

Cam teased the zipper down to the small of Blair's back, brushed the straps of Blair's midnight gown from her shoulders, and pulled her back against her chest. She kissed Blair's shoulder at the curve of her neck. "I would if I could, but we can't afford a leak. And the only way to contain a leak is to limit those in the know. Everyone who *does* know will need to be boots on the ground."

Blair stiffened but kept her voice light. "You're a deputy director of Homeland Security. You don't have to get your boots wet."

Cam pushed Blair's dress slowly down over her hips where it gathered at her feet like a glimmering pool under the moonlight. Sliding both hands up Blair's torso, she cupped her breasts and brushed her mouth over Blair's ear. "I know what you want. I'll do my best."

Blair's head fell back against Cam's shoulder, and she arched into Cam's hands. "I know you will. You always do."

"I love you, Blair." Cam turned Blair until Blair's breasts brushed against her chest. She kissed her, felt their bodies fuse, their spirits join, and the memories of loss and fears for the future faded. There was only Blair, and Blair was everything.

CHAPTER TWO

Senator Franklin Russo walked the last guest down the spacious central hall to the front door of his estate in Idaho Falls. His assistant held out a long sable coat for the doyen of the county, a widow who wielded the power her money could buy with the cold indifference of a threshing machine. Whoever was unfortunate enough to stand in the path of her plan to put a man worthy of God and country in the White House was destined to be mown down. Fortunately for him, he was that man.

"I'm so glad you could come tonight, Eleanor."

Eleanor Bigelow smiled at him thinly and turned her back so Russo's deferential assistant, a thirty-year-old man in a conservative navy blazer, charcoal pants, and narrow red-striped tie, could drape the coat over her shoulders. "I know how busy you are, Franklin, and I've been wanting a moment with you for some time. It's always wise to know what my money is buying."

Franklin kept his expression bland, reminding himself that once he sat in the Oval Office, no one would own him. The power would be his. Until then, he would ingratiate himself as need be. He had his own resources and his campaign coffers were healthy, but some expenditures he couldn't afford to have made public. Private benefactors rarely demanded an exact accounting of how their funds were spent. Knowledge might be power, but it was also culpability, and the rich coveted the illusion of clean hands. The language of politics was less what was said and more what was implied and inferred, and he had understood Mrs. Charles Bigelow quite well. She expected her candidate to put a gun back in every house, God in every school, and the white elite in every position of power. Since he happened to agree, he wasn't worried about placating her need to exercise her authority, at least on the surface.

He bowed ever so slightly. "You can be sure I'll see that your generosity is put to use in support of an agenda—"

"You can save the speech for the campaign, Franklin. Just see that Washington doesn't give away what's left of the country, and put the power back in the hands of those who know what to do with it."

"Yes, ma'am," Franklin said solicitously. "I surely will."

Franklin stood in the doorway, the brightly lit, expansive hall decked out in holiday trimmings at his back, until the limo driver hurried up the path from the driveway to escort his employer to the idling Town Car. Snow drifted into Franklin's face and coated his shoulders, but he didn't move until Bigelow departed. Then he dusted off his black cashmere jacket and stepped back inside.

Derrick was waiting. "I take it the meeting was a success?"

"She's promised us three million. For starters."

"Merry Christmas," Derrick murmured softly. He nodded toward the paneled door of Franklin's study across the hall. "Can I pour you a drink?"

"I'd say this calls for one." Franklin frowned. "Where's my wife?"

"She retired some time ago."

"Of course." Franklin followed Derrick into the study and settled behind his broad desk. His wife managed to perform her hostess duties out of some long-ingrained sense of decorum, a virtue of her Southern upbringing, but she was barely able to do much more. With every passing week, she became more of a liability than a benefit. Idly he wondered which would create a more sympathetic figure in the voters' eyes—a widower or a devoted husband to an infirm wife. Powell had certainly gotten a lot of mileage out of his widower status, and the absence of a first lady had given Powell the excuse to push his degenerate daughter onto the national stage. "Pour one for yourself."

"Thank you, sir," Derrick said, handing Franklin two fingers of scotch in a crystal rock glass and holding up a glass of his own. "To a victorious campaign."

"To winning." Franklin drained the whiskey in one long swallow. He had ten months until all his plans paid off, but he didn't intend to wait that long to take care of Andrew Powell.

❖

Loren noticed the redhead the instant she stepped into the bar. At three in the morning, the only people in the place should have been club members, their old ladies, and hopefuls, girls hoping to *become* somebody's old lady. The redhead looked too confident and too high-class to be a hopeful, unlike the two girls in skimpy halters and jeans cut so low their pubic hair would've shown if they hadn't shaved it all off who were slouched in a couple of battered chairs, sleeping off too much booze or too much sex or both. Nobody was behind the bar, but the redhead had a whiskey glass in front of her.

Realizing her steps had slowed as she took in the redhead's shoulder-length waves, smooth creamy complexion, sharp green eyes, and killer body, Loren averted her gaze and followed Quincy toward the hallway that led to the club rooms in the back.

Quincy stopped next to the redhead, and Loren pulled up behind him.

"You lost?" Quincy said.

The redhead swiveled on the stool, her long slender legs, encased in tight blue jeans, crossed at the knee and ending in shiny black leather boots with four-inch heels. Her leather jacket was open down the front, exposing a tight, scooped-neck turquoise T-shirt and no bra. She had nice breasts, just the right size. She had hot and sexy written all over her. Loren yanked her gaze up and saw the redhead watching her look.

Quincy tapped her chin with his fingertip and repeated, "Lost, sweetheart?"

"I don't think so," the redhead said in a throaty voice, finally giving him a slow smile. "I saw the bikes out front. I love bikes. Bikers too."

"The place is closed," Quincy said.

"The door was open."

"Look, honey—"

A gravelly rumble from the far end of the room said, "Let her stay. She brightens up the place. Nice change of scenery."

Loren, Quincy, and Armeo shifted in the direction of the club president. Ramsey slouched in the door, his muscled arms folded across his leather vest, the black T-shirt underneath tucked into broken-in jeans. His wide black belt sported a buckle with the club's logo on it—an American flag with wings. His wedding ring glinted on his left hand. His eyes glinted at the babe at the bar. Looked like the Prez had already staked out his territory, and Loren registered a flush of anger that she quickly brushed aside. None of her business who the president chose to bounce with.

Quincy started forward again, and Loren fell into step next to him.

The redhead murmured, "See you later," and Loren could've sworn she was talking directly to her.

They all filed into the club room, and the heavy wooden doors swung closed behind them. All the voting members were there: Ramsey—the president, Quincy—the VP, Armeo—the treasurer, Loren—exact description still open, but procurer was probably the best term, and Griffin—the enforcer. They all settled around the table in traditional order, with Ramsey at the head, Quincy at his left, Griffin to his right, then Loren across from Armeo. Ramsey pulled a cigar from the inside pocket of his black leather vest, bit off the end, spat it unerringly into the dented wastebasket leaning in the corner, and lit it with a silver Zippo. He drew in, savored the smoke, and exhaled slowly. His gaze moved over Loren and Armeo and landed on Quincy. "Everything all right tonight?"

Quincy said, "No problems."

"Terms?"

Quincy relayed the particulars of the meeting and the agreed-upon price. Ramsey nodded in satisfaction.

"Are we going to have any trouble filling the order?" He looked at Loren.

Loren shook her head. "It'll take at least two weeks, but there shouldn't be a problem." She thought about the calls she'd need to make, the guns she'd need to have moved into the warehouse. "For that quantity, though, we ought to make two runs on different days, different couriers in both directions."

Ramsey nodded in agreement. "Set it up."

"How sure are we these militia guys can be trusted?" Quincy said.

"The Bloods have dealt with them before and they say they're solid," Ramsey said.

"We're going to be inside their turf when we make the exchange," Quincy went on. "That's a lot of money and merchandise we're talking about."

Loren saw an opening, and she might not have another one. "I'm with Quincy on this. If we agree to make the transfer inside the Liberation compound, we'll be outmanned and outgunned. People disappear all the time up in the Bitterroots. And we can't exactly file a missing-persons report if some of us don't come back."

"So we'll take precautions," Ramsey said. "Can we get a backup team up in the mountains to cover the meet?"

Quincy shook his head. "No way up but the one road. They'll have that watched."

Ramsey grunted. "Anybody got any suggestions?"

"How about we request some kind of insurance policy before the meet," Loren said. "One of their guys comes down here and one of us goes up there. Nobody goes home until the money and the guns are transferred and everybody moves back to neutral space."

"What if they send somebody down here they don't care about losing?" Griffin said. "A hostage is only worth as much as his value to the other side. They could shoot up our guys, rip us off, and leave us with a useless body to deal with."

Quincy pointed a finger like he was shooting a gun. "The Bloods know these guys. We can get a rundown on the major players from them. Make sure they send someone with weight."

"Let me think about it," Ramsey said. "I don't like putting one of our guys out there with nothing but his dick for a weapon."

"No problem," Loren said. "I'll go."

Everybody laughed. Loren shrugged as if she didn't care, but her nerves jangled with anticipation. Things were finally coming together. She might finally be able to get a firsthand look at FALA.

Ramsey stubbed out his cigar. "Any more business or can we go home and enjoy what's left of Christmas?" When no one spoke, Ramsey rose. "Meeting adjourned. Nice work."

Loren pushed her chair back, feeling the fatigue for the first time. She'd been on edge for weeks setting up this buy, and it just might pay off.

The men started to file out, and Ramsey said, "McElroy, wait a minute, will you."

Quincy looked back, his eyes narrowing. When Ramsey didn't invite him to stay, he pulled the door closed, leaving Loren alone with Ramsey.

Ramsey edged his hip onto the corner of the long, scarred table. A Glock was tucked into the small of his back. Hers was still in her jacket, but she couldn't slide her hand into the pocket with him watching. She'd seen him execute a traitor to the club once. He'd smiled and patted the guy on the cheek, right before he'd pulled out his gun and shot him through the eye.

"See what you can find out about the squeeze at the bar."

Loren must have looked surprised because he laughed.

"Well, I can't ask my old lady to do it," Ramsey said. "And if I send one of the guys, they'll be sniffing around her pussy before they even get her name. Let me know what you find out."

"Sure, boss. You want me to call you?"

"In the morning, not too early. Trish likes to sleep in, and the kids are with the in-laws." He grinned.

She nodded. "Got it. Night."

"Yeah."

Loren strolled back into the bar. The lights in the hanging green-glass-shaded lamps were turned down low, making the place look less tacky than it did during the day. The few mismatched round tables looked less rickety, the felt on the pool table less worn, the bar less scarred. The two hopefuls were gone, probably sleeping it off with Armeo and Griffin—possibly together. The redhead still sat at the bar, a quarter inch of amber liquid in the rock glass in front of her. The hand that held the glass was long fingered and smooth, the nails shining sculpted ovals. Classy.

Loren sat on the stool next to her, leaned across the bar, fished a glass from underneath, and drew a beer from the tap. She skimmed off the foam with her index finger and took a long drink. "Why don't I think you're here by accident?"

The redhead half turned, her knee brushing Loren's thigh. "Because you don't look stupid to me."

"What's your name?"

"Lisa."

"Lisa…?"

She smiled. "Smith."

"Uh-huh. So, Lisa Smith—what are you doing here?"

"Jerome sent me."

Loren's spine stiffened. Jerome was international president of the Renegades—every local chapter along the Pacific Coast and as far east as Montana and Idaho paid tithe to him from the profits they made running drugs or guns or girls. "Why?"

"You've been busy here. Moving a lot of product. I'm an accountant."

Loren laughed. "Right, and I'm an undercover cop."

Lisa's smile widened as she traced a single finger down the center of Loren's chest. Goose bumps lifted on Loren's torso and her nipples tightened.

"I don't believe you," Lisa murmured. "You're too good-looking to be a cop. So why are *you* really here?"

Loren laughed again. "I'm here on a mission from the president. He's interested in you."

"Really?" Lisa emptied her glass and set it down. "He's not my type."

"Don't let the wedding ring bother you."

"It doesn't." Lisa leaned forward and kissed Loren on the mouth. "It's more the cock I'm not interested in."

"And I'm not interested in getting killed for a little bit of pussy."

Lisa ran her tongue slowly over the surface of Loren's lower lip. "How about for a *lot*?"

Loren eased back. Her clit was tight but she wasn't insane. No one got between Ramsey and a woman. "I'll have to give it some thought."

"You do that." Lisa slid off the stool, her high firm breasts brushing over Loren's arm. "Have a nice night, Loren."

Lisa turned to walk away, and Loren said, "I don't remember giving you my name."

Lisa winked over her shoulder. "You didn't. Night."

❖

Sky Dunbar slid behind the wheel of her crap rental car and pulled out of the gravel lot onto the deserted highway. The sky was crystal clear, an ebony blanket studded with stars and a full moon. The silver light was nearly bright as day. Before she accelerated away from the Ugly Rooster, she glanced at the big dark plate-glass window and wondered if Loren McElroy was looking out at her, or if she'd forgotten her the moment they'd parted. She didn't question why she cared.

McElroy wasn't exactly what she'd expected. Somehow, she'd thought McElroy would keep a lower profile, but apparently taking a backseat wasn't her style. Figured, really. A woman didn't get accepted into a biker club as one of the members and not one of the old ladies unless she had something special to offer. McElroy had that, and more. An Army vet, she'd started out as a grease monkey in the motor pool and worked her way up to commanding a supply company. Along the way, she'd made plenty of contacts, and soon her unofficial duty became procuring whatever needed to be gotten for the post. Everything from extra fuel, surplus body armor and machine parts to contraband of all description. The bureau had recruited her by then, and her illegal activities were sanctioned. Her cover story was a long time in the making, and by the time she'd reached Silver Lake, where she owned her own garage, her story was more than a cover. It was her reality.

They'd never met in person—in this kind of long-game, labyrinthine operation where the smallest breach could mean disaster, the fewer people who could identify one another, the better. Until an hour ago, she was just a voice to McElroy—her telephone voice that didn't resemble her natural tone at all—and McElroy was just a black-and-white photo clipped in the PDF of her classified file. The file with half the lines redacted. The photo had been of McElroy in desert camo. She looked a lot different now, decked out in leather, her unruly dark hair scattered around a face that would've been called beautiful if the edges had been a little softer and her coal-black eyes a little less piercing. Handsome wasn't quite right, either, but closer. Bold, brash, dangerous. In uniform she'd been imposing; in biker black she was tantalizing.

McElroy moved with the lethal kind of confidence that said she'd unhesitatingly use the weapon tucked into the right front pocket of the jacket that displayed the patch of the Renegades. The Renegades weren't a Sunday-afternoon club filled with lawyers and accountants and other weekend warriors. They were all longtime bikers, many of them friends since young adulthood, almost all of them with records, and they'd been on the FBI's and ATF's radar for a dozen years or more. But their threat level, and consequently their interest level, had waned as more dangerous groups had slowly infiltrated the West Coast—Salvadoran gangs and Mexican cartels, and the right-wing paramilitary groups that were hotbeds for domestic terrorism. The low-level drug, gun-running, and porn rings associated with most of the biker clubs didn't pose the kind of national security threat that the other groups did. So instead of arresting the bikers, they infiltrated them.

Sky pulled into the rambling, run-down motel complex where she'd taken a room late that afternoon. She'd signed in as Lisa Smith, the woman whose identity she'd assumed. Her orders, predictably vague, had been to tighten the leash on McElroy and be ready to escalate McElroy's involvement with the militia at short notice. She didn't know why, hadn't been read in on the big picture, and wasn't about to make that call from three thousand miles away. She wanted a closer look if she was sending her contact in deeper, and she was sick of flying a desk. She wanted a firsthand look. Her phone rang, and she slipped the smartphone from the right front pocket of her skintight jeans. She recognized the number, and she wasn't in the mood for a tongue-lashing. At least, not the kind she knew was coming after her disappearing act.

She hadn't made her way in the bureau by going through channels, but this time she was way outside the lines. But then, what were they going to do? Fire her? She smiled.

She unpacked the few articles of clothing she'd brought and slipped them into the rickety, chipped Goodwill dresser and sat on the bed to get rid of the god-awful high-heeled boots. Why anyone would choose to wear them was beyond her. She slid her feet into flip-flops, choosing not to look at the faded carpet too closely, and padded into the bathroom to turn on the shower. She was feeling just a little bit grimy. Maybe that had been more a result of the day's activities than the long hours, but she chose not to think about that too carefully, either.

CHAPTER THREE

Sky slept poorly and woke with her nerve endings vibrating beneath the surface of her skin. Trouble was coming, she could smell it. She had an uncanny knack for telling when an operation was heading south, just as she'd always had an inexplicable ability to tell when someone was lying, no matter how good they were at it. She'd honed the innate skill young, when learning to anticipate a blow from her father or a sly come-on from her older stepbrother had saved her from another assault. The trait had gotten her noticed when she was still a rookie agent, but it had been her ability to beat the polygraph that had gotten her fast-tracked into covert operations. She could regulate her biorhythms so completely she could fool the machines, repeatedly. She didn't sweat, not if she didn't want to.

She should have been a shoo-in for an undercover posting, and that's what she'd wanted. To go in deep, create her own persona, write her own rules. But the psych profiles pointed in another direction—she was better suited to handle the undercover operatives than to be one. She was the best at talking operatives off the ledge when they'd been under too long. She could read the terror or remorse or desperation in their psyches and say just what they needed to hear to get them grounded again. She could analyze their panic without being touched by it. She was an empath without empathy, at least that's what the psych evals said. She didn't bother to argue. Hell, maybe it was even true.

But she'd never lost an operative, and that made her untouchable. Maybe she'd gone off the reservation a few times—like now—but the higher-ups gave her a lot of rope, and she hadn't hanged herself yet.

Annoyed at the trickle of unrest scratching at the back of her mind, she threw off the thin covers and climbed out of bed. A shower would clear away the roaches in her head. No light filtered through the uneven slats of the dust-covered metal blinds. Her internal clock read 0630. Dawn came late in midwinter this far north.

A tap sounded on her door just as she was about to pull off the tank top she'd put on after her shower the night before. She dove for the gun in the suitcase she'd left open on the chair next to the bed and had it in her hand with the safety off in less than five seconds. No one knew where she was.

She eased toward the door, keeping away from the windows and turning sideways to present the smallest target if someone decided to pepper the door with rounds. She'd chained the door when she'd come in, but that wasn't any kind of protection.

"Who is it?" Sky asked.

"Room service."

"Good line, but not at this place. You've got the wrong room."

"I don't think so, *Lisa*."

Sky braced her gun at shoulder level and put her hand on the knob. "You want to give me a clue?"

"Jerome's VP verified your visit. Said he recommended you for the gig."

"Then we're all squared away, aren't we." She recognized Loren McElroy's voice.

"Not exactly. He happened to mention you were one hot Chicana. Funny, you don't look Hispanic to me."

Shit. She'd expected someone to check on her, but she'd taken a chance that they wouldn't discuss exactly what Lisa looked like. "He was probably thinking of someone else."

"He was very specific—apparently he has…personal knowledge. Think you better let me in."

Sky debated for about a second. Checkmate. She slipped the chain free and opened the door.

❖

Cam's cell phone rang while she was in the shower, and Blair picked it up to check the readout. She recognized the number and answered. "I thought you might take the day off—it's Boxing Day. Lots of great sales at all the shops."

Lucinda Washburn answered pleasantly. "The wheels of Washington never stop, even for fifty percent off."

"That's really a pity. You sure you don't want a girls' day out?"

Lucinda burst out laughing, a sound Blair hadn't heard much in the last three and a half years. She'd missed it. "You know, Luce, Dad would be lost without you."

"Your father is a resourceful man. He's going to be fine."

"I know that, but I'm not talking about President Powell. I'm talking about Dad. You have to take care of yourself, you know."

The line was silent for a long time, and Blair wondered if she'd finally overstepped. Lucinda had been more patient with her than anyone in her life except Cam, and Lucinda had seen her at her worst. Hopefully her best too, but she wasn't really sure. She wasn't certain that anyone except Cam really saw what was best about her. She couldn't go back and change the past. She couldn't unwrite her wild, resentful youth or those times when she'd disregarded her own best judgment to assert her independence, placing herself at risk and putting those who loved her in the untenable position of making her even more unhappy in order to protect her. Those days, hopefully, were past, although she knew she would never slip easily into line, never make the easy decisions about things that didn't strike her as right. Her father's and Cam's safety were the two most important things in her life. "Look, Luce, if I've—"

"No," Lucinda said softly. "You just caught me off guard."

Blair laughed. "That's not easy to do."

"I'm not sure you're right, though," Luce said, sounding uncharacteristically uncertain. Andrew Powell's chief of staff was never uncertain. Everything that happened in the White House and far beyond was channeled through her. She was the president's confidant, his buffer, some said his enforcer. She was the first one he came to for advice in a crisis or to discuss a new policy, and no one got through to him who didn't first have to deal with her. But she was also a woman who had been Andrew Powell's best friend his entire life, even more so since the untimely death of his wife.

"You know," Blair said carefully, "he might be the president, but he's also a man. And he's been alone for a long time. Well, I don't actually know that—nor do I want to," she said quickly, "but you might think about what's best for both of you sometimes."

"I wish I had one-tenth of your courage."

"It's not courage." Blair listened to the shower in the other room, thinking about Cam stepping out naked with water trickling over the smooth surface of her skin. Skin that was scarred in places from wounds that might've taken her away. Blair's heart froze for an instant until she banished the memories and the fear. "Selfishness. I wanted her, and the world be damned."

"Well, we can't have the president be damned with an election coming up," Luce said with a touch of the old steel returning to her voice. "And right now, our main concern is being sure that he's safe while he's out winning the minds and hearts of the people."

"All right, you win for now. No Boxing Day, no candlelit dinners. So, what can we do for you?"

"Ah, I was actually calling Director Roberts."

"Well lucky you, now you've got two of us."

Lucinda sighed. "We need a strategy meeting. Say, nine o'clock?"

Blair glanced at the clock. Not quite seven a.m. "That should work. See you then."

She ended the call and leaned across the bed to put the cell phone back on Cam's night table.

"Who was that?" Cam asked, walking into the room as she toweled off her hair.

Blair pushed the sheet aside and rose, naked also. She took the towel from Cam and kissed her. "Lucinda."

"Ah. What time?"

"Nine."

Cam turned toward the adjoining dressing room, and Blair caught her hand. "You're not dry yet. Stand still."

Cam raised an eyebrow but obeyed. Blair finished drying Cam's hair, then her chest and abdomen. She slipped behind her and drew the towel across her shoulders and down her back to the curve of her muscled ass. Tossing the towel into the bathroom, she wrapped her arms around Cam's waist and kissed the back of her neck.

"Mmm. Morning," Blair whispered, pressing her breasts to the warm skin of Cam's back.

"Blair," Cam said, "don't forget Lucinda."

"How could I?" Blair drew Cam back toward the bed. She sat on the edge, spun Cam to face her, and kissed the tight plane of her belly. "I don't need a lot of time. But I do need you."

Cam braced her hands on Blair's shoulders and parted her legs. "I'm all yours."

Blair kissed lower. "I know."

Cam shuddered and closed her eyes.

Blair took her deeper, her awareness eclipsed by the scent and taste of her. Time was something she would never take for granted. Cameron was hers, and she would yield that to no one. Ever.

❖

The plain white door to the motel room opened. The room beyond was shadowed, only a sliver of light leaking past a partially open door in the back corner—probably the bathroom. The redhead was just a dark outline, a slightly grayer silhouette in the gloom.

Loren stepped inside. "You don't need the gun."

"I guess we'll find out." The redhead, whose name was almost certainly not Lisa, motioned toward the single straight-backed wooden chair pushed into the corner next to the dresser. "Want to put your jacket over there and leave the gun in the pocket?"

"That hardly seems fair."

"Who said anything about fair? I didn't invite you."

Loren shrugged out of her jacket and dropped it onto the seat of the chair, leaving her Glock inside. She didn't like being without a weapon, but she wasn't inclined to get into a shootout, nor could she afford to. Now was not the time to draw attention to herself, and leaving a body in a roadside motel was likely to get her looked at.

She turned back, her eyes adjusting to the dim light. The redhead looked even better without clothes than she had in them. She was still wearing the turquoise tank, but the jeans were gone, and her long legs were bare except for white bikini panties. Loren lifted both hands. "You've got the advantage. Want to lose the gun now?"

The redhead lowered the gun to her side. "What do you want?"

"Answers."

The redhead laughed. "Those are rare commodities."

Loren smiled. "I know."

"Why don't we trade?"

Loren shook her head. "I don't think so. You're the one here under false pretenses."

"Really?"

"Where's the real Lisa Smith?"

"Taking a little vacation."

"You do know what Jerome will do to you when he finds out you're here using one of his people as a cover."

"I wasn't planning on telling him. Are you?"

"I guess that depends."

"On what?"

"On who you are and what you're doing here."

Sky weighed her options, which were slim to none. She hadn't been sure the night before if the club had recording devices in the Ugly Rooster, and she couldn't risk exposing her identity to Loren while they'd been sitting at the bar. She hadn't even been sure she wasn't going to just disappear into the night and continue to handle Loren from a distance. Now the decision was out of her hands.

"You haven't been checking in on schedule."

Loren, to her credit, didn't react. She hadn't survived undercover by being naïve or easily led. "I'm not following."

Sky smiled. "Sure you are. I never required regular reports, but not taking my calls?" She shook her head, feigning a frown. "Missing your weekly check-ins? What did you think was going to happen?"

"I don't know you."

Sky put her Sig on the rickety nightstand next to the bed, reached for her jeans, and pulled them on. She lifted the small suitcase onto the bed, pushed the clothes aside, and triggered the hidden lock. A portion of one inner wall popped open and she extracted the cell phone. She tapped 1 on the speed dial. A second later, Loren looked down at her leg. Sky murmured, "Answer your phone, Loren."

"Where'd you get my number?" Loren made no move to touch the phone she must have inside her leathers.

"Still don't believe me?"

"Like I said, I don't know you."

Skylar held Loren's gaze as she thumbed off the call. "Nobody does."

CHAPTER FOUR

Lucinda had scheduled the meeting for a briefing room on the ground floor of the West Wing. Cam and Blair were the first to arrive. A coffee service with bagels, muffins, and assorted spreads sat on a sideboard. They helped themselves and sat down around the long table in the center of the room. A few minutes later, a door opened, and Tom Turner, the special agent in charge of the Presidential Protective Division, walked in alone. His intense brown eyes focused on Cam and held for a few seconds before he nodded to Blair. "With all due respect, Ms. Powell, this might be something better discussed alone with the director."

"Why don't you sit down, Tom." Cam gestured to a nearby chair. "I'm happy for Blair to stay. She's been read in on all the details."

Tom's face contorted for a moment, an oddity for him. He was the epitome of calm in every situation and rarely showed any emotion, even in a crisis. Today, though, anger tinged his smooth dark features with an undertone of red. "I guess I'm the last one to know."

"That was my call." Cam had been expecting a confrontation after Tom had been excluded from the recent apprehension of a terrorist bent on assassinating the president—the man Tom was responsible for protecting. She suspected Lucinda had arranged for the three of them to have a few moments alone to sort things out. "By now, you've probably read the after-action report and can understand why you were out of the loop."

Tom remained standing, but his voice was calm. "I understand that one of the principal subjects under suspicion was named Tom, but I'm not sure I follow the connection to me."

Cam understood his anger. She would have been furious if someone had excluded her from an operation for any reason, but particularly if she was under suspicion. Trust was everything in their position. Personally, she would have been affronted and outraged, but professionally, she would have acknowledged the necessity of protecting not only the operation but, ultimately, the president. Their decisions were not personal, couldn't be personal, and Tom knew that as much as she did. Right now he was reacting as a man whose honor had been impugned, and the only answer was to reach out to the professional in him. "Every member of the team knew you weren't involved, but the president's life was at stake. The right call—the only call—had to be one that guaranteed security, a hundred and ten percent. Like I said, my call."

A muscle in Tom's jaw bunched, and Cam wondered if she had lost a friend. She'd worked closely with Tom when she'd been in charge of Blair's protection detail and would continue to work closely with him as long as he headed PPD. But duty trumped friendship. Duty trumped everything except one. Except Blair. Where Blair's life and happiness were concerned, Cam suspected she would do anything necessary to preserve them. Anything except betray what meant most to both of them, and because she knew Blair would never ask that, she never worried about what she might need to do.

Finally, Tom spoke. "I'd like to think I would've made the same call."

"You would have," Cam said quietly. "And I probably would've been just as pissed as you are now."

He smiled wryly. "Yeah. I think you would have." His shoulders relaxed as he turned toward the sideboard and poured himself a cup of coffee.

Silence fell over the room until, a moment later, Lucinda arrived, followed by Paula Stark—the chief of Blair's protection detail, Evyn Daniels—another PPD agent, and Wes Masters—the chief of the White House Medical Unit. Paula, Evyn, and Wes had all been part of the detail that apprehended Jennifer Pattee, a nurse in the WHMU who had been part of a plot to assassinate the president. She'd been captured a few days earlier with a stolen vial of avian flu that had been genetically mutated to enhance its transmission from human to human and was, even now, being studied at a Level 4 lab in Bethesda to ascertain all its properties. They didn't know who was behind the plot or how far the leak penetrated into the upper echelons of White House security, but Lucinda had appointed Cam to find out. This meeting—the entire operation—was off the record, because the records were no longer trustworthy.

Lucinda wasted no time. "The president is planning to embark on a cross-country campaign trip mid-month. He'll land in Chicago for a fund-raiser first, then travel by air and train throughout the Midwest, where the opposition's influence is the strongest right now. He'll be on the ground most of the time, and he'll be doing a lot of hand shaking."

Cam pictured the crowds, the impromptu photo ops, the last-minute itinerary changes. The president would be exposed, vulnerable, and Blair would be right by his side in the hot zone. When Kennedy had been assassinated, the governor of Texas, sitting in the same vehicle, had been wounded too. During the attempt on Reagan, the White House press secretary was shot and permanently paralyzed.

If Cam ordered Blair to remain behind, the president would support her decision, even though Blair had been a powerful, positive influence in his first election campaign. Family was always an important part of any platform, but never more than now when Russo was running on a family values ticket. The president's family was his daughter. She was smart and popular with voters of all ages, but especially with the young and women—critical segments of the electoral population. Andrew was often typecast as being part of the liberal-white-male elite, despite the fact that his personal wealth was far surpassed by Franklin Russo's. Blair helped humanize him, and the president needed to be seen as a man of the people.

Cam wouldn't demand that Blair stay home—*couldn't*—for any number of reasons. The choice wasn't hers to make, and even if it had been, the one thing she would never do was cage Blair to ease her own fears.

Blair said, "What are we going to do about his security?"

"Evyn will lead the advance teams, and we'll do exactly what we've always done," Cam said. "We'll know every inch of his route and be prepared to divert to secondary routes. We'll keep his exact movements among the people in this room. No one else will know more than they need to until right before we deploy."

"What about possible follow-up to the bioterrorism? Are we sure there isn't more of that stuff around?" Paula Stark asked. The chief of Blair's detail looked younger than her thirty years with her cap of dark hair and smooth regular features. She wasn't young in experience, having come under fire and been recently wounded. Recovered now, she was intense and focused. "He's going to be surrounded by hundreds of people every day. That would be a perfect time to release one of these agents."

"We'll interview the people at the lab where the agent went missing," Cam said. "Find out if we have everything they lost." She glanced at Wes Masters, a navy captain and the president's doctor. "I'm scheduled to fly down there tomorrow. I want you with me on this."

"Of course," Wes said.

"I'll also be interviewing Jennifer Pattee again," Cam said. "So far, she hasn't given us anything. Maybe a few days behind bars will have changed her mind."

"We have to assume secondary targets," Stark said quietly.

Cam's chest tightened. If the president was invulnerable, assassins would likely shift to secondary targets, and the most high-profile secondary target would be Blair. "We'll have to limit the number of people at potential risk and exclude them from the hot zone, especially when—"

"Don't even think about including me in there," Blair said as she sipped her coffee.

Stark wisely said nothing.

Cam said, "How about you wait a few weeks—"

"No," Blair said. "My presence with the president on these trips is expected, and any deviation from the expected is only going to let the other side know we anticipate something more is coming. We need them to think they still have the upper hand."

Cam couldn't argue. Blair was right. She'd been involved in this game since she was a teenager. She understood not only the politics but the strategy of those who were opposed to her father, politically and ideologically.

"I agree," Lucinda said, placing her cup and saucer onto a two-hundred-year-old end table. "We'll continue the public information releases as usual, but hold back what we can. I'll handle that. Director Roberts will be in charge." She walked to the door and paused, her smile polite as ever but her eyes hard blue stones. "Everyone knows what needs to be done. Enjoy the rest of the holidays."

❖

The redhead wanted her to believe she was Skylar Dunbar.

Loren hadn't stayed alive by trusting other people. She'd survived in Iraq and Afghanistan and with the Renegades by never believing what people said. Instead, she watched their eyes, searched for physical tells, hunted for the little inconsistencies that marked their words as false. She had no reason to believe this woman. What bothered her, what gnawed at the animal part of her brain, was that she wanted to trust her. She could still feel the heat of the redhead's fingertip tracing down the center of her T-shirt, as if the woman had stroked bare skin.

Loren wasn't easily seduced, even though she was no stranger to the casual touch of a woman. She didn't indulge often, and she didn't give sex much thought. When she'd been deployed, there hadn't been all that much opportunity, and even when there had been, stealing a private moment when the slightest lapse in concentration might get you dead sapped the pleasure from a casual encounter. She'd decided when she'd arrived in Silver Lake and the first members of the Renegades had sauntered into her garage for a look-see that she'd play things as close to the truth as she could. So when the opportunity'd arisen, she'd let it be known she liked women. In some strange way that bought her credibility, made her more like them. Still, she was careful. Careful not to get in between any of them and a woman. She didn't want to compete, not that way, and there hadn't been anyone she was willing to risk her standing in the club for. If she trusted this stranger, she'd be risking a lot more than just her position in the club. She risked her life every day, but that was for a purpose, a goal. Not for pleasure.

"Let's just say I believe you," Loren said, "and you know something about me. What are you doing here?"

"Look, I don't know about you, but it was a short night for me and I could use some coffee." Sky pulled her thick hair back and twisted it into a knot, a quick unconscious move Loren found unexpectedly sexy. "There's a diner a couple miles down the road. Why don't we go there and talk."

Loren couldn't see any downside to the suggestion, and the room was starting to feel stifling. Not from the trickle of warmth from the pinging baseboard heater, but from the closeness of the redhead who, even clothed, sent off waves of sexual heat. "So what do you want me to call you in public?"

Sky smiled. "How about baby?"

Loren laughed. "Not before the first date."

Sky's eyes widened a little, and her lips parted as if she was about to say something and then thought better of it. "Why don't you call me Red. Not very original, but I've heard it a lot."

"Okay. Red. Let's get coffee." Loren pulled on her jacket while Sky put on boots—low-heeled riding boots, not the biker-chick ones from the night before—and shrugged on the fitted black leather jacket.

Outside, the emerging sun filled the deserted parking lot with thin gray light. Loren glanced up at the blanket of clouds. "Snow's coming."

"There's a news flash." Sky grimaced. "Does it do anything else here?"

"Not between November and May." Loren nodded to the bike. "Extra helmet's hooked on the back there. Where you from?"

Sky hesitated as she pulled the skull cap off the rack and strapped it on. "I move around a lot."

"How about originally?"

"Texas," Sky said, surprising herself when she answered with the truth. Now, why would she do that? She never gave out personal info, even in personal situations, and for sure not when on the job.

Loren straddled the bike and Sky climbed on behind her, wrapping her arms around Loren's waist. Loren was lean and solid. Sky ducked her head down against Loren's back to keep the wind out of her face. Loren's body was hot despite the cold winter air, but that had to be her imagination. Sky closed her eyes.

"Hold on." Loren kicked up the stand and started the engine. Sky's arms tightened around her waist, and Sky's cheek pressed to the back of her shoulder. Ignoring the wave of heat that pulsed through her belly, she pulled out onto the highway and headed to the diner.

A few trucks dotted the unpaved lot, framed in dirty piles of snow. Condensation painted the inside of the plate-glass windows of the low-slung metal structure and ran down the streaked glass in uneven trails. Inside, the hot air hung heavy with the scent of cooking grease, fried meat, and eggs. Loren pulled off her jacket and slung it over her shoulder as she strode down the narrow aisle between the red-vinyl-topped stools on one side of the diner and the Formica tabletops in the booths lining the opposite wall. None of the booths were occupied, and she picked one well away from the men at the counter hunched over cups of coffee and white crockery plates heaped with bacon, eggs, and potatoes. A minute after they slid onto the stiff seats, a brunette in tight black jeans, a frilly white nylon blouse cut low and tight across her generous breasts, and a short black apron approached. She had a pad in one hand and a pen in the other. "What can I get you?"

"Coffee, scrambled eggs, and toast," Loren said.

"Make that two," Sky said.

The waitress scribbled and left without comment.

Loren eased back in the seat and stretched her left arm out along the top. "So, you were about to tell me what you're doing here."

Sky had the uneasy feeling she was being handled, and she didn't like it. McElroy was a smart, seasoned operative, and she'd been under a long time. Sometimes an operative lost sight of their objective and became so integrated into the culture of the world they had infiltrated they had a hard time getting out. It was a matter of pride for her that she'd never lost an agent, physically or psychologically. This one wasn't going to be the first, but she wasn't entirely sure how far she could trust her. "I've already told you who I am."

"So you said. If you're here under one false identity, why not two?"

Sky smiled. "Not a bad idea. A double-double."

Loren nodded.

"But there is the little fact that I've got your number." Sky smiled.

The heat in Loren's belly tightened. It was just a line, and not even true. No one had her number. No one knew her. Being known could get her killed. "Both of us being here is dangerous."

"Only if we make a mistake. I don't know about you, but I don't make mistakes."

"What do you think you can accomplish?"

"Look—" Sky waited while the waitress slid their coffee cups in front of them. Once alone, she leaned forward. "If you go deeper, then you need someone closer in case you need extraction."

"I've never needed to be retrieved. I won't now."

"We wouldn't send an unarmed soldier into the mountains without backup. This isn't any different."

"And you think you'd be enough to get me out?"

"Me and everyone at my disposal."

Loren blew out a breath. "Things are heating up here. We can't afford to raise suspicions."

"Then we won't. My cover is good. And if you get friendly-like, we'll have all the more reason to be seen together."

"Friendly," Loren said. The heat spiked up into her chest.

"The club members know you're interested in women." Sky smiled. "So go ahead and be interested."

"There might be a problem there. Ramsey is interested too."

Sky's eyes hardened. "Not happening."

"Maybe not, but there's no way I'm getting in his road."

"I'll handle him. You just do your part."

"And you'll be playing a part with me too?" Loren didn't know why she'd asked. She knew the answer.

"Does it matter?"

"No," Loren said. "It's all a game."

"Then we understand each other perfectly."

CHAPTER FIVE

Augustus Graves drove his Humvee through the barbed wire–topped gate into the FALA compound, eight hundred acres of undeveloped forest, invisible from the air and unapproachable by ground except for a single unmarked, double-track trail carved out of the dense mountainside. The sentries, a man and woman in fatigues carrying assault rifles and sidearms, saluted as he passed. Some of his forces lived full-time on the compound. Others lived off-base, maintaining important outside contacts who could be called upon for munitions and other supplies. And then there were those special ones spread farther afield—the ones who had been groomed since birth for the most important missions of all.

Each time he drove through the gates and saw the training courses, the barracks, and the armory dotting the wooded encampment, his chest swelled with pride and satisfaction. His loins tightened and his heart beat harder. After the massacres at Waco and Ruby Ridge, he'd purchased the tract of land in the unpopulated Bitterroot Range via a series of shell companies with funds contributed by ardent Second Amendment rights supporters across the country as well as some highly positioned politicians who needed him to push the agendas they couldn't embrace publicly. He'd known sooner than some of his fellow militiamen that a defensible, secure haven to train and plan was essential. And he'd been planning for thirty years, ever since he'd jumped on the last helo out of Saigon as the U.S. forces turned tail and ran in disgrace from the Communists. The U.S. government, and the castrated military that bowed down before it, had failed the nation and wasted the lives of his brothers-in-arms. He'd arrived home with a clear and certain vision of his mission, and at last, victory was at hand.

He'd never wanted public approval, wasn't interested in the adulation of faceless masses like the politicians who supported him. He wanted to see the conviction burning in the eyes of the men—and now the women—who believed as he did in a free and powerful America, and who were willing to place their honor and their lives on the line to restore the nation to its rightful glory.

A hundred troops occupied the compound at any one time, but he had five times that many at his immediate command throughout Idaho and neighboring states. He didn't contemplate outright war. His was a guerrilla action, carefully planned strikes designed to maximize destruction and destabilize institutions believed to be unassailable. Violent actions sent a message the public could not ignore: the government was corrupt and had been undermined by those who'd lost sight of the basic principles of the Constitution and Bill of Rights. The evidence was plain—every year saw a further erosion of a man's basic right to control his own destiny, but the complacent masses refused to acknowledge the dangers. His goal was to change that, to force the truth on those who refused to see. Blood was hard to ignore.

He parked next to the one-story wood-framed headquarters building and jumped out. He could outrun and out-bench-press most of the men half his age. Striding quickly across the snow-packed ground, he dashed up the steps to the timber-floored porch and inside. A beefy corporal with buzzed blond hair and windburned cheeks sat behind a simple gray metal desk, a computer by one hand and a phone by the other. His khaki shirt stretched tight across his linebacker shoulders. Williams—ex-high-school football star, a plumber's helper before Graves had elevated him in rank and given him a full-time job. He was loyal, fervent, and happy to take orders. A perfect soldier.

"Morning, sir," Williams said, saluting smartly.

"Anything to report, Corporal?" Grave saluted and unzipped his green nylon flak jacket.

"No, sir. Nothing at all on the news about the…incident."

Grave's stomach curdled when he thought about the failed mission in Washington. He'd relied too heavily on mercenaries—men he hadn't trained, go-betweens who didn't have the discipline and courage to risk their lives for a just cause. When the plot to release a deadly contagion that would cripple the nation's leaders had been discovered and foiled, he'd lost not only the element of surprise, he'd lost one valuable asset and had a second severely compromised. Years of careful planning had been wiped out all because of the cowardice of a few key agents. Agents who would pay.

"Very well," Graves said curtly, as if the report was of little consequence. It wouldn't do to have the troops know he was upset by this…setback.

"Ah," the corporal said hesitantly, his gaze cutting to the closed door to Graves's office.

Graves slowed, narrowed his eyes. "What is it?"

"Captain Graves arrived early this morning, sir." Williams seemed to shrink in his seat. "The captain said not to disturb you, so I didn't call—"

"Thank you, Corporal," Graves said, striding to the door emblazoned with the word *Commandant* in black block letters. He pushed through into his office and shut the door soundly behind him.

Jane, in combat fatigues with a Glock holstered on her left hip, stood by the window, looking out over the compound. It must have been almost two years since they'd last met in person. She was thinner than he remembered, and her profile was harsher. Fine lines radiated around her eyes, as if she'd spent a lot of time outside in the sun. She'd cut her glossy dark hair short, and it curled along her neck in an incongruously delicate fashion.

His eldest daughter turned and saluted. "Hello, Dad."

❖

Cam and Blair left the White House through the northwest entrance. Two SUVs idled in front of the gate. As soon as they exited the building, Stark stepped forward to follow them. Blair said to Cam, "Let's go to the gym."

"Feeling a little pent up?"

Blair laughed harshly. "Feeling a little *penned* up already. I wish there was some way he could avoid this campaign trip."

"You could always—"

"Please."

Cam took Blair's arm. Squeezed gently as she pulled her close. "It's going to be a long campaign. Plenty of time—"

"I know you have to try, and now you have. Enough."

"Okay." Cam wasn't about to let go, not when Blair's very life was on the line, but she could pick her battleground a little more wisely.

Someone—*some ones*—had staged a very elegantly planned assault on Blair's father. Blair was probably angry and frightened and feeling powerless, and her instinct would be to fight back. Maybe a workout would settle her down enough that she'd listen to reason. "I think the gym is an excellent idea."

"Just remember you said that," Blair muttered as they climbed into the SUV.

Stark leaned into the back. "Where to, Ms. Powell?"

Blair told her, and Stark climbed into the front passenger seat, relaying the destination to the other agents and the driver. Blair settled back beside Cam. "So, how angry are you?"

Cam cupped the back of Blair's neck and stroked lightly. "I'm not."

"So you're not going to try to kick my ass in the ring?"

"I didn't say that."

Blair laughed softly. "I know it's not what you want. I'm sorry about that."

"I know."

"You might not be angry, but I am." Blair rested her cheek against Cam's shoulder. She spoke quietly, her body vibrating with tension. "I'm so damn furious that someone we trusted could get so close to hurting Dad. That now we don't know who to trust. I know there's always risk, but this seems like such a betrayal. So wrong."

"It is a betrayal—of the worst kind." Cam slid her arm down around Blair's shoulders.

"Do you really think letting him take this trip now is wise?" Blair sighed.

"Not my call." Cam kissed the top of her head. "But we all know what to do."

"You didn't mention anything about having an inside line on the militia in the meeting just now."

"That's because I don't have anything definite yet. I've made a few calls and I'm getting stonewalled. I'm not sure why."

"Sometimes I think we have more secrets from the people who are supposed to be on our side than we do from those against us."

"Unfortunately, even the good guys are human."

"Yes." Blair slid her arm around Cam's waist and closed her eyes. Human and vulnerable. And that's what frightened her most of all.

❖

Franklin pushed his coffee cup aside and rose from his seat at the head of the formal dining-room table. He kissed his wife absently on the cheek as he passed her at the opposite end, his mind already on the interview he was doing for the Christian Broadcasting Channel that afternoon. Christmas was an excellent time to reinforce his image by linking it to that of the Messiah. His core constituents, far to the right of most Christians, would eventually forget the difference.

His wife's voice, soft and diffident, reached him just as he was about to step out into the hall. "I know how busy you are, darling, but can't you stay home this morning at least? Jac said she—"

The muscles in his back tensed and he kept his voice even with effort. "Jac couldn't manage to be present for Christmas services and missed an excellent opportunity to show the media a united family front. I don't see why I should change my plans for her today."

"Perhaps if we had invited her—"

"I've made it perfectly clear to Jac that as long as she insists on having this public relationship with another woman, she'll have to carry it on somewhere else." He turned and regarded his wife steadily. She shrank back in her chair. "You understand, don't you, my dear, that I'm only doing what's best for the family. We couldn't stop Jac from making the bad choices she's made over the years, but we must necessarily let the American people know we don't support her. She hasn't left us any other alternative. Whatever pain has come of all this, it's her fault."

Charlotte looked down at the table, her slender fingers picking anxiously at the fine linen napkin by her plate. "I understand you feel her choice of relationships is a problem, but even the president's daughter—"

Rage flared in Franklin's throat. "Yes, the president's daughter is a pervert. And so is ours. Jac has chosen to make her deviance a matter of public record, and I've labored under that black mark in the eyes of my supporters for years. She almost cost me the nomination. But the difference between Andrew Powell and me, among many things, is that I don't embrace her abnormality. And for that, I will be rewarded in November."

Charlotte's gaze rose to his, frightened, but unexpectedly resistant. "I know you must do what you think is best. But Jac is our child, and I want to see her."

"And that is your choice. It isn't mine." He turned and walked out. He'd tried for years to relegate Jac to the background, to keep her out of the public mind, and while she'd been deployed overseas he'd actually been able to put a positive spin on her service as a sacrifice he was willing to make for the sake of his country. But when she'd returned and made the ridiculous decision to become a smokejumper, the best he could do was call in a few favors and have her assigned to a remote outpost.

Even that hadn't worked. She simply would not remain invisible. Not only had she taken a woman for a lover, this time apparently permanently, but she'd insisted on being open about it. She'd even appeared at one of his fund-raisers with that—woman. Yes, Andrew Powell might choose to parade his dyke daughter around the national stage, assuming, almost certainly falsely, that his liberalism would garner him favor and ultimately votes. But Powell was wrong, and he would realize that sooner or later. Franklin rolled his shoulders, making a note to contact Nora and arrange a few hours alone with her after the broadcast. The tension in his groin reminded him he hadn't seen her much recently, what with all the necessary family obligations around the holidays. Nora was more than his campaign manager. She understood his needs.

Derrick appeared from the library where he had been researching scripture to pull appropriate quotes for Franklin's interview that afternoon. He stopped, a sheaf of paper in hand, when he saw Franklin striding toward him. "Is there anything I can get you, sir?"

"Just bring the car around. I want to stop by the campaign office before we head over to the studios."

"Of course." Derrick held out a square of note paper. "This is the only call you should return before you leave."

Franklin took the paper from him. It held nothing except a telephone number. "I'll see to it."

Derrick turned away, and Franklin detoured into his study and closed the door. He sat down behind his wide desk and adjusted his trousers absently, his erection uncomfortably restrained. The antique clock on the mantel over the fireplace chimed ten times. Perhaps he would have time to see Nora before the afternoon recording.

Hurriedly, he unlocked the top right-hand drawer of his desk and removed the unregistered phone. He punched in the number on the paper—this week's burn phone number. Hooker answered immediately.

"What is it?" Franklin asked.

"The mountain men need an infusion of funds."

Franklin rubbed his eyes and sighed. "Why?"

"Big weapons deal."

"Are you really sure it's worth doing business with them? They cost us a great deal with the last fiasco, and we cannot risk exposure."

"If you want direct action, they're the ones to provide it. It's your call."

"I suppose we have to keep them close for a while. Their methods might be crude, but they are effective. How much?"

"Two hundred and fifty thousand."

"We had better be buying more than just talk."

"You will be. When you're ready to point them at a target—if that's really the way you want to go—"

"Neither our objective nor our target has changed." Franklin registered a ripple of concern. Hooker seemed to be losing his will, questioning the direction of their shadow campaign more and more recently. If Hooker was growing soft, Franklin would need to find another mercenary to carry out his wishes. Hooker would bear watching. "Is there any word from DC?"

"Nothing so far. The White House will want to bury the story. Any sign of weakness now will hurt Powell's standing—and probably rekindle the gun control debate. He won't want that because he can't afford to look soft, and he can't support armed retaliation."

Franklin smiled. He loved closing the vise on Powell's nuts, and the screws were getting tighter all the time. "And the person responsible? Are we sure they won't be connected back to us?"

"No way. I used a number of go-betweens, none of whom knew each other or can be traced back to us."

"What about the woman in Georgia—the one who supplied the agent."

"She wouldn't talk. She'd be facing treason charges. Anyhow, she's disappeared. Gone to ground, probably indefinitely."

"Good." Franklin preferred she be under the ground, but that order of business could wait. "See that you're careful. This isn't over yet."

Hooker was silent for a few seconds. "Washington will be expecting something else."

"Of course. We'll just have to surprise them. I'll be in touch." Franklin clicked off the phone, dropped it into the drawer, and locked it up. When he stepped out into the hall, Derrick was waiting with Franklin's dark wool overcoat over one arm and his briefcase in the other hand. "Is the car ready?"

"Yes, sir."

"Good. Call Ms. Fleming, would you, and tell her I'll be dropping by for a pre-interview strategy meeting."

Derrick's face revealed nothing as he handed Franklin his coat. "Of course, sir. I'll inform the driver of our change in route."

Franklin followed him briskly down the hall. Thirty minutes with Nora would put him in top form to meet the press, and any day he had a chance to deliver his message was a good day indeed.

CHAPTER SIX

"D id you have any trouble getting here?" Graves asked his daughter. Jane took a few steps toward him and then hesitated when he made no move to meet her. He buried the strange, unbidden impulse to pull her close. He couldn't remember the last time he'd hugged any of his children. Perhaps he never had. From the time they were young, his focus had been to train them. To prepare them. They'd all done very well and he was proud of them. Good soldiers, each of the three—loyal and firm in their beliefs. A commander's responsibility wasn't to praise his soldiers, but to harden them for battle. The reward came in doing one's duty. That was praise enough.

"No, sir. No problems." Jane's slate-blue eyes, a shade grayer than her sister's, held his. "I took public transportation—buses and trains for the most part. Untraceable. It took me a while to get here, but I didn't want to risk a call."

Graves walked to his desk and sat behind it. Jane turned to face him at parade rest. He nodded approvingly when she finished her report. "Smart tactical maneuver."

"Sir." Jane focused on a spot to the left of Graves's shoulder, respectfully allowing him the superior position even though she was standing. "I left when I didn't hear from the lieutenant at the appointed time. Our orders were to protect our positions from any threat of exposure."

"Your orders were correct."

Jane's left eyelid twitched, the only sign she'd given of uncertainty. "If I may ask, what is the lieutenant's status?"

A fist tightened in Graves's innards. A gnawing sensation, like acid etching its way through steel, eroded his midsection. He ignored the burning pain as he had been doing since the failed operation in DC.

"Our last communication confirmed receipt of the contagion. Beyond that, we've had no contact."

"Do you think she's been apprehended?" A flicker of frank concern raced across Jane's face before she schooled her expression to neutrality again. Her hands clenched into fists at her sides.

He'd have to speak to her about those small breaks in discipline. A good interrogator would latch onto physical tells like leeches on bare skin.

"We have to make that assumption," Graves said.

"With respect, sir, are there plans to extract her? I'd like to volunteer."

"Not at this time," Graves said flatly. And possibly never. He could not risk further compromise for the sake of one soldier, even a highly valuable one. Jennifer would not betray them, of that he was certain. He trained all his soldiers well, but he had trained his children even better. They weren't raised to simply follow orders. They were instilled with the same dedication to the mission as he held. They burned with the same fervor. They believed as he did, that personal sacrifice was a small price to pay for success. He'd raised them to excel, to follow career paths that would place them in positions where they could be used to further the cause when the time was right.

Never had he expected such an opportunity as had been presented to him when a man named Hooker had approached him with a request for an unusual weapon. A WMD developed not by the Pentagon or DOD, but by the capitalist industrial complex. Graves didn't know Hooker's backer, although he had men working to find out, but the plan reeked of political ambition. For the time being, Graves was willing to lend the manpower and weapons of his militia in support. They had lost a battle in DC, and they would not lose the next one.

"Can we get word to her?"

"By the terms of the Patriot Act," Graves said, nearly choking on the hypocrisy of the term, "she can be held incommunicado indefinitely. With luck, she'll find a way to get word to us."

"And Robbie?"

"His position is still secure. He's safe."

"Good." Jane straightened her shoulders. "I'm prepared for new orders, sir."

Graves suspected Jennifer would be incarcerated until his mission was accomplished, which might take years. His middle child, only a year younger than Jane and very nearly her twin in appearance, had

managed to position herself at the very heart of the enemy's power—
the White House. Her loss was a major strategic setback. Jane, the most
cerebral of his children, had bypassed the military for a career in science
and research. He'd pushed her toward experimental labs where she
might gain access to high-level projects and lethal bio-agents. She had
surpassed his hopes as well, advancing rapidly at Eugen Corp until she
was assigned to a Level 4 lab. Now that the attempts to infect Powell
and high-ranking members of the government with a virulent contagion
had failed, and Jane's cover was almost certainly compromised, she
was no longer of value in covert operations. But she was still one of his
finest marksmen.

"I need snipers."

She smiled. "It will be good to carry a weapon larger than a test
tube again."

"Put your time in on the range, prove you are fit for field duty, and
I'll give you command of C Company."

She straightened to attention and saluted briskly. "Yes, sir. Thank
you, sir."

He rose and saluted. "It's good to have you back, Captain."

❖

The gym was nearly deserted. Most of the city had taken an
extended holiday, and the streets teemed with people carrying shopping
bags, darting in and out of stores, rushing to Metro platforms, and
generally enjoying the air of post-holiday celebration. Cam opened
the combination lock on the locker she and Blair kept at the gym a
few blocks from Dupont Circle. Unlike Blair's favorite gym in New
York City, this one was more a modern health club. All the lights
worked, the floors were clean industrial tiles—as opposed to scuffed
and pockmarked concrete, cracked and dinged from years of heavy
weights clanging on it—and the locker rooms, men's and women's,
were brightly lit, clean, and equipped with functional private showers.
While enjoying the amenities, Cam missed the smell of old leather and
rubber. She missed the grunts and curses of men pushing their bodies to
lift more, punch harder, move faster. She even missed the appreciative
stares Blair drew as she worked out in the ring, swift and lethal.

The DC gym had about equal numbers of men and women, and
for the most part the emphasis was on fitness, not fighting. But the
owners had partitioned off a part of the huge space for a sparring ring.

In a city filled with federal agents, the move had been a wise one. While every agency had its own gyms, many agents preferred to get away from work when they relaxed, and a workout was very often a major form of relaxation.

As Cam followed Blair to the ring, watching the muscles ripple in her bare shoulders and her thighs bunch with each determined stride, she considered that a workout might also be a form of seduction.

Blair slowed, looked back over her shoulder, and said, "Spar first. Play later."

"You should stop reading my mind."

Blair grinned. "I don't think so. But you'd better keep your mind on your guard. I'm not feeling friendly."

Cam laughed. "Well then, let's see what you've got."

❖

Loren watched Skylar finish her breakfast in a nonchalant, unhurried fashion, while trying to work out the angles—what would be in it for Skylar to come out of the dark like this if she actually were Loren's handler. Or, looking at the other side of the coin, who Skylar might be working for if her goal was to expose Loren as an undercover agent. Logic and Loren's experience told her the second was a much more likely scenario—Skylar was lying. Maybe one of the middlemen Loren used to procure arms had gotten suspicious and run a background trace. Her cover was good, but if anyone searched far enough back, they'd discover she didn't have much of a history before she went into the army. At least, no history that anyone could find. She had a family, though—parents and a younger brother. Her only demand when she'd accepted the offer of a nameless man who had appeared at her tent in the middle of the desert in the middle of the night offering her the opportunity to serve her country in a way, as he put it, "that would be far more significant than anything you might do if you stayed in the regular forces," had been that her family would be untouchable. He had assured her that was possible if she was willing to leave her past behind—all of it. He'd given her a week to decide, and she hadn't slept for most of it, wondering if there was some way to tell them what was happening without putting them at risk. The best she'd been able to do was ask them to trust her and to tell them she'd be in touch again when she could. She'd Skyped with her mother, and she could see her mother's brilliant mathematical mind analyzing what she wasn't saying, the way she always had. Her mother had looked at her for a long time in silence and finally said, "You've always made us proud. I know that will never change. Be careful. We'll talk to you soon."

Loren had talked to her father next, and he'd had that slightly befuddled look he got when he was concentrating on a new project and part of his mind was elsewhere, but at the very end, when she'd said good night, his focus had grown steady and clear. He'd smiled at her and said, "Good night is a good phrase. I never did like good-bye. I love you."

A deep background check might tag her past as questionable, but she would rather she be vulnerable than them. Maybe Skylar was the bait someone had sent to try to convince her that she was actually talking to her handler. Then again, Skylar had her burn-phone number, and no one except her handler had that. She bought the phones herself and sent the number by text to a drop-box number after rerouting it around the world half a dozen times. Someone might possibly have killed her handler and taken her phone, but the chances of that... She ran the probabilities in her mind nearly as fast as her mother would have and came up with a pretty small number.

"Make a decision yet?" Skylar asked.

"I guess you forgot to add mind reader to your list of accomplishments."

"Not really." Skylar wiped her mouth on a paper napkin, balled it up, and slid it into her pocket. She tugged another paper napkin from the holder and methodically cleaned each utensil she'd used as well as the rim of the cup. Her movements were practiced and, unless someone was watching her very carefully, not at all obvious.

"Okay, that's impressive."

Skylar laughed shortly. "Never can be too careful."

"I know."

Leaning back, Skylar shrugged. "There's not much else I can do to convince you. And, really, if you were an easy sell, I'd be worried. But we don't have a lot of time. Things are heating up, and I'm not sure we have a great picture of exactly where all the pieces are going to fall. We need to get out in front of this."

"There's nothing going on with the Renegades that hasn't been going on for the last couple of years. So you're here because of the militia."

Skylar's left eyebrow rose an eighth of an inch. "Well, I see you've made a decision."

She had, and it wasn't because of any conclusion she'd come to through logic or analysis. Her gut told her Skylar was on the level, and her gut had kept her alive this long. If she was wrong, then she could hope that she'd figure it out before Skylar reported back to whoever had hired her. If she took Skylar out and made it look like an accident, she'd buy time before someone else came looking. She'd just have to keep Skylar close. "So? What's going on with the militia?"

"That's what we want to find out. Right now, all we're hearing is a lot of chatter on the Internet and reports of high-level deals from various informants—details murky." Skylar leaned forward. "We need to compare notes."

Loren scanned the diner. No one was paying much attention to them, but she was never happy about staying in one place for too long. If they bumped into someone she knew, she wasn't sure how she'd explain her early-morning breakfast with the babe who'd showed up out of nowhere the night before. She pulled her wallet from her back pocket and laid a twenty on the table. "Let's go somewhere else to talk."

"Where do you suggest?"

"My place."

❖

Cam landed hard on her back and tucked her chin to prevent her skull from slamming into the thin canvas mat. Blair dropped beside her and trapped her right arm in a figure-four hold before flipping her onto her stomach. The pressure in her shoulder increased as Blair ratcheted her arm higher between her shoulder blades. Cam tapped the mat and the pressure disappeared. She rolled over and Blair knelt on the mat, her hands relaxed on her thighs.

"Nice move," Cam said.

"Your attention was wavering." Blair grinned.

"No, it wasn't. You were just a little faster that time."

"I've been wanting to try that move." Blair shrugged. "Had enough?"

They'd been at it for forty-five minutes. Cam's T-shirt was soaked with sweat. Blair's hair lay in dark golden strands along her neck, her face glowed, and her eyes gleamed bright and clear. "If you're satisfied, I could do with a shower and a late breakfast."

"Shower here or at home?" Blair asked.

Cam pushed herself up to a sitting position and flipped the wet hair off her forehead. She eyed Blair slowly. "I think home would be safer."

Blair laughed and rose gracefully to her feet. "Something you have in mind?"

"Yeah. A move I've been wanting to try."

CHAPTER SEVEN

Cam held the line while the operator at Quantico patched her through to Eddie Byrnes, an FBI special agent she'd worked with when she was in the investigative division. They'd run a few joint task forces together, chasing drug money being laundered through seemingly legal gambling operations in Atlantic City. Eddie had moved over into counterterrorism after the bombings, and she'd eventually been rerouted to Homeland Security. Counterterrorism covered a lot of potential threat areas, from monitoring terrorist activities overseas to ferreting out sleeper cells at home. Eddie would be working closely with teams monitoring subversive domestic groups, and he'd know who she ought to talk to. She just had to get the information from him without revealing exactly why she needed it.

"Byrnes," a raspy voice said.

"Eddie, it's Cam Roberts."

"Cam, hey. I hear congratulations are in order."

"Ah, thanks," Cam said, still not used to how her private life had suddenly become public. When you married the president's daughter, privacy became wishful thinking.

"Nice catch. Any advice?"

Cam laughed. "'Fraid not. Just lucky."

"Uh-huh. So—what's doing?"

"Can you spare me a few minutes?"

"Sure—what's your schedule like?"

"I was hoping today."

"Must be important," Eddie said, probing a little.

"It's time sensitive. I'll come to you—you still based out of Richmond?"

"So I heard you were HS now. They give you your own plane too?"

"A loaner."

Eddie snorted. "Hate to disappoint you, but I'm in DC. You can take a cab."

"Even better. When and where?"

"How about Duggin's around three?"

"I'll be there. Thanks, Eddie."

"Sure thing."

Cam hung up and checked a text that had come in while they'd talked. Lucinda. Meeting at 1345. Her office. Cam sighed. Back to the White House.

On my way, Cam texted back.

Blair had gone to the spare room she used as a studio to paint, and Cam stopped to say good-bye. Blair had her back to the doorway, applying background colors to a five-by-five canvas in broad, sweeping strokes of magenta and purple. She was listening to something through her earphones and swaying rhythmically with each bold stroke. She'd stripped off her shirt and wore just a faded green tank top and low-cut jeans. She was barefoot, her hair damp from the shower they'd finally shared after a fast and furious few moments in bed. The lovemaking had felt as cathartic as the workout in the gym and nearly as rigorous. Despite the intense connection they'd shared just a short while before, Cam chafed under the uneasy sense that something was off between them. She suspected she was the cause—she didn't want Blair anywhere near the campaign trail until the threat of reprisal for the thwarted attack and apprehension of Jennifer Pattee was resolved. And she couldn't do a damn thing to stop her. Deciding not to inflict her dark mood on Blair, she turned away.

"Call me if you're going to be late," Blair said from behind her.

Cam turned back. "Sorry, I didn't want to disturb you."

Blair studied her solemnly, her brilliant blue eyes stormy gray. "You bother me in many ways, Cameron, but being near me has never been one of them."

Cam walked over and kissed her. "I love to watch you paint."

Blair held both hands out away from Cam's crisp white shirt and tailored charcoal jacket. "You won't love me if I get paint on you."

Cam grinned. "I might. Depends on the circumstances."

Blair leaned in and nipped at Cam's lip. "Guess we'll have to see, then."

"I don't expect to be too late. Meetings. You know how that goes."

"All right. Whatever you need to do."

"I'm flying to Atlanta first thing in the morning."

Blair nodded. "If you don't mind, I think I'll go home for a while."

"Yes. Of course." Cam's condo was their Washington residence, but it'd never been home for Blair. The sanctuary she had made for herself in New York City across from Gramercy Park was home. The loft space, the wide-open studio, but perhaps most of all, the city itself— where she could step out the door and disappear into the throngs of people—were her touchstones. The city represented freedom to her like no other place ever had. Right now, facing the constraints of heightened security on the campaign trail, she probably needed that freedom, or at least the semblance of freedom, more than she had in a long time. "When?"

"Tomorrow after you leave."

"Do you want me to join you there?"

Blair's eyes softened and the storm clouds disappeared. She leaned her cheek against Cam's shoulder. "Of course I do. There's nowhere in the world I want to be without you."

Cam kissed her forehead. "Then I'll be there. Soon as I can."

Blair kissed her neck. "I know. I love you."

"I love you too," Cam said quietly.

❖

Lucinda's aide directed Cam into Lucinda's West Wing office as soon as she arrived. Paula Stark and Adam Eisley—Andrew Powell's political strategist and campaign manager, a fortysomething Ivy Leaguer with hawk-like eyes—were already waiting in the formal sitting area. Lucinda put aside a report and joined them.

"Can I order anything up from the kitchen for you, Cam?" Lucinda asked.

"No, I'm fine. Thanks." Cam nodded to the others and sat down.

"I won't keep you long, then," Lucinda said. "Paula and Adam have been discussing the itinerary, and since there's some difference of opinion as to just how we should proceed, I thought you ought to be here for the discussion."

Adam looked like he had developed an acute ulcer. "This is a waste of time, as I've already noted. There's nothing to discuss."

Stark's normally calm dark eyes sparked. "You can't just make unilateral decisions about areas outside your expertise."

"I can when my job takes precedence over everyone else's—which it does if any of you want to *have* a job in a few more months."

"We're not talking about job security here, we're—"

"If you did the job you were—"

Cam followed the thinly veiled insults being hurled back and forth, as to who knew what and who had the final say, for a few minutes, then interrupted. "I take it this is about Blair."

Paula and Adam looked at her as if just now realizing they were discussing her wife. Paula blushed. Adam just shook his head in apparent disgust.

Paula said, "For the record, I'm opposed to Ms. Powell accompanying the campaign entourage given the recent circumstances."

Adam made a sound like rocks tumbling down a metal chute. "What the hell does that mean?"

Lucinda said, "We've had a recent spate of death threats aimed at POTUS."

"So what else is new? That's part of the job description." He cocked his head at Cam. "Isn't the whole point of the Secret Service to see nothing comes of it?"

"Yes," Can said, aware that Lucinda had purposefully not told Adam about the actual attack, "but when the density of threats increases, we take notice."

"So—put more bodies around him."

"Then you'll complain we're keeping him away from the public," Stark muttered.

"Cam," Lucinda said calmly, "what are the chances the security threat level will be lowered by the time we depart?"

Cam sighed. "A situation like this can change quickly—there's no way to say."

Adam grunted. "There you have it. We can't keep the president under wraps, and if he goes on the trail, Blair goes."

"Blair isn't essential," Paula said. "Not enough to outweigh the risks. She's been a target before. She's an obvious secondary now." She glanced at Lucinda. "I can't order her to stay, but you or the president could."

"Look," Adam said. "No one wants anyone in harm's way, but that's the reality of the game. None of you can say whether next week, or next month, or four months from now will be any safer." He glared at Cam. "Right?"

"Yes," Cam said reluctantly.

Paula sat forward in her chair. "From a security point of view, it makes sound tactical sense to remove an obvious secondary target and put all our resources into securing the primary, at least until we can investigate some of the potential threats."

"I agree," Cam said. "If we could have a few weeks to get this cleared up before Blair—"

"You just said you can't guarantee a quick resolution," Adam said, "and the president has a fight on his hands *right now.*"

Lucinda rubbed her eyes. "Cam, I know how you feel, but I'm afraid Adam is right. The opposition is gaining strength all the time, and Andrew, right or wrong, has gotten the reputation of being remote and removed from the people. Never mind that he's working thirty-six hours a day handling foreign crises and economic upheaval here at home. The voters need to believe that he is one of them, that he understands their problems, that he can walk in their shoes. And the only way for him to do that is to get out there, with them."

Adam stood and looked pointedly at Cam. "You'll just have to see that the people assigned to protect them do their jobs."

"Thank you for your time," Lucinda said, rising. "Anything you need, Cam, just let me know."

Stark's jaw looked tight enough to crack, but she said nothing as Adam turned and walked out.

"Thank you." Cam appreciated Lucinda's offer of support, but the one thing she needed, Lucinda couldn't give her. A guarantee that Blair would be safe.

❖

"So," Sky said, glancing once around the cavernous garage. Three motorcycle bodies in various stages of disassembly occupied the center of the room, and one entire wall was taken up by a counter covered with tools. Shelves above and below sagged under jumbles of spare parts. A few small windows on one long wall let in a little light, casting everything in a gray pall. Despite the clutter, the place seemed unusually clean for a garage. "This is home?"

Loren hung her leather jacket on a peg beside the double-wide pull-down door and hit the button for the automatic closer. She kept the temperature in the garage in the high sixties—cool enough to weld damaged motorcycle chassis in comfort, but high enough to inhabit when not working. She pointed to a half wall toward the far end of the room. "I sleep down there."

"Cozy," Sky said.

"It suffices." Loren poured water into a glass coffeepot, filled the reservoir of a drip coffeemaker, dumped grounds into a filter, and set the pot to brew. Leaning against the counter, Loren braced her elbows on the wooden ledge and surveyed Sky. She'd unzipped her jacket and stood with her hands on her hips, looking sexy and cocky and unsettlingly seductive in her tight tank and hip-hugging jeans. Loren ignored the twinge of attraction. "So, why are you here?"

"I already told you," Sky answered with mock patience. "Things are heating up and I wanted a firsthand look."

"If Ramsey finds out you're not Lisa Smith, he'll kill you. Or worse."

"He won't find out. Lisa gave us all the details of her assignment, including when and how she's supposed to report to Jerome's man. As long as she checks in on time and provides them with some intel, they'll be happy."

"Is the international president really interested in the club's finances?"

Sky laughed. "The New Year's run is coming up and he heard about the guns. He wants to make sure he gets his share."

Loren swore. "So we have a leak."

"Possibly not on your end—maybe whoever you're buying from is talking around, looking to leverage your offer into something better."

"Whoever I'm dealing with?" Loren asked. If the redhead was who she said she was, she'd know.

Sky sighed. "You are a hard sell. The *Russians* don't care who they sell their guns to, only who is willing to pay the most."

"Okay—you pass," Loren said. And Sky was right—all the guns moving along the West Coast were coming by way of the Russian mob. Two and a half years ago, when she'd first set up shop in Silver Lake and put out the word she was in the business of procurement again, she'd called on contacts she'd made in the Middle East to vouch for her with the mob. Only this time, she was working for the Renegades and not the U.S. Army. "My arrangements with the Russians are solid—they won't try to outbid me."

"You know there's no such thing as loyalty with these guys. And if there's a struggle going on internally, someone may be trying to build a power base by allying with the Soledads."

"Stupid, then," Loren muttered.

"Yes, but no one ever said these guys were geniuses."

"So we need to move quickly before our guns end up in the Soledads' armory." The Soledads were a Salvadoran offshoot and one of the most violent gangs to spring up in the last decade. They were annexing territory all over the country by killing off their rivals. So far, they hadn't made a move on Renegades territory, but if they got their hands on two hundred assault rifles, they might.

"I'd say the sooner the better." Sky straddled a demo Harley—one Loren had rebuilt and outfitted herself. Sky leaned forward and gripped the handlebars, her legs hugging the smooth rise of the black tank with red flames dancing along its sultry curves. "Nice bike. Your work?"

"Yeah," Loren said, her throat unusually dry. She reached into the small fridge under the counter, pulled out a bottle of water, and took a long drink. The cold did little to extinguish the simmering heat that burned hotter the longer she looked at Skylar.

"Where is FALA getting that kind of money?" Sky asked casually.

"I don't know yet."

Sky peered at her from beneath a sweep of glossy red. "What are they going to do with them?"

"Don't know that, either."

"We can't afford to have a bunch of fringe lunatics use guns we helped them get in some kind of homegrown terrorist attack."

Loren's lust cooled. Her voice hardened. "They won't. By the time the exchange is set and the guns are moved to an intermediary holding point, we'll know what we need to know, and we can arrange for a raid by the ATF. The guns will never get into the militia's hands."

"Yes," Sky said, lifting one long leg gracefully over the bike and dismounting. "That's the plan. And I'm here to be sure it works."

Loren watched her silently. Sky hadn't really said very much, and what she hadn't said was telling—who'd sent her, why now, and what she was really looking for. Of course, that assumed anything she'd said was really true at all. Loren had no choice but to play along, and the game would have been simpler if Sky didn't have the unusual and unwelcome effect of clouding her mind with a haze of desire. A distraction like that could get her killed.

CHAPTER EIGHT

Duggin's was a corner bar in Adams Morgan that had escaped gentrification, projecting a casual air of disregard for appearances typical of local taprooms that had served DC neighborhoods for generations. The wood-paneled, low-ceilinged bar was lit by dusty, shadeless bulbs in sconces along the wall opposite the long wooden bar whose varnish had long since been scoured away by countless bartenders' rags and gallons of spilled beer. Behind the bar, liquor bottles stood sentry in rows, from rotgut on the counter within easy reach to top-shelf brands almost as dusty as the light fixtures. The big mirror behind the bottles threw back distorted images of bottles and faces, discolored in smoky patches from years gone by. The bartender was a burly Irishman in a white open-collared shirt and shapeless black pants who'd inherited the place from his father, whose father's father and those before him had stood behind this bar serving the local police and firemen and, eventually, scores of federal agents.

Duggin's was a cop bar, and though the bartender didn't know Cam, he knew her type. Cops were cops, whether local or feds. He tipped a finger to his forehead in acknowledgment as she walked by and then studiously ignored her. Eddie had picked a good place. Their presence would be forgotten before they'd even left. Eddie sat at the far end of the bar nursing a beer in a heavy glass mug. He hadn't changed in the nearly two years since she'd last seen him. His receding hairline and long, thin face made him look a decade older than late thirties, but his frame was still wiry and trim. In a Redskins sweatshirt and jeans, he could easily pass for one of the local LEOs, stopping off for a quick one after shift. No one sat nearby. Happy hour didn't start for an hour, and then the place would be wall-to-wall bodies. Now a few men at the bar watched sports on the television monitors angled in the corners of the room or contemplated the liquor in their glasses as if searching for answers that had long eluded them.

Cam slid onto a stool next to Eddie and held out her hand. "Thanks for meeting me."

He shook her hand. "No problem. How's it going at the big house?"

"No complaints."

The bartender approached and Cam said, "A beer—whatever you've got on tap that's dark."

He nodded and moved away, a silent shadow.

Eddie stared unself-consciously at the ring on her left hand. "Whoever would've thought, huh?"

"I know what you mean." She did know what he meant, although they were undoubtedly thinking of different things. For Eddie, the idea of a president who publicly acknowledged his child's homosexuality and supported her decision to marry her same-sex partner would have been inconceivable just a few years before. For Cam, the ring symbolized something she had never expected—to love so deeply that all else was secondary, even the duty that had motivated and guided her all her life. She closed her hand, felt the ring tighten on her finger, a tangible link to Blair that steadied her no matter how chaotic the circumstances.

"So," Eddie said into the silence.

Cam said, "I need some deep intelligence on the militias—more than I can get from reports. I want to talk to someone who's up close to what's happening on the ground. I've reached out to a few people, but every source I've tried has closed me down."

Eddie pursed his lips and suddenly became very interested in his beer.

"I know how to protect someone's cover," Cam said quietly. She waited while the bartender surreptitiously slid a heavy glass mug in front of her and instantly disappeared. Cam took a sip. The brew was dark and tangy. Duggin's served the best. "And this is top priority."

"You're a deputy director of Homeland Security—why ask me? You can pretty much get anything you want, can't you?" Eddie didn't sound angry or accusatory, mostly curious.

"You're right I can make it happen, but if I do, word is going to get out that I'm looking, and that's not good for anyone."

"You've been in the field, Cam," Eddie said. "You know something like this can get people killed."

"That's why I'm here talking to you and not throwing my weight around through channels."

Eddie took a deep breath and let it out slowly. Cam waited while he considered. She could and would start knocking on doors if she had to, and she'd use her position to force people to give her answers, but the risk increased for everyone that way. No department was leakproof— and her investigation as well as the identities of agents in the field might be jeopardized. All the same, she was putting Eddie in a tight spot. He had to protect his sources, or he'd have none left.

"Where you interested in looking?" Eddie finally said. "It's a big country with a lot of loonies running around in camo spouting Second Amendment rights. You ran into some of them yourself not long back, as I recall."

Cam grimaced. Blair had barely escaped being a casualty of a paramilitary group thought to have been secretly aiding the terrorists who'd struck the WTC. The war on terror had suddenly taken on a very personal face, with an enemy much closer than they'd realized. "I'm chasing a lead that dead-ends in Idaho."

"Doesn't surprise me." Eddie pushed his beer away. "I can put you in touch with someone who knows someone who's running an operation out there. He's several levels above ground zero, though. I don't know how close you'll be able to get to the people who might be able to name names."

"I won't know what I need until I can get someone to connect a few dots for me—all I need is a thread to pull. These organized militia groups can't exist without deep pockets backing them up. And following the money is always a smart move."

Eddie grinned. "Just like in the old days, huh?"

"New game, same strategy."

"Okay. The guy you want to talk to is Chuck Ferrell. FBI."

"He won't know how I got to him," Cam said. "I'm willing to go out there, meet his people face-to-face. Nothing gets reported. No names will surface."

"You tell that to Chuck, he might buy it."

Cam didn't bother to say Ferrell wouldn't have a choice. She took out money to pay for the tab. "I appreciate it."

Eddie swiveled on the stool and leaned close. "Some of these gangs and militias don't follow any laws we recognize. Some of them don't have to because they've got cops in their pockets." He grimaced.

"Not just the locals, either. You'll have to be careful that you don't mistake friends for foes. Or the other way around."

"I know." Cam had run enough ops where a little money was traded for drugs in order to track a middleman back to the real power to know that sometimes criminals were protected to keep them as informants or to use them to set up a sting on a more dangerous perp. "But I appreciate the advice. Thanks for the help. I owe you."

"You know what?" Eddie said. "I'm glad I don't have your job. I'd rather just chase crooks and drug runners."

"Some days," Cam said, rising, "so would I."

❖

Blair's cell phone danced on the small table next to her easel, its ringtone swallowed by the pounding beat of the rock music from the portable on the window ledge. She checked the big gymnasium-style clock on the wall. Cam had only been gone a few hours, so it probably wasn't her. For a brief second, she thought about letting it ring over to voice mail—she hadn't had a chance to really get into a painting in a long time and she was excited by this one—but she checked the Caller ID all the same. Too much had happened lately to ignore a call. When she saw the number, she scooped up her cell phone and swiped Answer. "Hi, Dad."

"Hi, honey," her father said. "Sorry I missed you this morning."

"No problem. Everything okay?"

"I was about to ask you the same thing."

Blair dropped her brush in a jar of cleaner and grabbed the faded dish towel she kept by the easel and wiped away stray streaks of paint from her hands. "Sorry?"

"I wanted to be sure Adam wasn't pressuring you to come along on the campaign kickoff. He's great at what he does, and I trust his instincts where strategizing is concerned, but he tends to miss the human element in all of this."

"I'm not following, Dad. I haven't seen Adam since before the wedding."

"Oh," her father said. "He had some sort of meeting a bit ago, and apparently Cam and Stark needed some convincing. Adam said they were on board, and I wanted to be sure you were."

Blair walked over and pulled her iPod out of the speaker cradle.

A whisper of cold trickled through her chest. "Cam and Stark met with Adam—about me going on the trip?"

"Ah—" Andrew said, "I'm not sure of the details. I might have gotten the details—"

"Dad."

Andrew sighed. "It was some kind of last-minute brainstorming session with Luce—"

"Luce was there?" The cold spread, and beneath it, anger simmered.

"Honey, you know Adam. He's in total campaign mode now. He's likely to call at two a.m. with some new plan to win the undecideds."

Blair would have laughed at the image, knowing it was true, if she hadn't been struggling to keep her temper. Adam was a handler—he handled everyone in her father's circle like pieces on a chessboard when it came time to campaign, positioning each one exactly where and how he wanted them for greatest effect, practically scripting their dialogue to play to the sensibilities of particular voter demographics. As much as her father loved politics, she knew he disliked political maneuvering— he had Adam for that. Her father was a charismatic speaker and he genuinely believed the message that he delivered, but he disdained spin of any kind. Sometimes that frankness got him into trouble, and Adam did his best to filter the president's sound bites before he had a chance to give the evening news something to chew on.

"Okay—what was Adam worried about?"

"Nothing…he just mentioned Cam and Stark weren't in favor of you coming along at first, at least not for a few weeks. I'm okay if you want to delay. Adam's against it, but—"

"I see," Blair said, carefully and quietly. "I'm totally fine, Dad. I've been planning on it, and I'm not concerned about anything at all."

"Good. You know I want you along, but more than anything else, I want you to feel safe."

"I do. And I'm coming," Blair said. "If Adam had asked me, I would have saved him some time."

"Okay, honey. I'll be glad to have you. Lucinda will keep you informed about the schedule."

"Great. Thanks, Dad." Blair threw a drop cloth over the painting with one hand. "Oh, by the way, I'll be in New York until we leave. Just call me if there's anything."

"I'll do that. See you soon, honey."

"Bye, Dad."

Blair disconnected the call, capped the open paint tubes, and washed her hands of any remaining paint in the small adjoining bathroom. She splashed cold water on her face and waited for the haze of fury to settle. She'd hated having her life dictated by her father's staff when she'd been too young to do anything about it—she was way past that point now. And to have Cam take part—

Blair pressed the number for her detail chief and Stark answered immediately.

"Ms. Powell? Can I help you?"

"I'm going to New York."

"Of course. When would you li—"

"I'm leaving as soon as I'm packed."

"The car will be waiting," Stark said. "How long do you plan to be there?"

"I haven't decided." Blair disconnected. She hadn't been quite so angry in a very long time, but venting her anger on Stark wouldn't help.

She threw a few clothes and other personal items into a suitcase and started for the door. She'd once promised Cam she wouldn't disappear when she was angry. Technically she wasn't running out—she *had* said she was going to New York. She was just going a little early. After all, she still had the right to determine her own schedule, if little else, and if she stayed here, she was going to say or do something she would regret.

CHAPTER NINE

Loren tuned the old transistor radio on the shelf above the workbench to a rhythm-and-blues station, stripped down to her T-shirt, and pulled the carburetor from the 1949 Indian she'd picked up at an auction in the fall. She laid the parts out on sheets of newspaper to clean and inspect them. Mechanical work was her form of meditation—the routine focused her mind and settled her nerves—first in the desert, during the endless hours of tedium interspersed with the few moments of chaos when artillery shells dug craters in the sand and IEDs made twisted sculptures out of vehicles and casualties out of her friends, and now in this battlefield, where a lapse in concentration and a wrong word could buy her a shallow grave in the wilderness.

The gun deal with the Russians was her way into FALA, and the anticipation had her jazzed in a good way. She had her bases covered—as much as was ever possible in an operation with so many volatile players involved. What had her nerves dancing with a rare combination of uneasiness and excitement was Sky. She was an unknown, a piece that didn't fit in the patchwork landscape of Loren's shifting reality, and that made Sky dangerous. Loren was an expert at thinking on her feet, changing strategies midgame, adjusting to the violent swings in power among the bikers, gangs, and crime bosses—all because she knew the players and planned for the unexpected. She didn't know Sky—only who Sky said she was. And that was the most unreliable intel of all. She'd talked to Skylar Dunbar, her handler, every few weeks for almost three years. Their conversations consisted of instructions, reports, and, on very rare occasions, updates on Loren's family. Dunbar could have been a computer for all Loren knew—nothing personal ever transpired between them. Dunbar asked how she was doing, if she needed anything, if she wanted backup, but when Loren repeatedly declined, Dunbar never pushed.

Loren never talked about the men who'd gotten her alone in the back of the clubhouse when she was a prospect, forcing her against a wall, running their hands over her body, letting her feel their physical dominance even as they reminded her of their place in the hierarchy. They'd stopped short of raping her, and she'd kept her expression blank while resisting the gut-deep desire to blow their brains out. Eventually, she earned her way in by offering the kinds of connections the club wanted with the Russians and other suppliers, and all she'd said to Dunbar was, "I'm in."

Now a woman who said she was Dunbar was here, and none of what had come before meant a damn. Sky might be the only person to actually know Loren's true identity—not who she had been, but who she was—and that was as terrifying as it was exhilarating. Because even Loren wasn't sure how much of Special Agent McElroy remained in the outlaw she had become.

She'd been working about an hour when the door to the shop creaked open and slammed closed. She only sold restorations she did herself or took on jobs for people she knew. She didn't keep regular business hours and wasn't expecting anyone. She slid her hand under the shelf onto the grip of the Glock in a holster attached beneath the ledge. She turned enough to shield her movements and looked over her shoulder.

Ramsey strolled across the room, a friendly smile on his face. As usual, he wore the club uniform of black T-shirt, jeans, wide leather belt, and biker boots. He was forty-five and just starting to get soft around the middle, but his shoulders and arms were bunched with muscle. His gray-streaked black hair was full and swept back from his forehead, shorter on the sides than a lot of the guys wore it. Clean-shaven, his lantern-jawed face was heavy and tough. She'd seen him fight, and he was not only skilled, but ruthless. He fought to win, no matter what it took.

"Hi," Loren said, leaning back against the counter and letting her hand drop to her side. She could reach the Glock in under a second if she had to. She'd seen him draw too, and he was fast. Probably a standoff if it came down to it.

He admired the Indian up on the work stand. "Nice. You get this running, you'll make some money on it."

"Yeah, I know. I might keep it for myself, though."

"Yeah, I can see that." He gave her another slow smile. "Maybe I'll outbid you for it."

She laughed at the unbidden reminder that if he wanted it, he'd have it. As president of the club, he could pretty much have anything or anyone he wanted.

"So, tell me more about the redhead," Ramsey said, hoisting a hip onto a stool in front of the workbench. He rubbed his jaw and his smile turned feral. "I wasn't exactly in a position to carry on a conversation this morning."

She'd called him after she'd reached out to the higher-ups in the national organization, before she'd decided to confront Sky. He'd been rushed, and Tricia's plaintive complaints in the background gave Loren a pretty good indication why. She'd given him the bare essentials, and that was all she planned to give him now. If she even hinted Sky's story was suspect, she'd be signing Sky's death warrant, no matter who she really was. Maybe Sky was there to take her down, but if she was, Loren would handle it herself—when she was sure. "I talked to her for a few minutes last night before I left the club. She was pretty up front about why she'd come—not smart enough to be hiding anything. Jerome wanted an accounting and maybe to throw his weight around a little—my words, not hers. Dougie knew her from somewhere and put in a word for her with Jerome. He verifies."

Ramsey pulled a toothpick from the pocket of his vest, stuck it in his mouth, rolled it back and forth a few times, and shrugged. "Jerome's never asked for an accounting before. You think it has to do with the guns?"

Loren's stomach tightened. She didn't want Ramsey connecting Sky to the guns or even contemplating a connection. She shook her head. "I don't think so. I haven't gotten wind of any interest in that from her or anyone else. The Russians wouldn't want word of the deal with the Soledads. They've got an uneasy truce, but the Russians aren't dumb enough to dangle a shipment like that in front of a competitor who shares a border with them."

"Maybe Jerome is contemplating moving in on our shipment. A big shipment like this would bring a lot of money on the streets."

"I can't argue with that." She didn't want to protest too much. "But Jerome is the president—if he wanted in, he'd just say so. He's going to get his cut anyhow."

The toothpick rolled lazily across Ramsey's full lower lip. "If he hijacked our guns before we made the exchange, he'd get a lot more than a cut."

"He'd be risking war with us and a lot of the chapters would back us."

Ramsey nodded. "Watch your back all the same. And watch this broad. I'll have Armeo give her a look at the books"—he smiled that lazy serpent smile again—"the ones we keep for public review, and see if that keeps her happy."

"Sure," Loren said.

Ramsey scratched his stomach, his fingers settling on the waistband of his jeans above the outline of his cock. "For now, she's free territory."

"Whatever you say."

He laughed. "Don't tell me you weren't looking."

Fire leapt in Loren's belly, and for one second she wanted to launch herself across the space between them and plant her fist in his face. She'd had to swallow a lot to prove herself with Ramsey and the others. Even when they'd stopped physically taunting her, she'd had to listen to them demean every woman who wasn't their old lady, swallow their racist and homophobic rhetoric, and pretend she agreed. But knowing he was undressing Skylar in his mind, sliding his hands over her body and his dick between her legs, came closer to breaking her restraint than anything she'd had to endure personally. She took a long breath and laughed, feeling as if her throat were filled with broken glass. "She's got a lot to look at."

"Yeah, sent me home with something to give the old lady last night."

Loren knew better than to comment about his wife. He could say what he wanted, but if anyone else so much as looked at her for too long, they'd pay for it.

"All right." He stood, stretched a little. "Keep me informed. When do you expect you'll be moving the merchandise?"

"It's a big order, it's gonna take a while to bring it in—we'll need to move the shipments piecemeal, get it all safely warehoused and inspected before we can set up the exchange. A week or two."

He nodded, glanced around the room. "Nice place you got here." He stared at her for a long moment. "You're a surprising woman, McElroy."

Loren tensed and smiled back at him. "How's that?"

"At least half the guys in the club want to bang you, and usually, dykes don't cause that kind of reaction. You can shoot better than most, ride as well as any, and you're smart. But you're willing to take orders. How is that?"

"I like being a soldier," Loren said truthfully. "I understand the necessity for taking orders. I don't mind following a leader I trust."

He laughed and pointed a thick finger at her. "Like I said, you're smart. Keep an eye on the broad."

"I'll do that," Loren said softly as she watched Ramsey stroll out. She wondered just exactly how much he suspected about Skylar. And about her.

❖

In the last hour of daylight when most of the troops were settling down in the barracks or mess tent, Jane worked her way through the obstacle course laid out in the forest behind the compound, trudging her way through thigh-high snow in some places with a rifle strapped to her back. Frost rimmed her nostrils and the frigid air burned her throat. Tears froze on her lashes. Every fifty yards or so, she stopped, unslung the assault rifle, took aim at human-shaped targets set out at various distances from the trail in the underbrush, on overhangs, and in trees. She was timing her run and, on the way back, would collect the targets and determine her accuracy. She'd show her father the proof that she was ready for command.

While she'd been in Georgia working in the lab, she'd had to keep in shape at the gym and with infrequent visits to shooting ranges. She'd always driven at least a hundred miles from home to shoot, so she wouldn't run into anyone she might possibly know while at the range. As far as those at the lab knew, she was a quiet, single woman whose main interests were her job, occasional trips to the theater, and bicycling along the many trails outside the city. She kept a low profile at work—friendly but not so friendly as to be included in casual after-work or weekend events. She didn't want to make an impression, and she didn't want to be forced into situations where she'd have to reveal personal information. Fortunately, when she'd volunteered to work the midnight shift, she no longer had to interact with colleagues. Only a skeleton crew worked at night, and the Level 4 lab precluded much in the way of conversation.

Now that she was home, nothing much would change. She and her siblings had always been kept apart from the other children of the survivalists, homeschooled by their father and mother, trained to be soldiers from the time they were old enough to shoot, and prepared to be leaders of the organization one day. She'd never had close friends other than her sister and brother. A sharp pain shot through her chest as she pulled herself up over an ice-covered embankment. Jennifer, only a year younger, almost her twin. Her closest friend, her comrade, her sister. Thinking of Jennifer caged, interrogated, imprisoned by the enemy filled her with rage and pain. She understood that theirs was a long-term war, but she wasn't going to leave Jennifer behind bars for years. She wanted her free, and somehow, she'd find a way to make that happen. If she couldn't, she'd make someone pay.

Cam's driver dropped her off a little before seven. She stopped just inside the lobby doors and scanned the foyer. None of Blair's protective detail was present. The doorman behind the desk nodded.

"Evening, Steven. Quiet night?"

"So far, Director Roberts."

She keyed the elevator to her floor, a frisson of wariness tingling along her spine. No one standing post. She paused at the door, listened. No music. Carefully, she let herself into her apartment. The only light came from the muted glow under the hood above the stove top. She knew the apartment was empty, but called out anyhow. "Blair?"

The silence was complete.

Without turning on the lights, she dropped her coat over the back of the sofa and strode through the empty living room, down the hall, and into the bedroom. She flipped the switch inside the door. The bed was made, the closet doors were closed. The nightstand on Blair's side of the bed was bare. Her iPad, phone, and wallet were gone. So was she.

Cam turned out the light, walked back into the living room, sat down on the sofa, and leaned her head back. Reflected light danced on the ceiling. A few weeks ago she'd strolled on the beach with Blair, awash with the amazing sensation of having just gotten married. For a very short time, the world had receded and there had been only Blair. She wondered what it would be like to live a life where the thing that mattered most to her would not be something she could only embrace in stolen moments out of time. She rubbed her eyes and unclipped her phone. She pressed Blair's number and waited. The call went to voice mail. She listened to the familiar sound of Blair's voice telling her to leave a message.

When Blair's voice faded away, she said, "Hi, it's me. I imagine you're in transit somewhere, so let me know when you've arrived. I've got a six a.m. shuttle, so I'll be out most of the day tomorrow. Be careful. I love you."

She pocketed the phone and contemplated the evening ahead of her. Then she pulled on her coat and walked out the door.

CHAPTER TEN

As soon as Blair arrived at her apartment, she showered, then dressed in a pair of black jeans, a black silk shirt, and black boots with chunky two-inch heels. She pulled a black leather duster from her closet and headed back out. Blair strode through the lobby and out onto the sidewalk, two agents from her detail trailing a dozen feet behind. The Suburban crouched at the curb across the street in front of Gramercy Park, a hulking beast with two shadowy figures in the front seat.

Blair hadn't taken ten strides before Stark jumped out and caught up to her. Stark fell into step on the side closest to the street and said, "I wasn't aware you were going out again tonight."

Blair cut her a look. "I'm not exactly hiding the fact."

Stark spoke into her wrist mic, and the Suburban rolled toward them, slowing to pick up the agents on foot. "It's helpful if we know ahead of time."

"Yes," Blair said. "I'm aware of that."

Stark said nothing as Blair headed west toward Chelsea. Stark wouldn't say anything further even if she was pissed, which she probably was. The Secret Service hated off-the-record trips. Well, too bad. She was pissed too.

"Would you prefer to ride?" Stark asked a few minutes later.

"No, I'd prefer to walk. Alone, actually." Blair balled her hands into fists inside her pockets. The January freeze hadn't yet set in, and the temperatures were in the low thirties. Brisk, but for someone walking fast and in a temper, the night was warm enough. The coat, unbuttoned, flared behind her like a gunslinger's. She smiled wryly at the irony. She was the one supposedly in danger and the only one of the entourage unarmed. She had no great love affair with guns, but she was a fair shot and knew with absolute certainty she could kill if her life depended upon it. It had and she had. But still they played this game—that the importance of her life trumped everyone else's, and since it did, she had no say over it.

"You can ride," Blair said. "I'm going to Francine's."

The bar was one of Blair's old hangouts, a cross between a happy-hour pit stop for yuppie office workers and, after hours, a pickup place for players interested in a little something spicier than a quick vanilla romp. Blair had spent many an evening picking up women at Francine's, especially in the days when she'd made a habit of eluding her protective detail and making the rounds incognito at various bars. She hadn't tried to hide her appearance tonight, although she'd left her hair down and, dressed the way she was, probably wouldn't be recognized by most people who weren't looking carefully. Stark didn't comment, but something about the set of her jaw suggested she was displeased. Hell. The silent standoff was almost as irritating as the rest of it.

"You know, Paula," Blair said, "if you had reservations about the upcoming campaign trip, you could have said something to me. We could've talked about modifying our routines."

"I didn't think you'd be receptive to that idea."

"But you didn't know, did you? You just assumed that it would be easier and more expedient to go behind my back to my wife and Lucinda. Did you make it as far as my father?"

"I followed protocol."

"Oh, bullshit," Blair snapped. "Do not sandbag me with the protocol excuse. All of you hide behind protocol when you don't want to bother with common courtesy."

Stark jerked to face Blair, her expression openly shocked. Maybe she really didn't realize how it felt to be on the other side of protocols.

Blair stopped in the middle of the sidewalk. "Do you honestly not have a clue what it feels like to have people sitting around discussing what you can and cannot do?"

Stark's brows drew down, confusion replacing the disbelief. "That's pretty much what happens every day for just about everything—what your father does, what we do, what you do. So, I guess, no...I don't think about it, and I don't consider doing it any other way."

"That's the problem. All of you are so well trained that you can't deviate from protocol, even when it might be better to do so."

Stark shook her head vehemently. "No. The minute you start

second-guessing your training, deviating from what's been proven to be the best, safest way to handle a situation, you make mistakes. You leave openings, create vulnerabilities."

Blair snorted. "That's your training talking."

"Yes, it is. And I trust it completely."

"God." Blair shook her head. "You sound just like Cam."

"I'm honored."

Stark meant it, and Blair understood why. Stark—hell, all the agents—would walk through fire for Cam because she'd die for any of them. She nearly had, more than once. An arrow of pain sliced through her, and Blair quickly pushed it aside. Cam would probably be home by now and realize that she'd left. She'd know why too. How could Cam know her so well, but not well enough to think she wouldn't care that Cam had gone behind her back? The thought still hurt as much as it had a few hours before.

The sign over Francine's came into view.

"Stay warm, Paula," Blair said. "Wait in the SUV."

"I'll wait inside."

"Suit yourself." Blair pushed through the door into the familiar heat of bodies on the hunt and hoped before too long she'd be able to forget about the pain for a little while.

Cam didn't bother to call her driver to come back for her but grabbed a cab in the street in front of her apartment. She gave him the address of the federal building where high-security prisoners were held, where encrypted records were buried so deep that someone searching the federal databases would not be able to find them. She showed her creds to the guard at a side entrance and was let into a long, narrow hall that ended at an unmarked bank of elevators. She inserted a key, rode down one floor, and badged her way past another security desk. Yet another drab hallway with closed, unmarked doors on either side ended at a glassed-in security station where three armed officers monitored video feeds from inside and outside the building. The sergeant rose and met her at the door. She showed her credentials yet again and said, "I'd like to see prisoner number 1329. Can you move her into an interrogation room."

"Yes, ma'am. Five minutes."

"Thank you. And turn the cameras off in that room, please."

He nodded. "Yes, ma'am." He turned, said something to one of the other officers, then keyed a door inside the security center and disappeared. A moment later one of the other guards escorted Cam through the same door and down another hallway to a windowless ten-by-ten room furnished with a plain steel table in the center. The metal folding chairs on either side of the table were bolted to the floor, as was the table. Soldered O-rings at various intervals along the table's edge provided anchors where restraints could be secured.

Cam sat with the table between her and the windowless door. Five minutes later a stone-faced guard escorted Jennifer Pattee into the room. She wore a nondescript gray jumpsuit that zipped up the front and shapeless slipper-shoes on her feet. Her dark hair appeared clean but hung in a loose tangle around her shoulders. She wore no makeup and, despite the shadows under her eyes, appeared alert and unintimidated. Her hands were shackled with steel handcuffs connected by a short length of chain, attached to the leather belt around her waist. Her ankles were free. When she sat in the chair opposite Cam, the guard attached the chain connecting her cuffs to the table. She could clasp her hands on the edge of the table but could not reach as far as her face or across the space between them.

The guard left silently and Cam stood, took off her coat, and laid it over the chair beside her. She sat back down and looked at Jennifer. "Tell me again about the man who delivered the virus to you."

Jennifer Pattee was a beautiful woman—luminous blue eyes, photogenic features, and a voluptuous body. Even in shapeless prison garb, she sat as if posing for a photo op, a seductive smile on her face. Her gaze slowly slid from Cam's face down her body and back again. "I know you haven't forgotten. You don't look like the kind of woman who forgets anything."

"I haven't forgotten," Cam said calmly. "I just don't believe you. The way I see it, the only way you can help yourself is to help us."

"I certainly would if I could," Jennifer said. "After all, that's my job. I signed on to the White House Medical Unit so I could help take care of the president. Why would I want to do anything to jeopardize him or my oath?"

"From where I'm sitting," Cam said conversationally, "you were in a perfect position to do exactly what you did—report the president's movements while moving in his inner circle unobserved and totally trusted. When the time was opportune, strike a death blow—or try to."

"You've seen my record. It's spotless. There's nothing to suggest I would ever do anything like that, because I wouldn't."

"Who is the man in the diner who gave you the virus?"

"I don't know," Jennifer said. "This is a mistake."

"You were prepared to shoot a federal agent. You drew a gun on Agent Daniels."

"I felt threatened. I wasn't sure what she was going to do. I have the right to defend myself, just like any other American citizen."

"You support the right to bear arms."

"Of course. I support the Constitution and the Bill of Rights."

"Is that what they taught you when you were homeschooled in Idaho?"

For just an instant, the expression on Jennifer's face flickered to one of uncertainty before her look of confidence returned. That look said there was something there. Jennifer hadn't expected them to know or care about that fact—which meant it mattered.

"I learned what every child learns in school—reading and writing and arithmetic." Jennifer smiled. "And the Pledge of Allegiance."

"Who did you go to school with?" Cam asked.

Jennifer's brows drew down. "What does this have to do with anything?"

"I think it might have to do with a lot of things. Where did you go to school? At home or at the training camp?"

"I don't know what you're talking about."

"Sure you do. Who did you go to school with, Jennifer? The sons and daughters of other righteous Americans who support the right to bear arms, even against the government?"

Jennifer laughed. "There's no law against being homeschooled, Director Roberts."

"No, there isn't. There is a law—quite a few of them, actually—against attempting to assassinate the president of the United States."

"I certainly didn't do that. I'm the victim here. I had no idea what was in that package."

"You know we can keep you here as long as we want, and until you start telling us the truth, we will."

"I'd like an attorney."

"I'm sure you would. We'll see that you get one." Cam rose and folded her coat over her arm. "Someday." Cam moved to the end of the table and paused. "I'm sure you have family you'd like to contact. As soon as you begin cooperating, you'll be able to do that."

"I'm not interested in making a phone call. But I appreciate the offer."

"Have a good night, Ms. Pattee."

"It's Lieutenant," Jennifer said coolly. "Lieutenant Jennifer Pattee, United States Navy Medical Corps."

"Good night, then, Lieutenant. We'll speak again, soon."

"I'll look forward to your visit."

❖

Blair sipped her wine and observed the woman wending her way through the crowd toward her. Heads turned to follow the sleek silver-blond beauty, and Blair smiled as she drew near. Turning as her best friend slid onto the stool beside her, Blair leaned over and kissed her on the cheek. "Thanks for coming so soon on such short notice."

Diane Bleeker waved an elegant hand. "No thanks needed. I'm always up for a night out on the town."

Blair laughed. "I don't think I said that."

"Yes, but we're at Francine's. What else would we be doing?" Diane gave the bartender a sultry wink. "Chardonnay, please. And not the house brand. Something daring and bold."

The bartender, a handsome Latino with liquid dark eyes and an appreciative grin, nodded. "I think I can come up with something for you."

"I'm sure you can."

"Now, now," Blair murmured. "Don't get his hopes up."

"Oh, I wouldn't think of it. I'm just keeping the rust off in case I ever have any reason to use my wiles again."

"Uh-huh." Blair laughed. "And how is Valerie these days?"

Diane's urbane expression softened. "Wonderful, when I see her, which is never enough. She's always off doing some big secret thing that I can't know about. That whole business is very tiresome."

"Yes," Blair said, turning her half-empty glass on the highly polished black granite bar top in front of her. "Isn't it."

Diane crossed her legs, her green silk skirt sliding midway up her thigh, drawing appreciative stares from men and a few women nearby. She lightly clasped Blair's forearm. "Is that what this impromptu visit is all about? Has Cameron done something loathsome again?"

Blair's chest filled with affection. Diane understood her and would support her, even while gently goading her to consider the real reasons behind her actions. "Don't take her part in this."

Diane pressed a hand to her breasts, the diamond and gold bracelets on her wrist sparkling against the champagne silk of her shirt. "I just said I knew she'd done something horrible again. How is that supporting her?"

"It's not what you said, it's the way you said it. And I know you've always had a soft spot for Cam."

"Darling," Diane said. "I have a soft spot for handsome women, and you have to admit, she is that."

"Yes," Blair said softly. "She is gorgeous."

Diane's hand slid down to Blair's and squeezed gently. "So," she said, no sarcasm in her tone, "what's happened?"

Blair sighed. "Oh, just more of the same. Some things have come up security-wise, and Cam wants me kept under wraps. Under glass, more like it."

"Oh, not that again. Is she back on that wanting to keep you safe at all costs kick?"

"Don't make light of it," Blair said grumpily, knowing she sounded petulant.

"I don't mean to. Only, at the risk of losing my oldest and dearest friend," Diane said, "sometimes I agree with her. I want you safe too, and I'm not married to you."

"Diane," Blair said, "you've known me longer than anyone except Tanner. I'm a lot more cautious now than I ever was before, and nothing ever happened even when I was running around half-crazy with no protection at all."

"Well, we were all young and foolish. But, you know, it was a different world then. Sure, there were always risks, but Blair"—Diane softly stroked Blair's cheek—"sweetheart, people *have* tried to hurt you. And there are threats now that we never even thought about when we were young. We didn't have to think about it because they weren't so close to home."

"Believe me, I know what the threats are. And I'm not young and wild or crazy any longer."

"No, you're not, and I know that. So does Cam."

"She didn't talk to me about it."

"Oh. Well." Diane sipped her wine and nodded at the bartender, who waited with an expectant look on his face. "Excellent."

He leaned forward, a conspiratorial grin on his face. "I thought you'd like that. You look like the sort of woman who appreciates something bold and a little daring. I do."

"Oh, so do I," Diane said. "I bet you and I probably appreciate the same things in women too."

He shook his head with mock sadness. "Oh well. Enjoy the wine."

She gave him a brilliant smile and turned back to Blair. "Well, there goes my chance for a wild evening. I guess you and I will just have to make our own fun."

"I guess it's a good thing I really love you, then."

Diane leaned over and kissed her cheek. "It is."

CHAPTER ELEVEN

Sky pulled the blinds on the single window facing the parking lot in her motel room and booted up her computer. She connected the hotspot, changed the encryption, and went online. The first thing she did was check her work e-mail. A dozen e-mails from her ATF counterpart over the last forty-eight hours, increasing in frequency during the last day. The message was pretty much the same in all of them, starting out with "Haven't heard from you, check in when you can" and progressing to "Where the hell are you? Need to confirm okay." She deleted those, scanned the many irrelevant bureaucratic updates, and deleted those too. Nothing else seemed urgent, and she closed the mail program.

Next she opened one of the protected files to requisition the funds Loren would need for the gun buy. Running an undercover operation could take years and cost hundreds of thousands, if not millions, of dollars to supply the cash the undercover operatives needed to build cases against the organizations they infiltrated. Operatives orchestrated drug buys, made weapons purchases, and bankrolled porn, all in the name of securing their cover stories.

Then the real work began—in order to safeguard an undercover operative's identity, handlers had to keep the number of those-in-the-know to the smallest number possible, which meant doing a lot of the case-building themselves. Every bit of evidence needed to be recorded, analyzed, and cataloged. Photographs, tapes, transcripts—everything had to be dated, referenced, and, in most cases, reviewed with the state's attorneys to ensure they were building the kind of case that would lead to federal convictions. As the lead agent, Sky oversaw all of the evidence collection, cataloging, and requisitions.

Sky had been burned before, trying to make charges stick against gang members. Idaho's anti-gang law looked good on paper—allowing for enhanced sentences for gang-related offenses—but proving the gang affiliation could be difficult. She'd seen convictions under similar state laws overturned, and that wasn't going to happen this time. Not after all the time, money, and resources they'd poured into Operation Bitterroot. Or the years of her life Loren McElroy had sacrificed. The case Sky wanted, what every federal agent wanted, to make against criminal gangs—including paramilitary organizations like FALA—was a RICO case. She needed evidence that showed a pattern of gang member behavior that included several offenses covered by the RICO Act— drug dealing, weapons trafficking, money laundering, prostitution, murder—the staples of gang life. McElroy had done a good job of compiling evidence so far, but this gun buy would be the lock.

Not that she was under any illusions about ending gang activity, no matter how many leaders they caught in their net. Racketeering charges carried the stiffest sentences and were likely to cripple the infrastructure of an organization from the top down, but the gangs and mob organizations were like hydras, many-headed. No one had yet been able to wipe out one of these groups. A new leader always seemed to spring up before the old one had reached his cell, but at least they could slow them down.

Sky ran half a dozen undercover operatives at a time, and she made sure each of them was as secure as she could make them. No one could predict what might happen out in the field, and an operative had to be ready to react swiftly and inventively when their cover was challenged. But she never sent any of them out there alone. She was always available and might end up hand-holding some of the newer ones, talking to them a dozen times a day in the beginning. Loren was an exception. Part of Loren's deal was she wouldn't meet anyone face-to-face—not even her handler. Sky had objected at first, but Loren's assets were so unique she'd been forced to accept the terms. The agency wanted Loren. Period.

Loren followed the rules—barely. Her reports were thorough, but she often neglected to relay her plans until after the fact. She generally made her requisite contacts with Sky, phoning in at more or less the expected intervals, but she never called for advice or backup. Loren was a lone ranger, and that behavior pattern was often a red flag, an indication an operative was going native—being seduced by the lifestyle and losing touch with their mission. It was too soon to tell if

Loren had succumbed to the allure of the outlaw life, but one thing was certain—she needed backup now, whether she liked it or not.

Sky's phone rang and she checked the readout. After a second's debate, she answered. "Hello, Dan."

"Jesus H., Dunbar. Where the fuck are you?"

"I'm on vacation. Skiing in the Bitterroots."

The silence was as heavy as a fist.

"How's SoCal?" Sky asked, picturing Dan's broad face turning as red as his carrot-top.

Dan cleared his throat. "Lonely. I need you back here. We might have visitors from the East Coast."

Sky doodled on the back of a fast-food receipt. Dan Bussy was a good guy, an experienced ATF agent who'd made some high-profile drug busts along the Mexico-California pipeline in the last few years. But he was nervous—always envisioning disaster scenarios. Worse, he was a stickler for regs. Sky tended to color outside the lines. A lot. Theirs was a bumpy marriage, but the powers that be had declared they would run this one together.

"Don't think I can do that. I'm booked in here for a while." Sky circled the initials *LMM* she'd penciled in bold. Loren Markham McElroy. "What's the word from back east?"

"Not sure just yet, but our territory might be overlapping someone else's. Like Homeland."

Sky's pulse jumped for a fraction of a second before she clamped down on the adrenaline surge and regulated her heartbeat. Not much caught her off guard, but the prospect of a bigger operation got her blood racing. "I'll leave you to set up a meet from your end."

"Fine—but answer your damn e-mail."

"Yes, dear." Sky scratched out Loren's initials, annoyed that McElroy had surfaced in her unconscious. She usually had much better control. An image of the dark-haired agent leaning back on the counter, seemingly relaxed but her rangy body seething with energy, shot a bolt of excitement through her middle. Another foreign and unwelcome sensation. Sky crumpled the paper and tossed it in the wastepaper basket. "Keep me informed."

"Yeah. Like you do me," Dan grumped.

"Sorry."

Dan sighed. "I'll be in touch."

"Me too." Sky disconnected, retrieved the tiny ball of paper from the trash, and flushed it down the toilet. Homeland Security. That could only mean the militia was into more than gun buying. And she was right here at ground zero. Now more than ever, she needed to be sure McElroy was solid.

She went back to her computer, filled out a requisition for a hundred thousand dollars for the gun buy, and sent it off to the regional office. The coffers were full this time of year, and she didn't anticipate any difficulties. She shut down the wireless, closed her laptop, and grabbed her coat. She planned to have something to eat at the diner, and then it was time to meet the boys and girls at the Ugly Rooster.

❖

Cam left the federal holding facility and headed down Pennsylvania Avenue toward the Treasury Building and her office. No point in going home to an empty apartment. She checked her phone as she walked. No message from Blair. She could call Stark and ask as to Blair's whereabouts. Stark would keep it between them, but she pocketed her phone, hunched her shoulders against the wind, and kept walking. Blair had the right to her privacy—as much as that was possible for someone who was the constant object of press attention and observation by a security detail. When Blair was ready to call, she would.

Why she'd left wasn't much of a mystery. Blair had heard she was the subject of the strategy meeting that afternoon, and she likely knew of Cam's opposition to her joining the campaign junket too. There were no real secrets in Washington, not even in the White House. She didn't blame Blair for being angry—especially since she couldn't honestly tell Blair she was sorry for trying to sway Eisley and Lucinda from including her in the early schedule. She hadn't called the meeting, but she'd been happy for the chance to try, one more time, to keep Blair out of the hot zone.

Cam badged her way past the guard at the door and made her way down the silent and mostly deserted halls to her impersonally furnished government office. She had to set personal issues aside for the time being. Stark would see that Blair was safe tonight. The best way she could ensure Blair's safety, and that of the president, was to discover who had orchestrated Jennifer Pattee's plan to attack the president.

Jennifer Pattee was her best lead and her biggest challenge. The lieutenant was disciplined, confident, and prepared to be interrogated. Some of her resistance to questioning might have been a result of her military training, but Cam suspected her self-possession went far deeper than that. She'd met Jennifer's kind of terrorist before—fanatical but not unbalanced. Absolutely dedicated to their cause, unshakable in their belief that what they were doing was right and, in many cases, righteous. Jennifer had the air of someone who had trained her whole life for exactly what she was doing now—waging war on the American government.

When Cam got to the office she rarely used, she hung up her coat and suit jacket, rolled up her sleeves, and booted up her computer. She was searching for a ghost, the ghost of Jennifer Pattee's past, because whoever Jennifer claimed to be today was not who she had been when someone had trained her for terrorism.

❖

Blair pushed aside her unfinished glass of wine, the third she had failed to finish that evening. The band was good—young, experimental, filled with wild energy and passion. She and Diane had moved on from Francine's after they'd been besieged by one too many offers of company. This club was just as crowded and seething with sexual tension, but she and Diane had scored a table close to the stage and sat close enough to send off couple vibes, keeping the hunters at bay.

The lead vocalist, an androgynous twentysomething in skinny black jeans, knee-high boots with heavy metal buckles, and a white shirt open between her breasts, moved with the barely suppressed rage of a tiger in a cage. Shock waves of sexual power radiated from her as she railed against a world that refused to see her. As she sang, her gaze returned to Blair again and again, the connection sizzling through the air between them.

Diane leaned close. "That girl is on fire."

"She's good," Blair said.

"She's *hot*."

Blair laughed softly. "Yeah, that too."

Diane glanced over her shoulder. "Where are your spookies?"

"They're here somewhere." Blair didn't bother looking for them anymore or care what they might observe of her life. If she did, she'd be accepting the prison that she had fought to break out of her entire life. The best she could do was accept their presence and then ignore it.

"You're not going to make me come up with some kind of distraction while you run off, are you?" Diane asked.

Blair watched the singer, recalling all the times she'd disappeared in a crowd while Diane covered for her. She'd made a career out of eluding her keepers and declaring her independence by bedding strangers—when she actually got as far as a bed. Sometimes she didn't even wait that long. She hadn't cared about the risk. All she'd cared about was the freedom.

"I thought I'd take care of that myself," Blair said.

"Really? What do you have planned?"

Blair looked away from the young animal on the stage, severing the tenuous strand of heat between them. She already knew the reality would leave her cold. "I actually thought we might head home. Is Valerie home tonight, or can you tolerate a houseguest?"

"Sweetie, I'm always happy to have you as a guest. Valerie won't mind, although I'm not expecting her."

"Good, let's go, then."

"What about…" Diane tilted her head toward the stage.

Blair laughed. "You're kidding, right? What would I do with that?"

"Oh, I can think of so many things."

"Thinking and doing are two different things." Blair slid her arm around Diane's waist as they walked toward the door, their coats over their arms. "And in case you missed the bulletin, I'm married now."

"I was there, remember?"

"Of course I do. Did you think it was all just for the media?"

Diane stopped, her expression completely serious. "Of course I didn't. I know exactly how much it meant to you. And I was kidding about fire girl."

"I know."

"You're not sorry, are you?"

"About marrying Cam?" Blair shrugged into her duster. Her anger warred with the ache of separation she always experienced when they were apart. "Not for a second. But I can still be pissed."

"Oh, absolutely. Let's stop for ice cream on the way home."

"All right. Just hold on a second." Blair took her phone from her pocket and texted Cam. *With Diane. Be careful tomorrow. I love you.*

CHAPTER TWELVE

Hooker rolled away from the blonde with the great breasts and fumbled in his pants pocket on the floor for his phone. The girl—Nancy? Nina, maybe?—reached around him and grabbed his cock.

"Don't answer that, baby. We've got all night, remember?"

Hooker grunted and moved her hand. Jesus, why didn't women understand you couldn't wring the damn thing like a dish towel? And since he'd paid for her company, he ought to know how long he had to go. He was just taking a break after she damn near sucked his eyeballs out through his dick. And as good as she was with her mouth, business was business.

"Yeah," he rasped when he got the phone turned around right.

"I kept up my end of things," an angry male voice said in a tight whisper. "Your turn to pay up. It wasn't supposed to go down this way. Where the fuck were you?"

"Look," Hooker said, "I can't talk right now. But my part was done when I handed off the goods. Delivery wasn't part of the deal."

"So you hire some flunky who blows the whole thing?"

"It wasn't him that queered the exchange. The woman was the one who tipped them, and that was *your* end of things." Hooker tensed as a warm mouth skated down the length of his cock and closed over him. He gripped the back of her head and pushed her lower.

"No way. Je—she wouldn't have given anything away."

"So you say."

"So what are we going to do about getting her out?"

"We?" Hooker laughed abruptly and tugged on the blonde's hair, pulling her off his cock. "You've got the wrong guy, buddy."

"Really? Then maybe I should ask your boss."

Hooker squeezed the phone. The little fuck had the balls to

threaten him. He couldn't know who Hooker worked for—he'd been very careful to keep Russo deep in the shadows. But he had to be sure of what the snitch really knew. "Look—let's talk this over. When can we meet?"

"I'll call you."

"What else have you got?"

Silence for a moment. "The daughter is definitely going. I'll have the advance info soon."

"Good. Then let me see what I can do on this other thing."

"Make it sooner rather than later—we want the woman out of there."

Yeah, right. And he wanted a ten-inch dick too. "That's asking for a miracle."

"We're not asking."

The line went dead and Hooker dropped the phone onto the pile of clothes next to the bed. "Fuck."

"Mmm, baby. Now you're talking."

The mouth went back to work on his cock while Hooker stared at the dark ceiling, wondering how long he could keep the snitch before he became more trouble than he was worth. One thing was for sure—he couldn't let Russo know his cover was at risk, or Hooker would be out of a job and possibly a dead man.

❖

The guard silently escorted Jennifer back to her cell, walking one step behind, the press of his stun gun against the middle of her spine a reminder that she could not escape. The chains connecting her cuffs grated softly with each step. The door of her cell stood open, a mocking invitation, but she walked through without slowing. She would not show weakness to her captors. The solid metal door with a foot-square window of reinforced glass swung closed behind her, and the lock ratcheted into place with the heavy sound of finality. The eight-by-eight windowless room was stark and barren: plain gray tile floors, blank white walls, air-conditioning and heating vents bolted in place, a stainless steel commode in one corner without benefit of a privacy screen, a stainless steel pedestal sink next to that, and a metal bed frame with a single mattress, utilitarian white sheets, and a plain gray wool blanket. No television, no radio, no computer, nothing to connect her to the outside world.

She wasn't being tortured. They fed her. She was warm and dry. And totally isolated. She had no watch, and the lights cycled on and off according to a schedule too random for her to judge the time. In an age where information was instant and the world was accessible with the press of a fingertip, she was as lost as a castaway on an uncharted island. She didn't know if any others had been captured, or if anyone even knew that *she* had been. She was completely at the mercy of her jailers. If they forgot her, and sometimes as the hours stretched, they seemed to—in her disoriented world, a few seconds could feel like hours—she could starve or die of thirst. But they always came, silently sliding plastic trays, bearing paper plates and cups filled with institutional food, through the slot in her door. She wasn't starving, but at times she hungered in a way she'd never known—for an instant's simple human connection to affirm she still existed.

She ran cold water in the sink and splashed her face, surprised to see that her hands were shaking. There were cameras trained on her, she knew that, but she couldn't be certain how much of her cell was actually under surveillance. She had to be always on guard. She wouldn't give them the satisfaction of thinking she was distressed. She dried her hands on the thin white cotton towel and sat on the side of her bed. Let them watch her. The guards didn't intimidate her—she didn't give them any thought. They held no real power.

The woman who'd questioned her tonight held all the power. Cameron Roberts, Deputy Director of Homeland Security. Roberts was the one trying to uncover her secrets, expose her identity. She would fail. They had planned for something like this, been prepared for it. She knew what to expect, and under no circumstances would she provide any information. Her father's words echoed in her mind as clearly as the many times he had repeated them. *You are stronger than them. Smarter than them. And you will never be alone. We will always come for you.* He would come. She just had to have faith.

Her father had prepared her for this, planned for it. Her identity was safe.

Roberts had asked her about being homeschooled. That wasn't in any of her background material. The question had caught her by surprise, and it'd taken her a few seconds to realize Roberts was fishing. It was no secret lots of independent Americans were homeschooled. Roberts didn't really know anything.

Fortunately, she hadn't given anything away. She shivered lightly, although the warm air trickled from the overhead vent. Her father had promised she wouldn't be abandoned, but she wasn't being held captive in some mountain compound where her father and his soldiers could launch an assault to free her. She was in a federal prison cell in the heart of the nation's capital. Maybe no one was coming for her.

Jennifer straightened her back and set her jaw. She knew what they were trying to do—they hadn't tortured her, probably wouldn't. But captivity was itself a form of torture, and they were trying to make her lose faith. They would fail. Her father and his soldiers would come, and if they couldn't, she would find her own way out.

❖

Sky parked her rental car at the far end of a long line of Harley choppers. The defrost in the rental was tepid, and her breath had misted the windshield until she'd had to wipe circles clear with her bare hand to see the road on her way to the Ugly Rooster. She pocketed the keys and jumped out of the car into the frigid night. She couldn't believe these bikers actually rode in this kind of weather. Leathers or not, they had to be freezing their balls off. Striding toward the door, she smiled to herself when she pictured Loren straddling the big Harley. At least one biker didn't have to worry about frostbite on her hot spots.

Still smiling, she sauntered into the bar packed with men in biker garb and women in as little as possible, despite the winter freeze outside. Halter tops, bared midriffs, and barely covered backsides shimmied and shook amid the shaved heads and tattooed torsos. The place looked like a convention for hookers on Santa Monica Boulevard. Sky had dressed to fit in and shed her jacket to display her calling cards. Skintight jeans, shiny black vinyl high-heeled boots, no bra, and a tight maroon shirt the color of blood that gaped a little across her chest, providing a peek at the pale skin of her breasts beneath. She got the desired effect. Men stared and women snarled as she strolled toward the bar and eased onto a free stool.

The bartender, one of the shaved-head, no-neck variety with the tattoo of a scythe and sickle extending from ear to collarbone, gave her a hard stare before glancing toward the far corner of the room. If he was looking for permission to serve her, he must've gotten it because he slid a slightly damp white square paper napkin in front of her. "What you want, honey?"

Sky smiled. "What you got?"

He laughed, his full face flushing as his eyes slid down to the opening in her blouse. "As much as you can handle."

"That's a pretty big promise."

"It's a pretty big chunk of prime beef." He grasped her wrist and tugged until she had to lean up over the bar to take the pressure off her shoulder. He smelled of sweat and beer. The position gave him a nice view of the rest of her breasts, and he took his time looking. "Keep that seat warm, baby, and I'll let you have a taste later."

"Why don't we—"

"That's a pretty lame line, Wheels." Loren stepped up beside Sky and put one hand on the middle of her back.

The bartender eyed Loren and shrugged. "Can't help but tell the truth. Ten inches of Idaho's finest."

"Well, keep your burger in the wrapper." Loren reached around Sky and tapped the bartender's hand where he still gripped Sky's wrist. "Red here is with me."

"You don't say?" Wheels eyed Sky, his mouth a hard line in his granite face.

Loren leaned down and brushed her mouth over Sky's ear. "What do you say, Red?"

Ignoring the grip on her wrist, Sky shifted on the bar stool and brought her mouth to Loren's. Loren had a nice mouth, and since she didn't have a lot of choice, she might as well take advantage of the opportunity. She took her time, running the tip of her tongue over Loren's lower lip before pressing her mouth harder to Loren's, breathing in the fresh, winter-white taste of her. When she eased back, a couple of the nearby bikers hooted.

Loren grinned. "Just got your answer, Wheels."

"You keep that up," the burly bartender growled, reluctantly releasing Sky's wrist, "and I'll have enough for both of you."

"How about two beers instead." Loren slid her arm around Sky's waist and slid her hand up until she cupped the underside of Sky's breast. Sky's nipple hardened against Loren's palm.

Wheels grunted and pulled two brews from a tap and slammed the mugs down in front of them. When he moved away, Loren nuzzled Sky's neck, her thighs pressed to Sky's hip, her fingers cradling Sky's breast. "You might have told me you were coming."

"Don't you like surprises?" Sky sounded a little breathless and her focus wavered for an instant as the brush of Loren's fingers over her nipple sent a chill down her spine. She'd anticipated they might have to get physical, she just hadn't expected to be affected by the contact. She had to struggle not to push harder into Loren's hand.

"I don't mind them, but if I'm headed into a fight, I like to be prepared." Loren figured she'd made her point to anyone watching. She'd just staked a claim on Sky, and for the night at least, the men would back off, waiting and watching to see what developed. But Ramsey was watching from across the room, and she didn't want to leave any doubt of her intentions. And Sky felt too good to let go—the softness of her breast and the lash of heat coming off her body kept her chained in place. She skimmed her mouth over Sky's neck. She even tasted sweet. Almonds and vanilla. "You took a chance waltzing in here. If the men didn't eat you alive, the women would have."

"I could've handled them."

Loren cradled Sky's chin with her free hand and rubbed her thumb over the faint dent that made her look both tough and vulnerable at same time. "Maybe. But since you're my girl, it's up to me to see that no one poaches."

"Your girl, huh?" Sky tilted her head until their eyes met and their mouths were in kissing range again. She knew they were playing, but she liked the game. And she really liked Loren's mouth.

Loren leaned down and kissed her. That nice mouth of Loren's was very talented, skimming lightly over Sky's lips at first, then more firmly, letting Sky taste her again. The kiss grew deeper and hotter until Sky had to pull back to ease the pressure building between her thighs. She almost couldn't think. Mistake. Big, big mistake.

Loren murmured against her mouth, "The safest place for you is with me. So yeah, you're my girl."

"All right," Sky whispered, following instinct. "I guess you've got yourself an old lady."

❖

Cam called Chuck Ferrell, the agent Eddie Byrnes had suggested. The man didn't sound surprised to hear from her, and she suspected Eddie had given him a heads-up about their conversation. She couldn't blame him. Eddie had to protect his sources and his reputation.

"Don't know that I can help you all that much, Director," the gruff voice said. "We've got agents and CIs undercover out there, sure, but we can't just pull them out because someone wants intel."

"Understood," Cam said calmly. "I'm willing to fly out, meet them on their own turf. No one has to know."

He laughed. "You know how much organizing that takes? Assuming they even agree to meet you?"

"I know. I'm asking politely to give you time to tell them I'm coming—one way or the other."

He sighed. "I'll make some calls. Give me your number."

She told him. "Thirty-six hours. Then I'm going to start opening files and digging up names."

"I hear you. I'll do what I can."

"Thanks."

She searched reports on survivalist activities, looking at known activists and paramilitary leaders who might have the resources to pose a realistic threat. She compiled a list of twenty possibles who had the experience, organizational expertise, and contacts to orchestrate the kind of plan Jennifer Pattee had been party to. The money to pull it off was another issue, and that thread was still eluding her. At close to 0200, when she'd done as much as she could from a desk, she closed the computer and caught a cab home.

She let herself into the empty condo, showered, and stretched out naked in bed. She hadn't slept there alone for a long time. She'd never slept well until Blair. With Blair in her arms, she didn't dream of her mistakes, wasn't haunted by those she had failed to protect. Blair chased her ghosts away.

As she stared at the ceiling, she thought about calling her. She left the phone on the table beside the bed. Not out of stubbornness or pride, but a phone call would have been about her need, not Blair's. Blair had texted, and her message had been clear. She wanted a little space. A little time to herself. That was something Cam could give her, and she couldn't give her the things that mattered most.

She rolled onto her side and stared into the dark. In a few hours she'd be on her way to Georgia and then off to Idaho. The closer she got to the answers she needed, the greater the risk of reprisal. Blair was probably safer exactly where she was.

Chapter Thirteen

Blair woke in the unfamiliar bed before dawn. The bedside clock said 5:05. She pulled on her jeans and the ancient sweatshirt, bearing the name of their prep school, Diane had lent her, and walked barefoot into the kitchen. On a clear day, Diane's high-rise condo had a million-dollar view of Central Park, but at the moment the only light came from a small table lamp on the circular bistro table in front of the opaque, dark windows. A woman sat there in one of the ornate wrought-iron chairs, leaning with her cheek on her hand, her back to Blair. Her blond hair was golden yellow, lighter than Blair's, and cut shorter than Blair remembered. Her thin shoulders seemed to sag inside her dark silk shirt. Her eyes were closed, her profile as elegant as a carved cameo.

Unwillingly entranced by Valerie's sad, solitary beauty, Blair stood still, watching her, wondering if she should wake her or just back away. She wanted to like Valerie because her best friend loved her. Part of her, most of her, *did* like her, and she owed her for many things. Valerie had saved Cam's life more than once. Valerie had also been Cam's lover, and some part of that connection still persisted between them. In her head and her heart, Blair knew Valerie was no threat, but the animal that lived deep in the primitive recesses of her mind urged her to mark her territory every time she and Valerie were in the same room. If she'd truly been the beast that prowled her subconscious, she would have growled a warning. Maybe she did.

Valerie opened her eyes and said in her husky alto, "I hope I didn't wake you."

"You didn't." Knowing she couldn't retreat without looking foolish, she walked the rest of the way into the kitchen and looked at the coffeepot. Thankfully, it was full and hot. Something else she owed Valerie. Shaking her head, she poured herself a cup, cradled the warm mug between her hands, and leaned against the counter. "When did you get in?"

"About an hour ago. I didn't want to wake Diane." Valerie smiled, and even the dark circles beneath her eyes could not mar her loveliness. "Fortunately, she can sleep through almost anything."

Blair laughed softly. "I know. Have you eaten anything?"

Valerie's brows drew down as if she was trying to remember. "I don't think…I'm not exactly sure when, but I'm not hungry."

Blair set her coffee cup aside and opened the refrigerator. "You just think you're not hungry. Believe me, I've seen Cam come in after a few days in the field ready to fall down from hunger, and too exhausted to tell. So…food first. Sleep second."

Valerie started to rise. "You don't have to—"

"Please." Blair waved Valerie back into her seat and took out eggs, butter, and cheese. She knew her way around Diane's kitchen as well as she did her own. It only took her a few minutes to scramble enough eggs and cheese for two. She slid toast into the toaster and put two plates on the small table. After the toast popped, she buttered it, scooped eggs onto both plates, and sat with her coffee across from Valerie. She nodded at the plate she'd placed in front of Diane's lover. "Go ahead. Eat that while it's hot. My guess is you'll be asleep in half an hour."

Valerie's elegant mouth quirked into a smile. "You think all of us are alike?"

Blair dug into her eggs. "Mostly, yes." She ate for a moment, then put her fork aside and leaned back. She wasn't all that hungry. She wondered if Cam had bothered to eat. Probably not. Coffee and a doughnut did not constitute a meal. Valerie was nothing like Cam—Valerie was secretive and changeable, while Cam was as honest and unwavering as bedrock. Valerie was as ephemeral as a melody drifting on a breeze, impossible to capture. Cam was a refrain that resonated in every cell, strong and unbending. Polar opposites, but they both accepted life-threatening danger in the name of duty, and each, in her own way, courted death. "Why do you do it?"

Valerie regarded her intently. "Shouldn't you be asking Cameron?"

"Probably." Blair smiled wryly and broke off a corner of toast. "I know what she'd say, but I'm still not sure I understand. Maybe you'll make more sense."

"I doubt it."

Blair laughed. "Because it's another secret-agent secret?"

"No." Valerie speared a mound of eggs, paused before lifting it to her mouth. She looked at Blair, her eyes appraising. "Because Cameron is motivated by a desire for justice. I'm not."

"You know, I really ought to hate you, but I just can't."

"Why?" Valerie asked in a curious tone. "Because I love Diane and I don't always make her happy?"

"That. And because you love Cam."

"Ah," Valerie said, not denying it. She finished the eggs and sipped her coffee. "We're fortunate, you and I. Diane loves me and Cameron loves you. I try not to think about why I'm lucky enough that she does."

"I know. It makes my head hurt when I do."

Valerie nodded slowly. "Yes, among other things."

"Well?"

Valerie leaned back and pushed a long, elegant hand through her hair. Her expression hardened and something dark moved through her eyes. "I do it because I'm angry. And because every time I win, I feel better. And, I suppose, I do it because I'm good at it."

Valerie had been a high-priced DC escort as part of her cover, but what—or who—she had been before that was a mystery. "Revenge?"

"Possibly. Isn't that just the other side of justice?"

Blair laughed. "Well, I might say so, but I know Cam wouldn't."

"No, Cameron is motivated by something far more righteous. She's probably the only truly noble person I've ever met."

"Me too."

"It must be very hard to be angry with her."

Blair laughed again, understanding a little why Diane loved this aloof, unapproachable woman. Why Cam had. Valerie saw beneath the surface as if long-defended barriers were only so much air. "It isn't hard at all to be angry with her. It's just really hard to stay angry."

"I suspect she knows that."

"You really shouldn't be so kind to me. I haven't exactly been gracious."

"I hadn't noticed." Valerie lifted a shoulder. "Besides, you love Diane, and that's enough for me."

Blair rose and took their plates and cups to the sink. "It's really tiresome being surrounded by people whom it's hard to dislike."

"Yes, I imagine it's a chore."

Blair looked over her shoulder and Valerie smiled. In that instant, she was nothing but pure beauty. "Go to bed, Valerie. Diane will be happy that you're home."

Valerie nodded and stood. "Do me a favor?"

"All right."

"If Cameron is in trouble, call me."

"What makes you think she's in trouble?" Blair wanted to trust Valerie, but she'd learned the hard way those who pretended friendship sometimes lied. And Valerie was a ghost—no one knew exactly who she worked for.

"You're here, unplanned, it appears." Valerie gestured to Blair's borrowed sweatshirt. "You're supposed to be on your honeymoon— or what passes for that for someone in your situation. My guess is, Cameron is working something urgent and you either don't know what, or you do and you're not happy about it. That usually spells danger."

"I'm back to hating you again."

Valerie shrugged. "All the same—I am very good at what I do. And I have friends."

"I'd deal with the devil if it meant keeping Cam safe."

"Sometimes the devil is the only option, but best to leave it to those of us who have already sold their souls." Valerie didn't laugh.

"I'll remember."

"Remember too that Cameron is the best. Good night, Blair."

"Sleep well, Valerie." Blair went back to bed and crawled under the covers with her clothes on, even though the room was warm. She didn't want to be naked alone.

5:35.

She reached for her phone and pressed Cam's number on speed dial.

Cam answered at once. "You're up early."

"I thought I might miss you. Boarding soon?"

"In line now."

"Fly back to New York when you're done down there."

Cam was silent.

"What?" Blair asked, sitting up in bed.

"I might not be able to get back there right away. Another meeting."

"Where?"

"West Coast. I might be gone a few days."

"I want to see you before you go."

"I'll try."

Blair's stomach tightened. "I mean it, Cameron. You don't disappear without explaining."

"I'm on the jetway. I have to go. I love you."

"I love you too, God damn it."

"I'll try."

"Cam?" But the line had gone silent.

Blair dropped the phone on the bed and closed her eyes. She hated that she couldn't keep Cam safe, but at least Valerie was the devil she knew.

❖

The Ugly Rooster finally stopped crowing about 0430, and the bar slowly emptied out. Members with old ladies left for home. Others paired off and drifted into the rooms in the back for a quick fuck or three, depending on the amount of alcohol they'd consumed. The club had a strict no-drugs policy at the Rooster—the local LEOs tended to drop in unannounced too frequently to risk getting busted for drugs. The prospects and hopefuls who didn't rate crib space and a few members too wasted to move were passed out on sofas, chairs, and even the pool table in the big back room off the bar.

When the action finally ground to a halt, Sky finished her second beer. She'd been nursing it all night and it was warm and flat. She made a face, leaned over the bar, and poured the dregs into the stainless steel sink. "God, that stuff tastes like panther piss."

Loren slid off the adjacent stool and wrapped her arms around Sky's waist from behind. Tugging Sky against her chest, she kissed the back of her neck. "I would've gotcha something in a bottle if you'd asked."

Sky turned and draped both arms around Loren's shoulders. She nibbled on her lower lip. "Do tell. You've got what I want in a bottle?"

"Not beer. Something better."

Sky wrapped one leg around Loren's and drew her calf slowly up the back of Loren's thigh until their lower bodies were entwined. Loren's heat radiated through Sky's jeans and made her throb. "You've been making a lot of promises tonight."

"Well, I guess I'll have to come through, then." Loren scanned the room. "Ready to leave?"

"I hate to break it to you, but I'm not getting on that bike at ten below zero. Not even for a promise."

Loren grinned. "How'd you get here tonight?"

"In a clunker of a rental that at least has something that passes for a heater."

"Then let's take that. Unless"—Loren nodded toward the remaining empty overstuffed chair. It listed to one side, and the springs looked as if they were about to explode out of the seat—"you'd rather stay here. You can curl up in my lap."

Sky considered the tactical aspects of leaving versus staying. If they left, she'd have to negotiate the next step in the plan with Loren, whereas she was right here in the middle of where she wanted to be right now. She could make something happen if she was here, keep on top of events. After all, that's why she'd come. "I suppose it wouldn't hurt to be seen."

Loren grinned. "Won't hurt my standing with the guys, that's for sure."

"God," Sky muttered. "Fine, as long as it's your ass on the springs."

Laughing, Loren took Sky's hand and pulled her to the far side of the room. She settled into the overstuffed chair and pulled Sky onto her lap.

Sky drew her knees up and curled into Loren's chest. Loren's body was hot and hard. She smelled good. Sky nuzzled her face in Loren's neck and because she wanted to kiss her, and there was no reason not to, she did. Loren murmured low in her throat and ran her hand up Sky's side and over the curve of her breast. Sky arched and pressed her mouth to Loren's ear. "I'm not fucking you in front of an audience."

"They've all checked out."

"Ramsey is somewhere in the back, and he was watching us."

"Somewhere else, then?"

"Nice try," Sky whispered. "But if we're alone, it won't be necessary."

"If you keep kissing me, it will."

"I guess I'll have to stop, then."

Loren slid a hand to the back of Sky's head and held her in place while she explored Sky's mouth in a slow, deep kiss. When she stopped, she murmured, "I'd rather you didn't."

"If we're staying, I'm going to sleep," Sky said, because what she wanted to do was push her hand under Loren's shirt and stroke her skin.

She wanted Loren's hands on her, with nothing between them, and the want was too foreign to analyze when she'd been awake for two and a half days and was surrounded by people who might kill her if she slipped. Lust curled in her belly, a hungry hot thing, and she pushed it away. "Sorry to break it to you."

"I'm patient." Loren tucked Sky's head beneath her chin and folded her arms around her. "Go ahead and catch a few. I'll be here."

The promise was just a line, but Sky liked the way it sounded. Too much. All the same, she closed her eyes and let herself fall.

❖

Cam settled into the aisle seat next to Captain Wes Masters. "Sorry to drag you away at such short notice."

Wes buckled her seat belt. "No problem. It comes with the job."

"Settling in okay?"

Wes Masters was the newly appointed chief of the White House Medical Unit—the president's doctor. She'd come on board the WHMU in the midst of an investigation for the source of a leak somewhere close to the president. Wes and her new lover Secret Service Special Agent Evyn Daniels had been instrumental in Jennifer Pattee's apprehension. In a few weeks when the president left for his campaign tour, Wes would be by his side the entire time.

"So far," Wes said, "there's been nothing about this job that resembles a routine to settle into. But I'm happy to be here." The plane taxied down the runway at a few minutes past six. Wes lowered her voice despite the revving engines. "Any idea what we're looking for?"

"I'm not sure. We know the virus was stolen from Eugen, but not the who or the how," Cam said. "We've got an AWOL lab tech named Angela Jones—an alias, I'm sure—and not much else. You might have a better chance than me to spot something that looks wrong."

Wes said, "I can talk to the team that developed the virus and find out how many people knew about it during the planning stages. This wasn't accidental or a crime of opportunity. This took time to orchestrate. Whoever stole it knew what they wanted and knew how to handle a Level Four contagion. The inside person was carefully positioned well in advance. We need to know who knew."

"We'll find out who had the skill and opportunity to get close to the virus, talk to fellow employees, run traces on employee records." Cam shrugged. "I suspect they'll be falsified, but you never know. A smart infiltrator uses part of the truth. Superficial background checks will often pick up those few factual references, and that will be enough to satisfy more employers than you might think. Even federal agencies."

"We need to be sure there isn't another batch missing," Wes said.

"Once we're on the trail, you'll need to be ready for anything."

Wes's gaze was steady, calm. "I will be."

Cam would have to trust that Wes and her unit would be able to deal with any emergency because the president wasn't the only one at risk. Her job was to see Wes was never needed.

CHAPTER FOURTEEN

When roll call ended at 0600, Jane followed her father to headquarters and asked permission to speak with him. Graves nodded and walked into his office. Jane handed him a half dozen human-silhouette shaped, time-stamped targets and silently stood at parade rest as he studied the bullet patterns on each one. He didn't look at her, and she could read nothing in his expression as he scanned first one, then another. After placing the last one face down on his desk, he walked around and sat behind it. "There's a little drift to the left that you'll want to attend to, but the head shots are tightly grouped and the body hits focused in the center of body mass. Kill shots, all of them. Well done."

"Thank you, sir."

"Your speed could be better. You're out of shape."

"Yes, sir," Jane said. "I know. I'll rectify that ASAP, sir."

"See that you do." He picked up his phone, punched a number, and said briskly, "As of now, Captain Graves will assume command of C Company. All soldiers billeted on the compound will report to the parade grounds at eleven hundred hours for the change of command." Graves switched off the phone and dropped it onto his desk. "The order will go out with the other daily briefing reports."

Pride and satisfaction swelled in Jane's chest. "I appreciate your faith in me, sir."

"I expect you won't disappoint, Captain."

Jane saluted briskly and swung around toward the door. She'd gone a few steps before her father's voice brought her to a halt.

"We've had some word on your sister."

Jane whipped around. "Where is she? What can I do?"

"She's still in DC, and right now, there's nothing you can do." Graves thrust his chin forward. "By reports, she's being held in an extremely well-guarded detention center."

"Our source is good?"

"Robbie's sources are excellent. It's impossible for a bloated bureaucracy like the one in charge of our country to do anything without leaving a trail. Men, weapons, food, money—all must be requisitioned, and everything leaves a fingerprint." Graves smiled thinly. "Your brother is well positioned and has made many friends. Guards boast. Aides gossip. Clerks speculate on the contents of the paperwork that passes their desks."

"Can he get a message to her?"

"Not yet. You will best honor your sister by continuing our mission. She has done her part and now it's time to do ours."

Jane's stomach curdled at the thought of Jennifer held captive. Alone. Even though they'd all been alone since they'd been old enough to leave home and actively pursue their parts in their father's plans. She'd lived alone, slept alone, and prepared alone. But, always, the others were there. She could reach out to them if she needed to. Every few months, she'd even been able to make physical contact with Robbie or Jenn. Her siblings were her fellow soldiers, her life-support system. To have Jenn severed from her now was akin to losing a limb, and she ached for her. Worst were those fleeting moments when she would forget, when she'd still think if she reached out, Jenn would be there. Then the realization flooded back—Jenn had been taken from her—and the pain rekindled like the phantom burn of a missing part, every bit as agonizing. "There must be some way."

"There might be," her father said. "What we need is the right kind of leverage."

She'd learned almost as soon as she could walk that her father's messages were often cloaked in innuendo and hidden suggestion. He wanted them to think for themselves, to learn to strategize as he did. Now he was waiting for her to make the connections, to put the pieces together. She thought about Jennifer in a cage and forced herself to analyze the problem coolly. What would it take to open the cage door when the jailers had all the power?

Anticipation swelled in her chest, and the sick feeling in her stomach burned away. "We need something to trade."

"Something?"

"We could threaten an offensive with mass casualties unless she is released."

Graves steepled his hands in front of his chest and regarded his oldest child. When she'd been born, he'd been disappointed she hadn't been a boy, but she'd turned out to be the best soldier of the three. They were all smart, all dedicated, but Jane had a killer's heart. She didn't shy away from the ultimate solution. "Such as?"

"Another biological agent—sarin, perhaps—or explosives targeting a high-density, high-profile objective—Wall Street, the Super Bowl, the Oscars."

He nodded. "That might work, although the plan would take time to set up, and we may not have much time. She'll be moved once they realize they're not going to get any information from her. Right now, she's in limbo. Once she's in the system and more people know about her, the chance of a trade is less likely. After all, they profess not to negotiate with terrorists."

"We know that's not true," Jane scoffed. "As long as the media doesn't know, all kinds of bargains are possible."

"Let's assume our window of opportunity is a week, two or three at the outside. What else?"

"A one-to-one trade would only be possible if we had someone highly valuable as a bargaining chip," Jane said, thinking as she spoke. She stared at her father. "But what if we had someone they'd *have* to trade for? Like Blair Powell?"

"Very possibly. Also very difficult. She'll probably be as heavily guarded as the president now." He smiled faintly. "But I think you might be onto something."

"I'll work on it. There has to be a way."

"Good. In the meantime, we have a substantial arms deal in the works. I want you to take point on that."

"Yes, sir," Jane said briskly, a sense of purpose replacing the lingering despair. This was what she needed. To be back in the action, with a gun on her hip and a rifle on her shoulder. She'd spent eighteen months undercover in the lab, and she didn't regret it. She'd been the one with the training to do it, but in her heart, she was a soldier. And now she had the most important mission of her life.

❖

When Blair woke again it was almost eight a.m. She showered in the bathroom adjoining the guest room and pulled on yet more borrowed clothes. Dressed in a long-sleeved navy T-shirt, dark sweatpants, and thick wool socks, she padded silently through the living room over the gleaming wood floors to the kitchen in search of more coffee. Diane sat in an emerald-green robe at the table where Valerie had been a few hours earlier, sipping tea and scanning her iPad.

"Morning," Blair said.

"Hi. I understand you took care of my girlfriend this morning."

"Hardly taking care of her." Blair poured a fresh cup of coffee and sat down across from Diane. "I just fed her a little bit."

"I appreciate it."

"Everything okay?"

Diane raised a shoulder and smiled wryly. "Who knows? She says so."

"How about with you?"

Diane pushed the iPad aside and cradled her cup between her hands. She stared into the tea as if hoping leaves would appear in the bottom of the cup with a message. "I love her. I never expected anyone to touch me the way she does. Not just physically, which is amazing in itself, but...I look at her and I feel things I never knew I could. She makes me ache, she makes me want, and she scares me."

"Yeah," Blair said, "that sounds like love to me. Especially the scary part."

"Well, we're a pair, aren't we?" Diane laughed softly. "How the hell did we end up with those two?"

Blair shook her head. "Beats me. I should've seduced you a long time ago."

Diane smiled over the rim of her cup, her crystal blue eyes warming as she took Blair in. "Oh no, we would've killed each other by now."

"Maybe. But I'm still glad I have you, hot monkey sex or not. Because I don't know what I'd do without you."

"Oh, sweetie." Diane grasped Blair's hand and entwined their fingers. "Want to tell me what's really going on?"

"I don't know, and that's what's making this so damn hard. Cam's not doing anything she hasn't done before, but I just have a really bad feeling—like we're being drawn into a very dangerous game and I can't see the shape of it. I feel like I'm fighting an army of ghosts."

"Maybe you should leave the fighting to Cam."

"I wish I could. But I'm part of the army—I got drafted when my father decided the next step after the governor's mansion was the White House. I love him, I really do. But his ambition has changed so many lives."

"I think that's part of the job description," Diane said.

"I'm not talking about his role as president. I mean as a man with people who love him."

"Would you change him, turn back time—if you could?"

Blair sighed. "No more than I would Cam. Never. I adore them both, but the cost to everyone…You know Luce is in love with him, right?"

"I've got eyes," Diane said. "I'm surprised the media hasn't been playing that tune for years."

"They're probably afraid to. Who wants Luce coming after them?"

"You're right about that." Diane ran the tie of her robe through her fingers, her expression pensive. "You know while he's a sitting president, they're not going to do anything about it. She's far too valuable as his chief of staff. She'd be wasted as First Lady."

"God, I didn't really think about them getting married." Blair's heart gave a little turn. She loved Luce, had since she'd been a child, but after her mother's death, it had been just her and her father against the world. But, to be fair, Luce had always been part of their struggles and triumphs. And she had Cam now. Her father deserved personal happiness too. "Luce as a stepmother. Oh my God."

"Well, I don't see Luce trying to be a mother figure. I wouldn't worry about it."

"I don't, but now I'm worried for her. If someone wanted to hurt my father, and they couldn't actually get to him, Luce would be a likely target."

"Just like you," Diane said softly. "I'm sure Cam knows that. And your spookies. They won't let anything happen to any of you."

"I know, I know." Blair drained her coffee. "Some days I just wish life was simple."

"And if it was, you wouldn't be who you are, and I don't think you'd be happy."

"Probably not, but I wouldn't mind trying." Blair gave Diane's hand a squeeze. "For now, I just want Cam home safe."

❖

A loud bang brought Sky jerking upright, reaching to her hip where her gun should be before she even registered her surroundings. Her hand came away empty. The hard body beneath hers tensed, and a hand tightened on her waist. Sky's heart thudded in her ears as she twisted around on Loren's lap and scanned the room.

"It's okay," Loren murmured.

Thin gray light flooded through the open front door and a buxom brunette in tight blue jeans and a clinging pink angora sweater stormed through the bar. "Where is he?"

"Uh-oh," Loren murmured. "Stay here."

Loren eased Sky to one side and casually strolled into the brunette's path, blocking the way to the hall at the back of the bar and the warren of rooms in the far rear. "Hi, Tricia. Things went really late last night and Ramsey decided to sleep here rather than wake you up at—"

"Oh, don't feed me that bullshit," the brunette snarled. Her dark eyes would have been beautiful if they weren't filled with so much venom. Her mouth twisted into an angry line. She pulled a handgun from the front pocket of her leather jacket. "First I'm gonna blow the tits off of the bimbo he's with, and then I'm going to nail him in the nuts."

"Whoa, whoa." Loren held up her hands. "Just take a minute here, Tricia. You don't want to go waving that around."

"You're right," Tricia snapped, pointing the gun squarely in the center of Loren's chest. "I'm not going to wave it around, I'm going to aim and fire."

Sky eased toward the woman, judging the distance between them, needing to get close enough to disarm her without endangering Loren.

Loren gave a tiny shake of her head and Sky paused, her muscles quivering with the strain of holding back.

"Look, Trish," Loren said calmly. "Take a breath. I'll go get Ramsey for you."

"I'll come with you. I want to see exactly who he's got back there."

"I'm telling you—"

Tricia waved the gun in a get-going motion. "No more talking. I want to see the snake for myself."

"Okay, okay…we'll find him."

Sky watched the two of them disappear into the back and fought the urge to follow. She had to let Loren take control—Loren was the biker, after all, and she was just the old lady. The impotence of the role rankled. She was used to being the one in charge, the one in control. Now she was relegated to the status of a second-class citizen. God, she missed her gun.

Feigning indifference, she walked around behind the bar and poured herself a glass of orange juice from the refrigerator tucked underneath. The distant sound of shouts carried through the thin plywood walls, but when she didn't hear a shot, she started to relax. She sipped the orange juice and watched the others begin to stir. Women sat up, their expressions dazed, their hair disheveled, and their makeup smeared. Men labored to their feet and shambled to the bar as if drawn by an invisible force.

"Pull me a beer, will you, baby," a heavyset bearded guy with scraggly brown hair muttered as he leaned on the bar. He smelled like he'd slept in his clothes for a week.

Sky drew a draft and slid it in front of him.

"I didn't get your name," he rasped.

"Red."

"So you'd rather suck pussy than dick, Red?"

She smiled and saluted him with her OJ. "Any day."

He grunted and drained half the beer. "That McElroy always has been a lucky bastard."

That moment, Loren emerged from the back hallway. "What's that you're saying about me, Spike?"

"I was saying to your old lady here you've always been lucky. Remember last year when three of the guys got picked up? You were supposed to be on that run, but your bike blew a tire before you could leave."

"Yeah. Close call." Loren edged around behind the bar and up to Sky. She kissed the back of her neck and slid an arm around her waist. Spike's attention immediately shifted to them, as she'd hoped.

"You ready to get out of here, baby?" Loren nuzzled Sky's ear.

Sky's nipples tightened with a will of their own and everything below her waist pulsated. God, she'd been aroused for hours, and her body felt as if it might shatter with a single stroke in the right place. She dropped her head back onto Loren's shoulder and kissed her neck. "More than ready."

"Fuck. Lucky bastard," Spike muttered and staggered back toward the hopeful he'd been tangled up in the night before.

Sky swiveled around and kissed Loren hard. "I want out of here, now."

Loren fisted Sky's hair and kissed her back. "My place."

"Yes," Sky whispered.

CHAPTER FIFTEEN

Hey, McElroy!" Ramsey called just as Loren and Sky reached the front door on their way out of the Rooster. "Can I talk to you for a minute."

Loren kept her arm around Sky's waist and turned, facing Ramsey at the back of the long bar. "Sure, Prez."

Ramsey grinned, his arm draped over Tricia's shoulders. Gone was the raging homicidal Valkyrie—now Tricia resembled a well-fed cat, a contented expression on her face as she pressed to his side, one hand clenching his wide leather belt. Luckily, Ramsey had been alone when Loren had led Tricia back to the room he kept in the members-only area. Whatever he'd said—or done—after Loren left the two of them alone had seemed to satisfy his old lady.

Loren kissed Sky and patted her on the ass. "Go ahead, baby. Take off."

Sky slid her hand behind Loren's neck, gripped her hair, and kissed her back, plastering her body to Loren's. Sky's breath was warm as it curled over Loren's ear. "I'm staying."

"Watch yourself," Loren muttered. "I'll be right back."

"Take your time," Sky said offhandedly, loud enough that Ramsey would hear.

Loren hesitated, a little breathless from the unexpected kiss. Sky managed to keep her off balance, and ordinarily that would be a problem. Hell, it was a problem. But she couldn't bring herself to mind. Sky had felt too good curled up in her lap in the dark hours of the night. Warm and soft and incongruously fragile, when Loren knew that wasn't true at all. No matter who Sky was, friend or foe, she was a dangerous, potentially deadly woman. All the same, Sky had been undeniably vulnerable as she'd slept, and she'd let Loren see her

that way. The trust she'd put in Loren moved her more than anything
had since her mother had reassured her that her family would always
believe in her. Since that phone call a lifetime ago, Loren hadn't let
anyone close enough to trust or be trusted.

And as much as she knew they were only playing their parts in
the charade her life had become, she wanted the game to go on. She
could still feel Sky's warm breath against her neck, the sensation so
exquisite she'd been more satisfied than her casual sexual encounters
had ever managed. She'd been naked with women who hadn't provided
the pleasure she'd experienced just drawing Sky's hair through her
fingers. As she'd slowly sifted the deep red strands, feeling Sky's heart
beat against her own, the press of Sky's fingertips against the bare skin
of her throat had eventually become the sole focus of sensation in her
body, until those small points of pleasure had magnified and filled her.
Until Sky was all she knew. Even now, pleasure coiled deep inside, and
she had the urge to bend her head and take another kiss. She didn't want
to walk away, didn't want to leave Sky alone.

Sky pulled away and sauntered down the length of the bar until
she was only a few feet from Ramsey. He watched her approach with
predatory interest. She edged a hip onto a bar stool, crossed her legs,
and smiled. "I guess you know why I'm here."

"I heard," Ramsey said.

"Is today a good time?"

His eyes narrowed, and Tricia suddenly focused on Sky as if
sizing her up for dinner. Loren couldn't figure out what the hell Sky
was doing, but antagonizing Ramsey or Tricia was not a good idea. She
strode past Sky and blocked her from Ramsey's line of sight.

"Ready when you are," Loren said.

Ramsey grunted and disappeared around the corner. Loren caught
up to him before the double doors that led to church, the members-only
meeting room where they held their tactical gatherings. Quincy was
there, and Armeo, both of them looking hungover and as confused as
Loren was about the sudden meeting. Ramsey closed the door after she
followed him inside.

Loren took her seat in the usual place and Ramsey slumped into
his at the head of the big table. "Jesus, what a night."

Loren waited for Ramsey to confront her about bringing Tricia
into the sanctuary, but he ignored her.

"Everything okay with Tricia?" Quincy asked. He was the only
one who could broach a personal subject with Ramsey—they'd been

friends since they were kids and now Quincy was Ramsey's VP. Quincy's number one job was to have Ramsey's back in all things.

Ramsey smiled wryly. "Still got my balls."

Everyone laughed and the tension in the air lessened.

"So what time is it? Fucking eight o'clock in the morning? Fucking militia." Ramsey rubbed his face, his palm producing a scratching sound as it rubbed over the bristles covering his heavy jaw. "Some broad who says she's in charge of the gun deal wants a look at the exchange point."

Loren's antenna went up and she stiffened. "Wait a minute. Somebody we don't know? How do we know she's even with the militia?"

"We don't," Ramsey said. "That's what I told her. Said I didn't know what she was talking about."

"What did she say?" Quincy asked.

"She gave me enough details to prove she was the real deal."

"You sure she couldn't have gotten the info from some kind of surveillance?" Loren asked. "Or a snitch?"

Sometimes an undercover operative's best defense was misdirection. She'd hardly raise the possibility of a snitch if she was one.

Ramsey shook his head. "She knew about your meeting with Graves the other night. Who was there, location—too many details she could only have gotten if she was on the inside."

"So what'd you tell her?" Armeo asked.

"That I'd have to get back to her." Ramsey looked at Loren. "We need to bump up the timetable. Get the money and get clear of this bunch. They're loose cannons."

Loren almost smiled but managed to shrug with a straight face. "I'll do what I can, but like I said, big shipments like this have to be moved carefully. Something tips off the feds, or even the locals, a lot of people could go down."

"Work your magic, McElroy."

"Do what I can."

"In the meantime, I told her we'd send someone to rendezvous with her. Discuss the exchange. Map it out."

"I can do that," Loren said before Ramsey suggested anyone else. If there was a new player, she wanted to know who it was, and another meeting could be her way in. "Tell them I want to meet on their ground first. That I need to be sure who I'm dealing with before I provide any details."

Ramsey's eyebrows went up. "What are you thinking?"

"I'm thinking a new player at this point doesn't feel right. We wanted a look at them, this is our chance."

Ramsey looked at Quincy and Armeo. They both nodded.

"Quincy and Armeo will provide backup. All of you, stay available."

"Sure," Loren said.

"What about the redhead?" Ramsey winced. "Jesus, what is it with the broads these days—now we have to negotiate with them? Whatever happened to the days when all they did was suck dick?"

Quincy and Armeo laughed. Ramsey looked at her.

"What's the story? You find out anything when you weren't busy extending a little hospitality?"

Loren's stomach tightened. "She checks out. The New Year's run is coming up, and you know national always wants more dues this time of year to finance the council's flight to Reno."

"Yeah, while the rest of us freeze our nuts off riding there," Quincy complained.

"Right," Loren said. "I think the leadership wants to be sure we're sending in our fair share."

"You get any vibes she's here looking for anything else?"

"Nope." Loren knew how things looked—she and Sky had set it up that way. "We haven't exactly been talking a lot of business, though."

Quincy snorted. "Hard to talk when her tongue's down your throat."

Loren grinned.

"Keep working on her," Ramsey said. "I don't want it to look like we're nervous, so do whatever you have to do to make it look like your interest is…personal."

"No problem," Loren said.

"Yeah, I'll bet it's not," Armeo muttered. "I get wood just watching her sip a beer. Wouldn't mind her lips around—"

"Fuck you, Armeo," Loren said.

Armeo made sucking sounds and laughed.

"If I get wind of any problem," Loren said to Ramsey, "you'll be the first to know."

Ramsey studied her silently and finally nodded.

❖

The brunette Loren had called Tricia stalked over to Sky like a lioness patrolling her hunting territory. "So, who are you?"

Sky smiled and held out her hand. "They call me Red. Name's Lisa."

Tricia gave her a surprisingly strong handshake. Her dark eyes, shrewd and appraising, dropped to Sky's chest and then lower in the same way most of the men's usually did, but she wasn't getting a sexual vibe from her. She was being sized up as potential competition, so Sky relaxed and let Ramsey's old lady take a good long look. When Tricia's gaze returned to hers, Sky said, "I think I have to get myself a gun."

"Oh yeah? Why is that?" Tricia said.

"Because I've had plenty of mornings when I've wanted to blow some bimbo's tits off, myself."

Tricia narrowed her eyes and finally grinned. "Ain't that the truth? Dick or no dick, every damn one of them has a problem keeping their fly zipped."

"True enough." Sky gestured to a coffeepot behind the counter. "Make you some coffee?"

"Sure." Trish settled onto a stool at the end of the bar like a queen.

Sky went around behind, rinsed the pot, and filled the coffeemaker with fresh cold water. She looked around, opened a drawer under the countertop, and found the coffee packets. In a minute, she had the coffee brewing. After rinsing a couple of mugs, she set them on the bar and folded her arms, facing Tricia. Tricia was the club president's old lady. That made her number one among all the women and more powerful than a lot of the men. If Sky wanted inside the club, she needed to make friends with her. The first step to acceptance was to show her respect for Tricia's position. "I'll have that for you in a minute."

"Appreciate it." Tricia reached down the bar and took a pack of cigarettes someone had abandoned. She lit one, blew a thin stream of smoke into the dust-filled, gray morning light. "Where you from?"

"Little place south of San Diego."

"Yeah? What the hell are you doing here?"

"A favor for a friend. Dougie up in Sacramento called me. Said they wanted some numbers crunched. I owed him. Otherwise you couldn't get me into this frozen hellhole for all the money in China."

Tricia laughed sharply. "I keep after Ramsey to take me to Palm Springs or Arizona or any damn place as long as it's warm in the winter, but he won't do it."

"Can't trust the club to anyone else, I guess," Sky said noncommittally. Tricia was fishing, and she wasn't going to throw herself onto a hook by criticizing Ramsey.

"Two weeks in the friggin' middle of January when nothing's happening. Wouldn't miss anything." Tricia ground her cigarette out angrily in an ashtray.

"Gotta be tough sometimes, I guess." Sky poured the coffee and placed the mug in front of Tricia. "A hell of a lot of fun, though."

"Yeah, mostly." Tricia laughed and sipped the coffee. "Thanks." She lit another cigarette. "So, does Dougie still ride that sweet little Harley Sportster?"

"Last time I saw him," Sky said, calling up the images in Douglas a.k.a. "Dougie" Holloway's file, "he was riding a Fat Boy."

"Oh yeah. I forgot he traded that old bike in."

"Yeah? He always told me he won the Fat Boy off a Soledad in an all-night poker game."

Tricia laughed. "Yeah, that sounds like him. Always got a story."

"Yeah."

"So how long you gonna be here?"

Sky took a chance. "I was only supposed to be here a day or two, but then…" She nodded toward the door leading to the back rooms. "I kinda like some of the scenery."

"I take it you don't mean Ramsey." Tricia raised a brow.

"Sorry, no."

"So you swing the other way?"

"Yeah."

"All the way or, you know, flexible?"

Sky lifted a shoulder. "Meaning no disrespect, but when I've got a soft mouth between my legs, I want someone who knows what they're doing from experience."

"No disrespect taken." Tricia laughed. "Good luck. I hear McElroy's very good at it, but she's not much for staying around."

"I'm not looking for a proposal. Just some fun." Sky glanced to the back of the bar as Loren walked in next to Ramsey. Some people would call Ramsey handsome with his powerful physique and dark, craggy looks, but Loren was just as strong and powerful with the added benefit of being gorgeous. "And that is some fun package."

"No denying that." Tricia put out her smoke, stood, and cocked a hip in Ramsey's direction. She gave Sky a last look. "If you're still here the end of the week, get Loren to bring you along on the New Year's run to Reno. I could use some company whose brains are bigger than their boobs for a change."

"I thought I needed an invitation."

"Consider yourself invited."

"In that case," Sky said with a satisfied smile, "I wouldn't miss it for the world."

CHAPTER SIXTEEN

I hope you had better luck than I did," Cam said to Wes after they'd cleared security and settled at a small table at one of the airport chain restaurants to wait for their flight.

A waitress flew by, barely pausing long enough to say, "Need menus?"

"Coffee and a turkey club would be fine," Cam said.

"Same." Wes draped her black topcoat over an adjacent chair.

Like Cam, Wes wore a tailored dark suit and white shirt, and she carried herself with the authoritative attitude and direct gaze of the naval officer she was. Cam had wanted someone with that cool, commanding demeanor to take on a group of what had to be defensive scientists and litigation-phobic corporate directors. No one at Eugen Corp had been briefed on exactly what had happened to the stolen viral agent. All they'd been told was that it had been used in a criminal undertaking. Cam had dealt with the security director—cop to cop—and she'd gotten nothing she hadn't known before the flight down.

"I reviewed the security tapes for the two days before and up to the night the virus went missing," Cam said. "There's nothing on them out of the ordinary. Angela Jones is the best suspect we have, since she's the only one missing, and she can be seen coming and going from the facility and the lab at her usual times. If she spirited that vial out, she was very good at it."

"She'd had plenty of time to plan," Wes said, sipping the coffee the waitress had deposited on another fly-by. "And if someone really wants to get something out, it's not that difficult. Almost all the security at research centers like this is directed at keeping would-be terrorists from getting in or creating physical barriers to prevent the agent itself from escaping via airborne contamination. Precautions against someone carrying it out are less rigorous. In private centers like Eugen, security isn't even federally regulated. Unless every person going in and out is scanned—thermally, radiographically, and radioactively—detecting a small quantity of an agent in a sealed vial is pretty impossible. And the cost of that kind of security is prohibitive."

"Did anyone strike you as being involved?" Cam asked.

Wes shook her head. "I talked to the lead investigator, and he seems solid. I know him by reputation, and he's devastated by the breach in security. This kind of exposure can call into question all the results of the team's work. If someone can spirit something out of the lab, someone can introduce foreign agents or sabotage the results in some other way. Basically, they're looking at repeating months if not years of work to validate what they've already proven."

"So what you're telling me is this guy would have no motive to be behind this, unless his sole focus is sabotage."

"Exactly, and I can't see that that's the case. He has a well-established career. He left academia when the funding dried up. A lot of the cutting-edge researchers did. They simply couldn't continue to support their work without federal funding, and that was one of the first things to disappear when the economy took a dive." Wes shook her head. "Unless you turn up something in the background checks on the other team members that points to an extremist connection or some kind of blackmail leverage, I don't see the leak being one of the primary investigators."

"We haven't, but I wanted your face-to-face assessment," Cam said. "How many people were in on the planning stages of the project?"

Wes sat back as the waitress slid club sandwiches in front of them. Once she'd left, Wes picked hers up and took a bite. After swallowing some coffee, she said, "The lead investigator, the co-investigator, and several research associates drafted the original plans for the project, but once it got under way, there were probably a dozen people who had at least some working knowledge of the project goals."

"So how hard would it be for someone interested in stealing one of the specimens to get themselves into a position to manage that?"

"Not that easy," Wes said. "Like I said, the project wasn't exactly top-secret, but it was pretty small. On the other hand, the nature of the work necessitated a Level Four environment, and lots of projects are going on in there. Someone working on a different project would have access, theoretically at least, to everything in that lab."

Cam frowned. "So we're back to looking at everyone who had clearance for that lab."

Wes nodded. "Anyone on the main project would just be too obvious. What about Jones? Anything more on her?"

"We knew Angela Jones was an alias," Cam said, "but I was hoping we could find out more about her—or turn up some other possible suspects. Her file here is as clean as the background I already ran. Strong credentials, been here almost two years." Cam paused. "Do you have to register this kind of project or something?"

"Ordinarily, yes, investigative projects of this nature are registered with the FDA. They receive a DIN—a drug investigation number—even if no drugs are expected to be produced."

"And there would've been a record, somewhere."

"Sure. Probably multiple places, especially if the PIs—the principal investigators—went outside Eugen Corp for funding."

"So let's say someone's looking for exactly this kind of project, discovers this place, maybe other places that do something similar, and applies for positions at all of them," Cam said. "Someone with Jones's credentials is likely to get one of those jobs, right?"

"Absolutely. I reviewed the copy of her CV you sent me. Stellar training, good previous experience, and apparently willing to relocate. That would make her an excellent potential candidate."

"So we dig deeper into her background. She's still the number one candidate," Cam said. "Eventually we'll find the place where her falsified identity breaks down." She thought she might already know where the truth stopped and the lies began. Some things couldn't be erased or repurposed. Angela Jones's birth certificate might be fake, her name, her driver's license, her social security number—all fabricated. But at some point she had come from somewhere, had to point to a trail that could be checked. Somewhere she had stopped being who she was and had become Angela Jones, and Cam was betting it was the day she'd left home and started college. The day she entered the system, she became Angela Jones. Before then, she and Jennifer Pattee had known one another—Cam was certain of that. An operation this long-range wasn't orchestrated by people who didn't know and trust each other completely. Who didn't have history. What she needed to do was follow them both back in time until their paths intersected, and then she'd find the ones who had trained them. Were very likely still training others just like them.

"We did catch one break," Wes said.

"Tell me nothing else is missing."

"The vial we confiscated is the only thing they've come up with that's not accounted for. Their inventory has been thorough. If there's another attack, it's not going to be viral. At least, not with this agent."

"No," Cam said slowly. "Next time, I think the focus is going to be much more directed. They were hoping for a big splash by releasing the virus at a public function with the president and high-ranking officials in attendance—they've lost the element of surprise now, and they know we'll be doubling security on those kinds of events. Having failed to create the kind of chaos that produces multiple casualties and throws confidence in the government into question, they'll want to make a strong statement of some other kind. The way to do that is to single out a well-known target of critical importance to as many people as possible."

Wes put her sandwich down, suddenly not hungry. "POTUS?"

"Or someone close to him—someone whose death could stand in for his, who represents the same kind of public symbol." Cam didn't need to name names. Wes knew. And so would whoever followed in Jennifer's wake—and she knew someone would. She needed to find them or draw them out first. But before that, she needed something else. She checked her watch and stood up. "Listen, I'm going to change flights. Sorry."

"No problem," Wes said. "What's up? Are you going to take a later flight?"

"No," Cam said, putting money on the table. "I'm going to change my destination."

❖

The late-morning sun finally burned off the gray clouds, and a trickle of warmth struck Sky's face as they walked out of the Rooster. She blinked in the thin sunlight. She'd been inside the windowless bar for twelve hours. Twelve hours that felt like twelve years, surrounded by clouds of smoke, testosterone, and barely concealed suspicion. She took a deep breath and hoped the cold, clean air would purge the smoke from her lungs and the taste of violence from the back of her throat. "God, I almost feel like climbing on the back of your bike just to blow the grime off me."

"We don't have that far to go," Loren said. She still had her arm around Sky's waist and steered toward her Harley in the line outside the bar. "I'm up for it."

"Not exactly dressed for it," Sky said, indicating her short jacket and skimpy top. "If I lean over on the back of that bike, my ass is going to freeze."

Loren laughed, but her voice held an edge. "Can't have that, although the way you risk it, I'm surprised you're that worried about it."

"Come on." Sky grabbed Loren's hand and dragged her past the bikes toward her car. They were alone, but anyone could walk out of the bar, and she didn't want to have this conversation outside. Besides, the look in Loren's eyes said she was pissed, and since they were supposed to be one step from jumping into bed, she didn't want to spoil the illusion. She yanked open the car door and climbed behind the wheel. Loren cut around the front and dropped into the seat beside her. Sky started the engine and said, "What are you talking about?"

The car was small and Loren seemed very close as she leaned toward Sky. "What the hell were you trying to prove in there? Pushing Ramsey about the audit, then getting chummy with Trish."

"Ramsey would have expected me to say something," Sky pointed out.

"And Trish? You do know she could chew you up and spit you out if she gets a wild hair. And, trust me, she gets a wild hair frequently."

"Listen, McElroy," Sky said, backing toward the road, "I came here to get inside, and that's what I'm going to do. Tricia is the perfect avenue."

"Tricia is smart and tough and more than a little crazy." Loren was so close, her breath streamed like a hot caress across Sky's cheek.

A ripple of sensation, shockingly swift and sweet, ran down her body and exploded in her center. Loren's heat overpowered the pathetic wheeze coming from the vents, or maybe it was just her own temperature spiking. Sky shivered. "If I wanted to be anything more than a faceless pair of tits you diddled for a night, I needed to be seen. Really seen. Being noticed by Tricia helps my cover."

"Well, now she's seen you. For better or worse. And you've managed to wrangle yourself an invitation to the New Year's run."

Sky cut Loren a look. Her eyes still flashed with temper. "Well, only if you offer me the bitch seat."

Loren grunted. "Do I have a choice?"

"Plenty, I'm sure." Sky imagined Loren had no trouble finding women to keep her company on the back of her bike whenever she wanted it. The idea left a sour note in her stomach. "Look, I might be able to get a look at things you can't. And women talk to other women the way they won't to you—not when you're a member first, a woman second."

"Is that how you see me?" Loren asked. "Or do you only see an operative you intend to handle?"

Sky watched the road, and for the first time in her memory, didn't know how to form her answer. She couldn't read Loren the way she could other people, couldn't discern what answer would produce the outcome she wanted. She didn't know what she wanted. Her feelings, or whatever it was Loren caused to swirl around inside her, throwing her off, confusing her, were getting in her way. "Can we agree to focus on the job?"

"Sure." Loren pulled back and the heat dissipated, leaving Sky cold even though the interior had warmed up.

"We're on the same side, Loren," she said softly.

"You'll get plenty of opportunity for a firsthand look on the run to Reno—all the chapters will be there, and so will the national officers," Loren went on as if they hadn't nearly crossed some unspoken line between the personal and the professional. "But I suggest you go through the books as quickly as possible and give them a clean bill of health. You don't want Ramsey getting nervous about what you might find, and you don't want him watching you any more than he already is."

"Okay, that makes sense. I'll go back this afternoon and make quick work of it." Sky ought to have been happy they were back on neutral professional ground, but instead a nagging emptiness spread through her. "If I close out the books, you and I will have to be seen together to maintain my cover. Frequently."

"I've got my own agenda—I can't spend all my time feeling you up for the benefit of the club members who might be watching."

"Darn, and I was so hoping you would."

Loren laughed and some of the weight lifted from Sky's chest. "Okay, it's not a hardship, true. But I may be out of town for a while, probably tomorrow."

"Doing what?" Sky asked.

Loren was silent.

"I thought we were past this, McElroy." Sky took the turn toward Loren's shop. "There's no reason for me to be here except the ones I gave you. If I'd come here to expose you, I've already got enough on you to do that."

"We'd still both be better off if you handled things from a distance."

"So what—you can take on this gun exchange with the militia with no backup of any kind?" Sky shook her head. "That's not happening. You get me, or you get the county sheriffs dogging your steps."

Loren snorted. "Well, that's guaranteed to get me dead. They've got more leaks than a faucet. Plus, I know two of them who work on the Renegades' payroll."

"Yeah, I know. We've been looking at them. So I'm as good as you get."

Loren blew out a breath. "Well, I guess I'll just have to keep feeling you up for the benefit of the boys, then."

"I'll try not to make it too much of a chore," Sky said dryly.

"The problem," Loren murmured, "is that it isn't."

Sky knew exactly what she should say. She should have put Loren off, put distance between them—safe, comfortable, anonymous distance. Her silence was as telling as a confession.

CHAPTER SEVENTEEN

Sky parked in the long lot behind Loren's garage. The fog and clouds had blown away on a rising wind, and the rambling, one-story automotive shop Loren also called home seemed desolate in the too-bright daylight. The nearest house was a quarter mile away around a bend in the snow-covered highway, and the mountain rose directly behind the narrow strip of uneven gravel where they'd parked, towering over them, dwarfing them in its shadow. Sky hesitated before cutting the engine, a sensation of foreboding urging her to back out onto the road and keep going. Irrational and completely not her. Irritated at feeling so out of her element, Sky turned off the car and got out.

Loren unlocked several deadbolts and stepped into the rectangle of blackness that appeared when she opened a blank-faced gray metal door. Sky followed Loren and the door swung shut behind her. The air inside was cool and smelled faintly of motor oil. She paused with the door at her back, waiting for her eyes to adjust to the semidarkness after the bright sunshine outside. A shadow moved across the room, and a small table lamp came on next to a single bed. An army-green footlocker stood at the foot of the bed, and if Sky hadn't known where she was, she'd have thought she'd walked into a military barracks. The plain wool blanket was stretched taut across the mattress, its corners folded with military precision. A plain boxlike nightstand next to the bed was the only other furniture, with the exception of a utilitarian plank bookcase overflowing with hardbound and paperback books. A braided rug lay on the concrete floor next to the bed. A partition at the opposite end of the room probably led to a bathroom. The plywood walls were painted a uniform tan. Overall, the space was neat, clean, and impersonal.

"Where do you do your cooking?" Sky asked. She knew from her first visit that the garage and workshop were directly through the curtained doorway on the opposite wall.

Loren pulled off her jacket, hung it on one of a row of hooks on the wall, and leaned against the curtained doorway ten feet away from Sky. "Hot plate in the shop. You'd be surprised what you can cook on a hot plate. After you spend a few months in the desert, you learn how to do a lot of things with a little."

Sky tried to imagine what it would be like, sleeping in that bed night after night and waking up to this barren space. Spending her days with men who would kill her if they knew who she was, risking her life, *forfeiting* her life in so many ways, in pursuit of a goal she might never attain. She needed to understand these things if she wanted to understand Loren. And she did. For the job, of course. But for more than that. For the woman who had held her while she'd slept, asking nothing and offering everything that mattered in that moment—safety and trust. "God, Loren, you don't have to live like you're still on the front line."

"Don't I?" Loren shrugged as if it didn't matter. "It works for me, and it suits the cover."

"Right. Okay." Sky took off her jacket and let the subject drop. Loren was right—and how she lived was no concern of Sky's. It just... bothered her. Bothered her to feel the loneliness of the place. Maybe that was just her projecting her own weird sense of being out of place— she must be more tired than she'd realized. Maybe Loren didn't feel the emptiness like a weight pressing down on her. Maybe she was past loneliness. Maybe she had to be.

Sky turned to the bookcase and perused the titles. Mysteries, thrillers, an odd Western too old to be currently popular. The subjects seemed to be in keeping with who Loren professed to be, perhaps with who she had always been. Sky didn't know, and the frustration returned. McElroy was a cipher, and Sky needed to solve the mystery of her for both their sakes. She pulled out one of the hardbound books with a plain spine, faded lettering, and a cover that was frayed at the corners. She opened it. A yellowed title page. Zane Grey. *Riders of the Purple Sage*—arguably the most popular Western ever written. The book had to be eighty years old, at least. "This looks like an original."

Loren smiled quickly. "Picked it up at a yard sale for fifty cents. It's easy to pick up old books if you're looking for them."

"Hobby?" Sky turned the book over in her hands. She could see Loren as a cowboy—riding free, living beyond the reach of law and convention.

"Not intentionally. They just follow me home." Loren's faintly crooked grin made her look devastatingly handsome.

Sky didn't want to think about how damn good-looking Loren was, or remember the feel of Loren's hands on her body when they'd been pretending—hell, she wasn't about to start lying to herself now, they hadn't been pretending, they'd been touching, and kissing, and doing what she'd wanted to do then and what she wanted to do again. She forced her mind away from the lingering images, ignored the tremor in her belly. "What else do you do, when you're not working on the bikes or riding with the Renegades?"

"I don't have a lot of time for anything else. A movie now and then. I keep busy."

"Yes. I imagine." Sky turned and put the book back in exactly the place she'd found it, noting without surprise that the titles were all alphabetized. Loren was careful, particular, with the things she cared about. Sky wondered if she'd be that way with a woman. If there was a woman. When she turned back, Loren was still watching her. "You said you had things to do the next few days—with the militia. Tell me what that's about."

Loren slid her hands into her pockets. The leather tightened across her thighs. "Everyone back at the Rooster thinks we're here fucking."

"Well, we'll let them think that, won't we."

"It's always best to keep your cover as close to the truth as possible."

Sky laughed, grateful for the humor that cut the sexual tension slowly closing her throat. "That has to be the most unromantic offer I've ever had."

Loren laughed too. "When I offer, you'll know it." The humor in her face faded and the outlaw returned, eyes deadly and hard. "A woman contacted Ramsey early this morning. Said she was in charge of their end of the weapons deal. Actually, she said *in command*. She wants a rundown of the op and a personal review of the rendezvous site. Maybe the warehouse too."

Sky looked around for a chair and didn't see one.

"You can sit on the bed." Loren tilted her chin toward the garage.

"Or we can go out there and you can straddle the Indian again. You looked good on it."

"I'll take the bed." Sky refused to let Loren's compliment affect her, even if her pulse did jump a little bit at Loren's admission. She sat in the center of the bed. "Is that usual? A request like that?"

"It's not totally out of the ordinary—bikers tend to be paranoid, militia too, apparently. Always expecting a double or triple cross. With good reason, oftentimes, especially with a deal this big. But we've already met with the militia leader, so this seems to be overkill."

"Why are you going?"

Loren shrugged. "We could make noise about it, but since they're asking, it gives me the opportunity to ask for something in return. I want a closer look at what's going on up there. If I can get some pictures, it'll help us ID the members and maybe find some connections. They're getting their money from somewhere. My guess is somewhere big."

"If you get caught up in those mountains taking pictures, they'll kill you."

"Well, I'll just have to be careful."

"Who's going with you?" The tension in Sky's belly ratcheted up along with her temper. Loren shouldn't be planning an op like this without discussing it with her first. She was Loren's handler.

"Quincy and Armeo will back me up, but chances are if I want to get anywhere near the compound, they'll want me to come alone."

Sky shook her head. "I don't like it. It's too isolated up there. We can't get aerial surveillance, we can't get a ground team in place. And all you have for backup is two bikers who won't save your ass if they get wind of who you are."

"Look, I've been doing this a long time. I know what I'm doing."

"I know. Even though you're lousy at reports, I know what you've been doing. I know more about you than anyone." Sky stood up. "And you know you should have run this by me."

Loren stiffened. Sky was right, and she didn't like it. Sky did know more about her than anyone, and she didn't know Sky at all. Loren didn't like being on an unequal playing field. She didn't like how much Sky affected her. Wrong. She liked it too much. She liked the way Sky's skin smelled, the way they fit, the way when they kissed the connection felt immediate, intense, right. She liked the way she felt every time she looked at Sky—like she wanted to touch more of her skin, taste more of her, drown in her. Loren raked a hand through her hair, cursed under her breath.

"What?" Sky asked. "You're going to have to talk to me."

Loren paced a few feet away, then whipped around. "You're a complication."

Sky's brows rose and heat prickled along the back of her neck. "Am I? Define *complication.*"

"You shouldn't be here. You've introduced an unknown element into an operation that's already in progress. We have to secure your cover right in the middle of the damn Renegades, with Ramsey and everyone else watching everything we do. And now you think I can just drag you up into the Bitterroots to a paramilitary compound with no way to explain who you are or why you're there. You're crazy if you think I'm doing that."

Sky stalked toward her and poked a finger into the center of Loren's chest. "Listen, McElroy. You might like being a lone ranger, but there's more going on here than we originally suspected, and we need intel now. We need to know who's funding them and what the hell they plan to do with two hundred assault weapons. You can't be the only person on the ground out here because even though you are very, very good, if something happens to you, we lose two years of effort on this project. So you're stuck with me."

Loren grabbed her wrist loosely, but firmly enough to send a message. She moved Sky's hand away from her body. "It warms my heart to know you want to keep me alive so the operation won't be a waste."

Sky's eyes flashed. "Do you enjoy being a pain in the ass?"

"Immensely," Loren half snarled.

"Well, so do I," Sky snapped. She gripped Loren's shirt, yanked her close, and kissed her hard on the mouth.

For a second, Loren's body tightened, and then she wrapped an arm around Sky and tethered her in a tight embrace. Sky tasted like her name—cool and bright. Loren drank her like she drank in the morning air after a fresh snowfall. She basked in her heat as she ran her hands over the smooth, firm planes of her back. "You're beautiful," she murmured against Sky's mouth when she paused for a breath.

Sky's fingers came into her hair, twisted there, trapping her as she had trapped Sky. "Shut up and kiss me."

Loren laughed, scooped an arm behind her legs, and picked her up.

She walked three steps and sat on the bed, Sky still in her arms. Dipped her head, took another taste. Snowflakes melting on her tongue. Sky tasted fresh and clean, something she hadn't realized how much she'd hungered for. She swung her legs onto the narrow bed and pulled Sky down beside her. Their legs intertwined and she pushed up Sky's top, pressing her hand to the bare skin of Sky's lower back. Sky moaned softly, and Loren groaned with the rush of blood into the pit of her stomach.

Sky pressed her palm to Loren's chest. "Slow down."

Loren sucked in a breath. "What?"

Sky was breathing hard, her heart racing. "We don't need this complication."

Loren's vision cleared and reality returned. She eased her grip and removed her hand from Sky's bare skin. Sky's eyes were dark, all pupil. Fathomless. "I'd say I'm sorry, but I'm not."

"That's all right, neither am I." Sky pushed away and sat up, rearranging her clothes. Her hands trembled. "I'm sorry I let things get out of hand. We don't need that."

"Do you think everything is your doing?"

Sky's jaw tensed. "No, but keeping order—that is my job. I'm sorry."

"It definitely wasn't orderly." Loren slid off the end of the bed and strode to the small bathroom. She ran water in the sink and splashed her face, then toweled dry. She hung the towel up and returned to the bed. Sky sat on the side. "Let's say what happened was mutual and let it go."

"Yes." Sky rose. "I need to go back to the Rooster later and look at the books."

"I need a ride back for my bike, and if we're supposed to have spent the last few hours rolling around here, it would make sense for you to take me back."

"All right. I'll grab some sleep in the car." Sky reached for her jacket. Loren stopped her with a hand on her arm.

"That's crazy. It's freezing out there, and if anybody drops by, they might see you and start wondering. That we don't need." Loren opened the trunk at the bottom of the bed and took out another blanket. She grabbed Sky's hand and pulled her toward the bed. "Lie down."

"I'm not taking your bed."

"Just lie down. Try taking an order once in a while."

Sky shot her a look but did as Loren asked, curling up on her side facing the wall. A second later, Loren lay beside her and pulled the blanket over them.

"Loren," Sky said, a warning in her tone.

"Don't worry, you're safe with me."

Sky believed her, even though she'd never heard anything further from the truth.

CHAPTER EIGHTEEN

Russo reached across Nora for the tumbler of scotch on the bedside table. He sat up against the pillows and sipped the smoky liquid. The burn left a spike of exhilaration in his stomach that tingled all the way down to his balls. Fine whiskey and fine sex. Not much more a man needed to feel satisfied, other than power over other men. And soon he'd have that too.

"The polls yesterday looked good," Nora murmured, her voice barely tinged with postcoital satisfaction. She turned on her side and wrapped an arm around his waist.

Russo congratulated himself on his choice of lover as well as campaign manager. Nora was considering his goals too. No pointless sentimentality for her, no demands for meaningless platitudes about love and devotion. He liked that about her—she was unrestrained in bed, shamelessly unbridled, demanding what she wanted with unabashed directness. And after they'd both gotten what they sought, she was back to her controlled, analytical self.

"I think the community meetings have won us some followers, don't you?" Russo asked. He counted on her to judge the tenor of the populace and adjust his message to keep out in front of those in both parties who cared more about ideology than actually winning. In the end, only winning mattered. He'd learned early in life to give people what they *thought* they wanted while maneuvering them into supporting his own goals.

With Nora's help, he planned on using the same strategy to win the upcoming election. People thought they wanted the right to govern themselves, the right to dictate law and order, the right to determine morality—especially other people's—and the right to ignore the rest of the world as if what happened outside the national borders had no impact on them. And his message was to tell them they were right. That their view of justice, morality, God, and the national conscience was correct, despite the fact their outlook was naïve and ultimately self-defeating. But until he controlled the reins of corporate financial power, religious influence, and military force, his first priority was to convince those who would carry him to Washington that he believed as they did.

Idly, he stroked Nora's breast. Her body was young and tight and as coolly efficient as she was. "Powell still has the heart of the nation. Until his ability to govern is called into question, we'll be playing catch-up."

"Hearts can be broken."

He laughed. "Yes. Powell needs to betray their faith, or at least be perceived that way. Right now, the people still believe he can keep them safe, free, and prosperous."

"I thought you had plans to change that," Nora said cautiously.

He hadn't kept her completely in the loop as far as his dealings with Hooker and his connections with the militia. Not that he didn't trust her…exactly. He never trusted anyone with anything that could ultimately be used against him. At least, not unless he was also willing to eliminate those who knew too much, and he rather wanted Nora by his side when he headed to Washington. Nora was ruthless when it came to manipulating people, but deep down he sensed she had a streak of moral conscience that would be at odds with some of his plans. So he didn't discuss all of them.

"I do have people working on putting some tarnish on Powell's shining armor, but it's a long-range kind of thing." He finished the scotch and set the glass aside.

"The recession has hurt him. A little more negative press, a few more instances of government ineffectiveness, and his popularity will take a nosedive." Nora casually stroked his abdomen. "The people only love a winner when he's winning. And you're going to win and keep on winning."

Russo watched her hand trail lower. Common lore suggested men of a certain age had difficulty in the bedroom. Some of his contemporaries had actually admitted it. He laughed to himself. If he was having trouble in that department, he certainly wouldn't make it public. A man who couldn't dominate in every area was hardly fit to lead. But he wasn't a common man, and he wasn't having any difficulty. He pushed Nora onto her back and rose over her, already primed. "You just keep refining my message and watching those numbers. I'll worry about Powell's popularity."

She reached down and guided him inside her, locking her legs behind him. Her body tensed like a bow, her pupils widening. "You're going to be absolutely invincible in the White House."

He settled himself deeper. "And you're going to look even better as my chief of staff."

Nora smiled and closed her eyes.

The cab let Cam out at the corner of East Twenty-first a little after nine. The gates surrounding Gramercy Park were locked and foot traffic was sparse. She glanced up at the loft on the top floor of the brownstone that sat midblock. A faint glow illuminated several windows, and she welcomed a rush of relief. Blair was home. She'd had to wait for a flight out of Georgia, and while she'd waited, she'd contemplated calling Blair to tell her she was coming. Finally, she'd decided not to interrupt Blair's plans and to just come ahead unannounced. If Blair hadn't been home, she would have let herself in and waited. Blair waited for her often enough, and she'd be asking her to wait again soon, and under circumstances Blair wasn't going to like. This detour to NYC was more for her than Blair, even though Blair had ordered her not to go anywhere without seeing her first.

Cam smiled as she looked up at the windows. Blair could be quite persuasive when she issued orders, and Cam had discovered she liked being the one to follow them, when she could. Unfortunately, often she couldn't.

When she'd left for Georgia, she'd expected to head directly out west to make contact with the undercover operatives tracking the militia. The viral theft and plot to attack the president had all the earmarks of domestic terrorism, and the only leads they had traced Jennifer Pattee to Idaho. She suspected Angela Jones's trail would also lead them back there. Ferrell hadn't contacted her about a meet with the undercover agents working the militia angle, but she'd told him she'd wait thirty-six hours before digging into the covert ops for a contact herself. He still had twelve hours before she started pressing him. Unfortunately, that timetable pushed her right into the New Year's weekend, and she doubted she'd be able to arrange a meet until after that, assuming Ferrell came through with some names. She was anxious to chase any lead, no matter how thin, but she was glad she had this small window of time to join Blair. She missed her.

Cam nodded slightly to the agents in the SUV parked across the street from Blair's as she angled up the block to the brownstone. Inside, she waved to Nunez, who had apparently drawn the night shift again, and keyed the elevator car that went only to Blair's residence floor. The Secret Service had the whole floor below as a command center. That used to be her base.

As the elevator car climbed, she remembered arriving here the first day and how much she hadn't wanted to be in charge of Blair Powell's protection detail. She'd only had Blair's reputation as a spoiled, irresponsible playgirl to go on and assumed she'd be babysitting a self-indulgent society brat. She'd quickly learned Blair had never been what the press made her out to be. Blair had been angry, and sometimes the anger erupted in ways that put her at risk, but she was also brave and intensely loyal to her father and her country. Blair's anger was still there, along with the frustration of not being in control of her own life at times, but Blair was also one of the bravest, most responsible people Cam knew. That bravery and sense of responsibility had put her life in danger more than once, and Cam wasn't going to let it happen again.

Cam let herself into the loft, set her suitcase by the door, and draped her topcoat over the back of the sofa. The living room was dark. She made her way past the open kitchen toward the bedroom in the rear, one of the only private spaces set off by half walls from the other areas in the open-plan loft. Blair was propped up in the king-sized bed, reading.

Blair put the book aside when Cam walked in, and smiled. "I heard the door open, and I was hoping it was you."

"Oh yes?" Cam removed her suit jacket and tossed it into the closet to go to the cleaners. She sat down on an easy chair in the corner to remove her shoes and socks and stood to pull off her belt, shirt, and trousers. She slid her badge and holstered weapon into the top drawer of the double oak dresser and walked to the side of the bed in her silk T-shirt and briefs. Leaning down, she kissed Blair. "Who else would it have been, coming in while you're in bed?"

"Oh, well…" Blair threaded her fingers through Cam's hair and kissed her back, taking her time. "An infinite number of choices. Paula…"

Cam laughed and climbed onto the bed.

"Mac." Blair nipped at Cam's lip.

Cam raised a brow and pushed the sheets aside. Blair wore only an oversized Giants football jersey that came down to her upper thighs. Cam leaned on an elbow and stroked Blair's bare thigh. Her skin was soft and warm, and the warmth settled into Cam's stomach like the heat from a welcoming hearth on a frigid winter night.

"Renée." Another swift kiss—just a tease of silky lips.

Cam skimmed her hand beneath the jersey and pushed it up. When she kissed Blair's abdomen, Blair made a humming noise, a deep reverberating sound of pleasure.

"Brock." Blair arched against Cam's mouth.

Cam laughed again and kissed a spot along the curve of Blair's hipbone. "Good thing I got here when I did, then."

Blair caught her breath. Her fingers came into Cam's hair, tugging impatiently. "You should have called. What if I'd gone out?"

Cam raised her head and pushed up until she was above Blair, supporting herself on her bent arms. "I would've found you."

"Would you?" Blair asked softly.

"Always. You can't get away from me."

"Promise?"

Cam kissed her softly on the mouth, then on her throat, lingering in the hollow between her collarbones. She settled her hips between Blair's thighs. Still poised above Blair's body, she read the uncertainty in Blair's eyes. She hadn't seen those questions there for a long time and knew Blair's doubts were more about the future than about her. Those fears were something she couldn't erase, but she could promise Blair she would never be alone. "I love you. No matter where you are, no matter where I am, I will always find you."

Blair wrapped her arms around Cam's shoulders and pulled her down until their bodies touched everywhere. Her mouth was against Cam's ear. "I need you so much."

"I'm here," Cam answered.

"And you're mine," Blair whispered, skating her hands down Cam's back to her ass, pulling her even tighter between her legs. The heat of Cam's body, the hard unyielding strength of her, was as exciting to her as the desire she'd seen in Cam's eyes. In a world where nothing was certain, this was. This, she counted on. She could never get close enough to Cam, never get her deep enough inside. The need for her, the desire for her, never lessened, and tonight—after they'd been apart—

the need was a living thing clawing at her insides. Her breasts ached, her belly trembled. She was wet and so ready. She skimmed her mouth over Cam's ear. "I want you inside me. Don't make me wait tonight."

"Anything. Always." Cam shifted and slid her hand between them, cupping Blair, squeezing lightly.

Blair's breath caught in her chest and electric heat streaked through her. "Don't tease me."

"I'm not." Cam's voice was rough and tight. "I'm teasing myself. I've been thinking about this for hours."

Blair arched, dug her nails into Cam's ass. "Then stop thinking and just fuck me."

"I plan to."

Cam filled her then, knowingly, exactly where she needed her. Blair cried out and closed down around her, the pressure as sharp as a blade, achingly exquisite. As much as she wanted to come, she wanted Cam to stay exactly where she was forever. She wrapped her legs around her, trapping Cam's hand between their bodies, inside her. "Don't move. Just…if you move, I'll come."

"I want you to. I need you to." Cam angled her body and withdrew just enough to make Blair cry out. Then she slid deeper again, then out, and deeper still.

All thought fled. No fears, no anger, no aching sense of distance and loss. All that remained was the connection, the perfect union that made Blair know beyond any doubt that she belonged. With Cam, to Cam. This moment, every moment. She clung to her, her face pressed to Cam's heart, and rose to meet each thrust, giving as much as she received. Everything.

CHAPTER NINETEEN

Loren woke to the completely foreign sensation of a warm body pressed against hers. She hadn't slept the night with a woman since college—before she'd joined the military. She'd only spent a few hours in the beds of those women she'd had sex with here in Silver Lake, and most of the time that suited them as well as it did her. She discouraged the occasional woman who wanted her to spend the night or hinted at something more than a casual encounter as gently as she could while making it clear she was all about sex and nothing else. She hadn't had to act, either. She'd never really wanted more than sex, and she'd always been careful not to let anyone think she was offering more. The brief connection a night with a woman provided was enough to satisfy her rare bouts of loneliness. Her nomadic lifestyle gave her an easy out when it came to avoiding entanglements—if she never stayed in one place long, she couldn't be guilty of disappointing anyone.

Moving around came naturally to her too. She'd always been restless, always been looking for the next challenge, the next adventure. Her mother used to say Loren had inherited her rapid-fire mind from her and needed the adrenaline rush to be content. Whereas her mother found her satisfaction working out the complex algorithms that always played through her mind, Loren found hers in the physical and mental challenges of her job. The military and then the bureau gave her the excuse to always be moving, and always moving on. Silver Lake was her longest billet since college.

Lying with Sky asleep in her arms wasn't anything she'd ever wished for, so she couldn't figure out why it felt completely right. Sure, Sky was beautiful and smart and sexy. She also had a way of cutting through all the layers of Loren's disguise, as if she was looking at Loren naked and unarmed. That should have made Loren put distance between them, but instead she kept getting closer, as if testing the heat of a flame with the palm of her hand—not really believing she could be burned. Somehow knowing Sky saw through the mask was as exhilarating as it was uncomfortable. She shouldn't have liked it, but she did.

She shouldn't have liked a lot about her feelings for Sky. She liked sleeping between Sky and the door and whatever lay outside in the dark, as if her presence made a difference. She'd been undercover for years, sustaining herself with the belief that what she was doing would make a difference, someday, somehow. Right this moment, being close to Sky had more meaning than anything she'd done in a very long time. Her arm lay around Sky's waist and she tightened her grip. Sky mumbled something Loren couldn't catch and rolled over onto her back.

"Sorry," Loren said, pulling away.

Sky grabbed the waistband of her jeans and kept her from moving. "For what?"

"Waking you."

"Feels good—you, I mean."

Loren went very still.

"Anyhow, thanks for…whatever." Sky gave a little laugh. "I slept really well. I have no idea how, considering everything that's going on and the fact I'm in bed with you."

"I'm not sure how to take that," Loren said dryly.

"Probably any way you want would be accurate."

"If you can tolerate the inconvenience," Loren said, "you should probably stay here for now. The members would expect us to be together, and it will be easier for us to coordinate our plans."

"Well, I'm all for coordination." Sky pushed a little away on the narrow bed. "But I'm not sure the sleeping arrangements will work."

Loren flushed. "I wasn't suggesting we sleep together—I'll take the floor. I've slept in worse places."

Sky snorted. "Right. How about we discuss accommodations later. It's after nine, time to head to the Rooster."

"How do you know what time it is?"

"I always know what time it is. Don't you?"

"Yeah, I do." Loren sat up on the side of the bed, instantly aware of the places where they were no longer touching. Those spots seemed instantly bereft. She shook off the momentary weakness and grabbed her boots.

"What?"

"Nothing," Loren said without looking around. Sky read her too damn well. She'd have to be careful about that. "Are you hungry?"

"What are my options?"

"I've got soup, bread and cheese, stew, and SpaghettiOs."

Sky sat up next to Loren, and their hips and thighs touched again. The sensation of rightness shot through her again, and Loren tried not to pay attention to it.

"Stew," Sky said, as if tasting the word on her tongue. "Would that be canned stew of the Dinty Moore variety?"

Loren laughed. "Did you think I cooked it up from scratch?"

"I'll take the SpaghettiOs, thanks."

"What's the matter, not adventurous?"

Sky gave her a long look, and Loren thought about the kiss earlier. The kiss that Sky had initiated. No, Sky was plenty adventurous. Loren still didn't know what the kiss meant. Maybe it didn't mean anything. People in a crisis situation often did things that didn't make any sense. People did, but she didn't. That wasn't her. She was careful—not cautious, but never rash. Kissing Sky back had been rash. Carrying her to the bed had been downright insane. Loren stood abruptly and moved a few feet away. Sky looked at her as if she'd been reading her thoughts again. "I'll get the food."

"I need a shower. Do you have one of those?"

Loren tipped her head toward the bathroom. "In there. It's small, but the water's hot."

"I suppose since you and I are supposed to be having monkey sex right now that I'll have to wear the same clothes back to the bar." Sky made a face. "I'm clearly out of practice at the one-night-stand thing."

Loren looked her over, while avoiding the question as to why it mattered to her whether Sky had a busy sex life or not. "I've got a T-shirt that shrank up when I dried it the first time. That will fit you. The jeans…" She lifted a shoulder. "I don't think I can help you there."

"A clean T-shirt would be great. Thanks."

Loren pointed to the bathroom. "Clean towels are on a shelf in there. Help yourself."

"Thanks." Sky walked toward the bathroom, then turned. "Really, Loren. Thanks. For last night and today."

Loren could've asked her for what, but she knew. Sky had felt it too. The moments they'd been together hadn't been about the job. She didn't know what those hours they'd spent holding one another were about, but she knew they were different. Special. "No problem."

Sky regarded her another long moment as if waiting for her to say something else before finally turning away and disappearing into the bathroom. Loren waited to hear the water come on, liking the sound of someone else in her space. Another feeling she shouldn't be having. Another feeling that was too right.

An hour later, they pulled up in front of the Rooster.

"You sure about this?" Loren asked.

"I'm sure." Sky turned off the engine and stepped out. When Loren came around to join her, Sky slid her arm through Loren's and pressed against her side. "You said yourself I had to get this audit over quickly. I can't do that unless I get started, and since that's why I'm supposed to be here, the sooner the better."

"Okay, but remember, they're going to be watching you when you're doing the books. Make sure you don't give them anything to worry about."

"I can handle this, Loren," Sky said. "Don't worry about it."

As soon as they walked into the bar, Sky pulled off her skimpy leather jacket and sashayed across the room to Ramsey, who was sitting at a back table with a couple of other members. She leaned down, giving him a good look down the front of the borrowed T-shirt that she'd slit down the center so it gaped between her breasts. The fact she wasn't wearing a bra would have been obvious even without the revealing gap. The thin cotton draped the curves of her full, firm breasts like a second skin. Loren remembered the warm weight of Sky's breast resting against her forearm as she'd held her a few hours before, and she thought about Ramsey running his eyes over Sky's breasts now, probably getting a hard-on thinking about how they'd feel in his hands.

A flash of heat so intense Loren nearly jerked shot straight to the top of her head. She'd never believed in the saying that someone could see red, but she was about there now. The rage stopped the breath in her chest. She wanted to drag Ramsey out of his chair and beat the hell out of him. All because he was looking, exactly as Sky wanted him to do. Sky was distracting him, diverting his suspicion. It was a smart move and it was making Loren crazy. She stalked to the bar and straddled the stool.

Grady pushed a beer in front of her and she drank half of it down just to cool off.

"What's doing?" Grady smirked as if he already knew the answer.

"Not much." The sound of Sky's laughter and Ramsey's satisfied growl set Loren's teeth on edge. She wanted to break something. Ramsey's face came instantly to mind.

"The Prez seems to have taken a liking to your squeeze."

Loren eyed Grady. Maybe *his* face would do.

He must have read her thoughts because he backed up. "Not me. Hey. I'm not going there."

"Just give me another beer and shut the fuck up."

Three hours later, Loren was still sitting there, staring at the dusty bottles lined up on the shelves and trying not to be obvious about watching the thin black hands of the Budweiser clock as they slowly crawled around the flickering face. Sky was somewhere in the back, still reviewing the club's accounts. Armeo had to be back there watching her. Ramsey wandered in and out from the back from time to time, and she pretended she didn't notice him. She didn't want to appear anxious, but as more time passed, the crawling sensation in her stomach mushroomed. No matter how good Sky was, she was alone back there.

Loren hadn't had to be responsible for anyone else in a very long time. Even when she'd been deployed, she usually worked alone. Procuring contraband or spiriting supplies and replacement parts destined for noncombatants to her base, where they could be put to use supporting the troops who were actually doing the fighting, was a solo mission. The fewer people who knew what she was doing, the safer for everyone concerned. Sure, she'd had troops under her command, but the dangerous jobs she did herself. She'd preferred it that way. If someone got caught doing what she was doing, the penalties extended far beyond a demotion in rank. Battlefield justice was swift, and often lethal, just like here. If Ramsey suspected Sky was not who she claimed to be, he'd kill her and ask questions later.

Loren drained her third beer and decided she'd waited long enough. Sky was her old lady. She was going after her.

A small cool hand curled around her bare forearm. "Hey, Lothario," a breathy voice crooned in her ear. Warm lips skimmed her earlobe and a touch of tongue teased along the edge of her jaw. Firm breasts, too firm to be real, pressed against her arm. Loren turned slightly on the stool and scanned the little blonde in the halter top and low low-riders. Despite the frigid weather outside, Candy was dressed for summer. Her augmented breasts spilled out over the top of the whisper of red silk that stretched across her stony nipples. Her flat stomach was bare all the way down to within an inch of her clit. Her hips flared in her skintight jeans. She had a cheerleader's body and the IQ of a rabbit. The interest of one too. She'd fuck anything in leather, male or female. Pretty and predatory, she'd been trying to get Loren to fuck her for six months. Loren had never been tempted. Candy wasn't her kind of woman, and since most everyone in the club had had a taste, she could decline just on the excuse she wasn't interested in leftovers.

Candy rubbed her pelvis against Loren's thigh and pushed her breasts harder against Loren's arm. Her bright red lips pursed into a pout as the tip of her pink tongue skated over her lower lip. "You're so mean. You keep avoiding me and all I can do is think about you. I love a hot mouth on my pussy."

"Well, you'll just have to love someone else's mouth, sweetheart," Sky said from a few feet away, "because Loren's isn't going to be on anybody's pussy but mine."

Candy turned while somehow managing to keep her breasts against Loren's. "I don't think you have anything to say about it. And I'm having a private conversation with Loren. *Sweetheart*."

"Let me set you straight," Sky said with a dangerous smile. "You're poaching on my territory. If Loren had wanted to fuck a Barbie doll, she probably would've done it already. Why don't you get the message and get lost."

"Why don't you go fuck yourself." Candy threw a straight right punch that caught Sky on the left cheek and snapped Sky's head back.

Loren made a grab for Candy. "What the fuck, Candy!"

Candy twisted away from Loren and hauled off with another punch. Sky caught Candy's wrist and twisted it sharply, forcing Candy to turn with it to relieve the pressure. With her other hand, Sky grabbed the back of Candy's head and pushed her face down onto the bar, hard enough to break her nose if she hadn't turned Candy's head at the last second. She locked Candy's wrist to keep her still and leaned over until her mouth was close to Candy's ear. She didn't lower her voice. "Listen carefully, you little bitch. Touch me again and I'll break your arm. Touch Loren, and I'll break even more than that."

Candy whimpered.

"What?" Sky asked.

"Okay. I…hear you."

"Good." Sky straightened, pulling Candy up with her, and pushed her away so hard that Candy caromed off a nearby table. She turned to Loren and poked her in the chest, hard. "I can't leave you alone for a couple of hours without finding some slut crawling all over you?"

"Come on, baby, let me get some ice," Loren said. Sky's left lower lid was purple and her upper lid rapidly closing.

"*Fuck* ice." Sky planted a hand in the center of Loren's chest and pushed, nearly knocking her backward off the stool. "I said, why can't you keep your nose out of strange pussy?"

"I'm telling you," Loren protested, aware they were being watched from all corners. She held her hands up. "I didn't do anything."

"This one time I'm going to believe you." Sky's voice vibrated with fury. "But if you don't keep your hands and your mouth where they belong from now, you're gonna be missing out on the best pussy of your life."

A couple of guys hooted and a few girls clapped. Loren looked around the room and grinned. "Anything you say, baby."

"Remember it." Sky grabbed her T-shirt in both fists and kissed her.

Loren forgot they had an audience. She gripped the back of Sky's neck and sank into the kiss, careful of the bruise on Sky's face. Sky's breasts against her chest were nothing like Candy's had been. The heat and soft pressure kindled fire in her belly. Sky twisted her hands in the material of Loren's shirt until the cotton abraded Loren's nipples, sending shock waves to her clit. Sky's tongue explored her mouth until her breath fled.

Loren moaned, aching to touch her. She pulled away, gasping. "Let's get out of here."

"I don't think so," Sky murmured, her voice thick and sensuous. "I'm ready for a beer."

"You okay?" Loren asked, trailing a finger down Sky's throat.

"Never better." Sky's eyes glittered, fever hot. She ran her fingers through Loren's hair. "Never better."

Chapter Twenty

Blair stood in a small square of moonlight by the living-room window, watching the trees sway in the park beyond the wrought-iron fence. Time hung suspended—even the streets were empty—as if waiting for a giant hand to start the hands of some celestial clock moving forward again. She almost wished the gears of time would protest, demand a respite from the inexorable march of change. Right now, she had everything she could ever want, except the promise she would never lose it. Never lose Cam. Foolish wishes that would vanish with the dawn.

"Can't sleep?" Cam said from behind her.

Blair wrapped her arms around herself, chilled even though the loft was warm. She'd woken shivering. "Sorry. I didn't want to wake you, and I was restless."

Cam joined her by the window and put an arm around her. Drawing her into the warm haven of her body, Cam kissed her temple softly. "What's on your mind?"

"Nothing, at least nothing I can put my finger on. Just…nothing." Blair shook her head, leaning her cheek against Cam's shoulder. Asking Cam for something she couldn't give would only hurt her, and Cam had always been honest about who she was. Blair loved her for all the things that scared her to death. She kissed Cam's throat. "I love you."

"Still angry at me?"

Blair laughed, her melancholy drifting away like mist at sunrise. "It's a lot easier to be angry at you when you're not next to me. When you are, I forget almost everything except how much I love you."

"Then I'll have to stay close more often."

"You won't get any argument from me."

Cam took Blair's hand. "Come on, let's go back to bed. You're cold."

"I'm not really, or at least I shouldn't be."

"It doesn't matter what should or shouldn't be." Cam tugged her hand. "All that matters is what is. Come on."

Blair followed Cam down the hall and into the bedroom. She crawled under the covers and into Cam's arms again. The cold vanished. Cam provided all the heat she needed, and she curled up against her, her head on Cam's shoulder. "How long will you be here?"

"Are you staying?"

"I thought I might. I like New Year's Eve in the city."

"Mmm. I like your birthday in the city." Cam stroked her back. "Let's celebrate with Diane. Or would you rather it be just us?"

"I wasn't sure you'd be here."

"I know. I'm sorry." Cam sighed. "I've got at least a few days."

"Then I vote for New Year's Eve with Diane and Valerie—if she hasn't disappeared again."

"Good. As to you being angry, I suppose by now you know what went on at that meeting."

"My father called and more or less told me." Blair ran her nails lightly down Cam's bare abdomen. Cam sucked in a breath, so Blair repeated the motion. A little torture seemed like fair payback. "Who instigated it?"

"Does it matter?"

"Only if it was you."

"I agreed."

"Not the same thing." Blair gripped Cam's T-shirt, bunched it in her fist, and pushed it higher. Cam was all lean muscle and elegant form. A beautiful warrior. "I already know how you feel about me going with my father, so the fact that you agreed with wanting me to stay behind doesn't surprise me. What bothers me…" Blair fanned her fingers back and forth over Cam's lower abdomen, making the muscles jump. Cam tensed. "Well, you know what bothers me, don't you."

"Yes," Cam said, sounding a little like she was in pain. Blair smiled. "A, ah…a meeting to discuss what you should or shouldn't do, held without your knowledge or consent." Blair skimmed her fingers over the triangle between Cam's thighs. "Blair—come on."

Blair smiled. "Sorry."

"Right." Cam exhaled sharply. "I know how much you hate other people trying to make decisions for you."

"That sums it up pretty well." Blair took pity and relented, resting her palm on the inside of Cam's thigh. "But what really bothered me was thinking you might have gone behind my back."

"I didn't, but I can't promise I won't at some point."

"I'm not asking you to swear to every moment of the future. All that matters is right now…at least, right now." Blair caressed her. She couldn't help it. She loved Cam's body—the breathtaking contradictions of silken skin over steely muscle. "I can't swear to the future either."

Cam laughed. "That feels like a slippery slope."

"Maybe, but it's the best I can do."

"Then it will do." Cam pulled Blair down and kissed her. "Your call, baby. Always."

Blair relaxed for the first time in a week. Cam never stopped loving her, never asked her to change. Never told her what she felt was unreasonable or selfish or irresponsible. And she couldn't ask Cam to change, either. "Did you find out anything in Georgia?"

"Not as much as I'd like. I still think we're on the right trail looking for a connection between Angela Jones and Jennifer Pattee, but the threads are still pretty loose." Cam ran her fingers through Blair's hair. "Similar age and similar backgrounds, including geographic, as near as we can tell. I'm betting they knew each other before this plan was put together."

"So what's your next step?"

"I need to meet with some people who are a lot closer to the situation than anyone in DC."

"People?"

"Some agents with more direct connections to groups capable of pulling this off."

Blair took a breath and let it out slowly, waiting for the reflex flash of temper to pass. "That sounds like double-talk for you getting up close and personal with some really dangerous people."

Cam shook her head. "It isn't. I'm not planning to confront suspects. Still in the information-gathering stage."

"Uh-huh. From undercover agents who are right in the thick of some pretty hairy situations."

Cam hesitated. "True," she said finally.

"And when you catch up to whoever's behind this, you're just going to sit back and let someone else go after them?"

"That depends."

"Oh bullshit, Cameron." Blair braced herself on her arms and glared at Cam. "It doesn't matter what kind of job they give you or what description they hang on it, you're always going to go after the bad guys yourself."

"I have to," Cam said quietly.

Blair sighed and closed her eyes. "I know."

"I'll be careful."

Blair rubbed her cheek against Cam's chest. The scar tissue above Cam's heart, a reminder of the bullet that had nearly claimed Cam's life, was still rough and hard. She would never forget, even without that constant reminder, the absolute devastation she'd experienced in those moments when she'd thought Cam was gone. She shuddered. "Be *very* careful."

"I will be, I promise. And I won't promise anything I don't intend to do."

"As much as you can."

"As much as I can."

"All right then. We're square." Blair slid on top of her, needing to feel all of her against every surface, every inch of her skin. Dawn was coming. Silver light, the first hint of the day, cast Cam's face in marble, a perfect profile etched in stone. Blair kissed her, the warmth of Cam's lips a shocking contrast to the coolness of her profile. "You're so beautiful. And I love you so much."

Cam arched beneath her, pulse hammering in her throat. "And I, you."

"Lie very still," Blair whispered.

Cam's breath shuddered out.

Blair took her time, touching, kissing, and stroking, luxuriating in every dip and curve and sensuous angle of Cam's body. She knew every line by heart, but the miracle of reclaiming what was hers was just as awe-inspiring as the first time. When she pressed her cheek against Cam's lower abdomen, Cam gripped her hand. Blair settled her breasts against Cam's center and watched Cam watching her. Cam's dark eyes had grown even deeper, shimmering with secrets only Blair knew. Smiling, she eased lower between Cam's legs and skated her mouth over Cam's clit.

"Blair," Cam groaned, her neck arching.

Blair slowed, just barely touching her, and Cam bowed off the bed. Blair skimmed a hand up Cam's torso and rested it between Cam's breasts, anchoring her as she took Cam into her mouth. She didn't hurry, didn't want the moment to be over too soon. She tasted and teased and took her time taking what was hers.

"Blair," Cam said, her voice hoarse and tight. "Enough. Please."

Blair laughed, a swell of pleasure nearly swamping her. Her body clenched. She was so ready. Too ready. She took a breath. Concentrated. Filled herself with Cam. Not enough. She would never have enough. Spreading her fingers between Cam's breasts, she let Cam's heartbeat guide her. She sped up, matching her movements to the thundering tempo of Cam's heart, until Cam exploded in her mouth.

Blair held her inside, held her safe. She couldn't predict the future, but she could revel in every second that Cam was hers.

❖

"Ready to go?" Sky toyed with the sleeve of Loren's T-shirt, tracing the tattoo of the Renegades' logo on her biceps.

"Yeah." Loren leaned close. "Way ready."

Sky agreed. They'd spent most of the night sitting at the bar—long enough to make a statement about Sky's place. Loren was a ranking member of the club, and Sky was now her old lady. She automatically had status by virtue of Loren's, but even more importantly, she'd proven she was perfectly capable of protecting her place and her woman all on her own. Her face hurt like hell but she didn't let on. The spreading bruise was as much a symbol of belonging as Loren's club patch. On and off since her altercation with Candy, men had dropped by to make random conversation with Loren while not so subtly giving her the eye. The old ladies didn't even bother with subtlety—some stared at her suspiciously, and some, like Trish, gave her a smile. Not too hard to see where the dividing line was between those who were sure of their stations—or their men—and those who weren't. She grabbed the back of Loren's leather pants as they walked out, just to make sure any of the hopefuls who'd missed the earlier drama got the message. Loren was off the menu.

"Let's take your car," Loren said. "You'll be more comfortable."

"Okay." Sky didn't mind not having to wrestle with a helmet. Her head felt as big as a pumpkin. She handed Loren her keys. "Why don't you drive."

"Why did you let Candy get that shot in?" Loren asked once they were in the car and headed back to her shop. "You could have blocked it."

"I could have," Sky said, leaning her head back. She fingered her cheek and winced. "Damn, she sure didn't punch like a girl."

"It was a pretty good shot," Loren agreed.

"I had to let her get a shot in—I didn't want to call attention to myself by being too good at self-defense." Sky smiled to herself. "Besides, it made the takedown all the more satisfying."

"That was a pretty slick move all the same." Loren glanced at her. "You could have hurt her more. Some of the other girls would have."

"Yes, and I would have made an enemy for life—one with a grudge to settle. It's all about saving face, you know that. Now all she has to complain about is not getting laid."

"Smart. Of course, you could have let me handle it. I'm sorry I let her get the first punch off."

"Thanks," Sky said dismissively, "but I needed to take care of her myself. After all, I didn't want to look like a pussy."

Loren burst out laughing. "Believe me, you didn't. How does it feel?"

"It smarts."

"I'll bet it does. As soon as we get to my place, we'll get some ice on it. We should have done that three hours ago."

"Listen, if I'm gonna be credible as your old lady, then I have to be tough. You know what it's like for those girls. They don't survive if they're not tough. They either kill each other off or their men do it for them."

Loren's hands tightened on the wheel. "All the same, I don't like seeing you get hurt."

"All the same," Sky said softly, "I appreciate it. And I'm all right."

Loren glanced at her, and her eyes were hot. Sky liked the look on her—Loren was always so cool. So controlled. Hell, even when Sky had lost her temper and pushed her, Loren had kept her cool. Heat looked good on her—especially the possessive kind that flared in her eyes right now.

Loren had kept a hand on her the entire time they were in the Rooster, but that might have been part of her act. They weren't acting now, though—and the look was still there. A look that had Sky aching for something she hadn't known she'd wanted. Belonging. Maybe it really was all an act, even now. Maybe. The enjoyment was harmless enough, as long as Loren didn't know exactly how much she enjoyed it.

"Had to help my cover," Sky said, breaking the spell. She couldn't afford to get caught up in feelings, real or otherwise.

"Anything in the books?"

Sky shrugged. "They're skimming a little off the meth sales. Not very much, and not on a regular basis. Armeo is pretty good at hiding it. Most people would probably miss it. But then, I'm not most people."

"You didn't let on you knew, did you?" Loren asked. Her hot, hard eyes were riveted to Sky again.

"Nope. That's not why we're here. I told them everything looked fine."

Loren let out a breath. "Good. Maybe now you'll consider backing off. Disappearing. You've had a look, you know the terrain."

"And you're about to set up a meet with the new contact for the militia. I told you, I'm staying."

"We'll be leaving soon for the New Year's run to Reno. Nothing's going to happen until after that."

"Well, in that case, we can relax a little and work on our cover."

"I wouldn't exactly call it *relaxing* so far," Loren muttered.

Sky shifted closer and rested her hand on Loren's thigh. Loren's leg turned to stone. Sky pressed a little harder, pleased at Loren's discomfort. After all, why should she be the only one who was in a constant state of frustration? "Guess we'll just have to practice a bit more."

CHAPTER TWENTY-ONE

Jane found her father at the shooting range. At 0700 on a cold December morning, they were the only ones around. She grabbed a pair of ear mufflers from the utility shed and joined him on the firing line. He didn't look in her direction as she stepped up beside him, but continued to fire rounds at paper targets fifty yards away. She sighted on the adjacent target and unholstered her Glock. Soon they were firing in unison, and at least from a distance, her grouping looked as tight as his. She emptied her clip, reloaded, and pushed the button on the automatic pulley for a new target. She moved from center mass to head shots. Fifteen minutes later, she ejected the last empty clip and holstered her weapon. She stepped back to wait for her father, who shot one more clip and then joined her. His face was ruddy from the wind. He never wore a hat and today, like most days, wore only a nylon flak jacket over his khaki uniform shirt.

"Captain," he said as he worked the mechanism to bring the targets forward for inspection. "Something on your mind?"

"I wanted to bring you up to date on the arms deal, sir."

He nodded and walked first to his target, where he stood for a few moments, then moved on to hers.

Jane waited, throat dry as it always was when her father scrutinized her performance, whether it was the way she'd set up a wilderness camp when she was ten years old or how she handled her weapon now.

"Better," he said. "You've corrected that drift."

"Yes, sir. Thank you, sir."

He pulled down the targets, folded them, and methodically tore them into small pieces. He dumped them in a nearby metal trash bin and faced her with his hands on his hips. "Some problem with the exchange?"

"Not on the surface, no, sir." Jane fell into stride beside him when he headed back to headquarters. "But with a purchase this big and several middlemen, I'm worried about security. I thought changing a few things might disrupt any attempt to sabotage the exchange if something was in the planning."

He glanced at her. "A surprise maneuver. Keeping the enemy off balance."

"Yes, sir." Jane wanted to unzip her jacket. His piercing scrutiny was making her sweat, but she couldn't let that show. He'd taught her the consequences of revealing her emotions.

"How do you expect to accomplish that?"

"Press on the timetable, for one thing." Jane jumped up the stairs to the company command post and followed her father inside. She waited until they were in his office with the door closed to continue. "And change the rendezvous site. I haven't suggested that yet."

"Hmm. We'll need the cash for the buy sooner, but that can be arranged." Her father hung his jacket on a peg by the door and walked to his desk. "Their response?"

"Cooperative, so far. The club president referred me to the member who is in direct contact with the supplier. He assured me she would meet with me to review details."

Graves paused. "She."

"Yes, sir."

"There was a woman there the night I met with the club's representative. That must be the one. What do we know about her?"

"Nothing, sir. At this point, I don't even know her name."

"Find out. We have a few associates in the county sheriff's department. I'm sure they have files on all the Renegades." He sat and regarded her steadily. "Remember, it always pays to know the enemy— better than they know themselves."

"Yes, sir. I'll get a file together on her."

"Anything else? Problems with the new company?"

"No, sir. All the men are ready and eager for action." She didn't bother to qualify the generic term. There were a handful of women in the ranks, and they preferred not to be distinguished by gender. She never had.

"Anything else?"

"About Jenn."

His eyes narrowed. "What about her?"

Jane took a breath, prepared to present her plan. She'd been thinking about nothing else since she'd learned of Jenn's incarceration. "I think we have a small window of opportunity to secure her release, but we need to move quickly—before news of her arrest gets out or she is moved to another facility and processed."

"And the bargaining chip?"

"A hostage," Jane said. "One who's not expendable."

His eyes glinted as he continued to probe her face. "And you have one in mind?"

"Several, sir."

He smiled. "Good. It's always important to have a contingency plan. Now let's hear the details of exactly how you plan to secure one of these individuals."

Jane hoped her flush of excitement would be attributed to the wind buffeting her out on the range. She wanted to appear cool and confident to her father, but her heart raced with excitement. This was her chance to prove herself beyond any doubt. She didn't want to spend another two years hiding, just another cog in some distant plan. She wanted to fight, and she was ready now.

❖

"Yes, what is it, Derrick?" Russo asked when Derrick tapped on his partially open study door.

"I just received a text, sir. Hooker would like you to make contact."

Sighing, Russo set his newspaper aside and looked at his wristwatch. Breakfast would be served in just a few minutes and he detested a meal gone cold. "Can it wait?"

"I don't know, sir. I'd recommend taking it."

Russo sighed again. "All right, fine. Thank you."

Derrick nodded and disappeared. Russo unlocked his desk drawer, took out the burn phone, and dialed Hooker's number. He hadn't given anyone this number and had expressly forbidden Hooker to call on his personal numbers. Now with the campaign gathering momentum, he had too much to lose and couldn't risk being publicly associated with the militia. He needed the moderates' votes as much as he needed the lobbying clout, and resources, of the far-right wing. With everyone from the Pentagon to the CIA leaking like a sieve, he didn't trust anyone's security, not even his own.

The phone rang three times before Hooker answered.

"Hooker."

"Yes, what is it?" Russo snapped.

"Our friends might want to move up the timetable for the exchange. I'll need the cash as soon as possible."

"You'll get it as soon as I can reasonably provide it without leaving a trail as wide as the interstate."

"I just wanted to give you advance notice."

"So noted." Russo checked the time. He thought it unlikely Hooker's phone was being monitored and he knew his wasn't, but he disliked speaking on the phone about matters of consequence. "And they understand we will expect repayment to be forthcoming without delay? I want something foolproof for my money this time."

"They know."

"We need an unambiguous statement that points to the ineffectual and deteriorating power base in Washington. Something that hits close to home and discredits our opponent. I don't care how you arrange it."

"Do you care who we use as a target for the...statement?"

"At this point, as long as we've got a high-profile target as close to him as we can get, I'll be happy. We can work with that."

"So can I."

"Any new developments in regard to the investigation?"

"Nothing substantial. We know they've been looking in Georgia."

"To be expected. Any word as to what they might have learned?"

"No. There's no paper trail—no reports being filed. Strictly need-to-know."

"Who's coordinating the investigation?"

"My sources can't be certain. My best guess would be Homeland and, considering the players, someone on Roberts's team."

"Are we watching them?"

"As well as we can."

"I want to know if and when they get close to anything that might lead to me."

"Of course."

"I don't want the new year to progress very far without him losing some of his shine, no matter what it takes."

"Understood," Hooker said.

"Good. Now, I'll be spending the holiday weekend in Palm Springs with my family. I don't expect to be disturbed with any unpleasant news."

"Right," Hooker said. "Happy New Year."

"I sincerely hope so." Russo disconnected and locked the phone back in his desk. It was about time he started getting what he paid for.

❖

Sky muttered a curse when her phone rang at some god-awful early hour. She rolled onto her side and felt around on the floor for her jeans. The phone was in the pocket. She was alone in Loren's bed. She blinked in the hazy light coming through the small windows set up high in the rear wall of the garage. Loren was asleep on a cot pushed against the opposite wall. Her clothes were folded over the only chair. Sky had a searing memory of sitting on the side of Loren's bed in her tank and panties with an ice pack pressed to her eye and watching Loren shed her clothes—all of them—with practiced ease before stretching out on the cot and pulling a blanket over her truly magnificent naked body. The quick glimpse had been enough to supercharge Sky's engines despite her very unsexy pose with the ice pack, but Loren had just muttered, "Leave it on for twenty minutes," and promptly fallen asleep. Or a good facsimile of that, at least. Sky had turned out the lights, crawled into Loren's bed—sans Loren—with a cold bag of ice and some decidedly hot images dancing in her head.

The hot images were still there, and Sky was feeling sore, horny, and bitchy. She did her best to banish the picture of small, firm breasts and lots of long lean muscle as she brought the phone to her ear. "What?"

"Morning," Dan Bussy said.

"It's not even eight o'clock yet," Sky snarled. "What could possibly be so important?"

"You secure?"

"Yes." Sky fell back on the bed and draped her arm over her eyes. The slight bit of pressure on the left side of her face sent a shock of pain through her jaw. "Ow."

"What's the matter?"

"Nothing." Sky shifted a little to take the pressure off the side of her face, but when she squinted she could see Loren, who had turned on her side. The blanket fell away, baring a lot of naked back. Sky gave up trying not to look. She was still human, after all. "Why are you calling me?"

"You're going to have a visitor."

"Believe me, I'm not in the mood for entertaining."

"It doesn't matter. We don't have any choice."

"Who?"

"Homeland. And someone serious."

"Listen," Sky said with patience she didn't feel. "Things are hot around here right now. We don't have time to give a sit rep to some bureaucrat who probably just wants to get credit for—"

"Deputy Director Roberts."

"Crap." Sky sat up, unmindful of the blanket dropping down to her waist. The room was warmer than she'd expected. Loren had started a fire in a potbellied stove in the other room, and the air smelled of wood smoke and pine. She'd pulled off her clothes, all of them, when she'd gone to sleep. They'd reeked of beer and bar smoke. "What the hell is going on?"

"Since when does Homeland ever tell anyone anything?" Dan said. "Maybe nothing. Word is, she's just looking for some information that might tie into another case. That's all I know, but if we don't accommodate, we're likely to have a lot more than Roberts poking into our open cases. None of us want that."

"No," Sky agreed. While all of the agencies paid lip service to interagency cooperation, in reality, they all ran their own operations because they didn't really trust anyone else to do it as well as they could. And, let's face it, after years of work, when a bust went down, no one wanted to share the glory. The last thing she wanted was Homeland Security digging around in their ongoing undercover ops. If it meant talking to some desk jockey for an hour or two, she'd manage it. "When?"

"I bought you a little time. Told them it would take me a while to contact an agent in the field. You tell me."

"Tomorrow we're headed for Reno. If you can get us seventy-two hours, that would work."

"I'll do my best." Dan cleared his throat. "You need anything?"

Sky immediately thought of Loren. "Not a thing."

"Okay then. I'll be in touch."

"Yeah," Sky said. "You do that."

She disconnected and dropped the phone back onto her pile of clothes. From across the room Loren said, "Trouble?"

"I don't know." But Sky didn't see how it could be anything else.

CHAPTER TWENTY-TWO

S ounds like something's going on you're not too happy with." Loren leaned over, snagged her T-shirt off the chair next to her cot, and pulled it over her head. She wasn't self-conscious about being naked, but both of them naked in the same space probably wasn't a good idea. Sky still seemed to be too consumed by her recent conversation to even register she was sitting up in bed wearing nothing but a scowl. And Loren wasn't about to tell her. Her imaginings hadn't come close to conjuring how beautiful Sky was. Her breasts were full, rose-tipped and perfectly shaped for holding. Her abdomen was sleek, a luscious curve disappearing beneath the folds of the blanket draped across Sky's hips. She didn't doubt for a second that the rich red-brown of her hair would be echoed in the delta between her thighs, and suddenly she wanted to confirm her suspicions. Stomach churning, she dragged her gaze up and away.

"Finished?" Sky asked.

Loren laughed, not in the least embarrassed by something so natural—and so pleasurable. "Not by choice. You're beautiful. Different time, different place, I'd show you how much."

Sky blushed. "You can save the line, McElroy."

"If I wanted a line, I'd come up with one better than that." Loren swung off the cot and went to the cubbies next to the bathroom where she kept her clean clothes stacked on shelves. She found a pair of jeans without too many holes and tugged into them. She walked barefoot back to the cot and sat down. "So what's going on?"

"That was my ATF counterpart. He says Homeland is poking around. They want to meet."

Loren shook her head. "Bad idea. The more people who get

involved, the greater the chance of a leak. It sounded to me like you agree."

"I do, but I don't think there's much we can do about this. It's a deputy director, and you don't say no to somebody at that level."

"The last thing we need with a big buy coming up is someone blundering around, giving away our cover." Loren had the prickly sensation in the back of her neck that, little by little, things were slipping out of her control. That kind of feeling usually ended up with someone being dead. In warfare, orders were orders and you did what you had to do. This was bureaucratic bullshit, and she didn't feel nearly as compelled to go along. "I say we conveniently forget to show up."

"I'll set things up. Since there's nothing you could tell her that I don't know, you won't even have to go." Sky grimaced. "It's politics and maybe bullshit, but I get paid to handle that."

"So you'll be the only one at risk, is that it?"

"All things considered, you're more important to the operation than I am."

Sky didn't seem concerned about her own welfare, and that pissed Loren off. "Is that all that matters to you? The operation?"

Sky gave her a look that would have withered stone. "Isn't that the song you've been singing since we met? Nothing else matters except getting the inside story on the militia. And now you're close. I'm expendable. You're not."

"That's bullshit," Loren said. The idea of Sky's cover being blown, of her at risk of being taken out by the Renegades or FALA, bothered her a lot more than the operation going south. She hadn't thought anything mattered to her except the operation, either. Nothing had mattered for so long it'd become the norm. Now something did matter. Sky mattered. She didn't want her going off without backup, and she didn't trust anyone except herself to keep her safe. "We're partners. We're in this together. I'm going with you."

"No, we're not, and no, you're not." Sky climbed out of bed, scooped up her clothes, and walked toward the bathroom. "When do we leave for Reno?"

"Tonight. It'll be a two-day drive, considering the weather. We'll have to stop more frequently."

"Good. I'm going to take a shower. Then I need to go get the rest of my clothes and move in here."

"Setting up house?"

Sky smiled over her shoulder. "Why not? I'm your old lady."

The curtain swung closed over the alcove and the water came on in the shower.

"To hell with this." Loren followed Sky.

❖

Cam's cell rang while they were in the middle of breakfast. She checked the readout and gave Blair an apologetic smile. "Sorry. Have to get this."

"No problem," Blair said, pouring them each more coffee. The next thing Cam would say was she was leaving. A small knot of disappointment formed in her stomach, but she brushed it away. She believed Cam wanted to stay with her, wanted to carve out time for them, and she understood too it wasn't always possible. She'd seen her father's life and understood the demands that duty made—on not just one person, but everyone around them. She smiled inwardly, thinking how, from the time she'd been old enough to recognize the cost, she had been so determined never to let her life be dictated by the obligations of others. And here she'd fallen in love with someone so much like her father that nothing had really changed. Except her. She wasn't angry at Cam, didn't feel her life had been hijacked. She'd made this choice and not for one second had she ever regretted it. There were times she wished things were different. She was only human, after all. She couldn't promise not to complain when Cam's obligations, or her own for that matter, derailed their personal plans. She wasn't going to torture Cam for being who she was or destroy the joy of what they shared because she couldn't always dictate the time and place when they could be together.

Cam ended her call and put her phone down on the table. "I'm sorry, I—"

"You have to go somewhere," Blair said, sparing her the apology she didn't need to hear.

Cam's smile was rueful. "I should, yes."

Blair reached across the table and took Cam's hand. "Do me a favor."

"Anything."

"Don't apologize to me for what you have to do. I don't need to hear it. All I need to hear is that you love me and you'll be back as soon as you can be."

"All right. But can I say, once more for the record, I would never cancel plans unless I didn't have any choice. The moments I'm with you are the happiest of my life." Cam lifted Blair's hand and kissed her knuckles. Her dark eyes deepened to obsidian. The look was one that often promised Cam's hands would be on her in seconds.

Blair's chest tightened. If the small table hadn't been between them, she might have shown Cam exactly where she wanted her hands. "You always know just what to say. That must be why I fell in love with you."

Laughing, Cam drew Blair's hand to her mouth again and kissed her fingers. "That and my many other charms."

"Don't push."

"Worth trying."

"So," Blair said, "tell me, what's come up?"

"That was my contact in the ATF. He's got someone who might be able to provide some names. Another place to look."

"You're convinced it's a militia group behind this?"

"Probably not alone, but yes, all of our intelligence suggests the only organized domestic organizations capable of this kind of long-range planning are the militia groups. I'm looking at Idaho because that's the last place I can track Jennifer Pattee. How much of her history is fabricated, I can't be sure, but I suspect that early in her life, whoever trained her tried to stay as close to the facts as possible. It's just not that easy to create an entirely new background for someone within the system."

"So you're going to Idaho."

"Yes."

"But not today?"

Cam shook her head. "No, today I'm going to DC to tell Jennifer Pattee about my trip."

"Hoping to surprise her into giving something away?"

"It's a possibility."

"If she's been trained her entire life for this, I can't imagine she's not prepared for something like that."

"Oh, she's prepared. She's as well trained as any professional soldier." Cam took a deep breath, her expression a mixture of anger and sadness. "Someone is training children, perhaps lots of them, to grow up to be traitors. It's worse than criminal."

Blair rubbed her thumb over the top of Cam's hand. "You know it happens everywhere, we just never thought it would happen here."

"I know. I'm just afraid the problem is a lot worse than we suspect."

"Do you think she'll talk this time?"

"Honestly? No," Cam said. "But I don't want her to think we've forgotten about her. And I want to see her reaction when I ask her about Angela Jones again."

"When are you leaving?"

Cam glanced at her watch. "I should grab a shower and get going." She smiled. "Then I can be back sooner."

"You *are* getting the hang of this."

"Thanks. I'm working on it." Cam rose, came around the table, and kissed Blair. "Thanks for understanding."

Blair stroked her cheek. "Just remember you're due back here tonight."

"Got it."

Blair watched her head toward the bathroom, knowing Cam meant it, and also knowing nothing was ever for certain. She contemplated joining her but decided she wouldn't be able to keep from delaying her. She showered second, and by the time she got out of the bathroom, Cam was already dressing.

"When will you be back?" Blair asked. She tossed her towel into the hamper and padded naked over to Cam.

Cam buttoned her shirt and pulled on black pants. "Ought to catch the four p.m. shuttle and be back in time for dinner."

"Good." Blair picked up Cam's belt from the bed and threaded it through the loops on Cam's pants. She slid the leather through the silver buckle and secured the hasp. Pressing close so the cool metal pressed into her belly just above the juncture of her thighs, she kissed Cam, careful not to wrinkle her perfectly ironed shirt. "I'll make reservations somewhere."

"Since we're eating at Diane's for your birthday," Cam said, cupping Blair's bare butt, "why don't we order in. I think I'd prefer you naked all evening."

Blair laughed. "Oh really. I suppose I could turn up the heat and work just like this all day—just in case you come home early."

"I'll do my best, but I'd prefer you wear clothes." Cam slipped an arm around Blair's waist. "I like undressing you."

"Mmm. Okay then." Blair kissed her again and stepped back. She needed to let her go, and the sooner she did, the sooner she'd have her back.

"Be careful."

Cam grabbed her jacket. "Always. See you soon."

Chilled, Blair grabbed a robe and walked out into the living room. The faint hum of the elevator was the only sound. Cam was already gone.

❖

"Excuse me," Sky said when the curtain slid back and Loren crowded into the small space in front of the shower stall. "Naked here. Taking a shower."

"I know you're naked," Loren said. "I noticed that quite a while ago."

The bathroom was little more than a closet, with a small toilet, a pedestal sink barely big enough for a quick rinse angled in one corner, and a two-by-two foot shower where you'd have to turn around to get both your front and your back wet. With Loren in the space along with her, Sky was forced to back up against the painted plywood wall to make a little breathing room. When Loren took a step closer, the miniscule space between them disappeared. Loren's jeans rubbed against her thighs, the unexpected friction as tantalizing as a caress. She felt herself swell, get wet, and her nipples tightened. She stared into Loren's eyes. "What are you doing?"

Loren braced her hands on either side of Sky's shoulders and pressed a little closer. She liked the look in Sky's eyes—a little wary, a little angry, a little aroused. She liked the way Sky's lips deepened to a ruby red and swelled as if waiting for a kiss. She decided not to make her wait. She kissed her. "I think I'm taking advantage of you."

Sky flattened her hands against Loren's shoulders, but didn't push her away. "I'm not the being-taken-advantage-of kind."

Loren's eyebrow arched. "No? Well then, maybe I'm just indulging myself. I said you were beautiful. That was an understatement."

"Loren," Sky murmured, "if you don't get out of here in the next twenty seconds, this game is going to get very serious."

"That's what I was hoping." Loren dipped her head again and kissed her. She wanted to drink her fill. She want to plunder—to fill her hands, her mouth, with warm flesh and sweet flavor. If she gave in for just an instant to those wants, she feared how far she would go. Where she would stop. If she could stop. She pulled herself back from the brink. Fought for breath. "Nineteen seconds."

Sky reached deep for control. She struggled not to grip Loren's T-shirt and tear it off. She wanted Loren naked. She wanted Loren inside her. "Go."

Without a word, Loren left. Sky stepped into the hot shower and closed her eyes. She hadn't gotten what she wanted, but she'd managed to get what she should want. Somehow without her being aware of it, those had become two different things, and Loren was the cause.

CHAPTER TWENTY-THREE

The two guards on duty were not the same ones who had been there the last time Cam questioned Jennifer. They obviously knew her, as they gave her ID only a cursory examination.

"Anything unusual reported in the last few days?" Cam asked.

The younger of the two guards, a husky, freckled blond who looked as if he'd be right at home on a Midwestern farm, turned to a computer and brought up a file. He scrolled through it quickly and swiveled back to face her. "Nothing out of the ordinary." He shrugged. "Actually, nothing much at all has happened."

"No visitation requests?" Cam didn't expect there to be any, but sometimes the simplest things could be overlooked. Again, the guard shook his head. "I'd like to see the video feeds for the last thirty hours."

"Sure thing." The guard gestured to an adjacent chair, and Cam took off her topcoat and laid it over the back. By the time she sat down, the guard had pulled up a video file.

"The controls will come up with the mouse," he said and went back to his work.

"Thanks." Cam positioned the mouse over the lower left-hand corner of the screen and clicked the play icon. The white-walled cell, lit as brightly as an office in daytime and looking about as coldly impersonal, came into view. Jennifer Pattee sat on her bed with her back to the wall and her knees drawn up, her arms folded around them. The timestamp said 0500 the previous day.

The prisoner didn't look particularly distressed. She was given daily access to a shower and a change of clothes, and she'd obviously been making use of the privilege. Her hair was washed and combed, her pale gray jumpsuit was clean. The faint circles under her eyes suggested she might not have been sleeping entirely well, but the casual observer would not automatically recognize her as a prisoner. Cam fast-forwarded and noted the times at which Jennifer's meals were provided. Jennifer took each tray, sat on the side of her bed, and methodically consumed all the food, her expression never betraying any reaction to how it tasted. She simply ate as if it were her duty. And perhaps it was. Fueling up to be ready for the fight to come. Whoever had trained her had anticipated this, and while Cam appreciated the necessity of preparing soldiers to withstand hardships, she could not fathom teaching children those lessons. But despite her abhorrence for what Jennifer likely experienced as a child, Cam had no sympathy for the woman. Jennifer was a criminal, and she had been ready to kill any number of individuals to make her statement.

The lights in the cell never went off, and a few hours after the third meal, Jennifer lay down on the bed and pulled the covers up to shield her face. Fast-forwarding, Cam noted she slept for almost six hours before waking. She suspected Jennifer had a very precise inner clock, as did most highly trained field agents. Jennifer then washed up in the tiny sink and stretched out on the tile floor to exercise. For exactly one hour. Cam timed her.

Nothing in any of the tapes indicated Jennifer's resolve was weakening. Cam hit Stop and stood. "Thanks."

"No problem," the guard said, diligently injecting enthusiasm into his voice as if trying to convince her he wasn't bored by his assignment. On the other hand, maybe he welcomed the low-stress post.

The older guard, a taciturn balding man, guided Cam through the maze of hallways to the familiar interrogation room. A few moments later, he escorted Jennifer, once again shackled at the wrists, into the room. Despite the fact that Jennifer was no real physical threat, Cam said nothing while the guard secured Jennifer's restraints to the table. She wanted to reinforce Jennifer's complete helplessness, to remind Jennifer she was a captive and completely at the will of her captors. Namely, Cam.

"I thought we'd finish our conversation about Idaho," Cam said.

Jennifer regarded her steadily. What hadn't shown in the video was the gleam of absolute fervor in her eyes. She might be a captive, but her devotion to whatever cause sustained her was unflagging. "I wasn't aware we were having a conversation."

Cam smiled. "It was a bit one-sided. I was hoping today you might be more communicative."

"I have nothing to say to you except to remind you that you can't keep me here without representation. It's against—"

"About that," Cam said softly, leaning forward, encroaching on the limited personal space the length of Jennifer's chains afforded her. "You are a terrorist. You have no rights. You forfeited those rights when you decided to attack the government that protects them."

For the briefest instant, shock dulled Jennifer's eyes. Fear doused the flames of her fanaticism. Just as quickly, her expression became completely blank, as if she had shuttered every emotion. She had been trained not to respond to threats, physical or emotional, but even the most rigorous training could not obliterate the involuntary responses buried deep in the animal brain. When threatened with extermination, every animal would run or fight. Cam wanted to force Jennifer into doing one or the other.

"On the other hand," Cam said casually, as if she were having a conversation with a trusted friend, "I'm in the position to make your life much more comfortable. I'm sure there are people who are worried about you. People you'd like to contact. Friends." Cam paused. "Family."

Again, Jennifer attempted to control her responses, and she was very, very good. But her pupils widened and constricted just enough to signal she'd experienced a surge of adrenaline at the suggestion of making contact with those close to her. Jennifer undoubtedly functioned in some sort of subunit, a terrorist cell isolated from the larger group—and she was waiting for them to find her.

"Do you really expect them to come for you?" Cam laughed and waved a hand around the room. "In a place like this? And just how do you expect that to happen?"

"Do you honestly expect me to tell you?" Jennifer made no attempt to hide her disdain.

"Not in so many words." Cam checked her watch. "I have a plane to catch to Boise." She looked up, caught Jennifer's stare. This time Jennifer failed to hide her hatred. "I'll tell Angela Jones you send your best."

"I don't know Angela Jones," Jennifer said flatly.

"No? You probably know her by another name. One of your school friends, I'd wager. And I'm sure there are others who know your name and hers. How many homeschooled children do you think went on to higher education from Idaho? The information is there, Jennifer. We'll find it." Cam stood. "And when we do, we'll find your leader."

"I hope you do," Jennifer said vehemently. "Because he'll kill you."

Cam was much better at controlling her emotions than Jennifer, and her satisfaction didn't show. But she had her confirmation. Jennifer and Angela were connected, and she was headed in the right direction.

She leaned forward, her palms flat on the table, her body looming over Jennifer's. "I sincerely hope he tries."

❖

The trip to the motel for Sky's scant belongings didn't take very long. On the way back, they stopped at the bar to pick up Loren's bike. When they returned to Loren's shop, Loren disappeared into the garage, and Sky put away her things on an empty shelf in the cubbies. The sound of an engine revving in the garage told her Loren was tuning up the bike for the seven-hundred-mile trip to Reno. At least they were heading south where it might be a little warmer.

The New Year's run was legendary. Bikers gathered to party and welcome in the New Year, and to have an excuse to consume excessive amounts of alcohol, gamble, and generally indulge in various forms of debauchery. In addition, the national club leaders used the occasion to remind the chapter presidents of their authority. Like the lords of old calling their earls to the castle for a great feast and vows of fealty, the national president and his inner circle reminded those who were not performing well that they could be replaced. No one missed the run if they wanted to maintain their status in the organization.

Sky didn't need to pack much. Follow trucks, filled with gear and spare parts, were driven by prospects who would accompany the members on their bikes. After packing a change of clothes and some personal items in a backpack, she left the pack on the bed and wandered into the shop. Loren crouched by the bike, tinkering with the engine. In a dark T-shirt, jeans, and biker boots, she looked enticingly tough and tremendously sexy.

Loren glanced in Sky's direction. "Hey."

Sky leaned against the nearby counter. "Hi. How's it going?"

Loren stood, set the tool aside, and dusted off her hands. "Just killing time. Everything looks good. What about you?"

Sky debated not telling her. At any other time, with any other operative, she wouldn't have given it a thought. But keeping Loren in the dark was getting harder and harder to do. "We had a potential problem, but it should be handled."

Loren frowned. "What?"

"My original plan was to be here a few days, make contact with you, and provide backup from behind the scenes. Now that's changed, and I don't want to chance running into Dougie in Reno."

"Fuck. There's no reason to think we will—there'll be a few hundred members there, but if Ramsey drags us into a meeting with Jerome, it's possible we could cross paths." Loren paced. "It's dangerous for you to be there."

"I know that." Sky anticipated Loren's next statement. "And I know what you're going to say, and I'm not staying behind." She held up a hand when Loren took a step forward, her expression darkening. "But it's handled. I called my ATF counterpart from the car on the way back here."

"To do what?"

"Dougie has an outstanding warrant on a concealed weapons charge in Oregon. No big surprise there. We'll pick him up on a routine traffic stop and hold him awhile."

"And you don't think it's going to look suspicious if he suddenly gets pulled in during the run?"

Sky laughed. "Why should it? No one's going to connect him to me, who Jerome has probably already forgotten about, especially when I'm five hundred miles away. We're just being cautious."

Loren slid her hands into her back pockets, and with her legs spread wide and her deepening scowl looked every inch the renegade she was. "You take too many chances. I don't like it."

"I'll be fine," Sky said softly, holding on to the counter on either side of her with both hands. She feared to move when every part of her ached to wrap her fingers around the corded muscles of her biceps, to sweep her palms over the hard muscles of her chest, press against the hot flame of her body. She swallowed against the desire filling her throat. "You just worry about your own cover, McElroy."

Loren took two steps closer, and before Sky could jerk away Loren's hand was in her hair, tethering her in place.

"Or what?" Loren said softly.

Sky slid her arms around Loren's neck and kissed her. "Or I'll be pissed."

"Then it'll make two of us."

Loren braced her arms on the counter behind Sky and leaned into her, effectively caging her. She kissed her mouth, her throat, and worked her way down. "You keep making me crazy, and there's going to be a lot more than a little trouble."

Sky arched against her, knowing she was losing the battle and not caring. She slid her calf around the back of Loren's thigh and locked her tight. "I can handle trouble."

Loren found the bottom of Sky's tight top and pulled it from her jeans. She was about to slide her hand underneath when Ramsey said from behind them, "Sorry to interrupt, but we've got places to be."

Loren raised her head but didn't ease away from Sky's body, glancing over her shoulder at the club president. "Your timing could've been better, Prez."

Ramsey, looking formidable in full leathers, shrugged, his gaze sliding down Sky's body. "Oh, I don't know. I'd say my timing was pretty good. A minute later would've been even better. Might even been able to lend you a hand."

When Loren stiffened, Sky dug her fingers into Loren's back and whispered, "Let it go, Loren."

Ramsey looked amused, as if enjoying Loren's temper.

Sky gave Loren a little push and laughed in Ramsey's direction. "Thanks for the offer, but she's got excellent hands already."

His grin widened. "You let me know if that changes."

"I'll do that." Sky nipped at Loren's lower lip and ran her fingertips down Loren's tight abs. "Come on, baby. We've got us a party to get to."

CHAPTER TWENTY-FOUR

The strip in Reno was visible from miles away, a glowing oasis blotting out the stars under a mushroom cloud of dusty orange light. The Renegades, fifty strong, roared into town with Ramsey in the lead, Tricia in the bitch seat behind him, and the ranking members following behind in order of hierarchy. Loren rode third in line behind Quincy and Armeo. People on the street stopped to stare.

Sky kept her cheek pressed to the back of Loren's shoulder to cut down on the windburn, riding with both arms around Loren's waist. They'd been on the road most of the night before and all afternoon to reach Reno by nightfall. At this moment, the only thing she wanted was to get off the bike and get warm. Despite the black leather chaps Loren had given her, the denim jeans beneath, and her heavy sweater and leather jacket, she was frozen. Her fingertips and toes were numb. The front of her body, though, was warm, and she imagined that was Loren's heat penetrating the layers between them. Fanciful, perhaps, but her body was convinced of the whimsy. Enough blood still flowed that her clit swelled and pulsed. Involuntarily, she tightened her hold around Loren's waist, and when Loren's gloved hand settled over hers, the pulsations turned to pounding. The casual touch might've been fingertips dancing along her naked flesh. Pleasure seared through her and she moaned softly into the wind.

"Hold on just another minute or two," Loren shouted above the roar of the engine throbbing between Sky's legs.

"I'm all right," Sky shouted back. Oddly, inconceivably, despite the danger ahead and the insanity of the two-day ride, she'd never felt more all right in her life. When they'd stopped the night before at a roadside motor court and she and Loren had staggered into their room, legs wooden from the cold and hours on the bike, she'd never felt more comfortable in her life. Because she'd been with Loren. They'd fallen onto the bed fully clothed, and sometime in the night when they'd shed their leathers, she had curled up in Loren's arms, and that's where she woke midmorning, her head on Loren's shoulder and Loren's arm around her waist. Loren's eyes were open, watching her with lazy privilege, and the heat had flared again.

"We better get something to eat," Loren finally said, her eyes still on Sky's. "We'll hit the road as soon as everyone is up."

"Why don't I go see what I can find for breakfast? You worked hard last night getting us here."

Loren's arm was loosely clasped around her waist and she stroked the curve of Sky's back slowly. Sky held very still, wanting the touch, wanting more.

"I'll shower while you're gone," Loren finally said. "Coffee. Bacon and egg sandwich would be great."

Sky smiled softly. Such a simple thing—bringing breakfast, but the idea gave her pleasure. The intimacy was more poignant than a kiss. All the same, she kissed Loren quickly and smiled again with satisfaction when Loren's eyes widened in surprise. "Don't take too long. I'm next." She slipped away. "And don't use all the hot water."

They'd barely had time to eat before the sound of engines revving in the courtyard signaled they were ready to go.

"We'd better get out there," Loren said. "Ramsey will be kicking in the door if we're not."

"I guess the concept of privacy doesn't extend to him."

Loren grimaced. "Nothing extends to him. He has absolute power—as long as he can hold on to it by force."

"And if he can't?"

"It's a wolf pack—the strongest rules."

"Even a woman?"

Loren smiled. "Never been done except in a women-only club, and there are some, but I don't see why not."

"You have aspirations?" Sky asked, half-serious. Loren had the physical and mental strength to dominate.

Loren shook her head. "Too visible." She grabbed her leather jacket. "And I don't like politics." She slung an arm around Sky's shoulder. "Come on, woman. Let's ride."

Sky had climbed on behind Loren feeling like the luckiest woman in the club. Three hundred miles later, all she could think about was getting off the bike and into a private room away from prying eyes, taking a hot shower, and finding a change of clothes. Maybe a nap. They'd be expected to party all night, and she'd need to be alert to protect her cover—and Loren's.

The line of bikes streamed around the corner off the strip and began to fill up a side street next to the Last Chance Casino. Eventually, bikes lined both sides of the small street and everyone climbed off. Loren grabbed her and pulled her close. "Doing all right?"

"I might survive if you can find me a couple of fingers of scotch and a two-inch steak."

Loren laughed. "That I can handle."

"What happens now?"

"We wait for Ramsey to sort out the room situation. Supposedly we all have reservations made by national. Doesn't always work out that way, though. You want to go to the bar first?"

"I want to go anywhere that isn't outside in the cold."

"Come on. I'll find Ramsey later."

Inside, the usual cacophony of dinging slots and loud voices filled the casino floor. The New Year's Eve crowds hadn't yet arrived, and they were able to find standing room at the bar. The scotch burned with a delicious bite, warming Sky all the way down. She sighed. "That is so much better."

Loren swallowed a quarter of a mug of beer. "About tonight—stick close to me and keep a low profile. I don't want people remembering your face—or wondering who you are."

"Don't worry. There's going to be so much going on, no one's going to be paying attention to us. We'll pretend to be having a wonderful time, and maybe if we're lucky, we can sneak away before dawn."

"I might get pulled away—a lot of chapter business gets done here behind the scenes. With this big deal coming up, you never know."

"I'll be fine. Don't worry."

Loren's eyes darkened. "Sorry. But I do."

The intensity of her words struck Sky like a fist. Dan was always worrying, fretting about her whenever she went into the field. His concern had never really registered with her, but Loren's did. That Loren cared what happened to her made her feel special in a way she never had and never thought she needed. Sky hooked her fingertips inside the wide strap of Loren's black leather chaps and tugged her forward by the heavy silver buckle. Loren's hard thighs collided with hers. "You know what?"

"What?" Loren's voice was husky, her black eyes blazing.

"I won't do anything crazy if you don't."

Loren smiled, a crooked smile that made her look impossibly handsome. "You ask a lot."

"I know."

Loren cupped Sky's jaw with the palm of her hand. "I liked you behind me on the bike today."

"I liked being there." Sky brushed her fingers over Loren's lower lip. "But I better warn you—don't get used to it."

"Oh yeah?"

"I don't plan on riding in the bitch seat forever. I expect my own bike if I'm going to be your old lady."

Loren's smile widened. "Optimistic."

"Always."

Ramsey was suddenly beside them, his hand clamped hard on Loren's shoulder. "There you are." He dangled a keycard in front of Loren. "Thought you might want this. Room 2010."

Without taking her eyes off Sky, Loren plucked the card from his hand. "Perfect timing again."

Ramsey smiled down at Sky. "See you later?"

Sky shot him a smile. "Wouldn't miss it for the world."

"Then I guess you'd better take care of business so you don't miss anything."

Loren took Sky's hand. "Exactly what I was thinking." Without glancing at Ramsey, she led Sky away.

"You're going to piss him off," Sky murmured, gripping the back of Loren's chaps.

"I don't care. He needs to get the message."

"What message is that?"

Loren stabbed the elevator button and slid her hand onto Sky's ass. "That you belong to me."

"Optimistic," Sky murmured.

"Nah." Loren yanked her into the elevator, pinned her to the wall, and kissed her. "Just sure."

❖

"Oh God." Blair leaned back on the sofa in Diane's living room and propped her feet on the coffee table. "I can't eat or drink another thing."

Laughing, Cam settled beside her and slid an arm around Blair's shoulders. "I think there's cake."

"No," Blair moaned.

Diane emerged from the kitchen with a tray bearing a chocolate layer cake with a single candle burning in the center. She placed it ceremoniously on the coffee table. "Happy birthday, Blair."

Valerie followed with a bottle of champagne and four flutes. She set them down and began to fill them. "It's not quite New Year's, but since it's your birthday now, we should start the celebration."

"This has been great." Blair threaded her fingers through Cam's. "The best birthday ever."

"We haven't even given you your presents yet," Diane protested.

"Believe me, you guys are the only presents I need."

Cam kissed her temple. "Happy birthday, baby."

Blair kissed her. "Thank you. I love you."

"I love you too."

Somehow, Blair managed to make it through the cake and her champagne, and before she knew it the countdown to the new year had begun on TV as the illuminated ball descended above Times Square.

"You sure you don't want to head down there?" Diane said.

"God, no." Blair pointed to the television. "I can do without the crowd and the cold. I'm happy right here." She was more than happy. Cam was with her and she was celebrating with friends. At the stroke of midnight, she kissed Cam. "Happy New Year, darling."

Shortly thereafter they said their good-byes and caught a cab home.

"Tonight was the perfect birthday," Blair said, shedding her clothes and climbing into bed. "Thank you for being here."

"I can't think of anywhere or any place I'd rather be right now than right here with you." Cam undressed quickly and joined her.

"Me neither. This is perfect." Blair slid on top of her and kissed her. "And I have you for two more whole days."

Cam kissed her. "You have me for a lot longer than that."

Blair rested her forehead on Cam's. "Like I said, perfect."

❖

Sky got her wish—a hot shower, a surprisingly good room-service steak, a quick nap, and clean clothes. Loren went out while Sky slept to check on her bike and collect the rest of their gear. Warm, full, and refreshed, Sky pulled on low-riding jeans and a stretchy scooped-neck tank that left a few inches of belly bare and a lot of breast showing. From the way Loren's eyes flared when she walked out of the bathroom, she figured the outfit would work. Loren was heart-stopping as usual in boot-cut jeans, heavy boots, and a black leather vest over nothing but skin and ink. Sky's throat was suddenly as dry as the desert. "You sure we have to go so soon?"

Loren grinned. "You want Ramsey in here?"

"I'll pass." Sky took Loren's hand. "Are you armed?"

"Just a blade. We get caught carrying here, the casino can lose its gaming license, and we lose our welcome."

"Be careful tonight," Sky murmured.

"You too."

They found the Renegades congregated six deep at the casino bar. Chapter after chapter poured in all evening, and bikers in leather and denim overflowed the bar onto the casino floor. Eventually, the noise and increasing advances from bikers toward any woman, attached or unattached, drove the ordinary citizens out into the night in search of less intimidating surroundings.

At midnight, a roar filled the casino. Loren grabbed Sky, slid a hand into her hair, and covered her mouth with a hard kiss. She'd been fending off men all night who'd wanted to get over on Sky before she could set them straight as to just whose old lady Sky was. Her patience was gone and her hold on her temper thinner than air. The ear-shattering din in the room was nothing compared to the thunder in her head when Sky's warm lips melted against hers. She hadn't been hungry earlier, but she was starving now.

"We need to get out of here," Loren gasped.

"It's still early," Sky whispered, running her hands up and down Loren's back. "And Ramsey has been watching us."

"Fuck Ramsey." Loren couldn't catch her breath. "I want you alone."

"Loren." Sky stroked her cheek. "Baby, we need—"

A heavy hand appeared out of nowhere, closed over Sky's upper arm, and pulled her away. A beery voice demanded, "Come on, sweet stuff. Give me a little of that."

The filament holding Loren's last sliver of control snapped. She caught the biker's arm, spun him to face her, and punched him in the face. Her knuckles screamed at the impact, but a flood of satisfaction filled her chest. The gratification ended just as quickly when the burly, bearded stranger rocked on his feet for a second, then shot out a fist the size of a cinder block and knocked her back into the bar. Someone grabbed her from behind, another fist connected with her abdomen, and she doubled over as all the air left her body. Her knees wobbled, and a blow to the back of the head put her down. She tried once to get up, but a boot to the side and a wave of nausea pulled her into the black.

CHAPTER TWENTY-FIVE

Russo checked his phone messages and saw a recent call from Derrick with an odd sense of relief. Business was infinitely preferable to watching any more of the New Year's Day parade with his wife, teenage daughter, and mother-in-law. If he'd had any plausible excuse for absenting himself from their Palm Springs retreat, he certainly would have, but his focusing on family for the holidays looked good to the electorate. Perhaps Derrick's call would provide him a reason to leave early.

At his wife's questioning look, he assumed an apologetic expression. "Sorry, my dear. Business. I won't be long."

She smiled absently before turning her attention back to the television. "Of course."

As he walked outside to the patio and closed the slider behind him, the thought crossed his mind that she was probably just as glad for the interruption as he was. When they were forced to spend more than a few hours together, their lack of common interests rapidly became painfully clear. He had no real idea how she occupied her time and didn't care. She took no interest in his political aspirations but faithfully fulfilled her obligations as the wife of a political figure as she had been raised to do. Their relationship functioned best when they each kept to their own separate spheres, in and out of the bedroom. Nora was expected back in Idaho after a short holiday with friends. A few days alone with her would be far preferable to enduring any more family time. While his wife accepted his attentions, she never relished them. And Nora—Nora threatened to burn him to cinders with her demand. Smiling at the image of Nora astride him, eyes wild and mouth open in a silent scream, Russo paused to adjust the sudden fullness in his trousers and called his assistant.

"Derrick," he said when the call was answered, "I got your message."

"Yes, sir," Derrick said. "I'm sorry to interrupt your holiday—"

"No matter. What is it?"

"Hooker wants to speak with you. I tried to put him off, but he says there's a problem. It sounded urgent."

"When isn't it?" Russo trusted Derrick nearly as much as he trusted Nora. He'd plucked him out of the state campaign office a number of years before when he'd been looking for loyal staffers to run his presidential campaign. Derrick was smart, aggressive, and loyal. He was the type of man who made a perfect number two—not likely to attempt to replace Russo, but quite willing to orchestrate the demise of anyone who threatened Russo's power. With Derrick handling the campaign machine and Nora orchestrating the public platform, Russo was well protected from any unfortunate outcomes. "I'll speak with him if you think it's prudent."

"I do."

"I'm going to take a drive and pick up another phone. If I need you, I'll call."

"Of course, sir. Anytime."

"I hope you've had a pleasant few days' vacation."

"Very nice. But truthfully, sir, I'm ready to go back to work." Derrick's tone was eager and completely genuine. "We've got a big year ahead of us."

Russo laughed. "We've got a big *eight* years ahead of us."

"Absolutely, sir."

Russo ended the call and walked inside to collect his car keys. He told the housekeeper to inform his wife he would be gone for an hour or so.

"Of course," answered the diffident middle-aged woman whose name he couldn't recall. "Should I hold lunch, sir?"

"I'll be back before then."

She nodded, never looking at him directly. "Very good, sir."

He didn't bother to tell his wife he was leaving. At a nearby shopping complex, he bought a disposable phone along with a bottle of iced tea at a Rite Aid. Back in his car, he called Hooker. "What couldn't wait?"

"Our friends in the mountains called me again," Hooker said.

"You need to remind them we're in charge here," Russo said. "I already told you I would arrange for the funds to be available early."

"This isn't about the funds. This is more serious than money."

Russo laughed. "I don't believe there is anything more serious."

"Try Homeland Security."

A cold wave churned through Russo's guts. "What are you talking about?"

"Our friends have friends in the local sheriff's department. They got wind of a meeting between someone in Homeland Security and an informant. Homeland is looking at the militia."

"That can't be unusual," Russo said, relaxing a little bit. "One agency or another is always looking at militias. It gives them an excuse to take a bigger piece of the budget than they deserve."

"The timing is suspicious, considering the situation in DC."

"It's very likely to be a coincidence," Russo said, aware that he was trying to convince himself as much as Hooker. "Do we know who the interested party is?"

"Not yet, but I've told our friends we need further details—who, when, and where."

"And you trust the source?"

"An ATF agent in Los Angeles called the sheriff's department requesting covert backup for a meet between an undercover agent and the Homeland agent. One of the sheriff's deputies is a member of the militia."

"And what about the undercover agent—are we exposed?"

"I don't think so, but I'm worried about the gun deal. We can't be sure what they know."

Russo paused, considered his options. His popularity was growing, and the gap between his polls and Powell's was narrowing. He'd wanted to cripple Powell's campaign by creating national doubt as to Powell's ability to keep the nation safe. Even without an assault, his odds of victory were improving, and he still had time to put together another plan. He didn't like giving up his long-range plans, but any connection to the militia and illegal activity would effectively destroy his chances of winning the White House. "How much time do we have before the exchange?"

"Not that long. Inside a week, probably. They'll want the money soon."

"Can we stall—perhaps suggest the exchange is too dangerous if there's a possible infiltrator?"

"If we pull out, there's going to be trouble."

"I'm sure you can handle it. After all, that's what I'm paying you for."

"We aren't the only people that can help supply this group with guns, and they're crazy."

"If we can't handle a rabscrabble pack of amateur soldiers, we can hardly expect to rule the country."

"I'll be in touch as soon as I know more."

"I want the name of exactly who is snooping around, and where they're getting their information."

"That's my top priority."

"I'll expect an update within twenty-four hours."

Hooker disconnected without bothering to reply.

Russo drummed his fingers on the steering wheel. Homeland Security. Even the suggestion of his involvement with the militia could taint his campaign. But if he showed himself to be capable of enforcing law and order on the home front, he might be able to counteract some of the criticism aimed at his support of the NRA. After all, a leader who took on the radical fringe would appeal to the liberals. Perhaps he could turn this investigation to his advantage, even if it meant sacrificing some useful connections.

❖

"I can walk," Loren muttered, pushing feebly at Quincy's arm.

"Sure you can," Quincy snorted, "on water too, I'll bet."

Sky checked over her shoulder to be sure they weren't going to do anything stupid like let Loren try walking on her own, and then hurried to unlock the hotel room door. "Put her on the bed."

Quincy and one of the prospects half carried, half walked Loren to the bed and none too gently deposited her on her back in the middle of the single king.

"Next time, wait till you got backup before you take on a bunch of Lobos," Quincy said good-naturedly. "Don't know who was watching the door, but Ramsey is probably chewing them a new one right about now for letting a rival club crash our party."

"Thanks," Sky said as Quincy and the prospect walked to the door.

"Keep her in here tonight," Quincy said.

"I plan to." Sky closed the door and turned all the lights off except for a small lamp on the desk. She searched in the TV cabinet for an ice bucket. "Don't move. I'll be right back."

"Where you going?"

"Ice." Sky studied Loren's eyes. Both pupils were equal and reactive although slightly unfocused. Her cheek was swollen, the corner of her mouth bleeding. Sky ran her fingers lightly along the edge of Loren's jaw, looking for any evidence a fist or foot had fractured it. She concentrated on what needed to be done and not the terror that had gripped her when Loren had gone down and she'd lost sight of her beneath a melee of flying fists and legs.

Loren gripped Sky's wrist. "You okay?"

Sky laughed wryly. "I wasn't the one getting hammered on back there."

"I should have stayed with you. Shouldn't have left you alone."

"You should've let me handle that asshole," Sky said sharply even as she gently brushed hair away from Loren's eyes. "Or, like Quincy said, waited until a few more of the Renegades were around before picking a fight with some gatecrashers."

"Tired of everyone pawing at you."

"No one was pawing. I don't allow pawing." Sky leaned down and kissed Loren's forehead. "Unless you're doing it."

"Don't be mad."

"I'm not mad. I'm worried. Just lie still. I'll be back in a minute. If we don't get ice on your face, you won't be able to open your jaw in the morning."

"Looks worse than it is."

"I sincerely hope so, because it looks bad." Sky laughed before she vented her anxiety and fear on Loren. Maybe Loren had been playing a part when she'd gone after the asshole who'd probably left finger marks on her arm, and maybe Loren really had reacted on instinct. Either way, Loren couldn't help being who she was, and browbeating her while she was hurt wasn't fair. "Stay put."

Sky filled the bucket with ice from a machine in an alcove down the hall and hurried back, afraid to leave Loren alone too long. Sure enough, Loren had managed to get to a sitting position and was trying to get her boots off.

"What part of lie down don't you understand?" Sky slammed the bucket down on the TV cabinet hard enough to spew ice cubes onto the floor. She stepped over the ice and grabbed Loren's right boot. "Lie back, I'll get these off."

"Don't like being helpless."

"No, I don't imagine you do." Carefully, Sky eased Loren's boots off and sat beside her on the bed. "I'm going to take off your vest and jeans. I'll go slowly, but I think it's going to hurt."

Loren tried for a grin, the swelling in her lower lip blunting her devastating smile but not completely obliterating the appeal. Even bruised and battered, she was the most exciting woman Sky had ever seen. "You have to stop trying to protect me."

"It's my job. You're my old lady."

"Don't try to manage me." Sky carefully unbuttoned Loren's vest and opened it. Loren was naked underneath and just as beautiful as Sky remembered. A multicolored dragon wended its way up her left side and ended along the curve of her breast. Sky had seen the tattoo from a distance, but now the backs of her fingers traced the graceful arch of the ancient warrior demon. "This is beautiful."

"Thanks." Loren raised a hand, caressed Sky's cheek. "You're beautiful."

"I'm going to pull this out from behind you. Don't try to sit up. I can get it." Sky concentrated on getting Loren's vest off and not on how striking her body was or how electrifying her touch. After dispensing with that, she unbuckled Loren's wide leather belt and opened her fly. Grasping the waistband of Loren's jeans, she tugged the pants down over her hips. She'd been prepared to find nothing beneath, but the impact of Loren's naked body was still a blow. Loren was beautiful, and if she hadn't been hurt, Sky wouldn't have resisted the urge to touch her. But a bruise as big as both her hands spread over Loren's right hip onto her lower abdomen, tempering her desire. Sky lightly stroked the purpling skin. "This looks bad."

"Doesn't feel too bad."

"You may have a bruised kidney."

"Don't think so. Had one before. Flipped the Jeep after an IED went off just in front of me. Peed blood for a week."

Sky's stomach tightened further. Loren was a soldier, then and now. She knew that, but thinking of Loren hurt, seeing her hurt, tore at her. She rested her fingers lightly on the center of Loren's abdomen. "I'm going to find you some Tylenol, and then you should try to get some sleep."

Loren shook her head. "A shot of Jim Beam will do just as well, and you can get that right in the minibar. I'm sorry."

Sky narrowed her eyes. "Sorry about what, exactly?"

Loren grinned as much as she was able. "Sorry I didn't get in a follow-up shot before that bastard clocked me."

"That's what I thought." Sky braced her arm on the opposite side of Loren's chest to keep her weight off Loren's body and leaned down until their faces were very close. "We're here to do a job. You need to be well enough to go on that gun run. You need to stop with the macho routine. If it hadn't been this guy, it would've been Ramsey. You've been challenging everyone with a dick for days."

Loren's eyes flared. "Maybe because everyone with a dick has been trying to get over on you."

"You have to expect that."

"And you have to expect me to stop them."

"I'm not interested. They know it. You ought to know it."

"Can't help it. Makes me crazy."

"You make me crazy too." Sky skimmed her mouth over Loren's. "I don't want you to be hurt. So stop."

"I thought of something I need besides the Jim Beam."

"What?"

"You. Lie down with me."

Sky laughed softly. "Loren, baby. I don't know if you've noticed, but I don't think you're capable of moving anything, so whatever you're thinking—"

"I'm thinking I want my mouth and my hands all over you."

Sky flamed inside, and for a second, she couldn't think. She took a breath and reason came flaring back along with her temper. "You're crazy. You're in no shape to be propositioning me, and even if you were, this is the wrong time and the wrong place and the wrong—"

"It's not wrong and you know it." Loren coughed slightly and winced. "Okay, possibly the wrong time. So that's why I'm only suggesting you lie down with me. The rest of it we can wait on a little bit."

"Oh, can we?"

Loren hooked a finger in the neck of Sky's tank and tugged until Sky was forced to lean down. Loren's mouth skated over hers, surprisingly sweet and incredibly soft.

"I'm done waiting," Loren whispered. "Soon as I can move more than this finger, I'm taking you."

"Maybe I'll have something to say about that."

"Say it now, Sky," Loren murmured. "What do you say?"

Sky stretched out on the bed as slowly and carefully as she could. She rested her arm across Loren's hips below the bruised area. She ought to know how to handle this, but she had to admit she didn't. She couldn't handle Loren any more than she could handle what she felt. All she was left with was the truth. "Yes."

CHAPTER TWENTY-SIX

Loren opened her eyes at midday on New Year's with Sky still asleep beside her. She lay still, breathing slowly, wanting to savor the weight of Sky's hand resting on her chest. The possessive spread of Sky's fingers on her skin sent sweet tendrils of pleasure coiling inside her, precious tethers she feared to break. A few details of the last part of the previous night were a bit fuzzy, but she remembered enough to work out that, all things considered, she was feeling better than she deserved. When she took a deep breath, a muscle twinged in her rib cage, but that was nothing she hadn't lived through before. Pushing up to a sitting position took a bit of effort, and her lower right side burned. Torn muscles, probably an inflamed nerve or two. But she was moving all fours, her head was clear, and she was hungry. All positive signs. She'd live. And a little pain was a small price to pay for putting that asshole in his place. She didn't regret punching his face in for a second.

All she'd been able to see had been his grasping fingers digging into Sky's arm as if she were a piece of meat to be passed around to whoever wanted a bite. Men had been looking at Sky with greedy eyes since they'd walked into the casino. At least back in Silver Lake, the Renegades accepted Sky was with Loren and had kept their distance, but here, just about any woman who wasn't glued to the side of a biker was fair game. And, of course, most of the men from other chapters thought Loren didn't have the right to claim a woman, being one herself. She should've known better than to let their attitude get to her. She should've been used to it, been cooler, kept a low profile. But where Sky was concerned, all bets were off. Sky elicited something primal from her deepest recesses, roused some instinctual possessiveness from a place where reason had no rule. Sky could take care of herself, she knew that, but she couldn't stop the soul-deep need to protect her, to claim her.

Loren brushed her fingers lightly over the crimson strands that clung to Sky's cheek and admitted she had a problem. She'd told herself she didn't need to be known for so long, didn't need to be touched by anyone who truly saw her, that she'd come to believe it. She'd believed her mission, her objective, her *duty*, was enough to satisfy. She'd never lied to herself and wasn't starting now. Sky had changed all that. Others only saw what she allowed them to see—the soldier, the biker, the outlaw. Sky had insisted on seeing past the façade, being on the inside, touching Loren with no pretense between them. And without truly believing she was capable of it, Loren had fallen in love.

Loren eased from the bed and made her way into the bathroom. A hot shower would help smooth out the cramps in her muscles and give her time to figure out what to do about this new revelation. Falling in love wasn't in the cards. Not part of her game plan, and certainly not now. Sky would leave, needed to leave, and the sooner the better. In fact, Loren had to do everything she could to get Sky to leave. Now more than ever. For the first time in her life, something mattered more than the mission.

Loren tilted her head back and let the hot water beat against the bruises on her face, ignoring the pain, welcoming the sharp clarity. The night before, she'd been ready to take Sky—had been consumed with the need to claim her. She hadn't been thinking, she'd only been driven by urges so deeply ingrained she couldn't have contained them had she wanted to. Now she was thinking. And she was done being selfish. Every day Sky remained exposed, the danger grew.

When the shower door opened and Sky stepped inside, Loren knew she had only seconds of restraint remaining before her body took control. She turned her back, braced her arms against the wall, let her head drop forward. Water cascaded around her like a screen, and she tried to pretend she welcomed the barrier. "I'll get out of here in a second and give you a little more room."

"I didn't get in here so you could leave." Sky pressed against Loren's back, her firm wet breasts a teasing torment. Her hands came around Loren's waist as she stroked Loren's abdomen in slow circles. "How are you feeling?"

Loren opened her eyes and watched Sky's hands move up and

down her torso through the veil of water. Her thighs clenched and her nipples tightened. Usually when she was in bed with a woman, her goal was to pleasure, gaining her satisfaction from that of her bedmate. Not so with Sky. Never had she ached for a woman's touch the way she craved Sky's. She shuddered. "You make me feel so good. I love your hands on me."

"I love touching you." Sky kissed the back of Loren's shoulder and pressed tight against her ass. "And I don't plan on stopping—but you still need to answer the question, McElroy. How do you feel?"

Loren turned and her breasts glided over Sky's. She moaned, her thighs trembling, and sagged against the shower wall. "Like I never want you to stop touching me."

"Oh yeah. You are so gorgeous." Sky's eyes widened and she caressed Loren's face. "You make me so crazy hot just looking at you. I want to touch you so bad—wanted to since the first second I saw you."

A flash of heat rolled through Loren's pelvis. "I've never felt better in my life. And I've wanted you since the first second I saw you sitting at the bar like you owned the place."

Sky braced her hands on the shower wall and carefully let her body rest gently against Loren's. She had to feel her, had to be connected more than she'd ever needed anything. "Not too sore?"

"For what?"

Sky smiled and caressed the dragon that curled around Loren's torso and invited her with every one of Loren's quickening breaths. "For what I have in mind."

Loren's lids lowered and she arched under Sky's hands. "I guess you have to show me and we'll find out."

Sky sucked in a breath, cupped Loren's jaw. She kissed her, tasting crystal water and liquid heat, sliding her mouth over Loren's, drinking her passion and reveling in the power to pleasure she'd hungered for all her life. She wanted Loren weak with satisfaction under her. "I want to make you come. I won't be able to stop."

Loren gripped her shoulders, pressed her down. "Then don't. Please, don't."

Sky dropped to her knees and rested her cheek against Loren's belly, gathering her fractured control. She didn't want to rush, feared she wouldn't be able to contain her need. She kissed Loren's navel and muscles tightened beneath her cheek. A tremulous shudder coursed through Loren's body and she moaned. Piercing desire eclipsed Sky's reason, suffusing her with blinding need. Her hands, her mouth moved by primitive direction, seeking and giving, reveling in the incredible touch and taste of Loren's body. She pressed her palms to the inside of Loren's thighs, opening her, easing her shoulders between Loren's legs, supporting her as she made way for what she wanted. Loren was hot and wet and swollen and ready for her. When she took her into her mouth, Loren bucked against her face. Sky grasped her ass in both hands, held her steady, and took her slowly. Time halted, every sensation coalesced into pure pleasure. She tasted and teased and stroked and sucked until Loren groaned and fisted a hand in her hair.

"Going to come, Sky."

Sky closed her eyes and waited for the moment she'd wanted since the first moment she'd seen Loren. When Loren came in her mouth, she knew a completion sweeter than she had ever dreamed.

❖

Cam lay on the sofa in the loft with her head in Blair's lap, enjoying Blair's look of relaxed pleasure. They'd spent the morning perusing the newspapers, discussing the latest movies and books and current events. Neither of them had mentioned Cam's imminent trip to the West Coast.

Blair set the book review section aside and ran her fingers through Cam's hair. "You're staring."

"Mmm. Awesome view." Cam rubbed her cheek against Blair's middle. "You look great."

Blair laughed. "Despite my advancing years?"

"Feeling your age?" Cam frowned. "Maybe I shouldn't have kept you up so late last night."

"Please." Blair snorted. "Who fell asleep first?"

Cam grinned. "I was going easy on you. Thought I'd give you a break."

Blair leaned down, kissed her. "Is that what you call it."

"I like you happy."

"I am. Really." Blair sighed, coiled a lock of Cam's hair around a finger. "But I keep expecting a call from Lucinda at any moment with an update on my father's itinerary and instructions as to when I should report for duty."

Cam smiled wryly. "You're probably right. It is the new year, after all, and the campaign year is upon us."

"I really should call her. Wish her a happy new year. I should call him—since I only talked to him a second last night." Blair shook her head. "I'm such a coward. I know if I do, I'll get her too."

Cam raised a brow. "You think?"

Blair laughed. "Don't you?"

"I try not to think about other people's personal lives, especially not the president of the United States."

"Even when he's your father-in-law?"

"Especially then." Cam reached over for the last of her coffee and took a sip. "It can't be easy for either of them, if what you think is true."

"Not when the public believes it has a right to know everything about you." Blair grimaced. "I understand it. I understand the imperative of elected officials being accountable, but the boundaries between what should be private and what is rightfully public knowledge don't seem to apply to him. Or anyone close to him."

"You don't have to campaign with him," Cam said. "I don't care if you drop out of sight and neither will he. No one knows me, except in relationship to you. We could disappear."

"Are you complaining about being a celebrity spouse?"

"Not at all," Cam said seriously. "But if you want to get out, we can move, find someplace where you can paint and keep a low profile."

"Believe me, I've thought of it more than once. But I'm proud of my father and I think what he's doing is important. If he believes I can help him, then I'm going to." Blair leaned over, kissed Cam hard. "And despite my occasional complaining, I'm proud of you too. What you do is important, and you're not replaceable. I'm sticking."

Cam sat up and slid an arm around Blair's shoulders, tugging her close. "Thanks. Just remember, no matter what you decide now, in the future, if you need to back off, make space for yourself, we'll find a way."

Blair rested her cheek against Cam's shoulder. "I know you mean that, and that's all I need. To know that you'll be there no matter what." She kissed the side of Cam's neck. "You will, won't you?"

Cam kissed her. "Always."

Blair played with the button on Cam's shirt. "When are you leaving?"

"First thing in the morning."

"Then let's not talk about politics or duty or anything else for the rest of the day."

"All right. What would you like to do?"

Blair grinned.

"*Besides* that."

Chapter Twenty-seven

"ith luck, we can get out of here later tonight," Loren said. "If we W hit the road by midnight, we can be home tomorrow night."

Sky focused on her in the misty mirror above the vanity in the small bathroom. The air still undulated with heat, and her skin steamed, inside and out. The surface of her brain burned, her thoughts scattered embers of sensation and desire. She couldn't seem to concentrate on anything other than the way Loren had felt against her mouth, under her hands, so pliant and open and incredibly hers. She watched as Loren pulled a towel off a shelf, rubbed her hair, and tossed the towel aside. Muscles rippled in Loren's shoulders, her dark hair feathered in sensuous strands along the taut column of her throat. Swallowing the sudden lump of desire that threatened to choke her, Sky said, "What?"

Loren's gaze grew heavy and she stepped closer, reaching around Sky's body to loosen the towel she'd knotted above her breasts. Pressing against Sky's back, her arms wending around Sky's waist, Loren whispered against Sky's neck, "We can beat the crowd home. I want you alone for a while."

Sky reached back and threaded her fingers into Loren's hair. She couldn't get enough of her. She wanted to be touching her everywhere. She wanted Loren touching *her* everywhere. "Ramsey won't care?"

"By tonight, he'll be too into the party to care who goes where." Loren breathed in the scent of vanilla shampoo and the lotion Sky had just rubbed on her arms, the kind they always stocked in hotels, but on Sky the aroma was as erotic as expensive perfume. Moisture beaded between their bodies, and when she cupped Sky's breasts, the nipples hardened in her palms. "Then again, we're alone right now."

"Loren," Sky whispered, a desperate sound that might have meant *stop* or *more*.

"Right here." Loren edged back, turned Sky with her hands on her hips, and kissed her. Sky arched into her and Loren filled her hands with smooth, hot flesh. Sky's fingers dove into her hair again, tightening, tugging, telegraphing urgency and desire. Loren kissed down Sky's throat, lifted her breast into her hand, and slipped Sky's nipple into her mouth.

"Oh God," Sky groaned.

Sky's head fell back and her thighs parted. Loren pressed a leg between Sky's, a welcoming heat flooding over her skin. "Right now."

"So good," Sky breathed, her eyes barely open, hazy and heavy-lidded.

Loren held her breasts in both hands and kissed between them, licking and sucking, edging her teeth over oh-so-sensitive flesh until Sky cried out.

When Sky slid a hand behind Loren's neck and pressed Loren's face harder to her breast, Loren slipped a hand between them, found Sky open and wet, and filled her.

"Yes," Sky hissed between clenched teeth, pressing down against Loren's hand, drawing her deeper. "Yes. Right now."

Loren surged within her, desperate to hear her sobs of pleasure, wild with the tight, slick invitation to take, to own. Her mind blanked, her heart beat furiously, she gave herself to the blinding need to claim. "I want you. I want you."

"Oh God," Sky cried, surprise and pleasure ringing in her voice. "You're making me come."

Loren drove her through her orgasm, and while Sky still pulsed and thrust against her hand, she dropped to her knees and took her into her mouth. Sky's startled gasp brought the blood pounding furiously in Loren's head, and she took her with her mouth and her hands, over and over in one long swell of desire, until Sky pushed weakly at her face. "Stop, please, no more, I can't."

Loren closed her eyes and rested her cheek against Sky's thigh, drinking in Sky's soft sobs of satisfaction. Finally, she rose on trembling legs, pulled her close, and kissed her. "You're amazing."

Sky dropped her head against Loren's shoulder and clung to her, more than a little afraid. She'd never given herself so completely, never wanted to be taken so thoroughly. She felt marked, branded, a sensation both terrifying and exhilarating. Loren's heart pounded furiously against her chest, as if she had run miles to reach her. Sky kissed Loren's neck, tasted salt and steam. "You're the one who's amazing. I'm not even sure what you did to me."

Loren rubbed her face against Sky's hair. "You're so sexy, you kill me."

Sky laughed, her voice shaking. "My intention is to keep you very healthy so you can do that again."

"When?"

"I might need a little nourishment first." Sky stroked Loren's back. "And I might have a few other things I want." Her hand dropped to Loren's ass, squeezed. "Like this."

Loren laughed softly and pressed her pelvis into Sky's thigh. "Works for me."

"Let's go put in an appearance so we can get out of here. But, Loren?"

"Hmm?" Loren stroked Sky's breast, thinking about tasting her again.

"You're pretty banged up. You might need to take the bitch seat."

Loren laughed. "You keep dreaming."

Sky kissed her, the expression in her eyes suddenly serious. "Maybe I am."

Loren wanted to tell her not to worry, wanted to keep her safe, and knew she could do neither. But she could give her the truth. "This is no dream. This is real."

❖

Sky's phone vibrated in the front pocket of her jeans, and she searched the casino for Loren. She found her at the far end of the bar, drinking with Ramsey, Quincy, and some biker she didn't know. The only other person who might be calling her was Dan. She said to Trish, "Gotta hit the ladies'. I'll catch you later, okay?"

"Sure, sweetie," Trish said. "Have fun."

Sky threaded her way through the crush of bikers in the direction of the restrooms but quickly ducked out a side door before she reached them. A few people congregated near the exit, a few smoking, others in various stages of working up to sex. None of them paid any attention to her. She strolled away from the cone of weak illumination thrown by the security light above the fire door and smiled at a younger woman in a short leather jacket with faux leopard fur at the throat, and pants that looked like they were made out of red latex painted onto her pencil-thin legs. She rocked back and forth on stiletto heels while she smoked furiously.

"Hey," Sky said brightly. "You got a fag I could borrow?"

"Sure," the girl said, pulling a crumpled pack from the tiny pocket of her jacket. She held it out to Sky, who extracted the filtered menthol, put it to her lips.

"Light?"

Wordlessly, the girl held out her cigarette and Sky lit hers off the glowing end. She hugged herself with one arm and took a drag. "Thanks. Too noisy in there."

"Yeah," the girl said absently, her eyes dull and vacant. Stoned or maybe drunk.

"Well, thanks," Sky said, drifting away. The girl paid her no attention. She walked on until she couldn't be overheard and returned the call. Dan answered immediately. "Not a good time."

"Where are you?"

"Out of town."

"You need to get back. Day after tomorrow, you've got an appointment."

Sky did some quick calculating. "It's gonna be tight for me to make that. Can you reschedule?"

"That would be awkward. There's some urgency."

Sky sighed. "I'll do what I can, but I've got some things going on that are more important."

"I don't get that sense. You need to be there."

"Fine." Sky dropped the cigarette and ground it out against the cracked macadam of the parking lot. "I'll call you when I know for sure. And let's keep this quiet. Too many eyes on this already."

"Yeah. Don't worry."

"No, why would I?" Sky ended the call and pushed the phone back into the pocket of her tight jeans. Dan was a decent guy to work with, but he was more of a manager than field agent. He worried a little too much about career advancement and performance reports. None of which made a damn bit of difference out here.

She found Loren still at the bar, but Ramsey was gone. She leaned into her and kissed her. "Hey, baby."

Loren wrapped an arm around her shoulders. "Hey."

Sky nuzzled Loren's ear. "We need to go."

"Then you better make this look good." Loren pulled Sky tight and kissed her.

Sky gripped the back of Loren's jeans to keep her balance and fought to keep her brain functioning. This show was for Ramsey and the others. But, God, Loren could kiss. A mind-melting few minutes later, Loren let her breathe.

"Let's go, baby," Loren said tightly, grabbing her hand and tugging her into the crowd. "I'm not done."

Sky followed, slipping with frightening ease across the border between reality and fantasy.

❖

Jane pretended to watch the football game in the small lounge on the first floor of the barracks. As soon as she'd arrived at the camp, she'd moved back into a spartan ten-by-ten room, just like the one she'd occupied during her breaks from college. Her only other option had been to find an apartment, and the expense and isolation made this a much better choice. Here, she was close to what mattered—her father, her mission, the men and women who shared her passion for justice and freedom. She was the only woman billeted in the barracks, but that was no problem. The soldiers treated her with friendly but distant regard. She'd come down to the lounge in hopes of finding something to divert her thoughts from Jenn, but nothing was working.

Her guilt made it hard to think of anything else. She was here, home, safe, and Jenn was alone somewhere. Imagining her sister's desolation kept Jane awake, plagued her through the day, even though she knew Jenn was prepared for it. They'd all been trained with the expectation that they could be imprisoned, interrogated, even physically abused. Jennifer would be able to endure, but Jane wasn't sure she could. The pain in her chest grew larger every hour.

Her phone rang and she read her father's number with a sense of relief. She needed a mission, something to fill the expanding void inside her. She hurried outside to answer in privacy. "Sir?"

"I need you over here now."

"Yes, sir. Right away, sir." She tucked her phone away and jogged across the compound, up the stairs to headquarters, and back to her father's office. She tapped on the door and entered. "Sir?"

Graves stood behind his desk, his hands on his hips, his face set. "We have a problem."

Dread snaked through Jane's insides. "Sir?"

"The Renegades may have been infiltrated."

The relief nearly made her gasp. Not Jennifer. Jenn was all right. "They're compromised?"

"Possibly." He walked to the windows that looked out over the training fields. His back stiffened, the hands he'd clasped behind his back tightened into fists. "My information is incomplete. My contact in the sheriff's department says there's a meeting being scheduled between an FBI agent who's infiltrated one of the local biker gangs and a Homeland Security agent."

"Homeland."

Graves turned, his eyes glinting with fury. "Yes. Interesting, isn't it."

"I don't like the timing."

"Neither do I."

"How exposed are we through those bikers?" Jane asked.

"We can't be sure what the agent knows, but my contact says the Homeland agent is interested in us."

"Us." Jane took a breath. "I'm sorry, sir, but I don't buy that this is a coincidence. I don't know how, but we must assume this is related to…the lieutenant."

"I agree. Especially considering who the agent is."

"Sir?"

"Cameron Roberts."

The air in the room seemed to chill, and Jane's blood drained from her head. She fought a wave of dizziness and clenched her jaw. "Roberts."

"Yes." Her father studied her intently, as if waiting for her to answer a question he hadn't asked.

Jane smiled and hope surged for the first time in weeks. "That's very good news, sir."

He grinned, a feral snarl that reminded her of a rabid wolf they'd come upon in the mountains when she'd been twelve. "I was hoping you would say that, Captain."

CHAPTER TWENTY-EIGHT

Blair walked Cam to the door and took her overcoat from the closet. She held it to her breasts as if that might keep Cam with her a moment longer. She'd wakened with a heaviness in her chest, as if the air had thickened during the night, pressing in around her with malevolent intent. Foolish, she knew. She just didn't want their private time to end, and that was natural enough. For a few days they'd been blessedly alone—even Lucinda had been quiet. But paradise was temporary. "Call me when you get there?"

"Of course." Cam took Blair's hand. "What are you going to do?"

Blair sighed. "I might as well head back to DC. I need to find out what Lucinda has planned." She laughed. "She's actually scarier when she's silent."

"Then I'll see you in a day or two." Cam kissed her. "Don't let her talk you into anything crazy."

"I'll do my best." Blair folded Cam's coat on top of her luggage. "One more thing."

Cam caressed her arm. "What?"

Blair threaded her arms around Cam's neck and leaned into her. "I don't know. Nothing. Just…I love you."

Cam kissed her. "I love you too. No matter where I am or what I'm doing, you're always there."

"For me too." Blair smiled shakily. Telling her to be careful was needless—Cam would do what she needed to do. "So. You've got a plane to catch. I'll be waiting."

Cam kissed her again. "Good. Because I count on it."

❖

Sky pocketed her cell phone and walked into the garage where Loren was offloading their gear from the bike. "The meet is set for tomorrow afternoon at a tavern called the Timberwolf Bar and Grill. Know it?"

Loren set the carriers she'd just removed from the motorcycle onto the counter. "Yes. It's a little out-of-the-way place about twenty miles from here. Why there?"

"Dan set it up. He figured it would be easy for me to get to, and I wouldn't be gone too long. Plus, in the middle of the day, the likelihood of any bikers being around is slim."

"I ought to be there," Loren said.

Sky understood. She'd feel the same way were the situations reversed, and she'd be complaining just as loudly. And Loren, no doubt, would be saying exactly what she was about to say. "No, you shouldn't be there. It's doesn't make good tactical sense."

Loren jammed her hands into the pockets of her jeans and leaned against her workbench, as if trying to keep from losing what remained of her temper. Sky picked up a rag from a bucket by the bike and started to wipe the snowmelt and salt from the chassis to give Loren a few minutes to get a grip. When she heard what sounded like a growl, she sighed and straightened. Guess not. "Look. You know the reasons why both of us being potentially exposed is unacceptable. I'm not going to repeat them. But, bottom line—I'm your handler, and ordinarily I'd be the one to meet with this Homeland agent anyhow. Just because I'm here doesn't change anything."

"Bull." Loren stalked over, took the rag from Sky's hand, and tossed it onto the counter. She gripped Sky's hips, her hold gentle despite the raging storm in her eyes. "Your being here changes everything. You're a cop, and if anyone in the Renegades, or the militia, or whoever is funding them gets the slightest whiff of that, you're dead."

"And the same is true for you." Sky shook her head, relying on procedural arguments so she didn't have to admit how much the thought of Loren disappearing one night terrified her—and that's just what would happen if Loren's cover was blown. She'd be executed and her body buried somewhere no one would ever find it, and Sky would be left empty and searching for the rest of her life. This was the safest way to ensure Loren's safety and her own sanity. "The chance of anyone getting on to me is practically zero, but even if it were to happen, your cover would be protected. I could pull out and the mission—"

"Fuck the mission," Loren said flatly. She tangled her fingers in Sky's hair and kissed her. "I don't care about the mission right now. What I care about is you."

The intensity of Loren's words, the fierceness in her eyes, left Sky breathless. She wanted to protest, wanted to argue, but how could she when all she could think was *Loren cares*. Sky forced herself to think, pushing her feelings aside. "I'm not the one who matters right now."

"The hell you don't. You matter to me," Loren said, tracing Sky's jaw. "And not because you're brilliant at what you do and tough when it counts." She kissed Sky softly. "You matter because you're stubborn and tender and brave and trusting. And because you don't let me hide. You matter to me."

Sky pressed her forehead to Loren's shoulder, feeling anything but competent and in control. No one had ever said the things Loren had said before. She'd known respect and begrudging appreciation from other agents, but she'd never experienced the joy of being special to someone. "I don't understand why."

Loren laughed softly. "Maybe that's one of the reasons." She kissed Sky again, none of the temper that had been in her eyes apparent in the soft, reverent glide of her mouth over Sky's. "You're beautiful and I trust you. With everything." Loren paused, kissed her again. "I love you, Sky."

Sky jerked, the words as piercing as a blade. "I—what?"

"I know. I didn't expect it either." Loren smiled. "But I do. I love you." She caressed Sky's cheek, traced her thumb over Sky's lower lip. "I think I could be happy with you in my arms for the rest of my life."

Sky caught her breath, stepped back. "This is...I don't know what this is."

"I don't expect you to say anything, and I know it's crazy." Fire flared in Loren's eyes again. "But no matter what is or isn't between us, it's still dangerous for you to meet with a high-profile agent like Roberts right now. Too many eyes on us. Too many people want a piece of this big gun buy coming up."

I love you, Sky. I love you... The astonishing words, the tender touches, the burning passion in Loren's eyes threatened to unravel her, and Sky panicked. By instinct she clung to what was safe, what was known—the mission, the protective cloak of the job. "I think we can trust Homeland Security."

"Really? I never took you for naïve."

Sky laughed shortly, staying far enough away that Loren couldn't touch her again. Another caress, another intimate glance from Loren, and her barriers would crumble. "All right, point taken. But in this particular instance, I can't see how they could have any interest in what we're doing. I believe Roberts is really here for information, and we certainly can trust her. If you know anything about her—"

"Who doesn't?" Loren said impatiently. "And I'm not saying we can't trust *her*. But we don't know who else might be read in on this."

"And I'll make that clear to her. I know how to protect my operatives."

Loren's jaw tightened. "Are we back to that again?"

"That's never changed." Sky wanted to tell her that she was so much more than just her operative now, had been since the first, but the timing was so wrong. Loren's life was still on the line, the entire operation was more complex than they'd ever expected, and there couldn't be a worse time for them to become involved. And they were, she knew it, but she couldn't think about it. Right now, the success of the mission was more important than ever—because if something went wrong, Loren could pay the price. Sky wasn't going to let that happen, and if it meant ignoring what she wanted, what she needed, she would. "You know I came here because this is a critical mission that I've spent months, years, overseeing. This is bigger than you and me, and we can't jeopardize it for anything, including a little personal diversion. I'm meeting with Roberts alone, and you need to concentrate on your job in all of this."

Loren stiffened. "Well, I guess that makes things clear."

"Good. Because we do need to be clear."

"Oh, we are. Crystal." Loren reached for her jacket and keys. "I'm going to the Rooster. Don't wait up."

Sky had made her choice and she had to play her part now. The sound of the motorcycle engine, an angry solitary roar, died into the distance, leaving the garage silent and nearly as barren as the emptiness that filled her chest. She gathered her clothes and few personal belongings from Loren's bedroom and carried them out to her car. Better to make the break official, especially since she'd be leaving as soon as the operation was over. Since Loren was known not to stay with anyone for long, no one would be very surprised that their short-lived relationship had burnt itself out. She climbed into the car and sat behind the wheel without turning on the ignition. She'd made the right decision for Loren and for the mission, and she didn't regret it. She just needed to hold on until the pain relented enough for her to breathe again.

❖

Arms shaking, Jane pushed the barbell up for the fifteenth time and let it drop into the cleats. Sweat ran into her eyes, and she kept them closed as she groped on the floor beside the weight bench for the towel. She looked up when someone pushed the towel into her hand. Her father stood over her.

"Sir," Jane said, quickly sitting up.

"I got a call. The federal agents are meeting tomorrow afternoon."

"You have a location?"

He smiled. "I do, and our local contact was able to suggest a meeting place that will be to our advantage. We'll brief in my office in thirty minutes."

"Yes, sir," Jane said, getting to her feet. "I'll be there, sir."

Her father turned abruptly and left the gym. Hurrying toward the shower, Jane glanced at the big clock on the far wall. Less than twenty-four hours. Less than twenty-four hours, and she would have all the ammunition she'd ever need to free her sister. Sometimes wars were won without bloodshed, and if her plan worked, she might avoid it. But nothing was going to stop her from freeing her sister.

CHAPTER TWENTY-NINE

"Flying solo tonight, Loren?" Trish said as she settled onto the adjacent bar stool.

"More or less." Loren finished the warm dregs in the bottom of her glass and held it out to Clyde, the prospect who'd been manning the bar at the Rooster since three when the regular staff had left. He dutifully jogged over, took her glass, and refilled it from the tap.

"Let me have a whiskey sour," Trish said when Clyde returned, and he hurried off to comply. She leaned her elbow on the bar and regarded Loren solemnly. "Just for the night or permanently?"

"Not quite sure."

"Too bad. I kind of liked her."

"Yeah, me too," Loren said, sticking to the truth. Always smart when undercover, but she couldn't bring herself to say anything else. She couldn't pretend she didn't care and she couldn't lie. Not about Sky. She was pissed off at her, but that didn't change anything. All she really wanted was to erase the sick feeling in her gut that surged every time she thought about Sky in danger. She knew better too. If she couldn't keep her head in the game, she was going to be a liability to Sky, and that was the very last thing she wanted.

"She's too much woman for you, though," Trish said casually and took the mixed drink from the prospect. She sipped it, a thoughtful expression on her face. She put the rock glass down on the bar and pushed it away. "That really sucks."

Clyde's face took on a sickly shade of gray. "I'm sorry, I'm really sorry. I'll make you another one."

"Yeah, and this time try putting a little whiskey in it."

"I will. I will. Just one minute." The skinny kid with a half-assed goatee grabbed the glass and bolted away.

"You keep busting their balls," Loren observed, "and Ramsey won't have anyone to ride with him before too long."

Trish laughed. "I'm a firm believer in busting balls. Helps you find out who the true men are." Trish took Loren's beer and swallowed a quarter of it. "Or the real women."

"I'm not going to ask about the particulars."

"No matter. You don't have to. I'm always happy to speak my mind."

Loren laughed. "Can't say I've noticed."

"See there? That's why you get all the girls. Because you know how to flirt."

Loren almost swallowed her tongue. The last thing she needed was Ramsey thinking she was flirting with his woman. "I...uh..."

"Relax, I know you weren't. Well, see, you *were* but you weren't meaning to, and that's even better. Actually talking to a woman, playing with her, that's exciting."

Loren resisted looking over her shoulder to see if Ramsey was in earshot. Trish definitely had something on her mind. "So, ah, what's your advice for an unworthy like me?"

"Now Lisa," Trish said with a pleased smile, "she's a woman with class. Smart and sassy, and sexy. In fact, I was a little surprised to see her in here at first."

Loren's stomach clenched. This was what she'd been afraid of. The men tended to discount women as being nothing more than entertainment, but the other women, they studied newcomers. Sky stood out, and Trish wasn't the queen of the pride just because she was Ramsey's old lady. She was street-smart, savvy, and tough. Loren needed to sell Sky's cover, and fast. "Lisa's in a league of her own, for sure, but she isn't the conforming type. She might be smart, but could you see her in an office?"

"No, but I get her being an accountant." Trish paused when the prospect handed her another whiskey sour. She tasted this one, grunted, and gave a little nod. "Better."

His sigh of relief was audible. "Thanks. Okay, thanks."

Trish waved him off with an absent flick of her hand, and he disappeared. "Lisa works with her head, and numbers mean you have to be quick and sharp. That fits. And, hey, working numbers for national? That's a power position. Smart again."

"Yeah, I see what you mean," Loren said, a swell of pride replacing the tension tying her insides into knots. Sky seemed to have sold her own cover just by being herself. Smart and sassy and sexy. And so much more.

Trish tilted her glass in Loren's direction, as if punctuating her words. "So she's the kind of woman it's good to know. Good to have on the side of the chapter, if you know what I mean."

Loren nodded slowly. "Important to treat her right."

"Exactly. And it wouldn't do you any harm, either. She's about a hundred steps up from the trash you usually bed."

"I wouldn't say they're trash."

"No, you wouldn't. That's another thing I like about you." Trish took a healthy swallow of her drink and patted Loren's thigh, her hand lingering until Loren wanted to jump up and run. "In fact, if I ever get tired of Ramsey, I think you'll be my next choice."

Loren stared from the hand on her leg to Trish's wickedly gleaming eyes. "Jesus, Trish. Are you trying to get me a one-way ticket out of here?"

Trish smiled sweetly and slid her hand back onto the bar. "Of course, I wouldn't bother you if you were already hooked up, you know?"

Loren nodded. "I think I'm getting the message."

"I always knew you were smart. Think about it." Trish slid off her stool and sauntered across the room to a table where three biker chicks had congregated with their drinks, leaving Loren to digest the not-so-subtle messages.

Trish liked Sky, but she also liked what Sky could potentially do for the Renegades, assuming of course she was actually the person Trish thought she was. And since she wasn't, the whole situation only meant Sky needed to disappear sooner rather than later. She'd already attracted too much attention.

Loren contemplated her beer and decided she didn't want any more. What she wanted she couldn't have. She wanted to climb into bed with Sky and spend the rest of the night wrapped up in her, immersed in the heat of her body and the sweet taste of her passion. She didn't want the mission driving a wedge between them, and she didn't want to be haunted by the specter of Sky being discovered—and eliminated. The idea of Sky disappearing from her life hurt more than she'd imagined possible, but at least if Sky headed back to LA before things got more complicated, she'd be safe. And above all, Loren wanted her safe.

But wanting was not the same as having, especially not when Sky wanted something else entirely. But maybe it wasn't too late. She'd made a mistake revealing her feelings—not that she regretted how she felt—but she'd pushed too hard. Maybe if she kept things between them strictly professional, she'd have a better chance of convincing Sky to go.

Loren left the bar and drove through the starless, frigid night to her shop. She parked her bike out back so she wouldn't wake Sky by raising the doors to the garage. When she let herself in, she knew instantly Sky was gone. The room held a stillness that could only mean it was devoid of life. She flicked on a light and scanned the space. Sky's few things were gone. She hadn't brought much, but the small touches of her had made the room come to life with a warmth it'd never had. Now it was once again a sterile place bounded by stark concrete and wood. A lot like her.

Loren dropped onto the bed and stared at the ceiling. All the things that mattered were still the same—the job she had to do, the need she had to pit herself against those who hoped to destroy the things she believed in. The only thing that had changed was her. Oh, she still believed, she still burned with the need to carry out her duty, but she bled now in places she never had before. Sky had touched her where no one else had ever dared to reach, and now she couldn't seal the wounds. She needed to be touched as only Sky could, something else she hadn't realized. She covered her eyes with her arm and wondered how she'd lived so long knowing so little about herself and what really mattered.

❖

Cam called the apartment late morning, Blair's time. Blair answered on the second ring. "Hi, baby."

"Hi," Blair said. "How's the hotel?"

Cam laughed. "Like every other hotel. Room service is pretty good, though."

"Well, that's important."

"How are things?"

Blair gave the barest hint of a sigh. "I was right, Lucinda was being merciful the last couple of days, seeing as how it was my birthday and the holidays. But she is back on Lucinda time now. I got a text at five a.m. instructing me to appear later to review the itinerary, the various venues where she'll need me to appear with my father, and backup plans for me to take his place if he gets diverted for any reason."

"Business as usual."

"Exactly. How's yours going?"

"Fairly smooth so far. I'll know more later today." Cam didn't discuss operations in progress. Blair wouldn't expect her to, and she'd learned that what mattered most was simply connecting. The sound of Blair's voice, the simple act of sharing a few moments of her day and hearing about Blair's settled her. Knowing Blair was safe and happy was all she needed to ground her.

"Okay." Blair was silent for a moment. "I hope that goes well. You'll let me know, as soon as you can?"

"Absolutely. Try to get some rest in between Lucinda briefings. You'll be busy soon enough."

"Same to you. And hurry home."

"I will. I love you."

"I love you. Talk to you soon."

Cam disconnected and packed the few things she'd removed the night before. She never fully unpacked, never knowing when she might need to check out in a hurry. Depending on how the day's meeting went, she might be leaving as early as the next morning. However, if she got anything in the way of reasonable leads from the FBI agent, she planned to follow them up. The rendezvous location was a two-hour drive from her hotel, and she wanted to arrive with plenty of time for reconnaissance. She didn't know any of the agents involved, and she couldn't be sure how good their security or intel was.

She owed it to everyone, especially Blair, to be cautious.

Sky slept fitfully, waking almost every hour to check the clock. By the time she decided to get out of bed, she was running mostly on adrenaline. She needed to settle, keep her mind clear for the meet later. Unfortunately, the one thing she needed in order to do that, she didn't have. She needed Loren. She couldn't stop wondering where Loren had ended up after the Rooster. In one of the club rooms in the back of the bar, with some young hopeful to keep her warm? Or back at the garage, alone in the silence? Or maybe she'd returned, found Sky gone, and decided that was all for the good. Maybe she'd slept perfectly.

That thought was so aggravating Sky threw the covers aside and stomped into the bathroom. The lukewarm shower helped clear her head, and she dressed in jeans, a button-down cotton shirt, a loose black sweater, and biker boots. She gathered her wallet and keys and decided to head to a diner for breakfast. She had plenty of time before she needed to set out for the tavern. She planned on arriving early enough to watch the comings and goings and get a sense of who, if anyone, frequented the place. According to Dan's intel, the place was usually deserted, so far off the beaten path it rarely got any customers except in the summer season. Locals had no reason to drop in, as it was on a road that led from nowhere to somewhere even less populated. On the whole, a perfect place for an out-of-the-way assignation, and for all anyone would know, she was meeting a lover somewhere they wouldn't be detected. All the same, she wanted a sense of the entrance and exit roads from the place, what foot traffic if any there might be, and plan her own strategy in case things went wrong. The only way to avoid problems was to see to the details herself.

❖

Jane stretched out on her stomach on the rocky ledge a hundred yards above the highway and two hundred yards from the turnoff to the Timberwolf Bar and Grill and peered through the high-powered binoculars at the building where the two federal agents were scheduled to meet. Her assault rifle lay by her side. Her thermal-lined, Kevlar-impregnated camo jacket and pants kept her warm. Three hours to go.

She'd arrived before sunrise and had nothing to eat but an MRE at dawn. The crackers, cheese, and candy bar were enough to keep her hands steady and her mind clear. She wasn't hungry, wasn't aware of the cold or the wind. A little discomfort was nothing compared to what Jenn was enduring, hour after hour and day after day. Jane's whole world had become the ramshackle one-story, split-log building framed by an L-shaped gravel parking lot. A thin trickle of sooty gray smoke streamed from the stone chimney, and the odor of burning pine carried to her when the wind shifted in her direction. Someone was inside although the parking lot was empty except for a run-down, rusted-out Ford pickup truck that presumably belonged to the owner. There'd been no traffic of any kind in or out of the restaurant in the hours she'd been there. A perfect place to carry out their plan.

"Com check," she whispered into her radio.

"Bravo one, check."

"Charlie one, check."

Jane nodded, satisfied. Even knowing where the others were stationed in the dense forest, she couldn't detect them. "Alpha one, check. Maintain radio silence. Out."

She settled down to wait. All that remained was for the prey to walk into the trap.

CHAPTER THIRTY

Cam drove past the Timberwolf Bar and Grill without slowing. The parking lot was empty, except for a ten-year-old pickup truck parked on the side of the building. Had she not known the place was actually in business, she would have assumed it had been abandoned long ago—the log timbers were gray with age and splintered in places, the roof had bare patches where the shingles had blown off, and the parking lot was little more than a muddy gravel turnaround. She drove on for another two miles, scanning both sides of the road for access trails or turnoffs where vehicles might be concealed, and saw nothing. Five miles down the road, a cluster of square single-story houses, a garage with a row of muddy pickups in front, and a small convenience store marked the village of Stromberg. A hand-lettered sign in front of the store advertised gas, pizza, coffee, and worms. She kept driving for another ten miles and saw nothing on either side of the road except forest. Eventually, she U-turned in a narrow fire road and headed back. A few cars passed her on the way. No one seemed to take notice.

She continued past the tavern, which still showed no signs of life, and on to the closest town, about twenty miles south. She went through the drive-thru at the McDonald's and sat in the parking lot to drink her coffee and wait. Thirty minutes before the meet time, she tossed her coffee cup into a trash can and completed the entire circuit again, eventually pulling into the tavern's lot. After parking the Pathfinder facing out toward the road in front of the low structure, she stepped out and looked around. She hadn't used the rear lot as she had no need to conceal her presence and every reason to want to be able to leave quickly if something went wrong. The two-lane road was empty, the forest quiet. She walked inside.

The musty bar was as empty and silent as the surrounding mountains. A grizzled, thin man in a red-and-black plaid flannel shirt and baggy khaki pants perched on a tall stool at the end of the bar with a newspaper spread out in front of him. He looked up and regarded her curiously, as if the presence of a potential customer was a surprise.

"Help you?" he said.

"Any chance of getting a coffee?"

He scratched his beard and nodded. "Don't see why not. You want something to eat?"

"I think I'm okay for now."

"Lost?"

"Not that I know of."

He nodded, slid off his stool, and disappeared through a door with a portal window into what Cam presumed was the kitchen. She unbuttoned her jacket to give herself access to her weapon in case he returned with more than her coffee. A few minutes later he emerged from the back with a white porcelain mug and a small carton of cream. He set them down on a round wooden table near the door.

"Need sugar?"

"I'm good, thanks," she said and handed him a five-dollar bill.

He took it and walked behind the bar to make change while she poured cream into her coffee. Real cream. The last thing she'd expected.

"Keep the change."

He looked at her over his shoulder, the curious expression back. "Thanks."

When he went back to his newspaper, Cam moved her coffee to another table near a window from which she could see both the door from the kitchen, which presumably opened into the rear parking lot, and the front door. Even though the window glass was streaked and gritty, she had a good view of the small lot in front of the building as well as the approach road in both directions. Five minutes later a dark blue sedan pulled in next to her rented SUV. A woman emerged matching the photo Cam had pulled from the FBI files when she'd gotten the name of the agent she would be meeting. Skylar Dunbar looked younger in person than her jacket photo, but she acted like an experienced field agent. Dunbar had backed her car in as well and, upon emerging from the vehicle, scanned the surroundings thoroughly before moving out from the cover afforded by the car.

The owner glanced up from his paper again as Dunbar walked toward Cam's table and called, "Get you something?"

Dunbar nodded toward Cam. "What she's having would be good."

"Be a minute." He slid off his stool and disappeared into the back.

Dunbar sat down across from Cam. "This place is a little off the beaten path."

"I noticed," Cam said. "I'd rather we had a little company."

"Yeah. Sometimes potential witnesses are a good thing." Dunbar looked around the room. "What do you think of the bartender?"

"Hard to say. He gave me cream for my coffee."

Dunbar laughed shortly. "I think that might be points for him, but I'm not sure it's a valid recommendation."

"How sure are you of the person who set up this meet site?"

"Totally sure," Dunbar said with conviction. "I've worked with the guy for years. He's solid."

"What about his intelligence?"

"There shouldn't be anybody else in on this. We've kept this operation quiet."

"All right, but let's make this quick all the same," Cam said. "What I'm looking for is a connection to someone in a militia in this state, particularly a well-organized group that is potentially growing their own from the ground up."

"Well, we've got plenty of paramilitary groups," Dunbar said, "but all of that's in the bureau files. You didn't come all the way here for background."

"What's in there is all pretty superficial. I'm looking to track specific individuals, and I need to cut through the camouflage quickly."

"Names?"

Cam shook her head. "Probably not real ones. The aliases are Jennifer Pattee and Angela Jones. I don't suppose that means anything to you?"

Dunbar shook her head. "No. We've got a few names, but we can't be sure that those are real, either. How'd you get this far?"

"My gut tells me this group probably homeschools their kids, then trains them to infiltrate organizations for later action. That takes sophisticated, long-range planning, and the radical fringe groups aren't stable enough to pull it off. We need to be looking at some of the grassroots paramilitary groups with professional leadership and resources."

"Putting people inside where?" Sky asked. "How high up are we talking, in terms of infiltration?"

Cam regarded her silently.

"So that's why you're here personally," Dunbar murmured. "Jesus. That takes a whole hell of a lot of resources, and a leader with charisma and power." Dunbar's sculpted red-brown brows creased. "The biggest group is right here in the Bitterroots, and from what we can tell, they're large, well established, and well organized. They've also got money behind them."

Cam felt the first stirring in her gut that usually meant she was on the right trail. "How big and how much money?"

"Enough that they can come up with a quarter of a million on short order."

"That's a lot of money. The kind of money that a group would need, to put together the type of operation I'm investigating." Cam took out a photo of Jennifer Pattee and the slightly blurry image of Angela Jones that had been on file in her Eugen Corp portfolio and passed them to Dunbar. "Have you ever seen these women?"

"No," Dunbar said after studying them for a few moments. "They look a little alike."

"Jones managed to pass off a faxed photo on her job app, so it's hard to tell, but I wouldn't be surprised if they're related. We can't connect them, but I think they are." Cam glanced at her watch. The tavern owner had been gone awhile. The building was silent. "Tell me about the group you're looking at."

"The main man running the militia goes by the name of Graves. Might be real, might be one of those identities cultivated so long ago that his original name would be tough to trace. We know he's got women in his organization, but that's about the best I can tell you."

"Do you have anyone on the inside?"

Dunbar didn't hesitate. "No."

"But you've got someone who can get close."

Dunbar held Cam's gaze for a long moment, nothing showing in her eyes. She was making a decision, and Cam wondered about the source of her reluctance. Someone she wanted to protect. Cam said, "I'm not going to jeopardize your operative."

"I don't know that," Dunbar said. "No disrespect intended."

"None taken. I'm not going to pull the national security card on you, either, because I don't have to, do I?"

Dunbar grimaced. "You don't have to. I've got someone who *will* be getting close. We might be able to get you some more information about the other members of the group."

"How long?"

"Soon. A matter of a week, maybe two."

"I take it you're after who's behind it? The moneyman?"

"We're after all of them," Dunbar said, steel in her voice.

"I need you to jump on this."

"Any chance the information highway will run both ways?"

"I can't promise you that. But if we need local help, you'll be my first call."

"Fair enough. I've got other contacts who might be able to help research people who fit the profile," Dunbar said. "If they're homeschooling, they'll eventually need an entry point into the official system, and they often use insiders who help pave the way. We might be able to track that."

"Good." Cam shook her head. "The coffee's taking too long."

Dunbar stood. "Yeah. I say we get out—"

The door from the kitchen swung wide, and the woman Cam knew as Angela Jones, dressed in camo and carrying a Glock in her hand, walked in.

"You're going to want to put your weapons on the floor," Jones said casually. She smiled almost pleasantly at Cam. The automatic looked like an extension of her arm, steady and comfortable. "Slowly. And then you'll want to come with me."

"I don't think so," Cam said quietly.

Jones fired, and Dunbar lurched back with a sharp cry and went down.

Cam drew her weapon and aimed at Jones, who was aiming at Dunbar on the floor, seemingly unconcerned by the automatic in Cam's hand.

"Please don't resist," Jones said, "or I'll shoot her in the head this time."

Dunbar writhed on the floor, blood seeping between the fingers she pressed to her upper arm, and gasped, "Forget about me. Fucking shoot her."

The tavern door behind Cam opened with a gust of cold air, and she knew by the look on Jones's face she was outnumbered. She lowered her weapon.

Jones nodded. "That's better. Now, come with me."

"She comes too," Cam said, indicating Dunbar. If she left without her, Jones would have Dunbar killed. No witnesses that way. "If she doesn't, neither do I."

"Why not," Jones said. "Maybe she'll be useful."

Cam leaned down, got an arm behind Dunbar's shoulders, and helped her up. "How bad is it?"

"Flesh wound, I think."

Someone prodded Cam in the back with a gun barrel.

Jones said, "Let's go."

Cam had no choice if she wanted to keep Dunbar alive. She went.

CHAPTER THIRTY-ONE

P at them down," Jones said to whoever was behind Cam.
The gun barrel in the small of Cam's back shifted away, and
someone quickly and efficiently checked her legs and torso for a backup
gun, then did the same with Dunbar.

"They're clean," a gruff male voice announced.

"Out the back." Jones gestured toward the kitchen with her Glock
as Cam and Dunbar walked toward her with another militiaman right
behind them. She pushed open the kitchen door, and a redhead who
didn't look more than twenty, dressed in combat gear and carrying an
assault rifle, pointed them down the aisle of a long, narrow kitchen.

The bartender lay face down on the floor in front of a chipped
cast-iron stove. Cam couldn't tell if he was dead or alive. Beside her,
Dunbar weaved unsteadily. "Can you make it?"

"I'll make it," Dunbar said through gritted teeth.

They proceeded in single file out the back, across the rickety porch,
and down three wobbly steps to the lot behind the tavern. Mounds of
dirty snow ringed the small parking area.

"Into the woods," Jones said from behind Cam, and they followed
the redhead up a shallow embankment to what looked to be a twisty
deer trail wending into the trees, the snow trampled flat by the passage
of many hooves. Neither Cam nor Dunbar was dressed for hiking.
Dunbar slipped on the snowy slope, and Cam grabbed her to keep her
from falling.

"I'm all right," Dunbar said, but her face was as white as the
surrounding snowpack.

Cam had no doubt if they were forced to leave Dunbar behind,
the militia would dispose of her, and she had no intention of letting the
agent fall. "You'll make it."

They stumbled through towering, dense pines for twenty minutes, as near as Cam could estimate. Perhaps half a mile. No wonder she hadn't seen any signs of an ambush. They hadn't come by the road. Two others, a man and a woman, fell in with them en route, automatic weapons at the ready. They made no attempt to hide their faces, which meant they planned to execute their captives when they were no longer of any strategic value, or they were confident their stronghold was unassailable.

Eventually they emerged into a small clearing where a Humvee awaited. A huge Dumpster with a sign reading *Caution, bear feeding area* took up the rest of the space. They'd walked into the back end of what was probably a campsite, almost certainly deserted this time of year. The redhead opened the rear of the Humvee and motioned them in. Cam half lifted Dunbar into the compartment, and she collapsed against the sidewall instantly. Cam pulled off her topcoat and threw it in before climbing in after her. Two of the four kept their weapons trained on them until Jones came around the side and climbed into the backseat. As soon as she knelt on the rear seat with her weapon trained on them, the others piled in, and the Humvee pulled away.

"I want to look at her wound," Cam said.

Jones appeared to deliberate.

"She's of no value to you dead."

"Don't make any sudden movements," Jones said in her persistently casual tone, "because I really don't want to have to kill you."

"What do you want?" Cam asked, gripping the neck of Dunbar's sweater in both hands and pulling hard. The material frayed around the bullet hole, and she was able to tear the material enough to see the wound. An entrance wound the size of a quarter in Dunbar's upper arm bled slowly. A larger ragged exit wound high on the back of her shoulder streamed copiously.

"I just want you to keep us company for a few days," Jones said. "Until we can trade you in."

Cam looked over her shoulder. "For Jennifer Pattee?"

Jones smiled. "You're quick."

"Now that I see you in person, the resemblance is clear. Sisters?"

Jones's mouth hardened. "She's one of ours. That's all that matters."

"Got a med kit in this truck? Letting her bleed out is not going to serve any purpose."

"She'll keep for a while."

Cam unbuttoned her shirt, stripped it off, and folded it into a makeshift field dressing. She pressed it firmly to Dunbar's shoulder. "Can you hold pressure on this?"

"Yeah," Dunbar said, gripping the shirt. Her eyes were glazed, but she was sitting up under her own power, which was as much as Cam could hope for.

Cam's T-shirt wasn't much of a barrier to the cold, but she leaned back against the side of the Humvee and folded her arms, contemplating Jones. She couldn't be much older than Pattee, and she had the same burning fervor in her eyes as her sister. They had to be on the way to the compound, and once they got there, their options would be limited. But they'd be better than they were right now, with a zero chance of escape. Cam settled down to wait. They'd be missed soon enough. Discovering their location in the heart of this wilderness might be more problematic.

❖

Loren hadn't slept, replaying her conversation with Sky over and over. She should have insisted on providing backup. She should have kept her mouth shut about her feelings—as if Sky had given her any reason to think how she felt mattered, anyhow. Sky had come to do a job and that was what mattered, all that mattered to her. They'd gotten into their roles, sure, and why not? No rule against physical attraction, or acting on it, for that matter. But Loren was the one who'd lost sight of reality. Maybe she'd been living in a shadow world so long, she couldn't tell the difference any longer.

And now Sky was out there alone.

She'd tried drowning her self-recriminations in a long hot shower, but as soon as she'd finished, she'd started watching the clock. She'd expected Sky to call an hour ago. No matter what was going on between them, Sky was a professional, and she would've kept Loren in the loop. When she didn't call, Loren got dressed, climbed on her bike, and rode to Sky's motel. Sky's rental car wasn't there. The meet had been almost three hours before, and Sky should've been back by now.

Loren straddled her bike, the engine rumbling, and considered options. She couldn't call Sky on the phone in case the meet had gotten complicated and she was in the middle of something. She could use the number she had to reach her handler in event of trouble, but she figured that number would go to Sky as well. She had a backup number she'd never used, but she suspected that would go to Sky's task-force partner. She'd try him if she didn't hear from Sky soon, but first, she'd take a look for herself. She wheeled her bike around and headed for the Timberwolf Bar and Grill.

❖

Sky shut her eyes and fought to keep the nausea at bay. The throbbing in her shoulder accelerated into a gut-wrenching stab of pain every time the Humvee hit a bump, which was every other second. Her head spun and her mind kept sliding away into a gray fog, where time morphed into one long trail of agony.

"How are you doing?" Loren asked.

No, not Loren.

Loren was gone.

Loren had said...she'd said...why had Loren walked out, left her?

"Dunbar," the voice came again, sharper. Command voice.

Sky opened her eyes. Cameron Roberts's eyes were winter gray, hard as ice. Sky's blood surged, her mind cleared. "I'm a little fuzzy," Dunbar said in a whisper.

"Let me check the wound."

Roberts lifted the makeshift bandage from her shoulder. She was gentle but unflinching.

"Looks like the bleeding is slowing. How's your hand?"

Sky flexed her fingers. The movement propelled searing shock waves through her arm. "Not so good."

"Numb?"

"I wish."

"That's good, then. The nerves are okay." Roberts pressed the folded shirt, soggy now with blood, back against her shoulder. "Keep holding. And I need you to stay awake."

"I will."

Roberts settled back beside her. Sky concentrated on staying awake. She had to stay awake, because if she didn't, they'd get rid of her and Roberts would try to stop them. She wasn't going to let that happen. She had to hang on. Couldn't let them use her against Roberts. Had to protect the mission, protect Loren.

Loren would miss her. At least Loren wouldn't know where to look. At least she'd be safe.

❖

Cam estimated they'd been riding an hour when the Humvee bounced off the highway onto an uneven trail. The windows were smoked and she couldn't see much outside, except that they were in a dense forest. They appeared to be climbing, and the Humvee was cold. Beside her, Dunbar shivered. "I'm going to get my coat and put it around her."

"Slowly," Jones said.

Cam pulled her topcoat over Dunbar. "You with me?"

"Yes," Dunbar said. "Better."

"Good." Cam settled back, and ten minutes later the Humvee stopped. Jones kept them in her sights while the others piled out. The rear door opened.

"Climb out," Jones ordered.

Cam helped Dunbar down from the vehicle and jumped out beside her. The camp was dark. All she could make out was a ring of buildings with a few lights showing through windows here and there. There could be a hundred militiamen in the place, or ten.

Jones appeared beside her and motioned to the left with her gun. "That way."

"If you've got a field hospital, she—"

Jones kicked Cam behind the knee and she went down, barely managing to catch herself before she fell flat. Small stones cut into her palms. Jones crouched beside her.

"You'd do well to worry about yourself."

"If you expect to trade us," Cam said, slowly pushing to a kneeling position, swallowing her rage, "it would probably be a good idea to keep us healthy."

"I didn't say I was going to trade both of you."

"I don't take you for a fool, and two hostages are always better than one."

Jones pushed the barrel of her Glock under Cam's chin until Cam had to lift her neck to ease the pressure. "And you might be wiser to stop giving orders. You're nothing here. You're no one."

Cam remained silent. Jones seemed rational, but she didn't want to push. What she needed was to remain as unfettered as possible, and antagonizing her captors would not accomplish that. She needed to get a sense of the physical space, of how many militiamen were billeted here, and find a way to communicate with someone she trusted. And she had to keep Dunbar from becoming a casualty. "You're calling the shots here. I just want to get her some medical help."

Jones stood. "Take them to the infirmary. Put a guard on the door and outside the windows. I'll be there in a minute."

Cam got to her feet, satisfied she'd won a small victory. Dunbar needed attention, and as long as they were together, she had a better chance of keeping her alive. And she'd learned that Jones could be reasoned with.

The infirmary turned out to be a single-story building little bigger than a garage, with two narrow beds, a single window above them, and a locked cabinet against one wall that probably held supplies. Their guards ordered them to sit on the beds. Dunbar slumped down facing Cam across the narrow aisle. Dark shadows of pain and fatigue rimmed her eyes, but her gaze was remarkably clear. She was tough. The guard by the door was a woman of about thirty with short blond hair and flat green eyes. She held her weapon with easy familiarity and regarded them with cold disdain. Cam considered rushing her and estimated she'd be wounded or dead before she reached her feet.

A few minutes later, Jones walked in, strode to the gray metal cabinet, unlocked it, and removed a field pack. She tossed it to Cam. "You should know what to do with this. Go ahead."

"Lie down," Cam said to Dunbar, who looked as if she was going to resist. "Go ahead. We need to get this cleaned up before you get infected."

Dunbar lay back against the thin pillow, wincing as she angled onto her right side so the wounded shoulder was elevated. Cam opened the field pack on top of the plain metal table that stood between the two beds. The guard kept her weapon trained on her while she worked. Jones stood at the foot of Dunbar's bed, her arms crossed, watching. Cam cut Dunbar's shirt up to her shoulder and peeled it back from the wound.

"Do you have any local anesthetic?" Cam asked.

"If we did, I wouldn't waste it on her."

"Go ahead," Dunbar said, the muscles around her mouth tight with strain. "I'll be fine."

Cam opened the Betadine pack and pulled out the swabs. "I'm sorry."

Dunbar's jaw clenched as Cam carefully cleansed the entrance and exit wounds, but she didn't make a sound. Cam paused, giving

Dunbar time to breathe. "I'll have to clean inside the track to make sure there's no foreign material from your clothes in the wound."

"I know."

Cam soaked the last swab in the remainder of the antiseptic and carefully worked it into the wound. Dunbar went rigid, her neck arching, sweat trickling down her temples into her dark auburn hair. Finished, Cam discarded the swabs, applied clean gauze, and wrapped a circular bandage around Dunbar's upper arm. She leaned back on her heels and looked at Jones. "What about antibiotics?"

"Maybe, if you cooperate," Jones said.

Cam rose. "What do you want?"

"The name of someone with the power to make decisions and get me what I want. Someone who isn't afraid to break rules."

Cam almost smiled. "Lucinda Washburn."

CHAPTER THIRTY-TWO

D o you think I should address same-sex marriage in Ohio?" Andrew Powell leaned back in his leather desk chair behind the broad walnut desk in the Oval Office.

Blair perched on an antique sofa, a cup of coffee steaming beside her. The valet had brought sandwiches, but she didn't have much of an appetite. She would rather have been at home, waiting for Cam to call, but when her father had asked her to come by during one of his rare free hours, she'd come. "I think you should if they raise the point. Otherwise, this early in the campaign, you should probably concentrate on the major issues—healthcare, the budget, and jobs."

"You don't think it's a major issue?" His tone wasn't challenging, just curious.

"It is to me and others who will be affected by the decision, but for the average voter, no. They don't really think about the things that don't affect them personally, and right now, what affects them is their paycheck, the cost and availability of healthcare, and their economic future."

"And the war?"

"Same issues—the war impacts all those things, but if you can keep the focus on the positives here at home, you'll avoid the topics that end up being a banner for the other side to wave while they avoid the real problems we face in the next four and a half years."

Andrew nodded. "I think you're right, although sometimes it frustrates—" His phone rang, signaling that his secretary needed to speak with him. She rarely interrupted him and never did when he was with his daughter, unless it was urgent. Frowning, he picked up the phone. "Yes, Kelly. Of course. Tell her to come right in."

He hung up, still frowning.

"Should I go?" Blair asked, assuming he'd received some notice of a new emergency.

"No, it's Lucinda. She asked that you stay."

"Me?" Blair said, the uneasy churning she'd had in her stomach all day blooming into roiling anxiety. "Did she say why?"

"No, but she'll be here any second—"

A loud knock reverberated on the door as it opened, and the secretary hurriedly stepped aside, allowing Lucinda Washburn to pass.

"Thank you, Kelly," Andrew said, when his secretary looked to him with a question in her eyes. "We've got this now."

Dutifully, the secretary closed the doors. Lucinda strode toward them, her eyes glittering blue chips of ice.

"What is it?" Blair said, holding onto her delicate china cup as if it were an anchor.

"I just got a call on my direct line. A woman claiming to have taken Cameron hostage—"

Blair knew Lucinda was speaking, but the words were indecipherable. All she heard was the roar of the ocean pounding in her head. From deep inside, rage welled up like a flaming geyser while a glacier carved its way through her heart. "I'm sorry. What did you say?"

"A woman said Cam had given her my number—that she was holding Cam captive."

"What does she want?" Blair said, her voice sounding eerily steady in her own ears. Her heart pounded so loudly she was surprised the other two couldn't hear it.

"She wants to trade for Jennifer Pattee."

"Get Averill in here and call the bureau chief." Powell sat rigid behind his desk, his palms flat on his blotter, his jaw a study in stone.

Lucinda took a slow breath. "I would advise against that, Mr. President."

Andrew's brows rose. "Why?"

Lucinda glanced at Blair. "Give us a minute?"

Blair carefully set her cup on the saucer beside her, pleased when it did not rattle, wondering how it was that electricity burned through her nerves but her hands did not shake. She rose on legs she could not feel. "You don't discuss Cameron without me here. Say what you have to say, Luce."

"We may want to make decisions that can go no further than this room. I don't believe involving any other agencies is wise."

"How do you intend to get her back if we don't bring in the FBI and Homeland?" Blair said.

"We have a few options, but if we have to discuss the possibility of a trade, we don't want a record—"

"No," Blair said. "No trade. You know as well as I do that that won't ensure Cameron's safety. And"—she had to stop to swallow the shards of glass that slashed at her throat—"Cam would never forgive any of us for doing that."

"Do you care, as long as she's safe?" her father asked gently.

Blair saw sympathy and what might be fear in his eyes. Her father was never afraid—even when she was young and her mother had been dying, he'd been a rock. The fear was for her suffering, she knew, and she let him see she was not going to break. "Cameron knows that I know what's important to her. She trusts me to know what matters. We don't compromise her. Jennifer Pattee stays where Cam put her."

"Do you know what Cam was doing out there?" Lucinda asked.

"Not precisely. She doesn't discuss these things with me in detail." Blair tried to think. It was so hard when terror ate at the edges of her mind. Cam—someone was holding her by force. Someone who would hurt her, who wanted to hurt them all. She wished for a gun. She wished for a target for her fury. She wished to hurt those who would hurt Cam and knew that was not what Cam needed. She had to think. "She had a contact who was going to set up a meet for her with some undercover agents. She was looking at the militia—she was fairly sure Pattee had ties to them, Jones too. Maybe she talked to Wes when they were in Atlanta. She used her cell phone, so I'm not sure who she called—"

"I can get someone to access her calls," Lucinda said.

"You can?"

Lucinda shrugged. "Let's keep that between the three of us."

"Do that," the president said.

"All right," Lucinda said. "As soon as I have the names of Cam's contacts, I'll make inquiries personally and find out who she was meeting."

"How long?" Blair asked.

"I should be able to track her calls—"

"No," said Blair sharply. "How long did they give us to deliver Pattee?"

"Twelve hours to make arrangements to transport the prisoner." Lucinda's fists tightened. "They'll call me again for the details tomorrow at zero six thirty their time."

"And if we say no?" Blair asked.

"They didn't say—"

"Luce," Blair said angrily, "you can't protect me from this. She's my wife."

Lucinda's expression softened. "I know, sweetheart. I know. We don't know what they'll do, and wondering, imagining, won't help Cam. All we can do is our best to stop them. Let that be enough."

"We'll stop them," Blair said, "but it won't be enough. It won't be enough until someone pays."

❖

Loren rode past the Timberwolf Bar and Grill, slowing slightly as her headlights swept the narrow lot in front of the building. A new black Pathfinder sat next to Sky's blue rental car. The tavern's roadside sign was dark, and no lights showed other than a flickering security bulb on one corner of the run-down building that threw an uneven cone of light in the direction of the road. The building appeared empty and deserted. On her return trip, nothing had changed, and she pulled beside Sky's car, cut the engine, and sat in the darkness. She listened for signs of life and heard nothing—no music, no rumble of voices, no clang and clatter to indicate the building was occupied. And yet, the vehicles suggested someone should be around. Her every sense screamed trouble.

She climbed off her bike and pulled her Glock from the inside pocket of her leather jacket, held it down to her side, and climbed up onto the wooden porch. Keeping close to the face of the building, she sidled up to the nearest window and took a quick look inside. A faint light above the counter coming from a beer sign revealed nothing but an empty room. She tried the front door and it opened. Cautiously, she pushed it wide and ducked low into the room, keeping her back toward the wall and fanning the space with her weapon. Nothing.

A sign indicated restrooms at the far end of the room, and she worked her way in that direction. She peeked into the men's room— single stall, the door open, empty. Same for the women's room. The only other door was behind the bar, probably leading to the kitchen. The room beyond was dark. Once more, she pushed the door open and went in low, making herself as small a target as possible. The place was small, crowded with appliances and a few boxes of supplies, and smelled like old grease and burnt coffee. It was also empty, except for the body lying on the floor in the moonlight just inside the back door.

She stepped over him, checked out the back door, and saw nothing other than a pickup truck. The two of them were alone. She knelt down and felt for a pulse. The faint ripple in his carotid artery told her he wasn't dead, just unconscious. She found a dish towel on the counter, ran it under cold water, wrung it out, and placed it on the back of his neck. A few seconds later, he stirred and moaned.

"Just hold still," Loren said. "I'm not going to hurt you."

The man on the floor didn't move but his eyelids flickered. "You the one who put me down here?"

"No. I'm looking for a redhead who came in earlier, probably met someone."

"Don't remember much," he muttered.

"Are you hurt anywhere besides your head?"

"Not's I can tell. Somebody hit me from behind, I guess. Came around once before, head hurt, went back to sleep."

"You've probably got a concussion. I'll call for an ambulance in a minute."

"No," he said with surprising strength. "Don't do that. I'll be all right."

"You might be hurt worse than you think."

"I've been hurt more than this before. Help me sit up."

Loren put her Glock back in her pocket, got her hands under his arms, and helped him sit up with his back against the counter. She found a light switch by the stove and turned it on. He blinked, focused on her.

"Who are you?" he asked.

"Just somebody looking for a friend."

"Nobody out there in the other room?"

She shook her head.

"Can't help you any. Didn't see anything."

"Hear anything?"

He frowned. "Like I said, I was kind of in and out. I think I dreamed there was a gunshot." He touched his chest as if to see if he was bleeding. "Guess it was a dream."

"Didn't see anyone?"

"Door opened behind me while I was getting coffee. Before I could turn, somebody hit me."

Ambush, Loren thought. Sky's partner had set her up, or someone had set him up to get to Sky. She needed to talk to him, find out who else knew about this meet. Both Sky and the Homeland Security agent were missing. There was only one conclusion. Someone had taken them by force.

"I'm going to check the other room."

"Yeah, I'll just stay here."

She found a light switch next to the door and hit the overhead lights in the bar. An overturned chair she hadn't seen in the dark lay next to a table by the windows. An irregular stain a foot in diameter marred the floor next to it, and she crouched down to look. She knew before she touched it what she'd find. Blood.

One of them had been hurt, fairly severely, and they were both gone. A storm of anger and self-recrimination surged through her. Sky was in trouble, and Loren should have been there. She'd played this all wrong, and now Sky was paying the price. She had to find her before the price became too much to pay.

CHAPTER THIRTY-THREE

"Where are you going?" Blair's father asked.

"I'm not sure," Blair said. She stifled the urge to run—she needed some air, some space, some room to collect herself. Her mind was whirling as if she might fragment into a thousand jagged shards of glass at any second. "Probably home. I need to move around, I can't just sit here."

"But Luce might find—"

"Luce will call me when she gets anything," Blair said. Inactivity was going to drive her mad. And she knew if she stayed, her father might feel compelled to do something he shouldn't do. She couldn't put him in the position of violating national policy because of who she was. But she couldn't stand by and do nothing, and short of negotiating with the terrorists for Cam's release, there was nothing that she considered beyond possibility. "Don't worry. I'm not going to do anything crazy."

He smiled sadly. "I wouldn't blame you if you did."

"I want her back. I don't care what it takes, and I'm not going to talk about it with you."

"I won't ask you to. But I want a promise."

"If I can."

"Don't trade yourself for her."

Blair smiled wanly. "I suppose I might consider that, if I didn't know how much it would piss her off."

"She loves you. So do I." He rubbed his face. "How can I be the most powerful man in the world and not be able to help my own daughter?"

"Because being the president means you have to put the personal aside."

"I'm sorry. For this—for all the times—"

"Don't. You don't have to apologize for anything. It hasn't always been what I wanted, but I never wanted you to change anything. I still don't."

He studied her for a long time, as if seeing her for the first time. "I love you, and you've always made me proud."

"I love you too. And you've always made me proud."

Blair grabbed her coat, left the Oval Office, and walked out of the White House alone. As soon as she reached the street, she made a call. "I need to talk to Valerie. Right away."

"All right." Diane must have heard the urgency in her voice. She didn't ask anything at all. "Is this number all right for her to call?"

"Yes. But tell her it's a private matter."

"I will. Do you need me to do anything?"

"I don't know. I guess, just be around."

"Sweetie, for you, I'm always around. I love you, stay safe."

"I will." Blair walked a few more blocks and then hailed a cab. She felt as if she were turning to stone inside, as if all her emotions were solidifying into hard edges and brittle planes. If her anger were a blade, the world around her would be a bloodbath. And she wouldn't care.

❖

Loren checked to make sure the tavern owner was stable and accepted he didn't want her to call for help. Outside, she straddled her bike and punched in the number she'd never used—her emergency backup number, the one she was supposed to call if Sky didn't answer. She got voice mail, identified herself, and disconnected. Five minutes later her phone rang.

"This is Dan Bussy. What do you need?"

"I need to know why you picked the Timberwolf for Sky's meeting."

"I…I don't understand."

"I don't care if you understand or not. Who gave you the name of the place?" If she'd been standing in front of him, she'd have had her hands around his throat. He was the weak link—he had to be.

"Look, let me talk to Sky."

"I'd really like to do that, but she's not available right now."

"What does that mean?"

"Unless you want me to come down there looking for you, you'll answer my questions. And I promise I won't ask nicely if I have to find you."

"I don't answer to you."

"You do now, or I'm going to start making calls to people you might not want me to be talking to."

"Look, I don't know what's going on there, and I haven't much to tell you. Sky needed backup, and I arranged for it."

Loren went cold. "Backup. Who knew?"

"Just the local sheriff. And they didn't know who she was—"

"What *did* they know?"

He sighed. "That one of our agents was meeting a VIP out-of-towner and we wanted backup."

"And did you happen to tell them who the VIP was?"

"I had to give them someone to identify. I couldn't keep them completely in the dark."

"Jesus, how stupid could you be. Who knew? *Names.*"

"I told you, I dealt with the local sheriff. We've used his guys before for backup. They're reliable and it's their turf. It's good for public relations."

"Right. Your public relations compromised Sky. We all might be. Find out what happened to the backup, because it doesn't look like there was any." She disconnected.

Someone had ambushed Sky and Roberts. Why? Who would benefit? Taking down federal agents was no small deal. The problem was, too many people were getting too close to the truth. Someone in the sheriff's department had leaked the intel about the meet. Ramsey had connections inside the department, undoubtedly the militia did too. If it had been Ramsey, he would have gone after Sky before the meet, and chances were she and Sky would both be dead by now. That left the militia. They wouldn't want Sky, they wouldn't even know who she was. They wanted Cameron Roberts.

She started her engine and pulled out onto the highway. In seconds the Timberwolf was swallowed by the night. By the time she reached home, she had a plan.

❖

Cam sat with her back against the wall, her legs stretched out on the narrow bed, waiting for Jones to make her next move. Jones must have contacted Lucinda by now, and if she had, Lucinda was tracking her. It wouldn't take that long to find out where she had been staying and who she'd been meeting. Narrowing in on this place was going to take some luck.

Blair would know by now too. And that was the thing worrying Cam the most, that Blair was going to suffer because of her. At least Blair would know she was doing everything she could to come home. Blair would know that nothing mattered more than that.

She was worried about Dunbar too. Dunbar was shivering despite the heat being thrown off by a space heater in the corner of the room. Cam got up to cover her with her topcoat.

"Thanks," Dunbar said unsteadily, her teeth chattering.

Cam laid her palm on the back of Dunbar's neck and looked over her shoulder at the guard on the door. The woman had been replaced by a heavyset bearded man in black BDUs carrying the ever-present assault rifle. "Hey, she's running a fever. Someone needs to dig up some antibiotics. You must have some around here."

He snorted. "In case you haven't noticed, this isn't Walter Reed and you're not in charge."

"Then get me the person who is."

"Like I said, you don't give orders around here."

"If you want my cooperation, you'll get someone in here with the authority to open up that drug cabinet."

"Or…?"

"Or I'm going to suddenly become very uncooperative. And nothing will happen in terms of a prisoner exchange unless I make it happen."

The guard looked uncertain for the first time. After a moment, he spoke into a radio.

Cam leaned down to Dunbar. "Just hang in there. We'll get you some medication."

Dunbar's eyes were glassy. "Don't worry about me. Don't make any decisions because of me. I'll be fine."

"I know." Cam squeezed her neck gently. "But I need you mobile if the time comes we have to move."

Dunbar grinned, a savage, wild light in her eyes. "I'm tough, I'll make it. Just say when."

Cam nodded. She'd have to trust Dunbar and hope they'd have a chance to find out just how tough she was.

CHAPTER THIRTY-FOUR

Lucinda answered her private line, expecting the call to be the technician in the communications center answering her priority request for a trace on Cam's recent calls. Instead, the White House operator said, "I'm sorry to interrupt you, Ms. Washburn, but I have a caller who insists on speaking to the president about a matter of national security. She says she's a federal agent, but she won't give me an identification number."

Lucinda sighed. "Tell her you'll connect her to the Secret Service—"

"Yes, ma'am. I offered that, but she said it had to do with Deputy Director Roberts, and I—"

"All right, I'll take care of it." Lucinda switched on the recorder attached to her phone. "Put her through and scramble the line, please."

"Of course."

A faint click was followed by silence.

"This is Lucinda Washburn. Who is this?"

"Special Agent Loren McElroy."

"Why are you calling?"

"I have reason to believe Deputy Director Roberts has been ambushed and taken prisoner by a paramilitary organization that goes by the name of FALA, and I thought I ought to start at the top. We don't have a lot of time to cut through red tape."

"Can you verify your identity?" Lucinda made notes on a yellow legal pad as she spoke, even though the tape was running. She might find it necessary to erase the tape. She used a shorthand code she'd created years ago, one no one was likely to identify as anything other than aimless doodling.

"I could give you the names of some people who would vouch

for me, but it would take some time," McElroy said, "and I'm not sure exactly who can be trusted. Roberts was out here to meet with an undercover agent, looking for leads in some case that had to do with the militia operating in this area. The meet was compromised and they're both missing. At least one of them has been wounded."

"How do you know all this?"

"Because I've been undercover for two and a half years and my... handler is the agent who met with Roberts."

"Give me your location."

"That's not going to help you any. You've probably already tracked Roberts's last known location. I'm no closer to them than that, but I think I know where they're being held. At least the general vicinity."

"Tell me."

"Here are the coordinates of the last meeting I had with members of the militia. My guess is they're somewhere within a fifty-mile radius."

Lucinda jotted down the coordinates. "That's a lot of area to cover."

"It's worse than it seems. That's undeveloped, densely forested land, and you can be certain they've done everything possible to camouflage their location. How long do you think it will take you to get some kind of aerial surveillance?"

"Not long."

"Did they give you a deadline for whatever it is they want?"

Lucinda hesitated. Every instinct told her this agent was being truthful. No one should know the things she knew, and the people who had taken Cam had no reason to try a ruse. They already held all the cards, and they knew it.

"About nine hours, now. What about the agent who was taken with Director Roberts?"

"FBI. Skylar Dunbar. You probably won't find much on her."

"How many people know she's missing?"

"As far as I know, just me and her partner in LA. I don't think he's completely trustworthy."

"Name?"

"Dan Bussy."

"Is there a number where I can reach you?"

"Hold on. This number will be good for tonight."

Lucinda jotted it down. "I'll call you in an hour. Stay available, and if you discover anything at all, call me."

"Fine. But listen—FALA is well organized and well trained, but they're basically fanatics. You can't trust anything they tell you. If they don't get what they want or even *think* they won't, they won't have any compulsion against killing hostages."

"I understand."

"Is there any possibility you'll be able to meet whatever demands they've made?"

Lucinda was silent.

"Then you have to find Sky and Roberts quickly. As soon as FALA figures out you're not going to play ball, they're going to make a statement, and what better way to do that than with two dead federal agents."

"I'll be in touch."

The line went dead and Lucinda switched over for another call. She reached the director of the FBI after three rings. "Mike, this is Lucinda Washburn. I need everything you have on a Skylar Dunbar, and I need you to pull an agent from the field and hold him for debriefing. No communication." She waited for the objection she knew would be coming. "I'm sorry, it's not something I can read you in on right now. The name is Dan Bussy. As soon as I can—yes. Thank you."

She hesitated, knowing she needed to brief Andrew. She made another call first. "Blair? We think we know where she might be. We're going to have some difficulties getting to her, however."

❖

"We've got trouble," Hooker said when Russo returned his urgent call.

"What is it now?"

"Graves just contacted me—they have a situation, and they want the money now."

"What situation?"

"He wouldn't say exactly, so I hit up my contact at the sheriff's. The details are sketchy, but it seems there's some snafu with a missing federal agent."

Russo stiffened. "They couldn't be that stupid. Here? They wouldn't try something like this on their own land?"

"If they've killed a federal agent, they're going to bring the ATF, FBI, and Homeland down on us like a fucking monsoon. It's going to be raining feds."

"We need to distance ourselves, and we need to end this quickly."

Russo thought furiously. If Graves and his people were in danger of being arrested, they would eventually give up Hooker, and that was too close to him to be tolerated. The only way he could be sure no one implicated him was to silence anyone in danger of arrest before they could talk. "What would happen if the Renegades were to discover that Graves was setting them up? That the whole gun deal was a ruse to entrap the Renegades, and that Graves was in bed with the ATF?"

"The Renegades would be out for blood—they'd go after Graves and burn his place to the ground." Hooker paused. "That would get us clear."

"Can we provide the Renegades with the incentive to do our work for us?"

"I might be able to get my guy in the sheriff's department to drop around to their bar and mention a rumor of a big bust in the making. Something to do with guns. That ought to get their attention."

"Good. Tell Graves you have his money."

❖

As soon as Blair finished talking to Lucinda, she called the number Valerie had given her. "Lucinda's had contact with an agent who might know where Cam is located."

"You understand that I have no jurisdiction."

"I don't care about jurisdiction. You have power, and that's what matters. I don't care about breaking rules. If someone has to be responsible, then I will be."

"That's not necessary," Valerie said. "Give me whatever information you have."

Blair relayed the few solid facts she had, but even doing that much made her feel as if she were closer to Cam. Until this moment, Cam could have been anywhere, somewhere beyond her reach, and the disorienting sensation of being disconnected from her was as debilitating as if her life's blood were draining away. Now, just knowing that there was something they could do, someplace they could begin to look, returned some of the strength to her wooden limbs. She felt warm for the first time in hours.

"That's a pretty big area to—"

"Bullshit. You can find a terrorist in a cave in the mountains in Afghanistan. There must be a way to find her in a forest in Idaho."

"There are things we can do in Afghanistan we can't do here."

"Listen to me. I don't care what you have to do. They're terrorists, and they haven't given us any choice. We can't negotiate with them, but we can't let them control us, either. Call it anything you want, but you find her. Do you hear me, Valerie? You find her."

"If anyone ever asks you, you knew nothing about what was happening."

"Do you think I care about that?"

"No, I don't," Valerie said softly. "But I can guarantee that Cameron would want you protected. And I'm doing this for her as much as for you."

"I know. That's why I called you."

❖

Loren pulled a Buster Brown Ale out of the small refrigerator she kept in her shop, popped the cap off against the edge of the counter, and took a long swallow. She hadn't had anything to eat all day and had no appetite. She hadn't smoked in a decade, but she longed for a cigarette. Something to do with her hands. Sky was out there, possibly hurt, definitely in danger, and she didn't know where to begin looking. She hated to be dependent upon others when something crucial was at stake. And something very crucial was at stake.

When she'd been in the service, she'd been tight with her platoon, but she'd never made significant attachments. Not because she feared losing them, but because she knew she could be most effective if she kept apart, if she moved in the shadows, if she adapted to circumstances like the chameleon she so easily became. After a while, keeping her distance not only came naturally, it was essential to survival.

All that had vanished when she met Sky. She hadn't managed to keep a single barrier between her and Sky. She'd been naked with her, on every level. Sky had touched her—heart, body, and soul. She needed her back to keep the structure of her world from collapsing. She had to find her.

Her cell rang and she checked the readout, hope a palpable weight in her chest. Just as quickly, her heart plummeted when she saw Ramsey's number. Not Sky.

"Hey, boss."

"How fast can you get those guns up here?"

"Here?" Loren's mind started scrambling. What the hell was going on—what was the rush? The militia must have pushed for an earlier exchange. It must have something to do with Sky.

"McElroy?"

"Sorry—just figuring. I can make some calls—if we rode out soon, six of us and a truck, we could make it round-trip in six hours. But a crew that big on the road would be obvious."

"You won't need that big a crew. You're not picking them all up. Just a quarter of the shipment."

"Okay. Then wha—"

"You, Quincy, and Armeo will go. Jetter in the truck. You'll take the guns to the original rendezvous point for the exchange."

Loren's breath slowed. "Up in the Bitterroots?"

"That's right," Ramsey said. "And we're going to tag along and convince our militia friends to take us home with them."

"How many of us?"

"All of us," Ramsey said. "Now get your ass over here and pick up the boys."

"Yes, sir. I'm on my way."

Loren didn't have time to wait for Washburn's return call. Her blood rushed with the thrill of the hunt. Now she had the quarry in her sights. The militia would lead her right to Sky and Roberts. Then all she had to do was keep them all alive and find a way out. She grabbed her leather jacket and punched in the number for the White House.

CHAPTER THIRTY-FIVE

B lair grabbed her cell on the first ring. "Hello?"
"An operation is under way to locate the compound and execute an aggressive rescue," Valerie said.

"You know where to look?" Blair held her breath, everything disappearing except the sound of Valerie's voice.

"We have a general area, and we have the kind of surveillance we need to locate individuals on the ground. The aircraft are being launched now from a secure location in Nevada. They ought to be in position within the hour."

"How will you get Cam out?"

"If the terrorists refuse to release her and the other hostage under threat of retaliation, there will be a coordinated strike from the air to enable a Delta Team to drop in."

"How did you—"

"I can't tell you anything further."

Blair didn't push for details, knowing the kind of operation Valerie had set in motion was not altogether sanctioned, at least not in the territorial U.S. "If you're in debt to someone, I'll pay the tab."

"That's not necessary. But thank you."

"Can you get me to Idaho?"

Valerie laughed softly. "I'm surprised you've waited this long to ask."

"I didn't want to be too far away in case Lucinda needed me or something changed. Now I want to be there when Cam comes out."

"I'll have transport for you within the hour at Andrews. Do you need a ride out there?"

"No. Stark can get me there."

"Don't plan on going up the mountain, Blair."

"I won't make any promises."

"No, I didn't think you would. Be careful."

"I will, and Valerie—thank you. More than I can say."

"Just don't get hurt. Cameron would not be happy."

❖

This time, when Loren called the White House, she was put through to Lucinda Washburn within seconds. "Something's come up. FALA wants guns in a hurry, and the bikers I ride with are set to deliver."

"How much firepower are we talking about?"

"I can't be sure. We're picking up fifty to a hundred automatic weapons, maybe more. You've got to figure they've got others stockpiled at their camp."

"When do you expect to make delivery?"

"If the current timetable holds," Loren said, "right about dawn."

"And you think this is the group holding Director Roberts and Special Agent Dunbar?" Lucinda asked.

"It's the only thing that makes sense. I don't know why the militia would target Roberts, but I assume you do. Sky is likely collateral damage, and if that's the case, her life isn't worth much. If we don't get them out of there soon, both are probably going to be casualties."

"Where's the gun exchange happening?"

"Somewhere up in the Bitterroots. The plan is to show up in numbers and force the militia to take us back to the compound. The Renegades seem to think FALA is working with the law. I don't know why, but I think someone is playing the two groups off each other."

Lucinda went silent, and Loren could practically hear the gears turning. Finally, the chief of staff said, "Who's bankrolling the gun buy?"

"That's what I'm here to find out."

"Best guess?"

"Someone on the far right with connections. Someone with solid supporters. My guess is the money is coming from powerful donors for promises of legislation they favor in the future."

"There are very few people who come to mind who have that kind of reach."

"I know, and that's why I'm in Idaho."

"Yes. And I wish I'd known that sooner."

Loren had a feeling someone at the FBI was in for an ass-chewing, but that wasn't her problem. Her cover was likely going to be blown before the night finished, not that she cared. Sky was all that mattered now. Washington could worry about the politics. "Not my call."

"I'm aware. Can you avoid going on this run?"

"Not possible. I'm part of it."

Washburn went quiet again, a sure sign there was trouble and she was trying to figure out how to approach it.

"What's going on?" Loren asked.

"We're commencing aerial surveillance momentarily. It might not be safe for you to try to penetrate the compound now."

"Surveillance? Something tells me you're not talking about sheriff's deputies in helicopters."

"Something a little less obvious than that."

Loren should've figured the White House would pull out all the stops for someone like Roberts. Someone was pulling strings, had to be. She knew her phone was secure and she hoped the White House line was too. Homeland and Customs and Border Patrol had been making noises about gearing up a fleet of unmanned Predator drones capable of monitoring cell phone communication and other on-the-ground electronic signals, as well as discriminating between individuals who were armed and unarmed. With facial recognition, they might be able to target specific individuals in FALA's compound, but the instant they launched an attack, FALA would counterattack. Potential witnesses would be the first to die. "Armed Predators?"

"Let's just say remote technology with the capability of identifying individuals on the ground and directing specific action as required."

"Ground transmission monitoring too?"

"Yes."

Hell. They were definitely planning an assault on the camp. "You might be able to blow up the place, but that's not going to get Roberts and Dunbar out of there. You need boots on the ground for that."

"Once the area is secured, we'll bring in—"

"You'll be too late. At the first sign of aggression, the militia is going to execute the two of them. This is a great way to lose the hostages."

"They've left us little choice. Experience has shown the longer we wait, the higher the losses. We prefer not to lose you as well. I can't order you—"

"No, you can't. Because we both know this conversation never happened. I'll call you with a new number if you need to reach me, but you'll have eyes and ears on all of us soon enough." Loren disconnected, crushed the cell phone under her boot, and put the remnants in her pocket. She'd ditch them somewhere along the highway on the way to pick up the guns. The chip was probably untraceable, but she couldn't take any chances. She had to keep her cover in place until she got to the camp.

She needed to get up that mountain and join the Renegades when they stormed the compound, and she had to do it before the Predators unleashed their missiles. If she could get Sky and Roberts into the woods, they all might have a chance of making it out alive.

❖

At the sound of footfalls approaching the door, Cam focused on staying as relaxed as she could manage. She kept her legs crossed at the ankles and her hands loosely clasped in her lap, telegraphing her confidence and that she and Dunbar were not afraid of their situation. The only weapons she had at her disposal were psychological—and the chance she might goad Jones into telling her something useful or distracting her enough to drop her guard.

Jones walked in, still in combat gear, and strode to the end of Cam's bed, her eyes glittering with triumph. "We'll bring you something to eat in a few minutes. You're going to do some marching in the morning, so you'd better eat it and get some sleep."

"We need some antibiotics." Cam gestured to Dunbar, whose eyes were closed. She was either feigning sleep, a smart move, or had fallen into a stupor. "She's running a temperature."

"I heard. I'll see to it."

"Is your name Pattee like your sister's?"

Jones smiled thinly. "You don't need to know anything about me."

"Actually, I already do. I know you and your sister were homeschooled, which really amounted to being indoctrinated and trained to infiltrate high-level organizations as part of a long-range plan to cripple the government. That's pretty impressive and a cut above usual paramilitary capability."

"We're not an ordinary unit. That should be obvious," Jones said curtly. "But even say you're right. So what?" She gripped the iron frame at the end of the bed and leaned forward. "You're *my* prisoner now. If you follow orders, you just might live a little while longer."

"Where do you plan on taking us?"

"You don't need to know that." Jones smiled. "All you need to know is I'm going to let you go—just as soon as we have my sister."

"Washington will never agree to that if they haven't talked to me. They'll require proof of life."

"Oh, they've asked. And we'll give it to them. On our timetable, not theirs." Jones's expression darkened. "We don't follow their orders."

"The antibiotics?"

Impatiently, Jones removed a set of keys from her right cargo pocket, crossed to the drug cabinet, opened it, and came out with a bottle of pills. She tossed it to Cam, who caught it one-handed. "Amoxicillin. Give her two now and another one in four hours."

"Thank you."

"Don't thank me. I'm just doing it so I can deliver her as part of the deal. But she's not the critical element. If she can't make the march, she'll have to…stay behind."

"She'll make it."

"That's on you, Director Roberts. Because I couldn't care less."

A knock sounded on the door, and a guard Cam hadn't seen before backed in, balancing food trays in each hand.

Jones said, "Your dinner's here. You'd do well to eat it. Have a good night."

Cam swung her legs over the side of the bed and sat up. She estimated Lucinda had until morning to find them and launch a rescue. Once they left the compound, their chances of survival dropped to near zero. An ache settled around her heart. She'd give anything to speak to Blair one more time.

"It's too soon to think about good-bye," Dunbar whispered, her gaze unwavering on Cam's.

"I thought you were asleep," Cam said.

"Just conserving energy."

"Good. You hungry?"

"No," Dunbar said, pushing herself up against the head of the bed with her uninjured arm. "But I'm going to eat. I've got a lot of reasons to get out of here." She smiled faintly. "One is personal. And I want the chance to tell her so."

CHAPTER THIRTY-SIX

L oren concentrated on the highway, refusing to think about the hours slipping away or about what might be happening to Sky. She couldn't think about Sky being hurt, helpless, alone and wondering if anyone was coming for her. When she did, the rage and fear welled up and clouded her mind. She couldn't allow that—had to be sharp now, on the most important mission of her life. She had to be in control like never before. In the past, the only one at risk if she failed was her. Now Sky would pay for her mistakes.

She gripped the throttle, held it steady, and ignored the cold wind clawing at her throat. Blinking back tears of ice coating her lashes, she rode on through the night next to Quincy, with Armeo and the truck behind them. Just a few more hours and she'd be heading back in the other direction into the Bitterroots, and when dawn broke, she would find Sky.

❖

The jet touched down at Mountain Home Air Force Base, forty miles southeast of Boise, Idaho, at 0300. Blair, Stark, and Mac climbed out and into the waiting Humvee. Stark leaned forward, spoke to the driver, and the Humvee headed for a gate in the twelve-foot chain-link fence that surrounded the landing zone. Blair looked out the window into the night. Mountains encircled them, massive and foreboding. As they left the bright lights of the base behind, stars blinked on in the velvet sky. The night would have been beautiful if it weren't filled with such terror.

"How far to Silver Lake?" she asked Stark.

"About an hour and a half."

"I want to talk to Lucinda about the timetable."

"As soon as we arrive."

Blair nodded. They wouldn't get much reception out here in the middle of nowhere, and Stark would want a secure line. Blair watched the night streak by and tried to let her mind go blank, but she failed. The mountains mocked her with their majestic and impenetrable presence. Somewhere in their depths, Cam was at the mercy of terrorists. She couldn't bear to imagine what might be happening to her. When the fear threatened to incapacitate her, she held on to the one thing of which she was absolutely certain. Cam would never give up. Cam would fight with everything at her disposal, and she would find her way home. Blair believed that with every beat of her heart.

"I want to know as soon as they pinpoint their location. I want to get as close as we can."

At any other time, Stark would have voiced some objection, but she didn't. From the instant Blair had called her and explained the situation, Stark had done everything possible to get Blair out here.

"As soon as I know anything, you will too," Stark said. "And as soon as we have a safe location for a base, I'll get you there."

Stark's face in the flickering light was solemn, strong. She still had the smooth features of youth, but only hard experience showed in her dark eyes. Affection welled up in Blair's chest.

"I don't think I've ever told you how glad I am that you're in charge of my detail. Cam made the right choice when she recommended putting you in charge. I trust you, like I do her."

Stark swallowed. "I'll do everything I can to deserve it."

"I know. Just find a way to get me to her."

Stark nodded.

Blair understood her silence. Cam never made promises she couldn't keep, either.

❖

Cam dozed, listening with part of her mind to Dunbar's breathing. The antibiotics seemed to be helping. Dunbar was less restless, her breathing slow and steady. The wound itself shouldn't be debilitating in the long run as long as they kept the infection under control, but she'd lost blood, enough to weaken her, and Cam worried she might not be able to tolerate a long hike in the near-freezing temperatures.

0330. The guards had cleared away the dinner trays and turned out the lights several hours ago. She could hear the low murmur of voices just outside—several guards, probably more stationed nearby. Their best chance of escape would be when they were being moved.

Jones had indicated they'd leave at first light. They'd been held roughly nine hours. Before morning, they'd have to let her speak to someone in DC. There wasn't much she could say that might help the authorities find them. She knew without doubt Lucinda would have a team looking for them, but she had no idea what information they had to go on. She was blind.

Since she couldn't do anything about what was happening on the outside, she passed the time piecing together the how and why of their capture. Someone had leaked the purpose of her meet with Skylar Dunbar, and Jennifer Pattee's organization had gotten wind of it. Kidnapping her was a desperate move, and one that suggested they were confident any reprisals would be minimal. That suggested they had powerful backers. Maybe that was the source of the leak—maybe this conspiracy reached all the way to DC, to areas they had yet to consider. She wanted to find out who their silent benefactor was. No matter what happened with FALA—and eventually they would be crushed as a result of this move—there would be others. Domestic terrorism was on the rise, and no matter how many they broke, until they cut off the power source, the problem would never end.

From the darkness, Dunbar said softly, "If you have a chance to get away tomorrow, take it."

"We came in together, we're going out together. And we're going home together."

"I'm not going to be as fast as usual. You need to get out of here— you need to find out who's behind this."

"We will."

"If we get separated tomorrow," Dunbar said, "I'd like you to give a message to someone."

"If I see them before you do, all right."

"There's an agent undercover with the Renegades—the biker club running guns in this area. Loren McElroy. She needs to be pulled out. Her cover's probably blown."

"Your operative."

Dunbar took an audible breath. "She was. She's more than that now. I need you to make sure she's all right."

"Done."

"Something else. I need you to tell her that I was an idiot. She'll know what I'm talking about." Dunbar laughed softly. "Tell her I should've mentioned I was in love with her too."

"Those exact words?"

"Yeah. Especially the part about being an idiot."

Cam sighed. "All the more reason for you to tell her yourself."

"I'll give it my best shot."

"Then that will be enough. Now get some sleep. We're going to be busy come morning."

CHAPTER THIRTY-SEVEN

A t the sound of a vehicle pulling into camp, Jane rose from the chair where she'd been waiting since her father had left to meet with Hooker and pick up the money for the guns. His footsteps were heavy and sure on the porch outside, as solid and formidable as him. The door opened and he strode in on a gust of cold wind, his lieutenants behind him. Jane saluted.

"Captain." Augustus Graves nodded toward his office, and Jane held the door open wide for him to walk in first. As if by unspoken command, the others stopped at the threshold, and only Jane followed him in. She closed the door behind her and stood at parade rest, waiting.

Graves set down the large black nylon duffel he carried in his right hand, then removed his flight jacket and hung it on a post by the door. Only then did he look at her. He smiled. "We have the money. What's your timetable for the guns and prisoner exchange?"

"I've arranged to have Roberts speak with Washington at zero four hundred. At that time, they will confirm that Jennifer is on a plane to be brought to the rendezvous point at zero six thirty. It should only take half an hour to pick up the weapons. Then I'll move Roberts and Dunbar down the other side of the mountain."

"The timetable is tight."

"Yes, I know," Jane said, making sure to look him in the eyes so he could see she was confident of her plans. "I wanted narrow windows to prevent Washington mobilizing countermeasures."

"You're confident Washington will have Lieutenant Graves here for the exchange?"

"Yes. They seemed very eager to have Roberts returned."

He snorted. "Yes, I imagine they are, considering the president's daughter has taken up with her."

"I made it clear that I would not let them talk to Roberts any sooner, and that once we gave them proof of life, we would expect to make the exchange within three hours. That forces them to follow our timetable."

He nodded. "Good. That leaves the power with us."

"Yes, that was my conclusion as well."

He lifted the duffel and handed it to her. "Hooker assures me there is a great deal more where this came from."

"Hooker has proved to be a valuable asset."

"Hooker is a mercenary and he's playing both sides of the street. He'll ally himself with whoever pays him the most and wields the most power. Mercenaries like him don't trust politicians, so his sympathies are likely to lie with us. For the moment." Graves sat behind his desk and regarded her thoughtfully. "You know, you and Hooker would make a very good team. We should think about it."

A frisson of fear shot through Jane's chest, but she was careful not to let it show. She'd met Hooker only briefly when she'd delivered the virus to him in Atlanta. He reminded her a little of her father—large, aggressive, sexual. He'd been attractive in a rough sort of way, but she couldn't imagine being intimate with him. But then, she rarely considered intimacy at all. She didn't have time for that kind of entanglement. Nevertheless, she nodded. "It's something to consider, when we've achieved our objectives."

"There will always be another mission. Never forget that."

She straightened to attention. "I won't. Thank you for trusting me with this one."

"As soon as you've given Washington their proof of life, pick up the guns. I want the camp fully armed when you set out for the exchange. I've called in another fifty troops. They'll be here before daybreak."

"I'll report back as soon as I have the guns."

"Good. Keep me apprised."

"Yes, sir." Jane saluted, picked up the duffel, and left the building. After stowing the money in a Humvee, she continued over to the infirmary. The guard at the door saluted and stepped aside so she could enter.

Inside, the room was shadowed, the only illumination coming

from a small light in the bathroom at the far end. Both captives were still on the cots where they'd been the last time she saw them. As she expected, Roberts was sitting up, awake.

"It's time for your television appearance." Jane unholstered her Glock and trained it on Roberts. "Let's go."

Roberts silently rose and walked toward her. Her T-shirt and dark trousers showed signs of wear, with patches of grime and a rip just below one knee. Nevertheless, other than her dark hair looking slightly disheveled, she appeared as cool as if she were the one in control. Jane found her arrogant demeanor so aggravating she had the irrational urge to pistol-whip her, just to show her who was in charge. The impulse was so unlike her, she nearly trembled. So much depended on her plan going right—bringing Jennifer home, proving her worth to her father, advancing the cause.

She satisfied herself with pushing the barrel of her gun into Roberts's back harder than was necessary.

"Let's go. And be careful what you say to your friends in Washington. Remember, we still have Dunbar, and I don't need to deliver her undamaged."

❖

The closed-circuit television image was being broadcast to Lucinda's office and the Oval Office simultaneously. She and the president were the only viewers. At precisely 0600, she connected to the link she'd been directed to use and an image flickered onto the monitor. The image was murky, the background just a gray haze, but Cam was recognizable enough, seated in a plain wooden chair with a bright light trained on her. Other than looking tired, she seemed fine. She stared straight into the camera, as if trying to reach Lucinda with the force of her gaze.

"Director Roberts," Lucinda said. "Are you well?"

"I'm unharmed," Cam said, emphasizing the pronoun.

"I want to assure you, we're doing everything we can to cooperate with your captors."

"I don't endorse releasing the prisoner," Cam said calmly.

"I understand, but these are extenuating circumstances," Lucinda said, understanding full well Cam would know she was lying. They would never negotiate with terrorists, foreign or domestic, so she hoped Cam would also deduce they had alternate plans under way. "We've already agreed to the exchange, and the prisoner is en route. The pilots have orders to continue on once we are assured of your well-being."

"I'm fine so far. If the weather holds, it should be an interesting day."

"Yes, well, I imagine you never can tell what might blow up in those parts."

"Time's up," a woman said.

"Tell Blair I'm fine," Cam said quickly as a shadow passed through the light trained on her.

"I'll let her know that you're all right and to expect you home soon," Lucinda said.

Cam's gaze burned brighter. "Tell her...tell her I'll see her soon."

The video disappeared, and the voice Lucinda recognized as that of the woman she'd talked to earlier came through. "Now you've had your proof. You are to deliver the prisoner at zero six thirty. The coordinates are as follows." Lucinda grabbed her pen and jotted down the coordinates.

"I'm not sure we have enough time—"

"If you're late, the exchange will be aborted. You're to bring one vehicle with a single driver. We'll be thermo-scanning to be sure that you comply. Turn off on the fire road at the location given to you and allow the lieutenant to leave the vehicle. She is to walk north on the road. Once she has crossed to us, we will release the director."

"And the FBI agent?"

"Yes."

"How do I know that you'll release them?"

The woman laughed. "You don't. But I can assure you if the lieutenant is not delivered to us, the director and the FBI agent will not be seen or heard from again."

"I understand. If we could have a little more time, we might be able to find common ground—"

"There is no common ground, and your time was up a long time ago. You have no options now."

"Where can I reach you if there's some change—"

"There won't be any changes. This is our final communication."

The transmission ended, and Lucinda sat for a moment staring at the blank screen. Her anger was a living beast raging to strike back at those who threatened all she held dear. Violence might beget violence, but in this case, they'd left her no choice. They were not open to a peaceful solution, and she didn't regret her decisions for a single second.

Still, she had to control the fury before she could rationally analyze the next course of action. The door to her office opened quietly and Andrew entered. She smiled wearily. "You heard?"

"I did," he said grimly. "What are our options?"

"I'll discuss it with command, but I agree with our previous conclusions. Attempting to secure the hostages at the rendezvous point is too dangerous. We can't bring in enough forces—they'd be seen before we ever arrived. A surprise assault before they leave the camp is still our best chance."

"Shock and awe." He shook his head. "Ironic, isn't it? The war abroad has prepared us to fight here at home. Still, it's risky. If the militia panic, they might kill the hostages."

"Yes. But the chaos may also give Cam and Dunbar a chance to escape. We have no choice but to play the odds."

Andrew sat heavily in the chair across from Lucinda's desk. "If something happens to Cam, I'll never forgive myself. And Blair"—he shook his head—"Blair will be beyond consolation."

"We're going to get them back, Andrew. We have the best people in the world at our disposal. You have to believe."

He smiled. "You've always told me that. And so far, you've always been right."

"Trust me this time." Lucinda came around the desk and held out her hand. He took it and stood beside her. She kissed him lightly. "You should get some rest. We've still got a little ways to go before the Predators are in position."

"You don't have to bear this all yourself, you know," he said.

"I'd rather you know as little as possible. Go now. I'll let you know when we're ready."

He sighed and cupped her cheek. "Sometimes I doubt I'd be here without you."

"You would. You belong here."

He left, closing the door quietly behind him. Luce leaned back against her desk, thinking about the next few hours. If they were wrong, if this didn't work, more than Blair's heart would break.

❖

Quincy pulled over at the last turnoff before the climb into the Bitterroots. While they waited, they all climbed off to stretch. They'd been riding nonstop for close to six hours with only a twenty-minute break to transfer the guns from the Russians into the truck. Quincy lit a cigarette and Loren bummed one. He raised an eyebrow as he flicked his lighter under the end of her cigarette.

"What's up?" he said.

"Just cold," Loren said, taking a drag. Thirty minutes until the meeting with the militia. Thirty minutes and then they could all be dead. That prospect didn't bother her nearly as much as the thought that if they couldn't infiltrate the camp, she wouldn't have a chance to find Sky. Finding her was all she could think about.

"Here they come," Quincy said.

Loren looked back down the road they'd just traveled and saw headlights approaching. Three vehicles—two trucks and a van. They all pulled into the turnaround and parked. Twenty men climbed out, Ramsey in the lead as they trooped over to Quincy and Loren.

"Any problems?" Ramsey said, looking at Loren.

"No. The exchange went fine." Loren lifted the gate on the truck Jetter had driven, piled to the roof with crates of weapons. "We can offload most of the guns now, stash them in the warehouse, and just take what we need to arm everyone here."

Ramsey motioned to a couple of the prospects. "You heard her. Move these crates into the truck and the van."

Once Jetter's truck was nearly empty, they stacked the remaining crates to form a barrier, leaving ample room behind them for ten men to crowd inside.

"I'll drive the other one with the rest of the men," Ramsey said. He looked over the Renegades congregated around. "Nobody shoots until we get to the compound. We need them to escort us inside. Everybody got that?"

A chorus of grunts responded in the affirmative.

"Once inside, you shoot anybody who gets in your way. We'll teach them that no one double-crosses us."

Loren dropped her cigarette on the gravel and ground it out. "Let's roll, then."

Ramsey nodded. "Yeah. Let's go get us some justice."

CHAPTER THIRTY-EIGHT

The woman in charge of the militiamen who'd come to pick up the guns wouldn't talk, even when Ramsey threatened to put a bullet between her eyes. Her second in command wasn't as brave, though. After staring down the gun barrel for a scant three seconds, he spilled his guts. Loren, sitting in the back of the truck with her Glock pointed at the woman in fatigues while Armeo followed the guy's directions, estimated they were within ten minutes of reaching FALA's encampment. No one had tried to stop them, and she doubted the militia had posted lookouts on this narrow fire trail in the middle of the night when they had no reason to expect a threat from the outside. She leaned close to the woman, pressing her gun against the woman's chest over her heart. She spoke quietly so the roar of the motor and churning of the tires on the uneven ground would cover her words. "I've got a cell phone in my pocket. You've got about five minutes to make a deal with me. Tell me where the captives are, and you can make a phone call to warn your people that a fight is coming unless they stand down and meet us unarmed and ready to talk peace."

The woman slowly turned her head and stared at Loren. Even in the dark interior of the truck, with only the dashboard lights filtering into the back for illumination, her eyes glowed as if on fire. She didn't blink. Not a muscle in her face moved. She wasn't wearing insignia of any kind, but Loren recognized her type—die-hard officer. Ooh-rah. "They're going to kill you all the second you step out of these trucks."

"You and your troops will be in the line of fire too."

She glanced at the traitor in the front seat as if she wanted to shoot him herself. "Wages of war."

Loren shook her head. "Are the two of them really worth it?"

She smiled thinly. "You wouldn't understand."

"Look, it's going to be a bloodbath. Why risk it? All I want is the FBI agent. I don't care what you do with the other one."

The woman laughed. "If you're after one, you're after both. And when the first shot is fired, they'll both be dead."

Loren tamped down her rage. She was so close, but this icy soldier was right. Once all hell broke loose, she'd have a minute, tops, to figure out where Sky and Roberts were being held. As soon as the bullets started flying and blood started flowing, there was no telling who might panic and shoot them or who might give the order to eliminate witnesses. If she was right there and still couldn't save Sky, she wasn't sure she wanted to walk away.

❖

The red phone on Lucinda's desk rang and she picked it up before the first ring had died away. "Yes?"

"We have targets in sight. Recommend we eliminate the weapons arsenal first."

"Are you able to locate the hostages?"

"Tentatively. The computers are working on imaging now." A brief interval of static muffled his words, and then he said clearly, "Two vehicles approaching the compound transporting armed forces, twenty-eight in all."

The bikers Loren had spoken of. Fighting was going to break out any moment. Cam and Dunbar would need all the diversion they could create if they were to escape. "Proceed with attack plan alpha."

"Roger that. Weapons arsenal and unmanned targets priority one."

"Thank you. I'll expect an update shortly."

"Roger and out."

She gently set the phone back in the cradle, musing with half a mind as to who had decided red was the appropriate color for a device used to order the destruction of life, while she debated calling Andrew. Decided his guilt and helplessness were a burden he didn't need. She felt no guilt, only anger she couldn't do more.

❖

An explosion rocked the building, and Cam jerked upright on the bed.

"What's that?" Dunbar asked, her voice surprisingly strong. She swung her legs over the side of the bed and gripped the mattress on either side as if trying to steady herself. "Damn. Dizzy."

"That's incoming artillery," Cam said. A second later, another closer explosion set off a series of earth-shaking tremors that rattled the doors and windows. A long cascade of secondary explosions boomed like cannon fire. Cam jumped up. "That was a weapons depot. We need to be ready to move. The camp is under assault."

Dunbar stood, took a step, and swayed unsteadily. Cam put an arm around her, pulled her over to the door, and stationed her with her back against the wall. "They'll be coming for us in a second. Let me handle it."

The door slammed open and a man in camo rushed in, sweeping his rifle in the direction of the beds as if expecting to see the two of them armed and taking aim at him. Cam hooked her arm around his neck, jerked him back against her chest, and twisted. He slumped, a deadweight in her arms, and she lowered him to the floor. Crouching, she yanked his rifle free and cradled it in one hand while reaching for his sidearm. A scuffle and a muffled grunt behind her got her attention, and she spun upright. Dunbar grappled with another soldier, both hands wrapped around the soldier's gun hand. The automatic was buried somewhere between them. Cam rammed the butt of the confiscated rifle into the back of the soldier's head, and he fell next to the first one on the floor. Dunbar sagged against the wall, panting hard.

"You okay?" Cam asked.

"Yeah," Dunbar gasped. "Who is it, do you think?"

"Hopefully the good guys. Either way, it's the best chance we'll have. You ready?"

"Hell, yes."

"Here." Cam passed her the rifle, grabbed the rifle from the second soldier, and shoved both handguns into the waistband of her trousers. "Can you handle the rifle?"

"In my sleep."

"Then let's get out of here. Stay low and close to me. We'll try working our way around the building and into the woods."

They made it as far as the porch before small-arms fire burst out across the compound. Wood fragments showered from the railing in front of them and peppered the air behind them. Cam grabbed Dunbar and dragged her onto the floor, covering as much of Dunbar's body as she could. Bullets pinged off the metal roof and ripped splinters a foot long from the building, hurling the spears of wood like deadly javelins. Something tore through Cam's calf and she grunted in surprise.

"You hit?" Dunbar asked, her face muffled against Cam's chest.

"No. You?"

"Don't think so."

"Can you crawl?"

"Point me."

"Straight ahead and over the side of the porch. We have to get away from the building before it gets hit with something bigger than bullets."

❖

The gunfire started before the trucks had even stopped. The windshield shattered, showering the men in the front seat and Loren and her prisoner with shards of glass. The side of her face stung, and blood ran down her neck. The men in the front shouted in pain, and the truck veered wildly, finally caroming into something, probably the side of a building. The impact knocked Loren to the floor. She held on to her weapon, but her prisoner launched herself out the back. By the time Loren got to her feet and jumped down to the ground, the camp was consumed by gunfire. People ran everywhere, shouting and shooting. Several buildings were ablaze.

Disoriented, uncertain of where to go, Loren advanced cautiously, keeping to the shelter of the trucks while trying to assess where the captives might be held. A whining sound she recognized split the air above her, and she threw herself to the ground. A missile hit a nearby truck, and it exploded in a fireball. The stench of burning rubber and diesel fuel coated her throat and stung her eyes. Rubbing tears from her face, blinking into the red-orange light cast by the soaring flames, she made out a figure running toward a low, narrow building across the compound. Loren lurched to her feet and raced after her.

CHAPTER THIRTY-NINE

Cam rolled off the far end of the porch and into foot-high brush. Dunbar landed beside her a few seconds later. Brambles and broken branches grabbed at her exposed skin. Rounds continued to dig up the twenty-five yards of open ground that stretched between the building and the surrounding forest, showering them with grit and debris. The fires blazing throughout the compound lit up the expanse as bright as day, the night sky blood red. Militia poured out of the few remaining buildings still standing, firing at anyone not in camo. From what she could make out, the ones firing back were civilians—men in hooded sweatshirts under denim vests and leather jackets. Whoever they were, they hadn't come to rescue her and Dunbar, but they were providing a welcome diversion. The Hellfires methodically targeting the buildings had to have come from Lucinda. Only Lucinda could have pulled those strings, with a little well-placed assistance.

The two dead guards she'd left inside would be missed, even in this chaos. Someone else would be coming for them soon. They had to go now.

"We'll have to run for it," Cam said. "You go first. I'll cover you."

"I'll be too slow." Dunbar gasped. "I'll draw them right to you."

"I'll worry about that." Cam gripped her shoulder. "Keep your head down and don't stop—now go!"

Dunbar rose, clutching her injured arm close to her body, and scrambled for the woods in a low crouch. Cam hugged the side of the building, scanning the ring of blackness beyond the crimson shadows, waiting to follow until Dunbar had reached cover in the trees. Dunbar was nearly there when the silhouette of a large man carrying an assault rifle seemed to step out of the flickering curtain of flames. He was bareheaded, with no body armor, just camo fatigues. Almost casually, he sighted his weapon on Dunbar. Cam stepped into the light and shouted, "Federal agent! Drop your weapon. Drop it now!"

A nearby explosion threw his face into bright relief as he turned to her, a faint smile on his face. The rifle swung in her direction and she fired.

❖

Loren raced across the center of the camp, skirting abandoned vehicles whenever she could, trying for cover and hoping to avoid getting caught up in the firefight. Ramsey crouched behind the hood of an overturned Humvee, firing his automatic at anything that moved. When he saw her, he screamed, "What the fuck is this? Are those fucking *missiles?*"

"I don't know," Loren yelled, crouching beside him. "But there's more than a fucking militia shooting at us!"

Ramsey hunched lower when another explosion kicked up rocks, and shards of metal clanged off the Humvee. "Motherfucker! We're outgunned with those things falling on us. We need to get out of here."

"Fucking A we do," she said, although she doubted he'd be able to organize the scattered bikers into any kind of retreat. At least he wouldn't see her searching for Sky. "Go ahead. I'll cover you."

He scuttled back a foot, stared at her. "Watch your ass, McElroy."

"You know it. I'll be right behind you!" Loren laid down cover fire, and Ramsey disappeared. She waited half a minute and took off running in the direction her prisoner had taken. Halfway to the building at the edge of the clearing, she saw a figure running for the woods. Sky.

A surge of triumph filled her. Sky was alive.

A man appeared, rifle aimed in Sky's direction.

She pulled up, aimed, but before her finger depressed the trigger, he fell. From ten feet away, a banshee howl split the air. She spun—the woman she'd been chasing stood backlit by flame, her face a contorted mask of rage. She pointed her Glock at a second woman running after Sky.

"Drop it," Loren yelled.

The woman dove and fired. Searing pain creased Loren's forehead, and she landed hard on her back. She tried to focus, struggled to aim her weapon, but the woman had already melted into the shadows. Dazed, she lay on the ground waiting for her ears to stop ringing, staring at the clouds swirling overhead in macabre death's-head constellations of terror and despair.

She couldn't stay here. Sky was waiting. Wiping the blood from her eyes, she staggered to her feet and stumbled toward the woods.

❖

Cam staggered a few feet into the woods, her right leg burning, and braced one arm against the trunk of a birch tree for support. She trained her weapon in the direction of the clearing they'd just left. Someone in the camp had to know they were gone by now. The sound of small-arms fire was slowing down to the occasional burst. Either ammo was running low or they'd managed to kill each other off. And she had no idea if help was on the way. "Keep going," she said to Dunbar. "Head downhill as much as you can. Come morning, they'll be looking for us."

"No way," Dunbar said, taking cover behind an adjacent tree. "You need all the firepower you can get."

"I'll follow you as soon as it's clear. That's an order."

Dunbar laughed. "Sorry, I don't work for Homeland."

"Everyone works for Homeland."

"Can't do it—if I left you hanging out to dry, my ass would be—"

A figure lurched out of the dark fifteen feet away.

Cam shouted, "Drop your weapon, federal agents."

"I'm FBI, I'm FBI," a woman called.

"Come forward slowly, keep your hands out to your sides," Cam said.

Sky pushed past Cam with a sharp cry. "Loren!" She threw her arm around Loren's waist. "Loren, God, you're hit."

"I'm okay. I'm okay." Loren leaned into Sky. "You hurt?"

"Nothing serious."

Loren peered at Cam. "Loren McElroy, Director Roberts. We ought to move our asses out of here."

"I agree." Cam motioned toward the forest. "They'll be looking for us before long. If we can find a defensible position, we might be able to hold them off until an extraction team finds us."

"We've already got aerial surveillance," Loren said. "They'll have eyes on us soon if they don't already, and a Delta Team on the ground before morning. I'm the least injured. You two go, and I'll guard the rear."

"I'm not leaving you," Sky said.

"Nobody's leaving anyone." Cam put some weight on her leg, gritted her teeth when pain knifed up her calf. "Everyone check your ammo, and then let's get the hell out of here."

CHAPTER FORTY

Blair's cell phone rang, followed half a second later by Stark's. Blair stood, pressed the phone to her ear. "Yes?"

"She's safe," Lucinda said.

Blair wrapped one arm around her middle, fighting off a wave of dizziness, as relief poured through her. Turning away from Stark, who spoke in a low murmur to someone, she walked to the hotel window and looked out over the snowy vista. The early-morning sun was so bright, tears filled her eyes. "Where is she?"

"They're en route by helo to the 366th Med Group at Mountain Home base. They might be there by now."

Hospital. The word cut her breath. "Is she hurt?"

"Blair," Lucinda said gently, "I don't have all the details. There are some injuries, yes. All of them have been through a lot. But they're all alive."

"Did you talk to her?"

"No. All I got was a sit rep from the Delta Team leader that they'd made contact and were extracting three agents. What matters is they're safe now."

"Thank you. Thank you, Luce." Blair's mind finally started working. "I need to get over there."

"Just be careful. We don't know the status of the kidnappers or how many others might be involved who weren't at the compound."

"Stark is here. I'll be fine. I have to go." Blair disconnected and slid the phone into a pocket. She took several deep breaths and turned to Stark. "How soon can we leave?"

"I've already called the team. We'll have a car downstairs by the time you're ready."

"Thanks." Blair threw her things into her suitcase, and they were on their way in less than five minutes.

Once on the road, Blair curled up in the corner of the SUV and stared out the window. Cam was alive. She couldn't think of a single thing that mattered beyond that. She just needed to see her, to know how badly she was hurt, to touch her. God, to touch her again.

"Here," Stark said, handing her a cup of coffee. "You'll need this. If you're hungry we've got doughnuts."

Blair stared at the takeout cup that said *Chrissie's* in big swirly pink letters. "Where did it come from?"

Stark smiled. "Diner across the street. I told Mac to grab something when he was bringing the car around."

"You're really going above and beyond the call, and I appreciate it."

"I don't think so." Stark sighed. "Sometimes it doesn't feel like enough."

"Believe me, I never want you to have to do more, because I know what that would mean."

"Don't misunderstand," Stark said. "I wouldn't want to do anything else. It's just that…I wanted to be out there looking for the commander as badly as you did."

"Just remember that Cam didn't have to spend any time worrying about me because of you. And that helped her do what she needed to do."

Stark blushed. "I hope so."

The SUV slowed at the gate, the guard checked their IDs, and then they moved onto the air force base and followed the signs to the medical center. Another guard directed them to the emergency entrance. Blair climbed out and, surrounded by her detail, made her way into the ER. A youngish man with short brown hair and flashing dark eyes, wearing scrubs, came forward immediately.

"Ms. Powell," he said, "I'm Captain Guzman. If you'll come with me."

"I need to see Director Roberts."

"Yes. Right this way."

The captain took her and the others down a hall past a warren of small rooms enclosed with curtains to a windowless waiting area with a vending machine, a few plain club chairs, and a TV that sat blank and silent in one corner. The doctor seemed to fade away as Blair stepped into the room, but that might have been her imagination. The only thing that mattered was that Cam was standing there. Blair hesitated, taking her in. She wore a scrub shirt that said *366th Medical Group* above the breast pocket and matching pants. She'd made an attempt to clean up— her hair was wet—but a spreading bruise shadowed her throat and a million tiny scratches marred the backs of her hands and her left cheek. Someone had hurt her, and Blair wanted them dead.

"I brought you a change of clothes," Blair finally said.

"Thanks." Cam caressed Blair's cheek, kissed her. "I'm glad you're here. I'm okay. How are you?"

"You're limping."

Cam smiled crookedly. "You're very observant. It wasn't a bullet."

Blair grasped Cam's shoulders gently, needing the solid substance of her beneath her fingers. She kissed the angle of Cam's jaw away from the bruise. "What was it?"

"A splinter the size of a redwood. It went right through. They stitched it up. Ought to be fine in a week or so."

"No other damage?" Blair let her hands drift down over Cam's chest, felt the beat of Cam's heart beneath her fingers. Strong. Steady. Her world righted. The terror that had haunted her for hours disappeared. Cam's arms came around her and she let herself be held. She pressed her cheek to Cam's shoulder. "Well? What else?"

Cam rubbed her cheek against Blair's hair. Sighed. "Just some scratches, a muscle strain or two. We did some hiking to get away from the compound."

"What about Agent Dunbar?"

"She got hit in the shoulder. They took her to the OR to clean her wound. She should be all right."

"And the kidnappers?"

Cam closed her eyes, drew in the sweet scent of Blair's shampoo and the summer rain aroma that was distinctly Blair. "We've got agents closing in on the compound from all directions. There was a firefight between the militia and a local biker gang. A lot of casualties. We don't have a count yet—I doubt we'll even have identification on most of them for a few days."

Blair wrapped her arms around Cam's waist and leaned back to study her. She was all right—she was Cam, resilient and sure. And very tired. Shadows deepened the hollows beneath her eyes. She took

Cam's hand, led her to the sofa against one wall, and curled up against Cam's side. Cam needed to rest, but she needed to talk out the pain and fear too. She was strong, not inhuman. And Blair needed to touch her. Needed her above all else. "What about the woman who took you? The one negotiating with Lucinda?"

"I don't know. She might be one of the dead or wounded. She could've gotten away. I'm sure some did."

"You have to find her."

"Oh, we will."

"Do you know who she is?"

"I have a pretty good idea. I know she's Jennifer Pattee's sister." Cam stroked Blair's arm, held her close. "But there's a lot we still don't know yet. I don't know where they came from. Or who the moneyman is behind it all. We don't know the true identities of the FALA leaders. We've got a lot more to go on, and after we scour the compound, or what's left of it, we'll know more."

"At least now you'll have help."

Cam sighed. "A blessing and a curse. The more people involved, the tougher the security."

"I called Valerie."

Cam laughed. "Well, now I know where the Predators came from."

"We owe her."

"Valerie won't think so. But I'll make sure there are no consequences."

Blair slid her hand under Cam's scrub shirt and stroked Cam's abdomen. The hard heat of her was enough to keep her warm for eternity. "This was scary."

"I know. I'm sorry."

"No, you don't need to be. I'm okay." Blair kissed Cam's throat. "But I'm really, really pissed. This kind of thing can't happen here. We have to do something about it."

Cam spread her fingers through Blair's hair and caressed the back of her neck. "It's going to be a long war."

"Maybe, but it's one that has to be fought. I have to travel with my father during the campaign. You know, that, right?"

"Yes. You'll be careful."

"You think we'll be targets?"

Cam's arm tightened around her. "We probably all will be."

"Well then, we'll just have to be prepared for anything."

"I love you. When I was out there, knowing you were counting on me, trusting me to come home—that made all the difference."

"I love you too." Blair settled her head on Cam's shoulder. "And that's what will let us win in the end."

CHAPTER FORTY-ONE

L oren paced outside the operating room, drinking a cup of vending-machine coffee she couldn't taste, searching for someone who could tell her something. Hospital personnel she couldn't classify streamed by, pushing stretchers, carrying specimens, talking in urgent tones. She was starting to feel invisible when a green-eyed blonde in scrubs who looked familiar did a double take and stopped in front of her. Her ID read *Captain Gabrielle Hill.* "Aren't you supposed to be in the ER for observation?"

Loren shook her head. "I'm fine. I need to be here."

"At least sit down. You've got a concussion. That *is* a bullet wound on your forehead, you know."

"Barely touched me."

Captain Hill rolled her eyes. "I so love taking care of alpha warriors."

Loren smiled. "See that a lot, I guess."

"All the time. Who are you waiting for?"

"The FBI agent with the gunshot wound to the shoulder. Can you find out how she's doing?"

"Who are you?" Hill asked.

Loren didn't have ID, but at least she was wearing the scrubs they'd given her in the receiving area and not her biker gear. Her jacket and pants had been trashed from tears, burn holes, and embedded grime and grit. She'd had to turn over her weapon to the Delta troops, but since the place was on an air force base and crawling with feds, she wasn't too worried about safety. So far, she'd been flying under the official radar and hadn't been questioned as to just how she fit into the big picture. She wasn't exactly authorized to be in on this operation, but since Roberts knew who she was, she figured her ass was covered.

"That's a tricky question. I'm federal, but I can't prove it. I think Director Roberts will vouch for me—I came in with her."

"I saw the three of you arrive." The captain looked like she was waiting for more.

"That's not what I'm doing here, though," Loren said. "The agent in there is my lover."

Hill nodded. "Wait here."

She donned paper booties and a cap from a shelf by the OR doors, entered a sequence of numbers on a keypad, and disappeared into the hallway beyond.

Alone again, Loren watched the second hand on a round clock with big black numbers, visible through the window in the closed OR door, go around three times before Hill reappeared.

After disposing of the cap and booties, Hill said, "Come with me and try to look like you work here. Lose the coffee."

Loren followed, dumping the paper cup in the first trash can she passed. Hill pushed the red button on another set of doors marked *Recovery.*

"She's in bay eleven. You've got five minutes," Hill murmured, "then you need to get out of here before we both get written up."

"Thanks."

Only two of the beds in the recovery room held patients, and bay eleven, nearest the door, was curtained off from the rest of the room. Loren slipped inside. Sky lay on a hospital bed covered by a thin white blanket. She appeared to be asleep. Her eyes were closed, her lids a bruised, fragile blue. Her lips were pale, her cheeks chalk white. Monitors beeped, a blood-pressure cuff automatically inflated and deflated on Sky's right arm, and clear fluids ran through intravenous lines into her wrist.

Loren eased up to the head of the bed, leaned over, and kissed Sky's forehead. "It's Loren, Sky. You're okay now."

Sky's eyes opened. "Hi."

"Hi." Loren's throat was so full she couldn't say more. Sky was alive. She couldn't think past that.

"You okay?" Sky whispered.

"I'm good." Loren brushed the backs of her fingers over Sky's cheek. Everything was clear now. Sky was alive and anything was possible. "Real good. How you feeling?"

"Like that bitch shot me."

Loren grinned. "You're in the recovery room at Mountain Home

Air Force Base. They just got done taking care of you. You're gonna
be okay."

"What about you?" Sky's brows drew down. "I remember blood.
You were hurt."

The beeping on one of the monitors increased, and the readouts for
Sky's pulse and blood pressure jumped. Loren leaned closer, stroked
her hair. "Hey, I'm fine. I'm up walking around. It was just a graze. You
know head wounds always bleed a lot."

"You sure?"

"Yeah. I'm sure."

"So…" Sky paused. Licked her lips. "Thirsty."

Loren looked around. Saw a Styrofoam container with a straw by
the bed. Figuring it wouldn't be there if it wasn't meant for Sky, she
placed the straw to her lips. "Just a little, baby."

Sky drank. Let out a long breath. "Thanks. How long will I be in
here?"

"I don't know."

"You can't go back to Silver Lake. Too risky. Your cover—"

"Shh. Don't worry about that. I'll figure it out."

Sky's eyes sharpened. She tried to sit up and failed. "Loren,
listen. Sooner or later, Ramsey will figure out someone was feeding
intelligence to the feds. He'll trace me and find out I wasn't Lisa. And
then he'll start looking at you. You can't—"

"There's a lot of casualties on the mountain," Loren said. "I'll just
have to be one."

Sky's eyes fluttered closed. A second later they opened again. "All
right. That will work. I'll get in touch with some of my people. Put out
a cover story."

"You'll keep your ass in bed and get better." Loren leaned down
and kissed her. "Just worry about getting better."

Sky was quiet a long moment. "Can you do that again?"

"Oh yeah." Loren cradled her cheek, kissed her again. "Sky, I'm not
going anywhere. I'll be here until you get out." She reached through the
bars on the side of the bed and gripped Sky's hand. "I meant what I said.
I love you. When I thought I might lose you up there on that mountain,
I about lost my mind. I've never been afraid of losing anything before,
but I can't lose you. You matter more to me than anything."

"You know," Sky laced her fingers through Loren's, "I wasn't
afraid to die. I would have been pissed, but I wasn't afraid. The only
thing I regretted was that I hadn't told you how much I love you."

Loren caught her breath. "Yeah?"

Sky nodded. "Oh yeah. I love you like crazy. I'm sorry I didn't say so sooner."

Loren reached behind her, pulled a chair next to the bed, and kissed Sky one more time before sitting down. She gripped Sky's hand again. "Then I guess you better get some sleep, because we've got some catching up to do. I'll be right here when you wake up."

EPILOGUE

R usso stood on the patio at sunrise, watching the fiery sky break over the Bitterroots. A few days before, he'd watched flames rise in the mountains and had seen blurry images on the endless televisior loops of a "conflagration of uncertain origin" as reporters hypothesize about the events without any real facts. The most recent story propose a local gun club had been storing weapons and ammunition against t day when gun regulation might become a reality, and their stockp had exploded. He doubted everyone believed it, but the governm was very good at spin, and new headlines quickly supplanted the st And for his own purposes, the cover story would do.

The door from the house opened and Derrick crossed the flags patio to join him.

"Here's your coffee, sir," Derrick said, handing him a ste mug.

"Thank you," Russo said.

"Do you want your coat, sir?" Derrick asked.

"No," Russo said. "I'm fine."

And he was. The cold didn't bother him. He was born v in his bones. And now that he'd put distance between hir Graves's organization, he felt confident that nothing would st path to the White House.

Why wouldn't he be fine?

❖

The motel didn't have room service, and the din highway was crowded with truckers at all hours. A lone looked like she'd been in a fight might stand out. She'd single barren room eating K-rations and cleaning the wound on her thigh three times a day with antiseptic, picking out the bits of metal as they worked their way to the surface. She barely limped at all now.

The charred black duffel sat on the floor next to her bed, within easy reach. She slept with a Glock beneath her pillow. And she planned.

When she'd seen Roberts gun down her father, she'd known that everything had changed. The compound was no longer a refuge, and she was now responsible for carrying out her father's mission. She could have gone into the mountains after Roberts and Dunbar, but she would have been outnumbered, and had she failed, she would have failed her father. She could not do that again.

She'd made a snap decision and run for the money. The biker who'd forced her at gunpoint into the back of the truck had gotten there first. He was just climbing out of the same truck with the bag in his hand when she pointed the gun at his forehead. "Why? Why attack the camp?"

He'd shrugged, as if the answer should be obvious. The gun she'd held to his head might as well have been invisible. "It's always better to strike first when you're walking into an ambush."

Her finger tightened on the trigger. "What ambush?"

"We had to hit you before you hit us. We got the word."

"Then you got it wrong. All we wanted were the guns." She nodded at the bag. "We had the money."

His face in the firelight was a pale red mask, but she saw his eyes clearly and they registered confusion.

"You were played." Rage scoured her nerves and her hand shook. If he and his gang hadn't started the firefight, she and the rest of FALA might have evacuated the compound at the first sign of the missile attack. Roberts might not have had the opportunity to escape. Roberts might not have had the chance to murder her father. Her father might still be alive. "Give me the money."

His gaze flickered to the right and relief passed over his face—a lethal tell. He thought rescue was at hand. She shot him between the eyes and dove to the ground, twisting in the air as she fell. She shot the other biker as she landed, then rolled onto her knees, grabbed the bag, and disappeared into the dark.

On the sixth day after the firefight, she showered, washed her hair, and dressed in clean plain black BDUs from the bag she'd taken from one of the trucks on her way out of camp. The diner was crowded with men at the counter and booths, and no one gave her more than a passing glance. She ate breakfast, paid with a twenty from the roll she'd taken from the duffel, and asked for five dollars in coins. Outside, she walked to the pay phone. Most diners along the truck routes where cell service was sketchy still had them. She called the number in DC, and her brother answered on the second ring.

"It's me," she said.

"Thank God, I thought...when I saw the news...what happened?"

"Someone gave us up to the feds. Dad's dead."

Her brother caught his breath. After a second, his voice came back, hard and flat and steady. "You?"

"I'm all right. Are you still secure?"

"Yes. What are you going to do?"

"I'm going to take care of the people responsible. I have a list." Jane watched the trucks streaming out of the parking lot. She shouldn't have any trouble getting a ride. "What about you?"

"He's getting ready to launch his first reelection campaign trip, and I've got a front seat on the bus."

"Good." Jane smiled although everything inside her was as frozen as the snowcaps on the towering Bitterroots. "That will make it all the easier for me to find Cameron Roberts."

About the Author

Radclyffe has written over forty romance and romantic intrigue novels, dozens of short stories, and, writing as L.L. Raand, has authored a paranormal romance series, The Midnight Hunters.

She is an eight-time Lambda Literary Award finalist in romance, mystery, and erotica—winning in both romance (*Distant Shores, Silent Thunder*) and erotica (*Erotic Interludes 2: Stolen Moments* edited with Stacia Seaman and *In Deep Waters 2: Cruising the Strip* written with Karin Kallmaker). A member of the Saints and Sinners Literary Hall of Fame, she is also a RWA Prism, Lories, Beanpot, Aspen Gold, and Laurel Wreath winner in multiple mainstream romance categories. She is also the President of Bold Strokes Books, an independent LGBTQ publisher.

Books Available From Bold Strokes Books

The Rarest Rose by I. Beacham. After a decade of living in her beloved house, Ele disturbs its past and finds her life being haunted by the presence of a ghost who will show her that true love never dies. (978-1-60282-884-1)

Code of Honor by Radclyffe. The face of terror is hard to recognize—especially when it's homegrown. The next book in the Honor series. (978-1-60282-885-8)

Does She Love You by Rachel Spangler. When Annabelle and Davis find out they are in a relationship with the same woman, it leaves them facing life-altering questions about trust, redemption, and the possibility of finding love in the wake of betrayal. (978-1-60282-886-5)

The Road to Her by KE Payne. Sparks fly when actress Holly Croft, star of UK soap *Portobello Road*, meets her new on-screen love interest, the enigmatic and sexy Elise Manford. (978-1-60282-887-2)

Shadows of Something Real by Sophia Kell Hagin. Trying to escape flashbacks and nightmares, ex-POW Jamie Gwynmorgan stumbles into the heart of former Red Cross worker Adele Sabellius and uncovers a deadly conspiracy against everything and everyone she loves. (978-1-60282-889-6)

Date with Destiny by Mason Dixon. When sophisticated bank executive Rashida Ivey meets unemployed blue-collar worker Destiny Jackson, will her life ever be the same? (978-1-60282-878-0)

The Devil's Orchard by Ali Vali. Cain and Emma plan a wedding before the birth of their third child while Juan Luis is still lurking, and as Cain plans for his death, an unexpected visitor arrives and challenges her belief in her father, Dalton Casey. (978-1-60282-879-7)

Secrets and Shadows by L.T. Marie. A bodyguard and the woman she protects run from a madman and into each other's arms. (978-1-60282-880-3)

Change Horizon: Three Novellas by Gun Brooke. Three stories of courageous women who dare to love as they fight to claim a future in a hostile universe. (978-1-60282-881-0)

Scarlett Thirst by Crin Claxton. When hot, feisty Rani meets cool vampire Rob, one lifetime isn't enough, and the road from human to vampire is shorter than you think… (978-1-60282-856-8)

Battle Axe by Carsen Taite. How close is too close? Bounty hunter Luca Bennett will soon find out. (978-1-60282-871-1)

Improvisation by Karis Walsh. High school geometry teacher Jan Carroll thinks she's figured out the shape of her life and her future, until graphic artist and fiddle player Tina Nelson comes along and teaches her to improvise. (978-1-60282-872-8)

For Want of a Fiend by Barbara Ann Wright. Without her Fiendish power, can Princess Katya and her consort Starbride stop a magic-wielding madman from sparking an uprising in the kingdom of Farraday? (978-1-60282-873-5)

Swans & Clons by Nora Olsen. In a future world where there are no males, sixteen-year-old Rubric and her girlfriend Salmon Jo must fight to survive when everything they believed in turns out to be a lie. (978-1-60282-874-2)

Broken in Soft Places by Fiona Zedde. The instant Sara Chambers meets the seductive and sinful Merille Thompson, she falls hard, but knowing the difference between love and a dangerous, all-consuming desire is just one of the lessons Sara must learn before it's too late. (978-1-60282-876-6)

Healing Hearts by Donna K. Ford. Running from tragedy, the women of Willow Springs find that with friendship, there is hope, and with love, there is everything. (978-1-60282-877-3)

Desolation Point by Cari Hunter. When a storm strands Sarah Kent in the North Cascades, Alex Pascal is determined to find her. Neither imagines the dangers they will face when a ruthless criminal begins to hunt them down. (978-1-60282-865-0)

I Remember by Julie Cannon. What happens when you can never forget the first kiss, the first touch, the first taste of lips on skin? What happens when you know you will remember every single detail of a mysterious woman? (978-1-60282-866-7)

The Gemini Deception by Kim Baldwin and Xenia Alexiou. The truth, the whole truth, and nothing but lies. Book six in the Elite Operatives series. (978-1-60282-867-4)

Scarlet Revenge by Sheri Lewis Wohl. When faith alone isn't enough, will the love of one woman be strong enough to save a vampire from damnation? (978-1-60282-868-1)

Ghost Trio by Lillian Q. Irwin. When Lee Howe hears the voice of her dead lover singing to her, is it a hallucination, a ghost, or something more sinister? (978-1-60282-869-8)

The Princess Affair by Nell Stark. Rhodes Scholar Kerry Donovan arrives at Oxford ready to focus on her studies, but her life and her priorities are thrown into chaos when she catches the eye of Her Royal Highness Princess Sasha. (978-1-60282-858-2)

The Chase by Jesse J. Thoma. When Isabelle Rochat's life is threatened, she receives the unwelcome protection and attention of bounty hunter Holt Lasher who vows to keep Isabelle safe at all costs. (978-1-60282-859-9)

The Lone Hunt by L.L. Raand. In a world where humans and Praeterns conspire for the ultimate power, violence is a way of life…and death. A Midnight Hunters novel. (978-1-60282-860-5)

The Supernatural Detective by Crin Claxton. Tony Carson sees dead people. With a drag queen for a spirit guide and a devastatingly attractive herbalist for a client, she's about to discover the spirit world can be a very dangerous world indeed. (978-1-60282-861-2)

Beloved Gomorrah by Justine Saracen. Undersea artists creating their own City on the Plain uncover the truth about Sodom and Gomorrah, whose "one righteous man" is a murderer, rapist, and conspirator in genocide. (978-1-60282-862-9)

The Left Hand of Justice by Jess Faraday. A kidnapped heiress, a heretical cult, a corrupt police chief, and an accused witch. Paris is burning, and the only one who can put out the fire is Detective Inspector Elise Corbeau…whose boss wants her dead. (978-1-60282-863-6)

Cut to the Chase by Lisa Girolami. Careful and methodical author Paige Cornish falls for brash and wild Hollywood actress Avalon Randolph, but can these opposites find a happy middle ground in a town that never lives in the middle? (978-1-60282-783-7)

Every Second Counts by D. Jackson Leigh. Every second counts in Bridgette LeRoy's desperate mission to protect her heart and stop Marc Ryder's suicidal return to riding rodeo bulls. (978-1-60282-785-1)

More Than Friends by Erin Dutton. Evelyn Fisher thinks she has the perfect role model for a long-term relationship, until her best friends, Kendall and Melanie, split up and all three women must reevaluate their lives and their relationships. (978-1-60282-784-4)

Dirty Money by Ashley Bartlett. Vivian Cooper and Reese DiGiovanni just found out that falling in love is hard. It's even harder when you're running for your life. (978-1-60282-786-8)

Sea Glass Inn by Karis Walsh. When Melinda Andrews commissions a series of mosaics by Pamela Whitford for her new inn, she doesn't expect to be more captivated by the artist than by the paintings. (978-1-60282-771-4)

The Awakening: A Sisterhood of Spirits novel by Yvonne Heidt. Sunny Skye has interacted with spirits her entire life, but when she runs into Officer Jordan Lawson during a ghost investigation, she discovers more than just facts in a missing girl's cold case file. (978-1-60282-772-1)

Blacker Than Blue by Rebekah Weatherspoon. Threatened with losing her first love to a powerful demon, vampire Cleo Jones is willing to break the ultimate law of the undead to rebuild the family she has lost. (978-1-60282-774-5)

Murphy's Law by Yolanda Wallace. No matter how high you climb, you can't escape your past. (978-1-60282-773-8)